AT SEA

AT SEA

AT SEA

EMMA FEDOR

G

GALLERY BOOKS

New York   London   Toronto   Sydney   New Delhi

G

Gallery Books
An Imprint of Simon & Schuster, Inc.
1230 Avenue of the Americas
New York, NY 10020

This book is a work of fiction. Any references to historical events, real people, or real places are used fictitiously. Other names, characters, places, and events are products of the author's imagination, and any resemblance to actual events or places or persons, living or dead, is entirely coincidental.

First Gallery Books hardcover edition July 2022

GALLERY BOOKS and colophon are registered trademarks of Simon & Schuster, Inc.

For information about special discounts for bulk purchases, please contact Simon & Schuster Special Sales at 1-866-506-1949 or business@simonandschuster.com.

The Simon & Schuster Speakers Bureau can bring authors to your live event. For more information or to book an event, contact the Simon & Schuster Speakers Bureau at 1-866-248-3049 or visit our website at www.simonspeakers.com.

Interior design by Laura Levatino

Manufactured in the United States of America

10 9 8 7 6 5 4 3 2 1

Library of Congress Cataloging-in-Publication Data is available.

ISBN 978-1-9821-7154-4
ISBN 978-1-9821-7156-8 (ebook)

For Mom and Dad

AT SEA

AT SEA

2014

Cara keeps her books in her car. Not all of them, just the ones she doesn't want her husband to find: an epic sci-fi novel about an underwater civilization; an Australian scientist's account on the future of marine exploration; a collection of Japanese folktales involving the *ningyo*, a human, fishlike creature. Her favorite, a memoir by a record-setting female free diver, slides out from under the passenger seat as she slams on the brakes, narrowly avoiding a mother with a stroller. Cara closes her eyes, takes a deep breath, and pushes the book back out of sight before continuing on down Basin Road.

She knows it's only a matter of time before Graham discovers it, this oddball collection of aquatic literature she's acquired over the years, but she's ready with an explanation. *It's research*, she will say. *For my paintings*.

When she gets out of the car, the water is at midtide, the currents still making up their minds which way to pull. Green seaweed clings to the sides of dock posts like wet hair. Barnacles fizz and gasp at exposure to the open air. In a few hours the water will rise to its peak, eclipsing the lingering smell of ocean rot. The winds have not picked up yet. A light breeze starts to awaken flags on ships, docks, and grassy seaside lawns.

Cara sees Tashtego, Dean's box-headed yellow Lab, before she sees Dean. His boat is in its usual spot, rhythmically bumping up against the water-swollen green posts of the Menemsha fishing docks. A larger boat has just pulled into the next slip over, drawing clusters of early-season tourists with hopeful delusions of seeing giant, iridescent blue-bodied tuna unloaded from below the ship's decks. They're disappointed when the catch turns out to be nothing more than a few icy crates of fluke.

Cara scratches behind Tashtego's ears and pulls herself aboard the *Incredible Hull*, cooing and baby-talking with the dog as a means of announcing her presence. The salt and oil of Tashtego's hair makes her hands smell. The deck is covered in a soup of fish scales, rusty water, and earwigs. Dean emerges from the cabin, wiping his hands with a blackened rag. He nods at Cara and offers a tight-lipped smile.

"Looks like Bette and Claude just brought in a nice haul of flounder," she says.

Dean squints, eyes ice-blue and sharp, over at the docks and adjusts his ball cap. The deep creases across his forehead and stubble on his cheeks betray the years he has spent out on the water as a boat captain. He is strong and lean, but walks with a limp.

"Good for them," he says. "Only been out a few days. Bitin' must have been good."

Cara smiles, but lets the topic drop there. "I got your message," she says. "Everything okay?"

She burrows her fingers deep into the back pockets of her jeans and rocks forward on her toes, pushing her hips up in a casual stretch. She avoids eye contact, working hard not to betray any sign of hope or expectation. He probably just wants to offer her first dibs at a fresh catch, she thinks. Or maybe he's found something that might be of use to her at the gallery.

"C'mon," says Dean. "Let's go for a stroll."

They walk down the dock toward the beach in silence. Any other day and Dean would be entertaining her with stupid fish puns.

You can tune a piano, but you can't tune a fish.

Not tonight, dear, I've got a haddock.

How do you make an octopus laugh? Ten tickles.

But today he is quiet. Nervous. He lights a cigarette when they reach the sand, taking in a long, slow drag.

Is Dean McIlroy about to tell her he's in love with her? Cara clenches her jaw and swallows at the thought. Dean is old. Old enough, at least, to allay any concern that her jokey jabs and witty teases toward him might ever be interpreted as something in the neighborhood of flirting. But then, he's not *that* old, Cara thinks, and she finds herself wondering, to her own consternation, if Dean is still able to get it up.

But that's not it and Cara knows it.

A little girl wanders the beach with a green bucket, filling it with treasures. A seagull feather. A sand-crab claw. The hollowed-out skeleton of an immature horseshoe crab. She can't be older than three, walking with a goofy, bowlegged stance.

"What's with you today?" Cara asks, forcing a laugh. "You're acting weird."

Dean opens his mouth and holds in the words with his breath, thinking carefully before uttering a sound.

"One of the guys says he saw something. Out at Gull's Ledge yesterday."

"What do you mean? Saw what?"

Dean blinks down and opens his eyes back up hard on Cara's face.

The gesture tells her everything she needs to know. Her internal sirens run on full alert, cautioning her against all hope. For nearly five years she's been waiting for this exact moment, and now that it's arrived, she isn't sure she's capable of the joy and relief she's always thought it would bring.

"I wouldn't say nothin' if I wasn't sure."

"But *are* you sure? I mean, did you see? Were you there?"

"I wasn't there, but my guys were. Good guys."

"Then how can you be sure? How could you come to me like this unless you *yourself* saw something?"

"I trust Jimmy. Jimmy Coughlin—who knows nothing about what happened with Brendan and your boy. Says he and the guys saw two people swimming in the water. Way far out. Not somewhere you see people swimming, you know what I mean? At first they thought it was just a couple of lobster traps or something. But when Jimmy looked through his binoculars, he swears he saw a man and a boy, treading water out there like it was normal. But by the time they got closer, the people were gone. Dove straight into the water. Just like that. Never came back up."

Cara shakes her head in disbelief and stares ahead, unblinking. Her legs buckle and she sinks down into the cool morning sand. Dean squats down next to her, fanning her with his dirty rag. The wafting smell of gasoline makes her temples ache.

"You okay, kid?"

"Why are you doing this?" Cara's voice breaks, and she turns her head away to hide the wave of emotion rising behind her eyes.

The child on the beach is singing now. Her song is unrecognizable. Made-up, probably, with references to fishies and starfish and mermaids.

Cara retreats into the safety of logic, halting the tears before they can come out.

"It could have been anything, Dean. You and your guys think you see all sorts of stuff when you're out there. All those stories . . ."

"I'm just telling you what was relayed to me," Dean says. "Seemed like a heck of a coincidence to me."

2008

They made everyone move out the day of graduation. Best not to let the new grads have free range of campus, the threat of taking away their diplomas no longer viable. Cara couldn't believe how quickly it all happened. One moment she was eating warm macaroni salad and a lettuce-bacon-turkey-tomato wrap under the tent with her dad, Drew, and Lucia, and the next she was in the passenger seat of Lindsay's Passat, headed toward Boston. She'd taken her robe off hours ago, but was still in the blue dress she'd chosen to wear underneath, a rare splurge at $150. The corner of her mortarboard poked out from the tote at her feet. She'd been too sentimental to throw it away.

She checked the clock on the dash. Her family was probably boarding their flight back to Phoenix by now, storing their baggage and settling into their seats. As hard as it had been to say good-bye to them—their forty-eight hours together had felt like much less—she was glad she wasn't with them. Phoenix in the summer was hell on earth for a girl from Vermont. They said the temperature had been close to 110 degrees when they left, and they expected it to be just as hot when they got back.

Phoenix would never be home to Cara, despite her father's best intentions. She'd never completely forgiven him for selling the Bennington house and moving the family thousands of miles to live in the desert. Worse, this had all transpired just three months after her mother had died, as if her father just couldn't get away from Vermont, and their life there, fast enough. He'd been raised in a military family, living in five states before he was eighteen, and had fond memories of Arizona, the dry heat, consistent sun. When Cara was growing up, he'd always complained about the harsh Vermont winters, jokingly threatening to move them all someplace warmer. She'd never thought he actually would.

Cara, fortunately, hadn't really had to spend much time in Phoenix beyond the few weeks before her freshman year of college and the school breaks and summers that followed. The move had been much harder on Drew, who'd had to start at a new high school at the onset of his junior year. But her brother had always been an outgoing kid, and made friends quickly. He grew to like Arizona, so much so that he'd chosen to stay there and work for a friend's mom this summer, ignoring Cara's pleas that he come east and spend it with her. It was hard to believe he would be a junior at UCLA in the fall.

Cara had looked at colleges in other states—as close as New York and as far away as California—but in the end had decided to stay in Vermont, initially so that she would be close enough to help take care of her mom. But even after her mother passed away, Cara had stuck by her decision, the idea of a departure still feeling too much like a betrayal.

She had orchestrated the past few days with her family very carefully. She'd taken them to Honey Meadow Farm for the world's most luscious, creamiest, hand-churned ice cream, and arranged for them all to take a sunset cruise on Lake Champlain. Somehow it felt like if she just reminded them of the very best that Vermont had to offer, they might be convinced to move back, or at least stay east a few days longer. "Don't you miss this?" she kept saying to Drew. Maybe they'd even decide to come to the Vineyard with her, she thought. But then, seemingly no sooner than she'd crossed the stage in her cap and gown, there they were in the parking lot, sliding down the handles of their roller suitcases and hefting them into the back of the rental.

Lindsay's family lived in Newton, a Boston suburb, so she'd offered to drop Cara at the bus station in Boston on her way home. From there, Cara would catch a bus to Woods Hole on the Cape and hop on a ferry to Martha's Vineyard to spend the summer with her aunt Moira and uncle Ed.

Lindsay tried to make it seem like she was jealous of Cara and all the beach time she was going to get over the next few weeks, but everyone knew Lindsay had the best future in store. In just a few days, she would be on her way to New York City to start an internship at *Self* magazine, a role that, in spite of its less than mediocre pay, evoked envy in Cara and the rest of their friend circle. Regardless of what the actual job entailed—which was likely to be coffee runs and scheduling—it conveyed a certain glossiness that none of the rest of them had been able to achieve. The next-best triumph was Melanie's temp position at Geico, which was really only cool because the company had those funny caveman commercials.

Cara had originally thought that she too might be headed to New York after graduation. That had been the plan, at least. She'd applied for dozens of entry-level positions at galleries all over the city, noting her experience working at the college gallery and her role as student supervisor of the art barn her senior year. Met by silence and auto-generated rejections, she tried for internships, but the paid opportunities ignored her and the unpaid roles required that she be a full-time student, which she of course no longer was.

It was only a few hours, but Cara was grateful for the time alone in the car with her closest friend. The pair had met in an introductory French class their freshman year. Despite having taken years of French in high school, both girls had somehow managed to fail the college's proficiency exam and were forced to enroll in a course far beneath their aptitude levels. They had bonded over the shared tedium of learning material they'd already been taught, amused at being the strongest students in class with minimal effort. It was the only A+ Cara ever got.

"I forgot to ask. How was it with the stepmom?" Lindsay asked. "She seemed fine."

"It was. She was," Cara admitted. "I think it helped being here, on my own turf. Did you see the way she was looking at our apartment, though? She was freaked out by the mess, you could tell."

Lucia, Cara's father's new wife, was a petite, attractive, but, Cara felt, age-appropriate woman of Ecuadorian descent. She'd come to the United States as a child, married, had a child of her own, and divorced at forty-two. She now worked as a special education teacher at an elementary school in Phoenix. She and Cara's father had met through church, and were married a year and a half later.

There was nothing overtly offensive or off-putting about Lucia, but in the time Cara had spent with her, they had never quite been able to connect. Cara blamed this in part on Lucia's demure aspect and scrupulous attention to cleanliness and detail. The condo she shared with Cara's father was always pristine—beds made, dishes put away, laundry folded—and Lucia herself was never seen with so much as a wrinkle in her clothing. It made Cara, by comparison, feel like a mess. She was always keenly aware of everything she touched in the condo, careful not to dirty a pillow or leave the blue grime of tooth-paste in the sink.

"Also, please don't call her my stepmom," Cara said. "She's my dad's wife. There's no mothering involved here."

"Sometimes I find myself preparing to be a stepmom one day," Lindsay said. "Like, I'll think about what kind I would be. Is that weird?"

"Yes."

"I mean, there are the ones who are, like, really young, and get the kids to like them by buying them cool clothes and taking them to Justin Timberlake concerts."

"Even for a boy?"

"Or whatever, sports games and paintball. You know what I mean. But that's one kind. And then the other kind is just this hippie-dippie, free-spirited one who leaves them alone and treats them like they're equals—like they're adults, almost to an inappropriate extent. And then finally there's the one that really embraces the mom thing and essen-tially, like, *becomes* the new mom. No hesitation. Packed lunches, soccer practice, bedtime stories, the whole thing."

"Okay, to start, I'm pretty sure there are other kinds of stepmoms besides the three you just named. But more importantly, are you se-cretly dating an older man with kids that I don't know about?"

Lindsay laughed. "No. I mean, not yet. But I've got this hunch, like that's what's going to happen. Like I need to mentally prepare myself for it now, just in case. Do you have anything like that?"

"Sometimes I think I play out worst-case scenarios in my head just so they *don't* happen," Cara said. "Like if I've already imagined it, the odds of it coming to fruition are way lower. Because apparently the track record of my daydreams actually coming true is really slim. Like, that's the pattern I've come to believe. If I've thought about it already, it won't happen."

Lindsay nodded. "Yeah, okay. Maybe that's kind of what I'm doing too."

"And like you said, you feel like you're more prepared once you've imagined it. So at least, if it does happen—which it won't—but if it does, and you *do* become a stepmom, you won't be totally shocked and devastated in that moment when you find out the guy you love has two bratty kids. You'll just be like, *Oh, okay, now this is really happening.*"

"So what's an example for you?"

Cara thought about it. The biggest thing she mentally prepared herself for was *not* making it as an artist. Deep in her heart, she was sure she'd one day make a living by painting and selling art, showing at galleries in cities across the country, and maybe even the world. But anytime she conjured up this possible future, she reminded herself that it probably wasn't going to happen—at least not overnight. She'd more likely end up a teacher. Or a gallery docent.

But such musings felt far too personal to share. It was too serious. Too important to her. Even with her closest friends, like Lindsay, Cara rarely showed vulnerability. Showing that you really wanted something that was seemingly unattainable—or, worse, making a clear and obvious effort to secure that something—was the most frightening and humiliating thing Cara could imagine.

"I'm already convinced that I can't have kids," Cara said. Somehow this felt less personal than her aspiration to be a successful artist. The idea of having kids still felt so far away. She wasn't even sure she wanted them, anyway. The mere thought of going through an experience as raw and emotional and affecting as motherhood, without her own mother there to witness it and to guide her, conjured a heavy, harrowing ache, a hurt that still hounded her all these years later, settling in quickly and often, without warning. Better to never be a mother at all.

"And I have no reason to believe this," she went on, blanketing the ache with a feigned nonchalance. "As far as I know, I am perfectly healthy. Yet it would not shock me one bit if I was totally infertile."

"Yeah, that's a good one," Lindsay said.

"But I think everyone probably worries about that."

"I don't."

Cara raised her eyebrows. "You don't?"

"No! It's never even occurred to me that I might struggle."

"See, and just hearing you say that makes me nervous for you," Cara said. "Like, because you're so confident, you're going to have the most trouble out of all of us."

"That makes no sense."

"I know, but that's how my brain works."

When they made it to downtown Boston, a woman flicked Lindsay off for almost running her down in a crosswalk. Cara put her hand to her mouth and sucked in a nervous breath. Lindsay was incredulous. Nothing was ever her fault. Cara, on the other hand, probably would have pulled the car over to get out, give the woman a bottle of water, and personally apologize.

"What?"

"You almost just hit that woman."

"She practically ran out into the middle of the road!"

"It's a crosswalk!"

Lindsay shrugged.

There was nowhere to park, so they said good-bye at the curb, Lindsay leaning over the gearshift and passenger seat to hug Cara through the door.

"I'm going to come visit you when my family goes to the Cape for Labor Day," she said. "And then I'm bringing you back to come live in New York with me."

"Deal," said Cara. "Just make friends with some cool gallery owner and convince them to give me a job."

"Sure," Lindsay said. "No problem."

A car behind Lindsay's honked. She rolled her eyes.

"Fucking Boston drivers. I gotta go."

Cara was anxious. She had to pee, but ignored it. She didn't like to leave the deck if she could help it, even to find a bathroom. Seasickness. It always hit her when she sat inside, the smells of reheated chowder, other people's sunscreen, and lingering antiseptic cleaner adding to the nausea.

The ferry was crowded and she'd arrived too late to grab a seat. That is, a seat that didn't require an *excuse me* or *is anyone . . .?* She stood at the railing instead, watching the giant hull of the ship cut through the water. Over the starboard side, the ocean tugged on a red nun buoy until it was nearly horizontal. Cara had heard that the waters of Vineyard Sound could be difficult to navigate if you didn't know what you were doing.

The Vineyard Haven harbor was a forest of masts on the horizon as they approached, the *Alabama* and the *Shenandoah* standing tall above the rest. The boats collectively pointed to the southwest, like an army of soldiers at attention. A white spaceship of a yacht with tinted black windows zoomed by them in the opposite direction. A woman who sat reclined on its deck waved up at the ferry, and Cara relied on the other passengers to wave back.

Her adrenaline kicked in when they rounded the stone seawall at the lip of the harbor. As the boat docked, she could faintly hear the music of halyards clinking against their masts below the sound of the ferry's engine. Leisure motors hummed and seagulls whined, hovering over the deck of the ship with an aggressive curiosity. A line of cars staked out the intersection of Union and Water. Families waited in line for brunch at the Black Dog. Cara followed the parade of strollers, roller bags, Labradors, L.L. Bean totes, and flip-flops down the ramp and toward the snarl of cars, white lines of paint guiding her path.

It felt strangely adult to be making the walk on her own. Trips to the Vineyard had always been a family affair. The four Hansens would pile into the twilight-blue Plymouth Voyager and make the four-hour drive down from Bennington to Woods Hole, stopping only once to pee and eat soggy chicken nuggets and french fries from McDonald's. The cup holders of the Voyager were always sticky with spilled Coke, and the fold-open ashtrays of the backseats seemed to contain endless treasures from the years prior. A gob of Winterfresh wrapped in its foil. Hair barrettes. Micro Machines. A pair of old fries and the greasy paper pouch they'd come in.

Cara's dad would drive while her mom played snack-master from the front seat. Cara sat in the middle seat next to their Newfie, Loretta, and Drew shared the wayback with boogie boards, bike wheels, and jumbo-sized bags of dog food. When they got to the ferry, Stanley and Siobhan Hansen would sit in line with the car while Cara and Drew gave Loretta one more chance to relieve herself before heading up the ramp as walk-ons, saving seats outside on the upper decks.

When their mom died, the tradition had passed away along with her in a manner so abrupt it nearly went unnoticed. August came and they stayed in Vermont, each of them hesitant to acknowledge the shift, as if doing so would breach the protective dam they'd built up around themselves. They weren't ready to go back. Not without her. Though disappointed, Cara said nothing, because she felt confident they would return the following year. Next year they would be ready. If not then, the year after that.

What she'd failed to understand was that the familial glue that tied her to the island didn't extend to her father, at least not in the same way. She couldn't yet grasp the reality of what it meant to marry into a family, versus having been born into one, the bond of law so much weaker than that of blood. It was her mother who had drawn their family to the Vineyard in the first place; Siobhan was the one with the family connection, an endless trove of memories pulling her out to the Atlantic each year. The bond wasn't as strong for Stanley. It broke when Cara's mother died.

Moira was there to pick her up in her 1995 Buick Park Avenue. She looked a little teary when she got out to hug Cara, which made Cara a little teary too.

"I'm so glad you decided to come, honey. I really am."

"Me too," said Cara, though she still wasn't sure.

"You know the Rosedales sold their place," said Moira as they drove away from town. "Two point six million. Ernie Schermer told me a movie director bought it. The guy who does all those war comedies? But I've never seen anyone over there. Not once."

"Jesus," said Cara. The place didn't even have indoor plumbing.

The cultural evolution of the island and its inhabitants had always been a favorite topic of discussion on Siobhan's side of the family. Community members took it personally every time one of their own was bought out by new money. Bexley House, named for Cara's maternal great grandfather John Bexley, had been passed down through the family and was now inhabited full-time by Cara's Aunt Moira, Siobhan's older sister by ten years, and Moira's husband, Ed. The house was located on the southwestern end of the island or "up-island," as locals referred to it, where the influx of new money was arguably less obvious. There were the quintessential summertime Vineyard-goers of Edgartown and Oak Bluffs ("down-island"), with their critter belts, boat shoes, Lilly dresses, and pearl earrings; and then there were the summer folk of Chilmark and Aquinnah ("up-island"), men and women in Birkenstocks, flowy dresses, worn-out cotton T-shirts, and ripped blue jeans.

It should be acknowledged, however, that the latter population, shabby and bohemian to the untrained eye, was not quite as it seemed. Shacks by the sea were tenanted not by starving writers and musicians, but by college presidents, record executives, and aging celebrities in casual disguise, desperate to *get away from it all*. High-end chefs from the mainland bought up mom-and-pop farms to sell local organic produce to said college presidents, record executives, and aging celebrities, hosting artificially idyllic farm-to table dinners in their fairy light–strewn barns for top dollar. Sunrise beach yoga classes had become commonplace, and the Menemsha parking lot was crowded each summer with Land Rovers, Beemers, and, for a tasteful balance, the occasional classic woody Jeep Wagoneer covered in bumper stickers.

The unspoken consensus, of course, was that since Great-Grandpa Bexley had bought the family property back in the early 1900s—when houses sold for hundreds versus hundreds of thousands of dollars—the family had a more legitimate claim to the land. They appreciated it more. Their history gave them license to roll their eyes at wash-ashores and island posers, even though not a single Bexley descendent had actually ever lived year-round on the island before Moira—never mind the natives who were there before anyone.

"How's Stanley?" Moira asked.

"Fine, I guess."

It struck Cara that Moira now referred to her dad by his first name, as if that's what Cara should be calling him now too. When her mother was alive, he was "your dad." Now he was Stanley.

"He's still with that woman? Lucia?" Moira said it the American way, *Loo-sha*.

"It's pronounced *Loo-see-ah*," Cara said in a mocking, hoity-toity voice, as if Lucia's preference on having her name pronounced correctly were demanding or pretentious.

"Well, *excuuuse* me!" said Moira.

"Anyway. Yes," said Cara. "They're still together. You know, they invited you to the wedding."

"Must have lost my invitation."

The BEXLEY HOUSE sign flapped on its hinges as they crunched down the shell-lined driveway toward the house. The Canadian goose mailbox was overtaken by honeysuckle and orange rose hips. Uncle Edward emerged from the back screen door with three Jack Russells at his ankles. Cara could hear the other dogs yapping inside.

"There she is," he said, going in for a hug. He'd just woken up from a snooze, his eyes puffy and his comb-over astray.

"Help her with her bag, Ed."

Cara noted the way her uncle hunched his shoulders, keeping his elbows locked and knuckles flexed for balance. She waved off their attempts to help and headed inside.

The house had changed since they'd winterized it. The once bare, shiplapped walls were now covered with insulation, drywall, and paint. It flattened the light, reducing shadows and muzzling the air. The built-in ledge where they used to exhibit beach treasures was gone.

But the old wood stove remained, as did the wall of buoys adorning the short hallway to the kitchen. Grandpa Bexley's painting of Gay Head Light still sat above the fireplace, and the same old taxidermized sandpipers, mallards, and solitary osprey continued to nest in the den.

"We thought you could stay in your mom's old room," said Moira.

"Are you sure? I don't mind staying in my usual spot."

"Whatever you're comfortable with."

Moira patted Cara's shoulder and smiled the familiar, sympathetic smile Cara had come to resent, the one that signaled that the beholder *knew*, that they could see Cara's pain, despite her best efforts to hide it. This kindness and tenderness from well-meaning friends and family members left Cara feeling vulnerable and exposed, the ache rising up inside, threatening.

"Yeah, I guess I will stay in the emerald room then," she said. "I mean, it's a bigger bed, right?"

She grabbed her bags and skipped up the stairs, two at a time, before her emotions could catch up with her.

What was wrong with her? She'd felt so good the past few months, and now suddenly it seemed as if she might burst into tears at any moment. She paused at the entrance of the room and took a deep breath. Everything looked as it always had—the white wrought-iron bed frame, the scallop shell pillows, the green crystalline curtain knobs, the emerald window-seat cushion. Books she could remember her mom reading leaned against a decorative brass anchor on the bureau. *The Poisonwood Bible. Memoirs of a Geisha. Summer Sisters.*

Cara shut the door behind her and opened the windows, letting in the full-bodied ocean air. There was a wedding photo of Cara's parents on the vanity. She picked it up to take a closer look. Siobhan was tilting her head back with a huge grin, looking up at Cara's much taller father. Stanley's expression conveyed a subtle smirk, which for him might as well have been an ear-to-ear smile, that's how seldom he showed any real emotion. He'd always been more reserved—not stern or cold, just reticent.

Both of them had been loving and supportive parents, showing up together for Cara and Drew's parent-teacher conferences and soccer games and art shows. But her mom always sat in the stands or mingled through the crowds with the other parents, remembering everyone's name and asking questions that showed she knew who they were and what their kids were interested in. Her dad, on the other hand, preferred to stand to the side by himself, taking in the scene, rarely engaging with anyone unless directly approached.

They'd met on a chairlift at Stowe, which Cara had always found very romantic.

"She got me so I had no chance of escape," Stanley liked to joke.

Cara replaced the picture frame and climbed onto the bed, lying on her belly and inhaling the salty must of the pillows. She was sad her dad and brother weren't there with her, but she could make this work. She'd feared this moment, being in a space so saturated with her mother's presence, and was surprised by her calm, the solitude a relief. She felt solace in knowing her mom would be glad she was here. New York would still be there at the end of the summer. She made a promise to herself to use this free, untethered time to paint and draw and build a portfolio for when she was ready to move to the city.

She turned onto her back, outstretched her arms, and closed her eyes, falling into the escape of a favorite fantasy. She imagined being at her very first show in New York, looking beautiful, glass of merlot in hand, laughing with friends and family about how crazy it was that so many people had showed up. Every piece would get sold. Agents and gallery owners would give her their cards. She would earn enough to buy her own place, where she'd host decadent parties for all her struggling college friends.

One night Paul Richard, the swimmer with the big blue eyes who was two years ahead of her, would stumble into one of her parties and they would fall in love, both of them reveling in how funny it was that they'd both always wanted to get to know the other back in college but had always been too shy to make a move. Later, when she'd earned enough money, they'd move back to Vermont where Cara would have her own studio space and shop, living and working as an artist in support of what would soon be their own little family, her mom looking down on them with pride from above.

But for now, it was the Vineyard with Aunt Moira and Uncle Ed.

Everyone knew the nudies hung out by the cliffs. That didn't bother Cara. She was an artist, after all. She'd sat in on countless figure drawing classes by now, learning the art of not only the male and female forms, but of making it seem like she was above the childlike giddiness of seeing other people's penises and vaginas. She was curious, to be sure, but made a point of keeping her head up as she walked down the beach. The quiet and seclusion were worth it, just far enough from the beach umbrellas, volleyball nets, and baby tents around the corner.

And then there were the cliffs, a brilliant canvas of clay, sand, and rock, baking in the sun. An island landmark. Only on the Vineyard would the site of one of the most famed tourist destinations and stunningly beautiful geographic formations also be a sanctuary for nudists. The cynic inside of her understood that the rules might change one day, but for now this small patch of beach had managed to retain the free-spirited flavor of the "old" Vineyard her family always talked about, though she herself was far too modest to shed her own swimsuit.

Dried barnacles scraped Cara's skin, leaving white zigzags in their wake as she climbed up the side of a granite boulder. She took out her sketchbook and charcoal kit and started to outline a cormorant drying its wings. She used a pencil to begin sketching, the edges of her palms lightly grazing the page. She didn't want to leave any marks that couldn't be erased.

Cara wasn't the kind of artist who liked to let her process show. She eschewed abstraction and strove for accuracy and realness, convinced that this was the best indication of true artistic talent. In college, she'd quietly resented her classmates who splattered clashing colors on a canvas and titled it *Apathy*, or *Man in Pinstriped Suit*. Her professors, in contrast, were enamored with it. The weirder a piece was, the longer they spent on it in critique, talking in circles about meaning and intent. When they got to Cara's pieces, the comments were always the same: "It's really good, but it doesn't make me feel anything."

Cara licked her finger and was attempting to wipe away a mark when a man in the water swam, naked, into her frame. She did her best to ignore him and continued to focus on the bird; she didn't want him to think she was looking at him. When he started to make his way out of the water, she averted her eyes and waited for him to pass so that she could get back to her work. But it seemed like he was walking right toward her. She allowed herself the briefest of glances to confirm as much before snapping her eyes back down to the page.

An attractive naked person was a rare sighting at the cliffs. It was usually just the wilty European men and women with saggy boobs who went nude, a parade of spare-tire bellies and cottage-cheese thighs. But this man was young and physically fit, his white hips and thighs contrasting sharply with the deep tan of his legs and torso. Dripping with salt water, his hair was a soaking mess on his head.

"Excuse me, miss, but I thought this was a nude beach," he said.

"I'm sorry?" Cara was too embarrassed to be afraid, too intrigued to be rude.

"This is a nude beach, isn't it?"

"I guess so. It's an option, at least."

"Well, then, what are you doing wearing clothes?"

The man had a thick Boston accent she'd heard only in Ben Affleck movies and from older, gruff tollbooth workers on I-90.

"Excuse me?"

"I just don't think it's fair that I'm here butt-naked and you're sitting there with shorts and T-shirt on. I mean, it's embarrassing—for me."

He looked down at his genitals with a goofy wince, licking up the salt water dripping down from his hair. His eyes were dark and sheltered by a heavy brow, but brandished a glint of playfulness. He had a strong, prominent nose with a small bump in the middle, and he looked young, but there were already permanent creases around his eyes and along the edges of his mouth.

"Well, first of all, it's optional," said Cara. "I don't *have* to be naked. And no one is forcing you to be naked. I certainly wouldn't stop you from putting your shorts back on."

"You wouldn't?"

"I wouldn't."

"See, I think you would. At least you'd want to."

"I . . . what?"

"I see you looking. Feast your eyes and enjoy. But I think you should get naked too. Partly because I feel a little nuts being naked alone, but mostly because I think you'd really enjoy it."

"I'm good, thanks."

Cara pretended to get back to her drawing. The man climbed up on the rock and sat down next to her.

"That's really good," he said, looking down at the page. Beads of water dripped off his skin, falling close to the sketchbook.

"I'm sorry, can I help you with something?" Cara fought to keep a serious expression. The sheer absurdity of the situation made it difficult to convey her annoyance.

"Yeah, you can," he said. "By getting naked."

Cara wondered for a moment if the man was foreign, but then she remembered the accent. This was the opposite of foreign. This was local.

"I'm sorry, but you're starting to creep me out a little bit," she said.

"Why? Because I'm naked?"

"Um, yeah, that's part of it. You do realize this is sexual harassment, what you're doing."

Cara wondered if she should leave. Grab her things and run. She glanced sideways to make sure there were still other people around. If he tried anything, she could scream, and people would save her, the saggy-skinned nudists now her only protection. But she didn't want to leave, and if she was truly being honest with herself, she didn't want him to leave either.

"I like to think of it as sexual liberation," he said. "The human body is a beautiful thing. But I don't need to tell you that. You're an artist, obviously."

He pointed to her drawing. Cara gave him a look.

21

"I'm Brendan," he said, reaching out his hand.

"Hi," Cara said, ignoring the gesture. This didn't seem to faze him.

"Aren't you going to tell me your name?"

"Nope."

"Please?"

"It's Cara. My name is Cara. Are we done?"

"*Sweeeeeeeeet Car–o–line*," sang Brendan.

"Nope. Just Cara." She didn't mind the song—she had fond memories of singing along to the Neil Diamond classic at Red Sox games with her parents and brother—but it had always annoyed her when people assumed her name was short for Caroline or Carolyn. Her name was Cara, just Cara.

Brendan shrugged. "Fair enough."

Cara let out an exasperated sigh.

"What's the matter?"

"My bird just left. The one I was drawing."

"I'm sorry to hear that, but I think this could be a good thing for us. See, now you can give me your full attention."

Cara let out a laugh. "Who are you? Where did you come from? And why are you so intent on talking to me?"

"I am Brendan, as I told you. I come from Gloucester, Mass., and I think you're very beautiful—like, very beautiful, sincerely—and I want to get to know you. That's it."

Cara had a skewed sense of her own attractiveness. She instinctively deflected compliments, as if acceptance or any semblance of gratitude made her complicit in what she deemed to be a glaring fallacy. People thought she was pretty, but she wasn't. Friends regularly told her how they wished they had her legs and brought her to the salon with them to show the colorist what they wanted. "Must be nice to be able to eat whatever you want and still have that body," they said. But the compliments never sank in. Cara never truly felt worthy. The curious eyes of men and jealous glares from women did little to bridle the overwhelming sense of insecurity she carried with her. She lived in perpetual fear of her admirers discovering the truth. That, up close, she wasn't *actually* that pretty. There was the bulb at the end of her nose; the gaping distance between her eyes; her crooked bottom teeth; her soft, pale belly; the cystic acne on her back.

"I'm sorry. I have to go," she said, closing her sketchbook and sliding down the side of the rock.

"Wait," said Brendan, jumping down and standing in her path. Cara kept her eyes up, but could feel a force radiating from the stark nakedness in front of her.

"Tell you what. You come for a swim with me now, and if I can hold my breath for four whole minutes, you have to go on a date with me tonight. If I come up a second before four minutes, I'll leave you alone."

"Four minutes?"

Cara and Drew used to time each other holding their breath in a neighbor's pool, and neither one of them ever made it past thirty seconds.

"I mean, I guess it's possible, but that's pretty long," said Cara. She couldn't figure out what his angle was and felt wary of being duped. Because four minutes was a really long time. At least, she thought it was.

"So do we have a deal?"

Cara pretended to think about it more, though her mind was already made up. She was intrigued. "Okay. But I'm going in in my bathing suit. I'm not getting naked."

"No worries, we've got time," said Brendan with a wink. "Here, take my watch."

He set the timer on his chunky digital watch to four minutes and handed it over to her.

Cara stripped off her shorts and shirt and followed him into the water. She told herself she'd been wanting to go for a swim anyway. It was a hot day and the seawater would soothe her sun-fried skin. She crossed her arms tightly around her chest and got into the water as fast as she could so as to avoid exposing her body to further inspection.

As they waded deeper, Cara noticed a giant tattoo diving down the left side of Brendan's back, a detailed rendering of a sperm whale.

"You into whales or something?"

"Oh, you mean this guy?" Brendan glanced over his shoulder. "Yeah, you could say that."

Cara assumed that Brendan wouldn't have made the wager if he thought he had no chance of winning. But four whole minutes? This was a scam to get her into the water with him. Still, having spent the last three days with her geriatric aunt and uncle, being with someone her own age was a welcome happenstance. She let the charade continue.

"All right. Let's see it."

"Four minutes. On the clock," said Brendan. "That's a long time, you know. You might start to miss me."

"I think I'll be okay."

"Okay then, I'll see you in four."

It happened so quickly it caught Cara off guard. She'd expected Brendan to make a big show of preparing for the dive, gulping in air and equipping his lungs, but it hardly looked like he'd taken in a breath at all. In a moment, he was gone, disappeared below the water's surface so fast that she didn't know where to look.

The longitude of the time frame became increasingly evident as Cara stood there in the water by herself, not sure what to do. She mentally prepared herself to be grabbed by the ankles and pulled below the water at any moment. She wouldn't put it past him to swim away and sneak a few gulps when she wasn't looking. She scanned the water for bubbles or ripples, anything that might hint at where he'd gone.

As the clock ticked past two minutes, she started to wonder if he'd swum to shore and was now over there getting a kick out of watching her. Determined not to be duped, she swiveled around on her right toe, her eyes scouring the water and the beach. It was getting close to four minutes now and there was still no sign of him. When the timer beeped and he still hadn't emerged, she felt certain she'd been conned.

Yet the thought that he could have drowned did also pass her mind. What if he never came up? Would she continue to look for him or go on her way with a new story to tell?

She heard a splash behind her and, swiveling, saw Brendan's body rising out of the water.

"Did I make it?"

He hardly seemed out of breath.

"To be determined," she said. "You were gone for over four minutes, but I'm not convinced you were holding your breath."

"What? Are you serious? I've been down there the whole time!"

"Have you?"

"Where would I have gone?"

"I don't know. You could have sneaked a breath when I wasn't looking or something."

"I swear to you I didn't," said Brendan. "I was just under there for four minutes! You owe me a date."

"You really held your breath for that long."

"Yes. I almost *died* for you."

"Yeah. Okay." Cara smirked.

"Okay, fine. It wasn't exactly death-defying—I'll give you that. But I did stay underwater for a really long time. You know, there are people out there who can hold their breath for close to thirty minutes. Deep-sea divers. It's a thing. Look it up."

"So you're a diver."

"I wouldn't say that, no."

"Then how were you able to just do that?"

"US Special Forces, baby. We got all kinds of talents."

"You're in the army?"

"Yes, ma'am. Got a big mission coming up in a couple of weeks too. Trying to get some R&R squeezed in before I ship out."

Cara felt a pinprick of disappointment. "Where are you going?" she asked.

"Afraid that's classified info."

"Well, aren't you important."

"Very important. And today is your lucky day, because you get to go on a date with me."

2014

Cara pours herself a glass of wine and sits in a beach chair outside the barn. Graham will be home any minute and she still isn't sure what she's going to say to him. She feels ridiculous for even allowing herself to consider the possibility that Jimmy Coughlin's story might be true. Because even if it is, it hardly changes things. Still, there's a part of her that's tempted to hop in the old Whaler and motor out to Gull's Ledge herself.

Dean said he'd alerted the coast guard out of an abundance of caution but would leave it to Cara to decide whether or not to contact the police. And while she appreciates his efforts to respect her privacy, she feels pressured by the weight of the decision now on her shoulders. On the one hand, the police would have the resources to perform an exhaustive search of the area. But what could she possibly say to them to convince them that it was worth it?

She'd dropped contact with Detective Sawyer a little over a year and a half ago. She and Graham had determined it was for the best. The agreement was that they'd only communicate with him if *he* reached out to *them*. But he never did.

She wonders now if Sawyer's even still working, if he's still the one assigned to the case. And if she were to contact him now, would he take her seriously? Would the past year and a half of sustained silence somehow add clout to her claim that she hadn't had before, back when she was calling him multiple times a week—sometimes multiple times a day? She winces at the thought, takes another gulp of wine.

The potential for humiliation is high. The potential for disappointment, even higher. She reminds herself that she has only a thirdhand account from a local fisherman to go by, and seamen aren't exactly known for their truthful storytelling. It could be nothing—just a pair of buoys some drunk fisherman mistook for humans. How many times has she herself mistaken seals for people, seeing their dark little heads bobbing up to the surface for air?

Cara hears Graham pull into the driveway and watches lights flick on as he makes his way through the house. He checks for her in the den and then moves upstairs, evidently thinking she might already be in bed. It's from the upstairs window that he finally locates her. She waves up to him from her chair and braces herself for the conversation to come.

Cara feels grateful to have Graham in her life. As she waits for him to come down, she commends her younger self for doing the smart thing. For marrying the good guy. To think she'd overlooked him . . . She'd fallen into the trap so many young women do of mistaking stability for insipidity; niceness for insecurity; humility for weakness. He isn't the man she always imagined she'd end up with. She had a track record of falling for the loudest, cockiest man in the room, quietly watching from afar and hoping he'd notice her.

Graham is different. His intelligence and creativity are sexy in ways she'd never realized they could be. He's smart, but unassuming. She loves introducing him to new people and showing off how thoughtful and bright he is. And she *likes* that his style is based entirely on comfort and practicality. He isn't trying to impress anybody, because he's confident in who he is. He's never been much of an athlete, but he keeps in shape with regular push-ups and a diligent cycling habit, and she loves how tall he is, how his long, toned arms can wrap all the way around her body nearly twice.

He'd been so gentle and patient with her during what had been the darkest period of her life. She'd been raised as a true New Englander, discreet with her emotions and tough in the face of adversity; the only thing worse than being unhappy was revealing said unhappiness to those around you. But all of that went out the window when she lost Micah—her beautiful, healthy, loving Micah.

Graham had let her grieve. He'd waited almost three and a half months for a first kiss—though of course they'd known each other for much longer than that. He was the one who'd gotten her eating again—coaxed her to get out of bed before ten, put in her contacts, wear clothes with buttons and seams. He helped her build a new life, and welcomed her into his.

She knew Graham had made serious sacrifices for her, though none of them were sacrifices she'd asked him to make. He had left a life in New York as a budding filmmaker to settle full-time on the island and take care of her. He'd invited Cara to help him with his grandfather's gallery, a gift she hadn't known she needed. The gallery had quickly become a place of peace and healing for her, art the only antidote to her madness.

She remembers how Graham used to watch her as she floated among the art, losing herself in the paintings' textures, and colors, and light. She could physically feel his love—could see it in the way he looked at her.

She'd waited until after they eloped to introduce him to her family. She knew it upset Graham, having to wait. She'd once listened patiently as he shared the narratives of insecurity he'd built up in his head to account for her hesitation. *She was embarrassed of him. She was embarrassed of them. She was hiding something.* The reality was far more complicated, impossible to convey in a single sentence.

After the ceremony, a private affair at the Edgartown courthouse, Cara had at last summoned the courage to call her father and brother to tell them about Graham. Just a few months later, she gave in to Graham's pleading for a small celebration with both their families, and was pleasantly surprised by the result. Everyone had gotten along. Graham and her brother had bonded over the intersection of music and film (Drew a musician, Graham a filmmaker), and although she knew Graham wasn't the sort of man her father generally surrounded himself with (the two had nearly nothing in common), it was clear to Stanley that Graham was kind, and trustworthy, and that he loved Cara. He would take care of her.

Even now, Cara marvels at the way Graham loves her. At his loyalty and his certainty. And she loves it. She loves how much he loves her.

"There you are. You had me worried," says Graham, folding open a chair beside her.

"Sorry."

"Everything okay?"

"Yeah. Yeah, no. I'm fine."

She wants to tell him about what she learned at the docks, but she knows what his reaction will be and doesn't want to hear it. He means well, but it's hard sometimes not to mistake Graham's natural leaning toward practicality and logic for condescension or judgment.

"You sure?" Graham pulls the chair closer and wraps his fingers around her forearm. "You have a tough day?"

Cara pulls her arm away. *Tough day* is their code phrase for depressive misery. *Did you contemplate suicide today?* But today has not been one of those days. In fact, it's been months since she's had a day like that, and even *that* day was nothing like the days she used to have.

"I'm fine."

"Okay. I just got a little worried when you weren't in the house. And then when I do find you, you're out here in the dark."

"I know. I'm sorry," she says. "I just had something weird happen today and I'm not really sure how to handle it."

"Do you want to talk about it?"

"I don't know. I'm worried you're not going to take it seriously."

Graham looks hurt. "Try me."

Only after having sent these warning signals does Cara feel like she can share her news. Graham knows now—regardless of what's about to come out of Cara's mouth—that he'll need to tone down his reaction, or risk being cut off completely by his stubborn wife.

"Someone thinks they saw Micah and Brendan," she says.

Graham takes a deep breath and sits back in his chair, staring upward at the night sky. "Who? Who saw them? Where?"

"One of Dean's guys."

"Here? In town? On the island?"

Cara can sense Graham getting nervous. If the story is true, and Micah and Brendan really have been found, where does that leave him? But she knows that the rest of the story will ease his concerns, transforming his trepidation into haughty skepticism. She wants to lie and tell him that, yes, they were in fact spotted in town, picking up groceries in Oak Bluffs, of all places! That's a story he might believe.

"Where does he think he saw them?" Graham presses again.

"By this place called Gull's Ledge. On Nantucket Sound."

"Like . . . in a boat?"

Cara can't bring herself to answer, but her silence is enough.

"Oh. I see."

This is all Graham says, but she knows what he is thinking. *Here we go again.*

"See. This is why I didn't want to tell you."

"Hold on," says Graham. "I didn't say anything. Give me a chance here. Tell me what happened."

Cara sighs. "One of Dean's boats was out on Nantucket Sound yesterday, and this guy Jimmy *swears* he saw a man and a boy in the water, just—treading water like it was nothing. And then as soon as he got closer, they dove back into the water and never came back up again."

"And so you think these people that this guy, Jeremy—"

"Jimmy."

"—Jimmy. Sorry. You think these people *Jimmy* saw were Micah and Brendan. That they're out there, in the ocean."

"Don't patronize me, Graham."

Graham puts a hand on her shoulder and softens his voice. "I'm not, I'm not. I'm just trying to get the facts straight."

"Yeah, but when you say it like that, it sounds ridiculous."

"Okay. I'm sorry. I didn't mean to."

"I know it sounds crazy, but you have to admit, it's weird, right? Why would two people be out there?"

"Totally. It's totally bizarre," Graham says.

"I know Dean and them are always making up stories and stuff, but I don't see why they would make this up."

Graham nods, then seems to reconsider, tilting his head to one side. "Well, you know Dean."

"What do you mean?"

"He's not the *most* credible."

"So you think he made it up."

"No . . ." Graham chooses his words carefully. "I believe one of his guys probably saw something. That is completely possible. But don't you think it's *also* possible that maybe this guy's eyes were playing tricks on him?"

"I know. But he said they saw them through their binoculars," Cara says. "That it was unmistakable."

"Okay. Fair enough. So, let's go through this. Let's say it really was them out there. In the water. What's our next step?"

Cara shakes her head.

"Do you want to contact the police?" asks Graham. "See if they can help?"

"No. I don't know," says Cara. "You're right. It was probably just some seals or something. It was stupid to let myself get my hopes up."

"I'm sorry. I feel like I just ruined this for you. Don't listen to me. If you trust the story, let's pursue it."

"No, you're right. The police wouldn't do anything anyway."

Graham's face brightens. "Or we could go look. We could borrow my uncle's boat and see if we see anything."

Cara is touched by Graham's efforts, his willingness to set aside his own disbelief to humor her irrational hopes. She even laughs a little, picturing the two of them aimlessly motoring around the Sound. "That's okay."

She pauses, looks over at him.

"I just miss him so much, Graham."

"I know you do." He stands and pulls Cara up with him, holding her in his arms.

"I really wanted it to be them."

2008

Cara told Moira and Ed that she was going out with a friend. She lied and said she'd run into a girl from school at the cliffs. She could see the relief in her aunt's eyes. It made Cara want to strangle her. She didn't want to be the lonely, pathetic girl they thought she was.

She was nervous, but when Cara thought back on the afternoon, she physically couldn't keep herself from smiling. The excitement brewed in the space below her earlobes and above her jawline and spread with a staticky tingle down her body. Brendan was undeniably handsome. She was both entranced and unnerved by his eyes, his expression perpetually in a sort of knowing smirk. Looks aside, he was masculine and uninhibited in a way that was either old-fashioned or just plain blue-collar. He was goofy, but witty. Fearless, but endearing.

She struggled to decide what to wear, standing on the bed to get a fuller image of herself in the mirror of her mom's old bureau as she tried on different outfits. She wanted to look her best, but was determined to maintain the air of indifference with feigned hints of resentment that made her and Brendan's banter so melodious. He was the smug but desperately smitten pursuer, and she the reluctant but coy object of his affection; she was only going on this date because she *had to*, indentured by the confines of a very (but really, not at all) serious bet. She couldn't let him see her try.

Against her better judgment, she went with a cotton dress with spaghetti straps. She was going to freeze in the evening sea breeze. She threw a cardigan into the basket of the bike she'd been borrowing from Moira and Ed, a vintage model with a horn and everything. It was the kind of bike the other art students at school would have drooled over, cool because it wasn't.

The brakes squeaked as she rolled up to the Menemsha harpooner statue, their agreed-upon meeting point. There was Brendan, in a T-shirt and shorts this time, sitting alone in the sand with his knees up and a backpack to his side. His face curved with an unabashed smile when he saw her. His hair, the color of walnuts, looked lighter now that it was dry. He had a habit of sweeping the longer pieces back away from his forehead with his hand.

A sickly twinge of pleasure spread through Cara's stomach and tightened up her throat. She tucked in her head and shoulders in an attempt to hide her smile.

"You put clothes on," she said.

"Yes. I'm afraid that's the nature of the society we live in. Wear clothes or get arrested."

"It's a wonder any of us can live with such oppression," Cara said.

"That's what I'm saying!" Brendan said, getting up and grabbing his things. "I can't believe you came. You look stunning."

He scanned her body with his eyes. Cara felt exposed. She silently wished she had gone with her second-choice outfit, a conservative T-shirt and jeans. Her efforts felt naked and obvious even in the dimming evening light of summer.

"Here," said Brendan, handing Cara a waxed paper cup with cap and straw. "You like frappes? Milk, chocolate, ice cream, the whole deal?"

"Yes, I like frappes. Who do you think I am?"

Brendan put his hands up in defense. "I don't know. Just checking. You seemed pretty averse to fun this morning."

"Are you trying to get me to leave?"

"Absolutely not. I'll have you know, Brendan McGrath doesn't buy a frappe for just anybody."

"I'm honored."

"Should we go sit? On the beach?"

Brendan put on his backpack and gestured for her to take the lead. They walked out to the sand together in silence. Cara stood to the side as Brendan removed a tattered, once-white bath towel from his pack and spread it out before them. At his invitation she took a seat, careful to cross her legs.

The small size of the towel afforded them little room to move. She could feel the heat radiating from his body in the inch of space between their arms.

"You want some Baileys?"

Brendan pulled out a bottle of the Irish whiskey and tilted it in Cara's direction. Just the thought of alcohol—and the sedation it might provide—helped to ease her nerves. Cara had been head of the SALSA group in high school—Students Advocating for Life without Substance Abuse—and had always turned her nose up at friends who didn't have the self-control to abstain from drinking the way she did. She could remember sitting to the side at parties, marveling at their embarrassing lack of self-awareness as they sloppily threw themselves at boys, shouting, dancing, and singing like fools.

And then Cara's mom died, and she went away to college, and thought, *Fuck it*. She didn't care if the kids from high school called her out as a hypocrite. Because as it turned out, she'd been wrong and they'd been right. Drinking was amazing. It was fun, and freeing, and exhilarating. It gave her the courage to go out in the ruffled cotton miniskirt she'd bought at Abercrombie and was always too scared to wear outside of the house, and sit on the laps of drunk boys at parties, who wore popped collars and puka shell necklaces. And while she'd made some rookie mistakes with mixing substances, to be sure, she'd eventually gotten the hang of it.

Cara pried off the lid of her shake and passed it to Brendan, who poured the stuff in with such a heavy hand that she had to pull the cup away. The brown liquid spilled over his fingers.

"You realize you just wasted about a gallon of deliciousness."

"Well, you just poured about five gallons of deliciousness into my frappe. Look at it, it's not even mixing in with the ice cream. It's just floating on the top!"

"Well, yeah. You gotta give it a little mixer-upper with the straw. It'll filter down. Just start drinking. You'll feel better soon."

"That's a very forward suggestion."

"Maybe. But am I wrong?"

Cara took a sip and coughed from the burn in her throat.

"Tasty, right?"

The sweet chocolatey essence of the shake was ruined, marred by the boozy torch of alcohol, but Cara slurped it up anyway, grimacing as she swallowed.

She was starving. Operating under the assumption she and Brendan would be getting dinner, Cara had foolishly declined Moira's offer to heat up yesterday night's cod cakes. She now had to clear her throat and hope for crashing waves to obscure the sound of her twisting stomach. It didn't work.

"Was that your stomach? Are you hungry?"

"No, I don't know what that was. I already ate."

"Are you sure? We can go back to the Galley and get food. They've got burgers and stuff."

"Oh, no. I'm fine, really," Cara lied. "I already ate."

She felt stupid for having expected they would be getting food. Like her expectations for the date were too high. Like she liked him more than he liked her. She felt even dumber for dismissing the visit to the Galley. She was always doing this, lying to make other people comfortable at her own expense. Saying she'd seen movies she hadn't. Pretending that she didn't have to pee, when she'd been holding it for hours. Acting like she wasn't cold when she was freezing.

"I'm sorry. This is, like, the worst date in the history of mankind," said Brendan.

"Oh, stop. It's fine."

"No, seriously. Look at those people over there."

Brendan pointed to a couple sitting together on a giant beach towel with a flannel blanket over their shoulders and glasses of wine in their hands. Cara longed for the warmth of a blanket. Goose bumps revealed the spiky blond hairs on her knees.

"They've got the Cadillac of picnics over there, and I roll up in my—I don't even know what—my 1993 beige Camry with the bumper falling off."

"This towel is so small," Cara managed to say before letting out a laugh.

"I know," agreed Brendan. "And you'd think I planned it as, like, a scheme to get closer to you. But this is seriously all I had. This is the best I can do, right here."

"I like it," said Cara, the whiskey making her bolder. "It's cute." She took another sip of her shake.

"So, what else?" asked Brendan. "Tell me your story."

"My story?"

"Yeah. Wait, actually—basics first. How old are you?"

"Guess."

"No way. I'm not falling for that."

"Falling for what?"

"Guessing a woman's age."

Cara was struck by being called a woman.

"That's only dangerous with middle-aged women," she said. "I'm still young enough to think it's funny if you overshoot."

"Fair enough. Twenty-two."

"What, did you google me or something?"

"Why? Is your age listed on your Wikipedia page?"

"*No.* But I can't believe you just guessed right on the first try."

"I guess you just look your age."

"Is that another trick you learned in the army? Age detection training?"

"Nope. You just look twenty-two."

"Speaking of age," said Cara, "*you* seem a little young to be special forces. Don't you have to, like, work your way up for that? For years?"

Brendan shrugged, avoiding eye contact.

"What does *that* mean? Were you lying before, or are you not allowed to talk about it?"

"I wasn't lying."

"So you're not allowed to talk about it."

"I would talk about it with you."

"Then tell me," Cara pressed.

"I'd rather talk about you."

"You can't do that. I'm interested now."

"Fine. I'll tell you whatever you want to know. But then it's your turn. Deal?"

"Deal."

"I joined the army after high school. Did a few tours. After that it was just sort of a right-place-right-time kind of thing. They had a need and I fit it."

"Did you go to Iraq?"

"Yup."

With this casual admission, Cara's perception of Brendan changed. She didn't want to assume that because he'd served overseas, that somehow made him damaged or laden with trauma, but she felt meek and ordinary sitting there next to him, suddenly so self-conscious of her relatively sheltered life. She wondered if he'd ever killed anyone.

"You don't have to get all quiet about it," said Brendan. "I'm proud of what I've accomplished. There's no reason to feel sorry for me."

"I don't," Cara said. "My dad served in Kuwait when I was little. So I get it."

She was glad to have this fact to point to, but she didn't really—*get it*. Her dad never talked about his time overseas. Ever. In fact, she often forgot that he had served. To her, he was just an insurance salesman. She could remember meeting his friends from the military just once. She must have been ten or eleven years old. It was Veterans Day or Memorial Day or something like that, and her family had hosted a barbecue at their house. They'd set up a slip-and-slide in the backyard for her and the other kids, whom she'd never met before, and never saw again. She could remember the men—she pictured them all with mustaches, but it was probably just the one—standing by the grill with their beers while the moms sat in fold-out chairs and supervised the children.

There'd been an incident that day with her brother, Drew, and the hose. He'd picked it up and pointed it at the dads, playfully spraying them as boys of his age were wont to do. But one of the dads hadn't found it funny. To the contrary, Drew's antics had made him very, very angry. She'd never forgotten the way he ripped the hose from Drew's hands and yelled in his face. She'd drawn a picture of it in her journal later—Drew holding a hose and the man with the mustache, red-faced, with lines drawn outward diagonally from his mouth to connote yelling.

Brendan's military ties made him instantly more attractive to Cara, and she wondered if this was in part because it made him seem tougher—manlier—or if it stemmed from some latent Oedipus complex. The people she'd grown up with and gone to college with were all far too privileged to have experienced actual hardship. The boys she'd dated in the past were tough and cool because they played football or grew up in Detroit, and not because they'd actually faced any real sort of adversity. That didn't mean they weren't good people, with plenty to offer the world, but it was clear that their personal sense of hardiness would have crumbled in the face of someone like Brendan. She found herself fending off waves of self-reproach in response to the strong feelings of fascination and attraction that Brendan evoked. She changed the subject.

"Where did you go to school?"

Brendan's shoulders shrank. His eyes pitched back and forth, avoiding hers.

"No college for me," he said. "Maybe someday. Put it on Uncle Sam's tab."

Cara blushed. "Oh, right. Sorry. You said that. I'm an idiot. But anyway, I mean, I *did* go to college and it's hardly helped me so far. Getting a job, I mean."

Cara told him about her failed attempts to find work in New York City, leaving her with two options: summer in the desert with her dad and stepmom, or out on the island with Aunt Moira and Uncle Ed.

"What about your real mom? Is she dead?"

The way that he asked it, so forthright and candid, Cara couldn't decide if it was offensive or refreshing. *Is she dead?*

Brendan sat with one leg stretched out in front of him, the other bent, supported by his toes, his knee bouncing with agitation. He continued to look at her, waiting for an answer as if his question had been perfectly normal.

"Yeah. Yeah, she's dead."

"How?"

"How did she die?"

Brendan nodded.

"Ovarian cancer."

Before Cara could squelch it, a swell of emotion overtook her. Her shock at Brendan's question. Her nerves about being there. Her empty stomach. Her disappointment at having struck out on the job market. The chill in the air. The Baileys. An uncontrollable feeling of listlessness.

"I'm sorry. Shit, are you crying? I'm sorry, we can talk about something else."

Brendan tucked an arm around her waist.

"No, *I'm* sorry," said Cara, wiping her cheeks. "I don't know where these tears came from. I think I'm just tired or something. Sorry. God, this is so embarrassing."

She'd been so successful at staving off the ache so far, but something about Brendan had left her defenseless, unable to keep pretending. It was humiliating. She wanted to get up and leave. Get on her bike, ride away, and never see Brendan again. She glanced back up the beach toward the parking lot.

"You must think I'm crazy," she said.

"Yeah, I do. One, I think you're crazy for thinking you're crazy," said Brendan. "And two, I think you're crazy for staying here with me at what has to be the world's worst picnic."

"I told you, I love it," said Cara, laughing through her tears. "It's a great picnic. At least, it was until I went and made it all dark. Out of nowhere. Like a crazy person."

"Listen, I get it. My mom's dead too."

She wasn't glad to hear this revelation—of course not—but as soon as he said it, she felt closer to him. She'd often felt an unspoken connection to others who had experienced grief like hers, a shared understanding that you were both indelibly injured. You didn't have to try to articulate your pain or hide it in shame, because they knew. You both knew.

"She is?"

"Yeah. She died in a car accident a few years ago. Drunk behind the wheel. Hit a tree." He took a drag on his straw, swallowing down a gulp of his frappe. "The good news is that no one else was injured. At least there's that."

Brendan laughed. He spoke rapidly, blundering on with a rehearsed lightheartedness that shook with insecurity.

"Yeah. She loved the bottle. It was hard sometimes, growing up, but it still hurt. When she died. You know that, though. Your mom's dead too. Life can be shit sometimes. But hey, I'm out here with you, so I guess I'm doing all right. I promise I'm not an alcoholic too, in case you're worried about that. They say it's hereditary, I know."

Cara sensed this was her cue to laugh, as if what Brendan was telling her was somehow funny. But it wasn't. She couldn't.

"I'm really sorry," she whispered. "About your mom."

"Nah, don't be. Don't be sorry. It's all good."

Cara felt another round of tears coming. She covered her face with her hands. The sudden onslaught of very different emotions she was feeling, all at the same time, overwhelmed her.

"Hey, hey, stop that," said Brendan, hugging her to his side. "Look at me. I'm okay. I'm here on a beautiful beach watching the sunset with you. None of that shit matters. All right? You've got to stop crying. You're killing me here."

Cara took in a deep breath, the air still unsettled in her passageways.

"Losing my mom was the worst thing that's ever happened to me," she said. "But it was years ago. I don't know why it's still so hard for me to talk about it without crying—like you can. And I can't begin to imagine growing up with an alcoholic parent. That must have been really tough. You must think I'm such a baby. And I am. I know I am. It's just . . . I'm embarrassed."

"Hey. This isn't a who's got the saddest story competition, okay?" Brendan zeroed his eyes in on Cara's until she looked back at him. "It isn't. So stop beating yourself up. I'm not judging you like you think I am. Believe me. I've been judged enough myself in my life. But I swear I'm not trying to one-up you or something. I'm just trying to relate, to show you that I understand. And that it's nothing to be ashamed of. Okay? You loved your mom and you miss her. You're human."

Cara nodded. She looked back at him and hiccupped, making both of them laugh. She leaned in closer, her heart beating fast. Hands shaking, she grabbed Brendan's and kissed him. The salt of her tears permeated their mouths and mixed with the chocolatey booze of the Baileys. What started as a blundering lip smush shortly evolved into a genuine, fluid kiss. Cara was relieved to feel Brendan kissing her back.

When they pulled apart, he gave her a disapproving look.

"Was that just a pity kiss right there? Did you just do that because you feel bad for me?"

"No—"

"Poor soldier son of an alkie? 'I feel really bad for him and I don't know what to do, so I think I'll just kiss him'?"

"*No*," said Cara again with more force. "Listen to me." She gripped his shoulders and focused his body toward hers.

Maybe it was the Baileys or the unguarded state her spontaneous tears had left her in, but Cara trusted Brendan. She felt at ease with him in a way she rarely did with someone she'd just met, let alone someone she felt so attracted to. His open affection toward her—automatic, unwavering, unconditional—felt like an antidote to the grief that just being on the island had awakened.

45

"I kissed you because I like you. God, I hardly know you, but I like you. You're so funny. And clever. I can hardly keep up. But I want you to know that I'm having a really nice time." She shrugged and wiped her face. "Tears and all."

Another man, Cara thought, might have taken the compliment and said thank you. But not Brendan. In their brief time together, she'd already observed his tendency to cut through the serious—the sentimental—with a self-deprecating remark or hyperbolic return compliment. She'd noticed it because she often did this herself. Brendan, however, was one of those people who never seemed able to find their personal "off" switch, perpetually in a protective "on" position.

So what he said was, "Thank you, but you forgot handsome."

Brendan was staying on a friend's boat—a guy he'd served with in Fallujah. Of course, the boat wasn't in the water, but perched up on pine blocks and metal jack stands beside the guy's driveway in Chilmark. Cara and Brendan rode their bikes there in the dark, a move Cara knew would have given Moira a heart attack had she known. She swerved aggressively off the asphalt and into the grass almost every time a pair of headlights approached, an overly cautious approach that Brendan seemed to find endearing.

The boat was nearly forty feet long and they had to climb up a stepladder to get into it.

"Are you sure this is safe?" Cara felt the structure wobble as she climbed aboard.

She waited on the deck while Brendan went below and turned on the lights. She could see through the trees that a light was on in the main house down the driveway. The anxious teenager inside of her worried about being caught, as if her presence here were somehow

46

against the rules. She was relieved to descend into the safe cover of the ship's cabin.

While the interior of the vessel was far more spacious than it looked from the outside, the furnishings hearkened back to a time when a gallon of gas cost sixty cents and itchy tweed reigned supreme. The walls and cabinets were a honey-brown teak, accented with olive-green and blood-red plaid cushions and deep-crimson velveteen curtains. There was a cordoned-off kitchen area with a mini fridge and sink to the right of the stairs. The counter shelving opposite the kitchenette was strewn with rusty nails, fraying ropes, wrinkled maps, and greasy lubricants; colored wires splayed out from a black box to the side. A tattered rug ran the length of the ship like a runway, between two facing settees: a port-side double berth and a starboard-side single. Brendan's sleeping bag lay strewn on the port side with a sad airline pillow. The place smelled like moldy fabric and sawdust.

They weren't actually in the water, but the mere act of being there in the boat felt adventurous. It was as if they'd already traveled hundreds of miles from civilization. It was just them now.

"You want a drink?" Brendan asked. "I've got Bud Light and half a bottle of Popov."

Cara opted for the Bud Light and sat down on the starboard side of the ship, intentionally staying away from the "bed," as if there were still a chance she might later ride home by herself in the dark.

"So this is where you live," she said.

"For now," said Brendan. "I don't actually live anywhere anymore. Not really."

He sat down next to Cara, cracking open his beer can.

"I guess I don't either," she said, before catching herself. "Well, I do. You probably *really* don't live anywhere. I still technically live at my dad's. A lot of my stuff is there, but it's never really felt like home."

"How come?"

"Lucia."

"Ugh, Lucia. She is the worst."

"The *worst*."

"Evil stepmom?"

"Stepmom, yes. Evil? No. Just . . . a little uptight. And hard to read. We never have anything to talk about besides, like, the weather and her plants."

"Hmm."

"I know what you're thinking. Could be worse. And I know that. It's more bizarre than anything else. My dad was raised Catholic, but we never went to church growing up. I think he maybe went a couple of times on his own, but almost never—until my mom got sick, and then I guess he felt like he needed it again. I don't know. After she died, he started going even more. Moved to Phoenix, found a church he liked, met Lucia, and got married, all in under two years."

Cara couldn't believe how quickly the words were coming out of her mouth. Why was she treating this guy like he was her therapist or something? She blamed the island—the isolation of living with two old people, surrounded by ocean on all sides, with no job, no direction. That, combined with the loneliness of being away from all of her friends, whom she was accustomed to being surrounded by 24/7.

But Brendan seemed genuinely interested. "You think it helped him grieve? The church?"

"I guess so, yeah. I went with him a few times, but I just didn't get it."

"I always feel a little jealous of the guys I serve with who have religion," said Brendan. "They have a faith in the order and meaning of things that I can never grasp. On the one hand, they're brainwashed as shit, sure. But they're more at peace than I am. They accept things that I can't."

Cara rested her beer on the floor and looked at Brendan.

"What?"

"I feel a little sad for you," she said.

"Why? Don't. I told you, I'm proud of what I do."

"But it doesn't scare you? Being a soldier?"

"Of course it does."

"So why do you do it? You're so bright. You could do anything."

The thought came out more insulting than Cara had anticipated. Brendan either didn't notice or chose to let it slide.

"I try not to think about it too much. It's just what I do."

"Are you really shipping out again soon?"

"Yeah."

"How soon?" Cara wasn't sure she wanted to know the answer.

"About two months."

"Are you going back? To the Middle East?"

"No."

"Are you allowed to tell me where you're going?"

"No, but I will."

"You don't have to. You said earlier it was classified."

"North Korea. I'm going to North Korea."

"You really don't have to tell me this. I don't want to get you in trouble."

"I want to tell you. I've got no one else to tell."

Cara wasn't quite sure what to do with this information. Brendan spoke so matter-of-factly that she questioned whether he was telling the truth, though he had no reason to lie. She didn't know much about North Korea, only what she'd seen in news clips and documentary shorts, but she knew enough to understand that it was a dangerous place for Westerners. Merely hearing him mention it made her nervous, as if she shouldn't have asked.

Fatigue from the excitement of the day was beginning to set in. Cara felt herself relaxing into a long, crazy-eyed stare. Her daze did not go unnoticed.

"You're tired."

"A little bit. Yeah."

"Let's lie down."

"Right here?"

"There's more room on that side."

"But that's your bed," said Cara. "I don't want to take over your space."

Brendan laughed. "Seriously?"

"What?"

"Never mind. You're right. You sleep on this side and I'll sleep over there. Alone. I'd really prefer not to have to share with you. In fact, it's probably best that we have as little physical contact as possible from here on out."

Cara smirked. "Is that right?"

"Yeah. Actually, you don't mind sleeping up in the bow, do you?" Brendan nodded to the crowded wedge of cushions at the front of the boat. "I don't want to breathe in too much of your recycled air. You're small, so you should fit."

Cara pursed her lips to keep from smiling and shook her head in mock disdain.

They looked at each other like two little kids with secrets. Cara picked at the dirt under her fingernails and waited to see what Brendan would do. She'd look at him, and then the ceiling, then back at him, and to the floor, while Brendan remained locked on her, charmed and in no way dissuaded by her obvious nerves.

"Come on, let's lie down."

Brendan stood up and extended a hand toward Cara. His palms were warm, but dry. He pulled her up to standing and held on to her hand as he lay down on the other side of the aisle. Ever fearful of misinterpreting even the most obvious of come-ons, Cara remained standing at Brendan's side, forcing him to reel her in by the arm and then the waist, pulling her down and in close to his side.

The last person Cara had been with was Simon Danews. It was one of those bizarre senior-week hookups blooming from the mixture of nostalgic sadness and nervous excitement associated with graduation. She and Simon were both art majors and had taken countless classes together, without ever really getting to know each other. His work was abstract and hard to grasp, while hers was tight and true to life. She went to frat parties and drank cheap beer while he hot-boxed his apartment and drew political cartoons with friends. He was skinny, with a scraggly, greasy blond ponytail, and always wore the same pair of wine-colored corduroys. She remembered enjoying the sex simply because he'd been so different, so unexpected. They'd both known it was nothing more than a spontaneous, one-night-only event. *This is weird, but let's just go with it.*

The feeling with Brendan was different. Everything about him—the touch of his skin, the smell of his body, the warmth of his mouth—inspired an exhilarating pulsing deep within her that drew so strongly from her muscles and nerves that it was almost hard to breathe. She clung to him as if out of desperation, pressing her palms and fingertips against his shoulder blades, pulling his body close to her own as he kissed her and slowly slipped off her underwear and dress. Keeping her close, Brendan pulled Cara upright, guiding her hips with his hands.

She'd known this would happen—could feel it all day—yet the thrill of it happening now, for real, was even more exhilarating than the physical act itself. To be this close, this intimate, with this man she barely knew, who made her so giddy and nervous and excited all at once, created a surge of energy and turmoil that made it hard for her brain to slow down. In the moment it was chaotic and frantic and disorienting, and afterward it was quiet, damp, tranquil.

———

Three days passed before Cara heard from Brendan again. It was longer than she'd expected. Long enough to awaken her hushed insecurities. As the minutes crept by without word, the lens through which she viewed her initial encounter with him began to cloud. She replayed her eighteen hours with him in her head, searching for missteps, moments where she'd perhaps said the wrong thing or interpreted his actions and words to mean something contrary to his intent.

The morning after their night together on the boat, they had gone to the General Store for breakfast sandwiches. Cara got a mango Nantucket Nectar juice, and Brendan got an A&W root beer, which Cara thought was a funny choice for 10:30 a.m. The way she remembered it, the conversation had been light and unobtrusive. They'd reminisced about their childhoods in the nineties, laughing about the shows they'd watched and the cereal they loved.

Cara was admittedly, as Brendan described it, "one of those PBS kids who loved learning shows like *Arthur* and *Wishbone*," though in her defense, Cara's TV-watching privileges had been tightly controlled by her parents. Brendan's were not. He was a pure Nickelodeon boy, addicted to shows like *Rugrats* and *Ren and Stimpy*, the latter of which had repulsed Cara as a child in the rare viewings she was able to sneak at friends' houses. Neither of them had anything good to say about *Scooby-Doo*.

They'd parted when Cara got a call from Moira, checking in to make sure she was okay. Brendan had kissed her good-bye, on the lips (which Cara now considered a very significant detail), clasping his arms around her waist and teasingly refusing to let go. She had played her usual part and pulled away, promising that it wouldn't be long before he saw her again. She would have been happy to see him again as soon as that same evening.

But Brendan never reached out.

Of course, there was no reason that Cara couldn't contact him herself. If she wanted to see him, and was confident that he would be happy to see her too, she had little to fear. But each time she brought up his number on her cell phone, she could only look at it, memorizing the sequence of numbers, careful not to press send by mistake.

In the beginning, it was her ego that held her back. If Brendan wanted to see her, then it was up to him to make that happen. She wasn't about to throw herself at him and make it easy. Though she'd never say it out loud, she liked the feeling of being pursued, although perhaps more from fear of rejection than from pride.

By noon on the second day of waiting, any sense of control Cara felt she had over the game she and Brendan were playing was dissipating. She began to seriously question why he would remain silent. Their time together was still relatively fresh in her mind, and she felt sure she'd done nothing to push him away. He'd kissed her when they parted. Was that not a good sign?

She tried to give him the benefit of the doubt. Brendan was an active member of the US military, and he'd told her he was shipping out in two months. It was entirely possible that he'd been called away sooner. At least, Cara imagined it was. She didn't know how these things worked.

In bed later that night, she drafted out sample text messages. There were many iterations, but the final words read as follows:

Hey, u still around? Free to meet up tomorrow?

She'd sent it. It was done. She regretted it as soon as she did it, but there was nothing to do now but wait for a response. Cara made sure her phone's alert sounds were on, and revved up the volume as high as it went. Then she turned out her light and tossed and turned for hours, even sitting up once to make sure the phone wasn't dead, before falling asleep sometime between three and four in the morning. When she woke up the next day (day three, because, yes, she was counting), there was still no response.

She was sure of it now. She'd been conned. Used for sex. It was her own fault for trusting a stranger, a man she knew nothing about, who'd hinted at a troubled past. He'd flat-out told her that his mom was a serious alcoholic. Then there was the detail that he was a soldier on leave. She was confident that most soldiers were noble, honorable men, but didn't many also have the reputation of being playboys? Life was different overseas. It changed people, made them act out. Caused them to behave in ways they were once taught not to. There were no rules in war.

And yet she'd ignored what she now saw to be these flaming red flags, seduced by Brendan's sense of humor and good looks. Because she had to hand it to him, the guy was charming. Not just charming, but magnetic. He'd completely fooled her, knowing full well what he was doing the whole time. She felt even worse when she realized he'd probably used the same moves on other girls before—showing up naked at the cliffs, pretending to hold his breath for a long time, the spiked frappes, the boat.

Anger and rage turned to self-admonishment and shame, before settling into a deeply felt sense of loneliness and, at last, disappointment.

I t was close to midnight when the dogs started barking. Someone was knocking on the door. Cara was awake in her bedroom, mindlessly paging through an old sketchbook. She froze and listened to the sound of Moira getting up and padding down the stairs.

She could hear muffled voices from below, her breath catching at the sound of her own name. Suddenly conscious that she didn't have a bra on, she quickly pulled a hoodie on over her thin cotton T-shirt when she heard Moira ascending the stairs, the toenails of the pack of terriers clicking against the steps as they raced up along with her. There was a light tap at the door.

"Bear? Are you asleep?"

The nickname brought up the ache, but only for a moment. Cara's mother used to call her Bear. She hadn't heard it since she'd passed.

Cara beckoned Moira inside and felt a thread of guilt when she saw her, decked out in her evening uniform, a flannel gown with a split ruffled collar, a Breath Right strip, and chintzy shark slippers from a novelty shop in Edgartown. It wasn't that late, not for a twenty-two-year-old, but Moira was nearing seventy; this was practically the middle of the night for her.

"There's a gentleman at the door for you. Are you expecting someone named Brendan?"

"I'm sorry, Moira. He shouldn't have come here this late. I don't know why he's here. He didn't tell me he was coming. Go back to sleep. I'll deal with it."

"Are you all right? Is everything okay?"

"Yeah. He's just—I don't know. I'll go talk to him. He's a friend of mine. You go to bed. I'm sorry you had to get up."

Cara was baffled by Brendan's behavior, showing up so late at night, without warning; yet she was equally grateful for a fresh reason to be mad at him, a reason seemingly unrelated to the lingering sting of rejection.

She found him pacing outside the back door, hands in the pockets of his shorts. His posture stiffened when he saw her. He smiled as if his visit were expected.

"Brendan, what are you doing here? You can't just show up like this."

"I know. I'm sorry, but I had to see you. I have to tell you something."

"Right now?"

"Yeah, right now. Can you come outside?"

Brendan glanced nervously over Cara's shoulders, as someone might appear behind her at any moment. Cara hesitated, not sure whether he deserved her cooperation. That's when Angus, the Boston terrier, slipped by Cara's feet and sped outside. She swore under her breath, pushed Brendan aside, and carefully shut the door behind her, shoving the noses of other flight-risk pups back inside with her toes. Angus reveled in the ensuing chase, scampering around the yard just out of reach.

"Fuck. Fuck, I'm sorry," said Brendan. "Is he not supposed to be out?"

"No, Brendan. He's not."

Cold blades of wet grass and shards of white seashell stuck to Cara's feet as she jogged around the yard on her toes. Eventually, with Brendan's help, she was able to corner the dog against the shed door and scoop him up, his legs wiggling with excitement. She brought Angus back inside, slid on some flip-flops, and rejoined Brendan in the cool evening fog.

The air was thick with moisture and the sound of crickets. Cara had her hood pulled up to keep her face and ears warm. Her bare legs shook from the cold.

"Are you mad at me now?"

"What?"

"Are you mad at me now? Because I set Angus free?"

"It's fine."

"Sorry. He seemed like he needed some air. Stretch his legs a little. Go on a thirty-second adventure."

Cara made a point of not laughing.

"You're mad."

"I'm not mad. I'm just . . . confused."

"About why Angus would want to run away from such a nice home? Me too. It's selfish. He doesn't know how good he has it."

Cara sighed. "Brendan. What are you doing here? It's almost midnight."

"I wanted to see you."

"You could have seen me anytime you wanted over the past *three days*."

"I know. I'm sorry. I have this thing where I get lost in my head sometimes. And I just need to be alone. Even though I wanted to see you. I really, really wanted to see you. I've been going back and forth about telling you something. And I wasn't going to, but then I decided that I was. Tonight, I decided that I was—*that I am*—going to tell you. And I had to come see you before I changed my mind. So now I'm here. So I can tell you."

Brendan was breathing heavily, using his hands to smooth back his hair, over and over. Cara didn't know what to make of him. She was glad he was there, she couldn't deny that, but his explanation for his absence confounded her. Seeing him now, in his T-shirt and shorts, so excited to see her, made it difficult to sustain her anger. The embarrassment and frustration she'd been feeling began to melt away, replaced by curiosity and concern.

"Come on," she said. "Let's go inside."

"What about them?"

"Who? Moira and Ed? They're sleeping. Come on, it's freezing out here."

"I feel like maybe we should talk outside."

"I'm really cold, Brendan. If there's something you need to say, just say it now. I'm not standing out here all night."

"Promise you won't freak out?"

"I think it's a little late for that. You're acting really strange. Should I be worried?"

"No, no, it's fine. It's just—you can't tell anybody, okay? Not even them." Brendan pointed to the house.

"Okay, Brendan, I won't tell my geriatric aunt and uncle your secret."

Cara mentally scrolled through possible confessions. She'd initially hoped, then feared, then hoped again that he was going to tell her that he had fallen in love with her, after just one day. That it was crazy, but he was already certain that he couldn't live without her.

Now she was sure that this wasn't it. She braced herself for a heart-wrenching war story—a tale of murder or betrayal. Maybe he had killed someone and regretted it. Or shamefully abandoned a fellow soldier in the field. Worse, maybe he had been lying to her the whole time. Maybe he wasn't a soldier at all. Maybe he had a girlfriend. Or a wife.

Brendan moved closer,

"Okay. So remember the other day? At the cliffs? When I went underwater?"

"Yeah."

"Well . . ." Brendan leaned in, whispering the next part so close to Cara's ear she could feel the warmth of his breath. "I was breathing."

He stepped back now, watching intently for a reaction.

"Wait. What?"

"I know. I can explain."

"So you cheated."

"No. Well, yeah, kind of. I'm not sure you get what I'm saying."

"That's it? You came here at midnight to tell me you cheated on our bet? Brendan, I already knew you were lying. I don't know *how* you did it, but I'm not an idiot. It's fine. I'm over it."

"No. I mean, I was *breathing*," said Brendan. "Underwater. I have these incisions. Under my arms. They allow me to extract oxygen in the water and excrete carbon dioxide. So I can stay underwater for indefinite periods of time."

Cara laughed, not because she thought it was funny, but because she was uncomfortable.

"What are you talking about? Are you sure you're all right?"

"Yes, here. I'll show you."

Brendan grabbed at the back collar of his shirt, pulling it up over his head and dropping it onto the ground. A fleck of something stirred inside Cara at the sight of his naked torso, the dim light of the moon reflecting off his hip bones.

"Come here. Feel."

Brendan took Cara's hand and placed her fingers deep in his armpit. Where there should have been hair was smooth, bald skin, something Cara had failed to notice the night they slept together. She felt an opening in the skin, a deep, horizontal slit that felt so alien, she quickly snapped her hand away.

"Brendan, what was that?"

"I just told you."

"Is this some kind of weird joke?"

Brendan shook his head.

"Do you have it on the other side too?"

"Yeah."

"Can I feel it again?"

Brendan lifted up his elbow, allowing Cara to touch the other side.

"I don't want to hurt you." Cara's fingers were shaking.

"You won't. Just don't dig your fingers in it or something."

The skin at the very edge of the opening felt thicker and tougher, protecting the softness that lay within. With the moon and stars their only source of light, Cara had to rely on touch alone to even begin to visualize what she was feeling.

"I feel like I'm dreaming," she said, starting to get light-headed. "Am I dreaming?"

"No. Are you freaked out? It's too much, isn't it? I'm totally freaking you out."

"No, it's okay."

"I mean, it's fucking weird. I get that. So, I guess you're allowed to be a little freaked. Maybe I shouldn't have told you."

Cara was wide awake now, her pulse a dull pounding in her ears. She was wary of being tricked. It could all be a cruel joke. Yet she'd felt it. The nervousness in Brendan's voice. The unnatural opening of his skin. The deformity of it. He was telling the truth. Whether or not Brendan could actually breathe underwater, Cara couldn't be certain, but she knew that he believed that he could, that this was his truth.

She made a commitment in that moment not to let her discomfort show. She would be there for him, to listen and to share in his secret. Regardless of whether or not Brendan's claim was real, he had chosen *her* to share it with, and that made her feel special. She felt touched by his vulnerability, and wanted only to confirm that he could trust her.

Cara wrapped her arms around Brendan's waist, resting her head on his bare, clammy breast. She could hear his heart thumping within, a slow, steady bass.

"It's okay," she whispered. "I'm glad you told me."

"You're not freaked out?"

"No."

Brendan put his shirt back on, and Cara invited him inside. This time, he accepted. They held hands as they walked on tippy-toes, careful not to disturb the slumbering dogs in the den. They didn't bother with the light when they got to the emerald room. Cara navigated them to the bed, a path she'd by now memorized, and pulled Brendan under the covers with her. They lay on their sides, facing one another with their bodies curved like *S*'s. Brendan brushed a piece of Cara's hair from her forehead.

"How long have you had them?" she whispered.

"Four years," said Brendan. "They were surgically put in. Or built. Constructed. Whatever. And it's not just these. They did a procedure on my lungs and gave me injections for a year."

"Who did? Doctors?"

"Yeah. Military doctors." He laughed. "Hundreds of thousands of soldiers out there, and they chose me as their guinea pig."

"You must have been so scared."

"I was."

"But you knew what was happening. You were okay with it."

"Yes."

"But why did they do it?"

"Think about it," said Brendan. "I can swim anywhere, without equipment, for however long I need to. That's a pretty valuable asset."

"Are you the only one?"

"As far as I know. But I have no idea. I think they chose me because they knew I'd have no one to tell."

"What would happen if they found out you told? That you're telling me right now?"

"I don't know. Maybe nothing."

"I promise I won't tell," she said.

"I know you won't."

"Have you told anyone else?"

"No one."

"Not even, like, a therapist or another army person?"

Brendan shook his head.

"And you can really breathe underwater."

"Yes."

The story felt more real somehow, there in the warm safety of her bed. Her mother's bed. Cara allowed herself to suspend her disbelief and let herself imagine that everything Brendan was saying was true. Even though it probably wasn't. It couldn't be. But if it was, it was remarkable.

"What is it like?" she asked.

"What's what like?"

"Breathing. *Underwater*."

"At first it was terrifying. I couldn't get myself to stay down. Everything in your mind is telling you you're going to suffocate if you don't swim back up. I'll always remember my first few days in the test pool. It felt like they were asking me to drown myself. But after a while, I started to calm down. I realized I wasn't going to die, and

I let myself adjust to my new body. After that, it was the opposite. Sometimes I think I feel more relaxed alone in the water than I do in the open air."

Cara could hardly keep her eyes open. Brendan's breathing was heavy and lumbering at her side. But she had one last question.

"What's the longest you've been under?"

Brendan didn't answer, evidently lost to sleep. Cara let it go and turned over, pulling the comforter tight around her body. Five more ticks of the clock passed before he responded.

"Two days."

Cara quietly led Brendan down the stairs, skipping the step that always creaked. It wasn't the one with the big black crack in it, but the innocuously smooth and sturdy-looking one just past it. She'd been fooled by it dozens of times as a girl. Not this time. They crept carefully past a newspaper-shielded Ed in the study and out the door into the white light of morning. They kissed good-bye, and Brendan promised that he wouldn't disappear the way he had the last time, and Cara believed him.

When she went back inside, she forgot to catch the door before it slammed shut with a whiny chord from the spring and a loud slap, provoking Moira to call out her name from the sun porch. Cara pretended not to hear and ran up the stairs. She shut herself in the second-floor bathroom and locked the door. She didn't take a breath until the tub faucet was on, sending a shuddering, whitewashed echo through the old house pipes. No one would bother her now.

Cara had never sneaked a boy home before. She wouldn't have dared to in high school, the prospect of being caught by her parents too humiliating to imagine. And she felt a little guilty now, for taking advantage of Moira and Ed's obliviousness in this way. She prayed they hadn't heard the creak of the floor and the *tap tap* of the iron headboard rails against the wall. Of course, they would never say anything if they had, which almost made it worse.

Bexley House was a place so intrinsically tied to Cara's childhood and familial memory that to succumb to sexual desire there had initially felt immoral and corruptive. The bed in which Cara had clasped Brendan's naked body last night was the very same place she and Drew used to pretend was a boat with their mom, using their dad's neckties as fishing rods to catch the sandals, sneakers, and high heels on the floor. She'd once convinced Drew that the giant quahog shells perched on the built-in shelving of the eastern corner were from the bra of a real mermaid.

And yet to assume that the house had never before experienced the telltale creaks, taps, and moans of sex was surely naïve. It was entirely possible that Cara's own mother had brought boys home to the emerald room, capping off a night of making out next to a beach bonfire with explorative cuddling beneath the sheets.

Cara stripped down to nothing and sat on the cold seat of the toilet as she waited for the tub to fill. She wanted to be alone, as if speaking of Brendan and all that had happened might spoil the thrill. On the tip of her tongue perched what was surely the biggest secret she had ever been privy to, and she wasn't sure she trusted herself not to divulge it. Brendan's claim was quite literally unbelievable, yet she trusted it to be true. She'd felt the incisions herself.

This was the kind of thing you discussed and dissected with a friend. Cara felt the urge to pick up the phone and call Lindsay. *You would NOT believe what just happened to me,* she would say. But she held herself back. Instead, she barricaded her newfound knowledge deep inside of herself, the impulse to tell perpetually on the brink of bursting through. The sensation was electrifying, burning and pleasing at the same time. She crawled into the bath and laid her pubic bone under the stream of water in an attempt to release the tension, her head a wobbly orb on the porcelain tub floor. But she'd come with Brendan only hours earlier and couldn't attain the release she needed, achieving only a muted, carbon-copy orgasm.

She let the tub fill and sank her head beneath the surface, keeping only her knees, nipples, and face above water. Her ears flooded with liquid, blurring the sound of the faucet into a dull churning. She took a deep breath and submerged her head, opening her eyes up toward the surface, the ceiling distorted by the light-bending water.

How odd that by merely holding her breath—by putting her respiratory system on pause—she could prevent the water from sneaking up her nostrils, two gaping passageways to her lungs. She opened her mouth and let the water filter in between her cheeks, using her mind to keep the throat closed.

Was it possible?

Defying all instinct, she allowed an attempt at a breath, her mouth and nose wanting oxygen where there was only water. The sense of hopeful curiosity lasted only a fleeting moment before she erupted from the water, coughing, choking, and burping. Her throat felt locked, each desperate breath squeaking through with a wheeze. Cara put a hand on her chest and felt as it rose and fell, calming herself back down to a natural rhythm.

She pulled the beaded chain of the rubber plug and got out of the tub, using one end of a towel to squeeze the moisture from her hair and the other to pat down her body. After, Cara wiped off the mirror and stood naked in front of it. She sucked in all the air she could to reveal the bony xylophone of her rib cage and watched as it slowly disappeared in pace with her exhale. She put her hands up and moved closer to the mirror. The glass fogged from the heat of her body as she examined her armpits, squeezing the flesh with her fingertips and visualizing the bone, blood, nerves, and tissue beneath.

Was it possible?

2014

Cara wakes up early the next morning to go for a run. She starts out on her regular route, heading south toward Gay Head. There is a chill to the air, which is thick and saturated with moisture. It settles on her skin and makes the tiny hairs on her shoulders stand on end. She usually runs with headphones, the sound of her labored breathing an auditory torture, but she's going without them today. The upbeat tunes of her running playlist don't appeal.

Suddenly she takes a sharp right, as if pulled by an invisible force radiating down the rocky dirt road. The decision feels spontaneous, though she's not sure it is. This isn't the first time she's considered taking this turn. The fog gets denser as she travels farther. She keeps waiting for someone to appear and tell her she can't be there.

She stops in her tracks when she sees it. The old 1970s bungalow by the sea. The beach house. *Their house*, with its salt-washed deck and sandy, scrubby lawn. She is disappointed to see a car in the driveway. A Jaguar. Hardly surprising on an island like Martha's Vineyard. It's safe to assume they've renovated the inside. She can't imagine a buyer who would have left it as it was—at least, not one who could realistically afford it. It's a wonder the original structure is even still standing. Most would have taken it for a teardown.

She's almost relieved there's a car in the driveway. It scares her off from pressing further, getting closer and peeking in the windows, seeing the full extent of the house's evolution. She imagines another family inside, the parents cooking breakfast in her kitchen while their kids play with beach treasures on the sandy wood floor, the morning sun shining in on them through the wall of windows.

Being here reminds her why she's stayed away all this time, taking the long way around just to avoid the street sign. It doesn't matter that you can't even see the house from the road. The mere knowledge of its presence, the sea breeze blowing in through the trees, would have been enough to break her heart.

Cara starts to feel light-headed. She looks for something to sit on— nothing, so she squats down low and puts her head between her legs. She coughs and dry-heaves a few times into the mix of poison ivy, weeds, and sand at the side of the road, but nothing comes up. Feeling unsatisfied, she wipes the drool from her face with her forearm, rises, and turns back toward the main road.

She runs faster, harder, as if in defiance of the feelings brought on by the house. She heads toward the beach, eager for the calm of the ocean. It's still early enough in the season that the beaches are empty. In just a few weeks the summer folk will begin to arrive in droves, riding the ferries across the Sound from Woods Hole and New Bedford. But today it's just her and the seabirds. She takes off her shoes and walks her sweaty, sock-creased feet into the water, sinking into the sand up to her ankles. The water is cold, but swimmable.

She can't help but imagine the two of them, her former lover and her son, out there at sea, living in the water. It's a ludicrous thought, and one she was sure she no longer believed until she heard Dean's story. And now here she is again, wondering whether they're wearing wetsuits or if they're warm enough in their own skins. What they talk about. What they eat. If their fingers are pruney. Humans can only be submerged for so long before the skin starts to break down. She learned that in her research.

She's spent the bulk of the past five years considering these details over and over in her mind, and the logical conclusion is always the same: there is absolutely, positively no way Micah and Brendan have been living in the water all this time. Brendan was crazy. Disturbed. And if there's a part of her that still believes him—his delusional claims of superhuman powers—she must be crazy too.

If they are still alive, she imagines them living undercover as new people with new lives. But this would mean that they've been gone all this time without attempting to contact her, and that hurts. It would almost be better if they were dead—both of them tragically drowned under Brendan's delusion.

Cara steps away from the water and walks farther up the beach. She feels guilty for rejecting Graham's advances this morning. Her refusal to engage in what's come to be a daily routine for them is a clear signal that she's taken a step backward in her recovery. But whereas Graham is likely to believe that she sincerely wasn't in the mood—that her mind was simply elsewhere—Cara's not sure she even wants a baby anymore. She wonders if it's Dean's news that's changed her mind or if perhaps she never really wanted a second child at all. She certainly thought she did. Mere days ago, she was sure. A baby, she thought, would re-instill her with purpose. But in an instant, all that desire has gone; the glimmer of possibility that Micah might be near is enough to change her mind.

She balances herself on a rock as she uses her socks to wipe the wet sand from her feet. While tying her shoes, she notices something out of the corner of her eye, an object on the boulder she's leaning on—probably just a piece of driftwood, she thinks, but bends over to take a closer look. Perched on the center of the rock, in a shallow indent, is a small wooden whale figurine. The sculpture is waterworn and rotted, but its resemblance to a leviathan is unmistakable. Her fingers shake as she picks it up, the object feeling weightless in her hands.

Cara runs as fast as she can to her aunt and uncle's cottage, kicking up a cloud of dust as she turns down the driveway. The dogs run out to greet her when she reaches the clothesline, five of them wagging their tails and sniffing her legs with wet noses. She pushes her way through hanging sheets and rows of towels that smell like lavender to the blue side door. It's unlocked, as always, swinging open with a metallic creak and slamming shut behind her.

"Moira, are you here?"

She thumps through the house in her sneakers. The sink is full of dishes and there's dog food and chew toys all over the floor. The Mamas and the Papas play in the background. The kitchen table is stacked with old newspapers littered with mildewy tea bags.

"Moira, it's Cara. Are you here?"

Moira emerges from the sun porch in her bathrobe and slippers with a glass of tomato juice in her hands.

"Carebear!" she exclaims, setting it down. "I was wondering why the babies were barking. Come sit on the porch. You want some tomato juice? I'll make you some juice." She pronounces it *toe-MAH-toe*, the way old-timey Americans and British people do.

"No thanks, Moira. I'm fine."

"You sure? Geraldine LaCroix brought me these tree tomatoes from her greenhouse. She says they drink it this way in South America."

"No. C'mon, let's just go on the porch. I need to talk to you about something."

"Okay, but let me just make sure the babies are all here. Was Pee Wee out there when you came in? He runs, so you've got to watch him."

"I don't know. Which one's Pee Wee? The Scottie?"

"The Newfie. I'm fostering him."

"Moira, listen to me. I need to tell you something," says Cara. "Something I can't even tell Graham. At least, not yet."

Moira puts down the dog in her arms and rushes to Cara's side, placing a hand on each of her shoulders. "What is it? What's wrong?"

"I think Micah and Brendan might be on the island," says Cara. "Or near it. Whatever."

The shock in Moira's eyes is magnified by her comically strong prescription lenses.

"What do you mean? What happened? I can't think in here. Let's go to the porch."

The two women walk out to the screened-in sitting area, taking seats in facing wicker rockers. Moira's attention is fully on Cara.

"So yesterday Dean McIlroy tells me that one of his guys saw something. On Nantucket Sound. And of course, I'm skeptical because, like, everyone knows those guys make things up. But here's the thing: the guy says he saw a man and a boy. *A man and a boy*. And not in a place where you would see swimmers or divers or something. With no other boat in sight."

"Hold on, Bear, back up a second," says Moira. "What exactly did they say happened?"

"Well, it was this one guy. Jimmy Coughlin—who I don't even know. And so I *know* he didn't know Brendan. He said he saw a man and a boy in the middle of the water, way far out. Gull's Ledge, it's called. But when the boat got closer, they just dove in the water and never came back up. That's what he said."

"Dear Lord."

"So, like, fine," says Cara. "Of course I want to believe it's them, but there's a good chance the guys are making this up. Or maybe Jimmy thought he saw something he didn't. Who knows? But Graham is convinced it's all a sham. So I was ready to let it go too. Until today."

"Today? It's not even nine."

"Just listen," urges Cara. "I ran to Aquinnah this morning, and when I was down by the cliffs, I found this."

She passes Moira the wooden whale. Moira fingers the idol and slowly nods.

"And it wasn't just, like, washed ashore or something," says Cara. "It looked like it had carefully been placed on a rock. *The* rock where Brendan and I met."

"You think?"

"I mean, I don't know for sure that it was the exact same rock," Cara admits, "but it could have been. It was at least right around there."

"Well, it's certainly a sign of something," says Moira. "Even if they didn't leave it, I believe you were meant to find this whale for a reason."

Cara knows she can rely on Moira to indulge in her theories, regardless of how delusional they may be.

"But do you think it's possible? That they're here?"

"Hard to say for sure," says Moira. "My advice to you is to keep your eyes open for signs. Visit places that were important to you two and see what you discover. Keep them in your thoughts. If you can establish a spiritual connection with them, it may lead you closer."

Cara nods. She can practically feel Graham's eyes rolling, miles away. While it's clear that both Graham and Moira have Cara's best interests in mind, the two have never seen eye to eye with their guidance and support tactics. Cara goes to Graham when she wants a reality check; she goes to Moira when she doesn't.

On her way back from Moira's, wooden whale in hand, Cara breaks her own rule and jogs over to Brendan's old boat. The boat with no name. It's still there, perched just off Middle Road, vines of poison ivy crawling up the stilts and onto the deck. The hull of the ship looks as though it's tilted even farther over to the starboard side since she last saw it.

Cara has been really good lately; she hasn't visited the old sloop for at least six months now. There was a time when she visited it every day, waiting inside for Brendan and Micah to return until she'd fallen asleep, waking up disoriented, confused, and still very much alone. She's lost track of how many times Graham has had to drive out to pick her up, listening to her quiet sobs the whole ride home.

She agreed a few years ago to stop visiting the boat, and has only slipped up a few times since then, like an addict sneaking the occasional fix. But like an addict, a visit to the boat is never just a visit. Each time she goes, she propels herself back into a downward spiral.

Graham has threatened many times to submit a complaint to the town and have the boat removed, but she's always begged him not to. The boat is the last remaining vestige of Brendan on the island. Over the years she's convinced herself that if the boat were to disappear, she would most certainly never see Brendan or, by extension, Micah ever again, the ship a magical totem of their existence.

And so it is with great caution and apprehension that she approaches the boat today. The practical, protective side of herself urges her to turn around. Run home. Avoid this self-sabotage.

But what about Dean's story? And what of the whale she at this very moment holds in her hand? What if Brendan and Micah are in there, now, waiting for her to find them? At the very least she should check for another clue, another symbol left behind for her to find.

Moira's words echo in her mind: *Keep your eyes open for signs. Visit places that were important to you two and see what you discover.*

She walks up to the boat, stops, turns back, then pushes forward once more. A glance in the window can't hurt, she thinks. She climbs up onto the deck and wipes the grime from a porthole. She is disappointed to find the ship's cabin empty and unchanged. Too far into the mission to abort now, she pushes the long-rusted hatch back as far as she can and slides out the cabin door to get inside. She digs through moldy tools and animal nests, searching for any kind of clue. By the time she is done she is covered in dirt and dust; her hands leave smears on her sweaty gray T-shirt. She finds nothing.

Defeated, she sprints the whole way home, the throbbing of her knees and the burning in her lungs a self-inflicted punishment for her relapse.

2008

As far as Cara was concerned, the day at Gay Head didn't count. The first time Cara felt like she truly, indisputably witnessed Brendan's ability in action came days later on a sailing expedition to Menemsha Pond—though she would years later begin to doubt what she had seen. Brendan couldn't believe it when Cara admitted that she'd never actually been sailing before, despite years of summers on the Vineyard. Her family was more of a sit-on-the-beach-and-read kind of family, she'd explained. Plus the fact that boats were hardly affordable. Which was why it was so surprising that Brendan knew how to sail.

Maybe it was the way he said *Chil-mahk* and *Chappawidick*. Or the notion that he'd chosen the military over college. But it had never occurred to her that Brendan might have come from a wealthy family. Not that sailing necessarily implied wealth. But didn't it? A little?

They met at Quitsa Pond, walking through strangers' yards to get to the water. Brendan had a neon-green snorkel set under his arm. It was still vacuum-sealed in thick, sharp plastic.

"Hold this while I swim out to the boat?" Brendan handed the new toy over to Cara.

"Is this for me?"

"Yes, it's for you. I've evolved past the need for such aids."

Brendan took off his shirt and tossed it at her. The faded red cotton was still warm in Cara's hands. She resisted the creepy urge to smell it and watched as Brendan waded out into the cloudy water, his arms reflexively raised above his head as the cold-water line lapped at his belly button. He swam past a Boston Whaler and a Beetle Cat before unhooking the algae-covered line of a Sunfish and swimming it back to shore.

The mast and rolled-up sail lay flaccid on the deck; the wooden rudder angled up out of the water at the stern. Cara crunched over the dry noodles of dead seaweed and through the soft silt of decaying sea muck to the ankle-deep water where Brendan had positioned the boat.

She'd never seen a Sunfish up close and was surprised by how big and heavy the hull was, with a hollowed-out cavity for sitting. She'd always imagined the little white boats to be flat and thin like surfboards.

Cara held the vessel steady while Brendan erected the mast and unfolded the vibrant pink and blue of the sail, using a pulley to hoist it into a giant triangle and securing it with what he told her was a cleat knot on the deck.

Brendan spotted Cara as she climbed aboard, before pushing her out into deeper water. The small boat lurched to the side when Brendan pulled himself onto the deck belly-first like a harbor seal, splashing up water as he did so. He thrust the rudder down and slid the centerboard in with a thunk. He gently nudged Cara's head down as he pulled on the sail and compelled the boom to the starboard side of the boat. The sail cupped the air and they were off.

74

After the chaos of rigging and launching, the vibe was noticeably serene. Cara couldn't believe how quietly the boat cut through the water and with such great speed. She was dizzy with excitement, feeling like they could go anywhere without fear of disruption. It was her first introduction to the tranquility of sailing.

"I'm afraid to ask whose boat this is," she said.

"Don't worry about it," said Brendan. "Though I notice you waited until we were at full sail to bring it up."

"Well, I didn't want to *not* go sailing. Just promise me we won't get arrested."

"We won't get arrested," assured Brendan. "Besides, if you leave your boat fully rigged at all times, I feel like you're kind of asking for it. They even left the centerboard out here. I'll admit I took a gamble with that one. Just keep an eye out for the coast guard."

They tacked back and forth through Quitsa and into Menemsha Pond, with Cara on centerboard duty, pulling it up and shoving it back down into its slot whenever Brendan told her to.

"The board counterbalances the sail," he explained when Cara asked what it was for. "Otherwise we'd just get pushed downwind the whole time."

"Where did you learn all this?"

"My dad was in the navy. He taught me when I was a kid."

Cara and Brendan had discussed his mother, but this was the first he had ever spoken of his father.

"What's your dad like?" Cara said. "Assuming he's still alive, I hope?"

"Yeah." Brendan pushed back his hair. "Yeah, he's still alive. Kind of."

Cara laughed. "Kind of?"

"It's not something I like to talk about," he said. "My dad."

He wouldn't look at her. She put her hand on his knee.

"I'll tell you, but . . . it's kind of intense," he said.

"You mean like you telling me you have gills?"

Brendan smiled. "Touché. No, but seriously, I don't want you to think differently of me once I tell you. And you might. Even if you say you won't, you don't know."

"You can trust me," she said. "I promise."

He sighed. "My dad's in prison."

Cara was surprised, but oddly relieved. She wasn't sure what she'd been expecting, but this didn't seem worth Brendan's highly cryptic and cautionary introduction.

"Okay. That's not so bad. You think I would judge you for that?"

"He killed someone."

Cara felt a chill rush down her spine, but made a point of keeping her face neutral. "Okay."

She found herself imagining a street crime. A botched robbery. A drug deal gone wrong. These were narratives she could handle. Or maybe it was an accident—manslaughter. Brendan hadn't explicitly used the world *murder*.

"Was it an accident?"

Brendan laughed through his nose. "No. He killed a woman. In college. And for years he got away with it—graduated from school, got a job, married my mom, had me. It wasn't until years later, when the technology was better, that they got him."

Up until this point, Cara realized, she had been imagining the victim as a man. The fact that it was a woman made her feel sick. But she'd promised Brendan that no matter what he said, she wouldn't let the story change her opinion of him, and she was determined to stick to that promise, even if it was only outwardly.

Brendan continued, "He says he was madly in love with her. But no one knew because their relationship was a secret. Turns out the girl was actually engaged to someone else. And when she broke things off with my dad, he cracked—strangled her and threw her body in the ocean. The other guy, the fiancé, had a strong alibi, so the case went unsolved for years."

"Oh, Brendan," Cara said. "I don't know what to say."

She wanted to hug him, but his hands were occupied holding the sail and steering the boat. So instead she sat there, looking at her feet.

"You're spooked now. I knew it."

"No, Brendan, I'm not. It's fine." Cara asked another question to prove her comfort. "How old were you? When he was arrested?"

"I was twelve. He did a horrible thing. And he deserves to be where he is. But it was really confusing at the time. It had happened such a long time ago—before I was born. Which doesn't erase it, but it made it seem less real. It made it harder to think about the victim—the woman. I've spent more years being pissed about him having to go away than about what he actually did. You know? It's fucked up."

Cara clasped and unclasped her hands. They were shaking.

"And so then what happened? After he went away. Did you live with your mom?"

"Technically, yeah. But I mostly stayed with friends. The case was pretty much her undoing. The whole thing was humiliating. She started drinking. It was bad. I waited it out until I turned eighteen and could enlist. Not long after, I got a note saying she'd checked into rehab. She was good for a while after that, but it always came back."

Brendan turned to Cara now, the first time in the whole conversation that he'd taken his eyes off the horizon.

"You know that I'd never, ever hurt you, right?"

Before Cara could answer, the boat ran aground suddenly with a jolting pulse. She braced herself with her legs and tightened her grip on the edge of the boat, startled.

"What was that? What happened?"

"Wasn't paying attention. It's too shallow here," Brendan explained. "My bad. Watch your head."

They both hunched over as the boom swung back and forth overhead, the now slack lines making pinging sounds against the hollow aluminum mast.

"This is good, actually," said Brendan, getting out of the boat and lowering the sail. "We don't even need an anchor. We can swim here."

He pulled out a pocketknife and cut a hole into the plastic casing of the snorkel. He had to use his teeth to slide the layer of plastic back. Once the gear was free, he hopped out of the boat and into knee-deep water. Cara climbed out behind him, surprised by how shallow it was.

"Have you ever snorkeled before?"

"Yes, I've snorkeled before," Cara said with mock impatience, though she was pretty sure the last set she'd used had been *Little Mermaid*–themed, complete with a purple scallop-shell bra top she'd been too embarrassed to wear outside of the bath.

Cara let herself relax. She took the information she'd just learned from Brendan about his family and safely tucked it away somewhere she didn't have to look at it. She would take it back out later, when she was alone and better able to process what he had told her.

She crouched down and dunked her head underwater to smooth out her hair, then suctioned the rubber edges of the mask to her face. The pressure made her ears pop.

"This seems a little unfair," she said, attaching the snorkel. "You get to be all normal and I look like a giant bug."

"Yeah, you've definitely got a solid insect vibe going on," said Brendan. "You'd have made a great Japanese movie monster. In, like, the sixties."

"Thank you, Brendan. That's really sweet."

"You're welcome."

They waded out to a deeper section of sandbar and Cara dove slowly forward, relaxing herself into a belly-down float. Her body was markedly buoyant. Her breath echoed loudly in her ears like Darth Vader's, but fast and panicked. She focused on slowing down her breathing and re-minded herself not to be afraid. She chased off a school of minnows and watched a pair of hermit crabs shuffle along the sandy bottom.

Brendan sank his body down underwater next to hers. His hair floated away from his head in waves of silk. His arms hovered buoyant at his sides. He smiled with eyes open and said hi. Gloopy beads of air simmered up around his body in a shower of bubbles. Cara let out a laugh that echoed distorted and loud through the shaft of her snorkel. She said hi back and waved her hand. The hairs on her body stood on end when she noticed the delicate flaps of skin beneath Brendan's arms—soft, sweeping valves opening and closing to a calm rhythm. He took her hand and pulled her along at his side, propelling them forward together with frog kicks.

They swam until they reached the edge of the sandbar. Cara could still see the bottom, but was unnerved by the darkness created by the eelgrass and underwater growth. She kept her body afloat at the surface so as to avoid getting tickled by the tendrils of seaweed below. Her pulse sped up every time she saw a fish. Sensing her fear, Brendan let out garbled laughs and petted her arm to let her know that she was okay.

But Cara couldn't get herself to relax, not completely. There was something about being submerged there in the deeper, darker water that scared her. She could hear her own heartbeat thumping in her head, the sound somehow amplified by the surrounding water. The tiniest movements from seaweed and bottom-feeding critters set off streams of anxiety from deep within her rib cage. She reached her limit when she saw a flash of light reflecting off of something big swimming in the near distance. Panicked, she swam as fast as she could back to the sandbar, planted her feet, and stood up tall out of the water, ripping off the snorkel and mask. The relief was immediate. She was glad to be safe, back in the open air.

One week before he was scheduled to leave the island, Brendan disappeared. They'd made plans to meet at the cliffs. Cara packed a cooler with Coronas, bags of Cape Cod chips, and plastic baggies stuffed with turkey, mayo, and cheese sandwiches on potato bread. She'd even remembered to bring a paddleboard and a rubber ball so Brendan could entertain himself while she tried out the new watercolor set she'd picked up in Oak Bluffs.

She finished two paintings before she started to worry. The first was yet another rendering of the cliffs to add to the thousands that existed in the world, most no different from the rest. The second was of a baby in a diaper and yellow bonnet, playing in the tide pools with a neon-green sand mold in the shape of a fish.

Cara ate her sandwich, and then she ate Brendan's, swallowing it down with her third Corona. Around four o'clock, she packed up her things and wheeled her bike out to the main road, her head spinning from the sun, alcohol, and resulting dehydration. She rode slowly, the bike's wobbling wheels leaving curvy, snakelike prints in the traces of sand that lined the side of the road.

She expected to find him at the boat, imagining he'd fallen asleep or simply forgotten about their plans, distracted by a project or repair that needed to get done. But when she peeked down from the deck and into the darkness of the cabin below, there was no one inside.

It had been a few days since she'd been there, and while the place had never been neat and clean by any standards, what Cara now observed was beyond messy. As she lowered herself inside, she was hit with a wave of hot, humid air tinged with the scent of mildew and rot. There was garbage all over the floor, wrappers still sticky with crumbs and oils from things like Kit Kats, Slim Jims, Ho Hos, and Doritos—so many empty bags of Doritos, the orange dust leaving its mark on books, maps, pillows. On the stove was a bong half-full of sepia water with disks of black mold floating on the surface. Two slices of pizza still attached at the side sat atop Brendan's sleeping bag, the nylon beneath stained with grease.

The shelves along the walls were filled with glass bottles and aluminum cans, a mix of cheap domestics and root beer. Cara picked one up and realized it was full. But when she poured it out in the sink, she discovered the liquid inside wasn't soda or beer, but human urine, its putrid, ammonia smell unmistakable.

Although the boat had a functioning toilet, Cara knew Brendan preferred to use it for emergencies only, generally opting to pee off the side of the boat or use public restrooms (they joked that his visits to see her at Moira's were really just an excuse to use the indoor plumbing). So why he would choose to urinate in bottles, and then not even make the effort of pouring them out, was beyond her comprehension.

She threw the bottle she'd picked up into the sink and was about to leave when a book on the bed caught her eye.

It lay on the mattress, tucked under the overhanging shelving with a pair of red-handled paper scissors on top. On the cover was pasted a magazine photo of a sperm whale, pockets of air raising the paper in the gaps between glue. Cara grabbed the book and took it outside. She sat with it in her lap, her legs stretched out to the opposite seat.

The book itself was an old copy of *Where's Waldo? The Fantastic Journey*, the one with the yellow cover. Cara had owned a copy as a kid, yet she hardly recognized this one now. The outer covers and interior pages were plastered with pasted-on cutouts and maps. There were torn-out atlas pages from around the world and navigation charts from as close as Long Island Sound to as far as Osaka Bay. Many of these maps and charts were marked with circles and dotted lines in red and black ink. Most odd were the book's center pages, which contained descriptions of whale migratory patterns—sperm whales, minke whales, humpback whales, all kinds of species—that had been printed out from the internet.

Cara didn't know what the book was, but she knew it wasn't meant for her eyes. The attention and time that had obviously gone into its construction made it feel ominously intimate, as if she were reading a journal or diary. Except there were no reflections or personal confessions, only pages and pages of maps and charts, with the occasional coordinate or date written in.

She was still sifting through it when she saw Brendan walking down the street, headed toward the boat. Acting on intuition, she tossed the book back down into the cabin, trying to aim it in the direction of the bed. She didn't want him to know that she had seen it. Despite her curiosity, the idea of putting Brendan on the spot like that, of forcing him to explain what was possibly a very private anthology, made her uneasy.

Not wanting to arouse suspicion, Cara pushed aside the anger she felt at being stood up that afternoon and put on a happy face. She stood up on the ship's deck and waved to Brendan, letting him know that she was there. But he didn't wave or smile with his usual enthusiasm; his arms remained limp at his sides and his face conveyed a look of confusion and disorientation, as if her being there was not just surprising but perplexing and disconcerting. As he traveled closer, his body heavy and forlorn, Cara realized with concern that Brendan was soaking wet.

"Hey, mister, you'd better have one heck of an excuse for standing me up today," she said, hands on her hips. She looked down from the deck at Brendan, who stood on the ground below, showing no intention to climb aboard.

"Yeah. I'm sorry," he said, his eyes slowly examining the metal scaffolds and supports perched beneath the hull. His teeth were chattering. "I needed some time to think."

"Oh, well, that's okay," said Cara, softening. He'd used the same phrase the last time he'd gone missing, back when he was contemplating sharing his secret with her. She wondered what he could be pondering now. "I just wish you'd told me, is all."

"I'm sorry. It's not fair to treat you like this."

"It's fine, Brendan. Don't worry about it. We all need our alone time."

Brendan continued to brood at the foot of the ladder.

"Will you please come up here?" asked Cara, trying again to break the tension with a laugh. "It feels weird having this conversation with me looming over you like this. Like you're my royal subject or something."

Brendan climbed up the ladder now, slowly, and sat down next to her.

"That's better," said Cara with a smile. "Now, tell me, why are you all wet?"

"I went for a swim," said Brendan. "In the harbor."

"In your clothes?"

Brendan shrugged.

His behavior was so changed, so obviously altered from what it normally was, that Cara began to wonder if it was intentional, if Brendan was trying to tell her something through his actions that he was hesitant to say with words. She'd pulled similar maneuvers with friends and family before, acting distant to elicit wariness and, eventually, confrontation, so that she wouldn't have to be the one to initiate a difficult conversation. Was that what Brendan was doing now? He was scheduled to leave in a week. Perhaps their relationship was coming to an end, and this was his way of showing her. He would leave, and they would continue on in their separate lives without each other.

He'd gone for a swim—what did that mean? Cara suspected he didn't mean it in the usual sense, the way a normal person referred to an afternoon of laps or a quick dip after a run. She imagined him hovering suspended under the water somewhere, deliberating whether he should break up with her. It occurred to her that Brendan might be regretting having told her his secret. It wasn't the sort of secret shared with a summer fling. It was a forever secret, a confession offered only in the presence of love you hoped might last. Perhaps Brendan's hope had run out.

"So is this it?" she asked. "Is this your way of breaking up with me?"

At last Brendan turned to look at her, his eyes emanating pure dejection.

"No," he said. "No, of course not. Why would you say that?"

"Because you're acting so strange. Not to mention that you completely stood me up today. I mean, what am I supposed to think?"

"I don't want to break up with you," said Brendan. "Please don't think that. In fact, you're the one thing that's keeping me going. I don't want to leave here. That's why I'm like this. I have to leave soon, and I don't know if I can do it. It's driving me crazy thinking about it. I just want to stay here on this island with you and never go anywhere else."

"You aren't seriously considering staying."

"Of course not," he said. "I can't. They'll always find me. I'll be damned if there isn't a tracking device implanted in me somewhere. And I have to go. It's my job. I signed up for this, and I'm proud of what I do. Really, I am. I know it sounds like I'm not, but I am. But I'm so anxious. I'm so anxious it makes me sick. My whole body hurts. I hate it."

"Maybe you're just a little nervous," said Cara. She slid an arm around Brendan's waist. His T-shirt was wet and cold against her skin.

"I didn't want you to see me like this," said Brendan.

"It's okay."

"No—it's not. This isn't me."

Cara helped Brendan change into dry clothes. She felt like his mother, telling him to put his hands up so she could tug the heavy wet T-shirt up over his head. She set the sodden clothes on the deck to dry before helping him find a pair of flannel pants and a T-shirt. She asked if she could help clean up, and Brendan said that she could. Finding a trash bag in a drawer under the sink, Cara started to fill it with the old food and garbage littered throughout the cabin. She was surprised when he let her pour out the bottles of urine she'd discovered on the shelving. Either he'd forgotten what they were filled with, or he simply didn't care. Not wanting to embarrass him, Cara breathed through her mouth and got it over with as quickly as she could.

Brendan's detached behavior gave her the courage to bring up the book, the strange collection of maps and charts she'd found earlier. If he didn't mind her handling his old pee, she thought, maybe he'd be open to sharing the book's contents with her. She pretended to stumble upon it, and asked him what it was and if he needed it. As soon as he saw it, Brendan grabbed it from her hands. He told her it was nothing, not to worry about it, and shoved it into a cabinet near the bow filled with crinkled papers.

Cara knew better than to press the issue. Not when Brendan was in a mood like this. And in truth, it was a relief to know the book was locked away, beyond the reach of her curiosity. In the days and weeks that followed, she made every effort to do the same, to tuck the book away into a dark corner of her brain where she didn't have to think about it. It was easier that way.

The night before Brendan shipped out, he came over for dinner at Moira and Ed's, acting very much like his usual self. He showed up at the door half an hour late with a Stop & Shop bouquet wrapped in cellophane. He didn't own any khakis so he wore the next best thing: similarly hued cargo pants paired with a wrinkled blue button-down.

"Look at you, all fancy," said Cara when she opened the door.

"Is this okay? I didn't know what to wear. These are for your aunt."

He thrust the turquoise and magenta flowers toward her.

"You did not have to get these," she said. "Don't get me wrong—Moira will love them—but this isn't, like, a formal dinner or something. So don't be nervous."

"Why? Do I look nervous?"

"A little bit, yeah."

"I'm not."

"Okay."

"No, seriously. I'm not. I'm Special Forces, remember? Plus, aunts love me."

"Oh?"

"Yeah. It's like, I'll be walking down the street minding my own business, and then, boom—I'm surrounded by aunts who are like, 'Hey, we love you. We're aunts.'"

"Is that right?"

"Yeah. It's almost annoying how often it happens. But I know it won't be with your aunt. Your aunt's going to be the best aunt. I can feel it."

Cara smiled and exhaled. This was the Brendan she knew. They only had a few hours left together, and it was important to her that they parted on a positive note. And while she couldn't erase the questions and concerns Brendan's behavior had raised the other day, she knew she could push them away for at least a few hours. Because maybe he had been telling the truth. Maybe he really *was* anxious about leaving, and that was all. He was sad, and nervous, and afraid. Cara hadn't a clue what sorts of things would be required of Brendan while he was away. For all she knew, his work could be incredibly demanding and dangerous. That would explain the mess. And the need to withdraw. He was dealing with complex emotions and had trouble opening up about it. That was normal. She could understand that.

The kitchen smelled like warm butter and melted cheese when

they walked in. Moira was at the stove in her cow apron with the pink fabric udder protruding out the front. She was making her seafood casserole with lobster, sea scallops, shrimp, and scrod tossed in butter, sherry, cream, and cheese, and served over angel-hair pasta. Mermaid vomit, she called it.

"Bear said you liked seafood and that you're going overseas soon and probably won't get a home-cooked meal for a while," Moira told Brendan. "So she said I should make my casserole."

"It's *amazing*," cooed Cara.

"Well, it's tasty, but it's heavy. I only make it on nights when Ed's at cribbage. Not good for sensitive bowels," said Moira. "Do you have sensitive bowels, Brendan?"

Cara hid her face in her hands.

"Oh, no, ma'am. My bowels are very strong," said Brendan. "*Very* strong. Don't you worry."

Brendan asked if he could help with the prep, and Moira gave him the task of chopping the onion. Cara watched him out of the corner of her eye as she cleaned the lettuce for the salad. Brendan stabbed a butter knife into the bulb like a flagpole.

"Do you want a different knife?"

She handed him a wider blade. Brendan continued to consider the onion like a foreign object. She watched him fumble with the knife a few ticks longer until she witnessed him nearly amputate his own finger, and stepped in to help.

When they sat down to eat, Brendan burned the top of his mouth on his first bite. He dropped his fork with a loud clang and made an O with his mouth, frantically sucking in cooler air. A still-sizzling shrimp fell from his lips.

"Hot," he managed to say, his mouth still open.

"Drink some water." Moira nudged his glass closer.

Brendan proceeded to blow on each forkful of food he ate, strangling the utensil in tentacles of spaghetti, spearing chunks of shellfish on top, and pile-driving each mouthful into his face.

"This is really good," he said between bites. "I don't know if I've ever eaten anything this good."

"Well, you'll have to come back again and have some more," offered Moira.

"He can't. He's leaving."

"Well, you should have invited him over sooner."

"Right?" Brendan chimed in. "We've been hanging out for months now and she waits until my very last night here to invite me over."

Cara rolled her eyes.

"Cara says you've been staying off Middle Road. With friends. On a boat?"

"That's right."

"Well, when you come back, you can stay here," said Moira.

"He's going to be gone for a while," said Cara. "I probably won't even still be here by the time he gets back."

"Oh, and just where are you going?" asked Moira.

"I don't know. New York? Boston? I've got to find a job eventually."

"Well, while she's in New York doing her job, you can come here and relax with me."

"Brendan's not coming back here, Moira. This was just a onetime thing."

"Hey, that's not true," said Brendan. "If I want to come back, I'll find a way. With food like this on the table, you won't be able to keep me away."

He winked at Moira, who gleamed.

Cara was surprised by her own behavior—the childish bitterness of her words. The more they talked about Brendan's impending departure, the more resentful she felt. She'd read somewhere that high school seniors on the cusp of college life often lashed out at their parents in unexpected and illogical ways as a means of distancing them-selves in preparation for change. They got angry because they were sad and nervous about leaving. She wondered if that was what she was doing now. She'd never had this experience with her own parents. She didn't have the luxury when one of her parents was dying. She'd been angry at the world, yes, but she'd never once taken that anger out on her mother.

Her behavior now wasn't fair to Brendan. She knew that. The mil-itary was his whole livelihood. He was literally built to perform his given duties. But it was starting to occur to her that her presence might have been little more than a welcome interruption in his life, and it saddened her to know that it wasn't the other way around.

What life would she go back to after Brendan was gone? She loved being on the Vineyard with Moira and Ed, but it wasn't real life. She was too young to be living in such seclusion. Her plan had been to spend the summer creating art, without the burden of rent checks and electric bills or the distraction of bars and nightclubs. She'd create an amazing portfolio of work to bring to the city and make a name for herself, skipping the monotony of entry-level work her friends now faced. But it was almost August, and she'd hardly painted a thing.

Moira offered to do the dishes so that Brendan and Cara could walk down to the water and watch the sunset. Covered in spongy white sand just a couple months earlier, the ever-evolving beach was now in the midst of a rocky cycle. They tiptoed across rocks pocked with barnacles, arms outstretched for balance. The ocean water foamed as it ebbed and flowed through the gravelly sand between the stones.

"Are you mad that I'm leaving?" Brendan asked when they reached the smooth safety of the jetty boulders.

"Am I mad? No, I'm not *mad*."

"You seemed mad at dinner."

"I'm not mad," said Cara. "You're just doing your job."

"It's okay if you are," said Brendan. "I'm a little mad. Not at you, but at the situation. For what it's worth, I'd rather stay here with you. And it makes me mad that I can't. It's like they own me. My own body isn't even mine."

"But it is yours. They might have changed it, but it's still yours."

They walked to the end of the point and sat on a pink granite slab. A fishing boat with tall, skeletal antennae and globular, neon-orange bumper buoys passed in front of them, a swarm of seabirds chasing after it like fruit flies. A bell buoy tolled in the distance.

"I've never had to do this before," said Brendan. "Not really."

"Do what?"

"Say good-bye to someone."

"Never?"

"Not like this," said Brendan. "Usually, when I leave for missions, I don't really think about if or when I'll be back. It's just never really mattered to me before."

Cara paused. She didn't want to pry, but she'd been wondering about something and she wanted to know more.

"What about your dad? Do you ever think about how it might affect him? If something happened to you?"

"My relationship with my dad is complicated. I told you that."

"What about other family? You must have aunts and uncles or some-thing."

"I don't. I only have you. That's what makes this time so hard. I wasn't afraid before you. I was fearless. For years I've felt invincible. And I'm not sure I feel that anymore. I think I feel a little scared. You know we won't be able to communicate when I'm gone."

"Not at all?"

"Nothing. So I need to ask you now. Would you want to see me? When I come back?"

"Well, yeah. Don't you?"

"Of course I do. But you should know that it could be a while. I can't make contact until they say I can."

Cara tried to imagine where Brendan would be going—what he might be doing—that would prevent him from sending an email, picking up a phone, or tapping out a text message for months on end. And who were *they*, these people dictating his every move, nameless men in uniform without personality?

She was already afraid that he would forget her. That *they* would steal him back.

"So how does this work? We exchange email addresses and then I sit here and do nothing and wait to hear from you for as long as I can stand it?"

"You don't have to do anything. That's why I asked you. You're acting like I'm abandoning you on purpose. Like I'm choosing to go. It kills me to have to leave you right now. Do you not see that? My chest literally hurts. My brain hurts. I can't sleep. I stay up fantasizing about going AWOL with you."

"I would never make you do that."

"But I think I would. For you. If that's what you wanted."

There it was. At last Cara's resentful, self-pitying prodding had yielded the response she'd unknowingly been after, a genuine declaration of exhaustive adoration. Proof of sincerity. Self-sacrifice in her name.

It felt amazing for a moment, before it felt like too much.

"Don't be crazy. I'll be here for you when you come back."

Because what was she going to do? Abandon her whole life to live god-knows-where in hiding? She pictured the two of them living in an abandoned cabin in the woods stocked with cans of tuna and cup-o-soups.

Cara knew little about military law, but had seen enough movies to deduce the gravity of what Brendan was proposing.

"Are you sure? I'll stay here with you if you want me to. I swear to you, I will."

The way he said it, looking her in the eye with unblinking assertion. Like all she had to do was say, *Yes, that's what I want*, and he would really do it. It weakened her to be given so much power.

"I'm sure," she said. "Just promise me you'll be safe. You get home safely and I'll be here for you when you get back."

"All I want for you is to live your life," said Brendan. "Stay here. Move to New York. Fly to Guam. Do whatever makes you happy, and I'll meet you there when I can. If you'll let me."

Cara placed a palm on Brendan's hand and nodded. Brendan leaned in and kissed her lips.

Cara woke to the smell of ocean rot, wafting in through the window screen, engaging the curtains in a rhythmic sway. The protective comforter of the sea had been pulled away from the shore, leaving the life beneath naked and vulnerable to the blinding morning light. Dead crabs. Dried open oysters. Clumps of seaweed. Beached minnows.

Cara used to love exploring the tide pools, searching for ocean refugees and collecting them in a plastic bucket of seawater. Periwinkles adhered themselves to the sides while hermit crabs tumbled about the bottom, crawling over eggplant-purple starfish and midnight-blue mussels. Her mom had taught her to pick up the bigger crabs from behind, pinching their backs and underbellies with her forefinger and thumb. The terrified creatures would extend their front arms in a wide arc, like a world leader greeting his followers, holding their pincers in a flexed open position.

It was supposed to be a rainy day. That's what the weather report in the paper had threatened, and that's what Cara wanted. An excuse to stay in. Damp, cold melancholy. Instead it was bright and sunny, the glare of the wall paint preventing her from sleeping any later than nine.

It was the first day in weeks that she would not see Brendan. The torment of their separation was still ripe with a sticky sweetness, and she basked in the thickness of it, lying in bed and conjuring up the memories of their weeks together.

It had been different when her mother died. That had been real loss. There was no beauty in it, no glorification of misery. Memories, no matter how lovely they might have been, inevitably led back to the final moments of the ugly present, her mother's body shrunken and feeble. Cara's response had been to block it all out completely. Get the required ceremonies of reflection over with. Move forward. Stay busy. Head to college and begin anew, as if the worst had never happened. Make friends, but keep them at a comfortable distance.

In the wake of Brendan's departure, she found herself doing the opposite. She allowed herself to feel. She was willing to play the victim now, because she felt certain that Brendan would be coming back. There was a romantic glamour to her loneliness that made it less painful and more indulgent. Only a night had passed since they'd said good-bye and she was already designing their reunion in her head.

She filled her sketchbook with drawings of Brendan's face. His hands. His body. She couldn't draw anything else. She'd never been one to draw from memory, always reliant upon models, still lifes, or photographs. She used to envy the people who could draw elephants and steam engines using only the images in their heads. But Brendan's likeness came easily. She'd memorized the narrow half-pipe of skin that channeled down his lower back and the bend of the thick vein that curved through his forearm into the back of his hand.

When she wasn't drawing him, she was thinking about where he might be. She imagined him on an aircraft carrier in the dark of night, getting ready to be released down into the cold ocean water below.

He wore a full-body wetsuit with a skullcap hiding his hair, a pair of special waterproof night goggles on his face, and a high-tech watch and tracking device on his wrist. Other days she pictured him in the daytime, lying in a hammock and writing her letters. She wondered if he was scared.

She could feel her thoughts pulling her in a direction she did not want to go, but the pull was too strong, her curiosity unyielding. She inevitably found herself thinking once more—as she would again and again in the months to come—about the book. Brendan's book. That odd compilation of scribbles and drawings and pasted-in charts she'd found amongst the mess of his home on the boat.

She supposed there were a number of things the book could be. The most logical explanation was that it was work-related. It was possible, she supposed, that the maps and notes Cara had seen were part of a military mission of some kind. That might explain why Brendan didn't want her to see it; it was classified information.

But there'd been something so raw, so disheveled about it. And it was constructed from a *Where's Waldo?* book from the 1990s. What modern military outfit would utilize an old children's book to present important information in this way? It made no sense. Not really.

The mere knowledge of its existence filled her with an unnerving adrenaline, similar to the way one felt driving past a crashed vehicle on the side of the highway, the shattered glass and crushed metal inciting a sick excitement. She wanted to look closer, to sift through the pages and search for meaning in the notes and photos, fully aware that doing so could expose a side of Brendan she might not be ready to see.

She'd caught glimpses of it, this other side of Brendan, like the cool darkness that descends before a storm on an otherwise sunny day. Twice he'd disappeared on her, retreating into a cloud only he could see. But the sun always came back out, the lingering wetness of the rain the only evidence that the clouds had ever passed through.

The boredom hit her almost immediately. Or maybe it was that the loneliness had finally set in, the boredom just a symptom. Cara felt unmoored, floating without any sense of where to find dry land, or if she even wanted to find it. She started staying up until two or three in the morning, making mazes and intricate patterned designs with black Pilot pens in her sketchbook and watching pirated episodes of *Planet Earth* and *Grey's Anatomy* on her laptop. She draped her aunt's silk-trimmed, scratchy wool blankets over the windows to block out the morning sun, enabling her to sleep until one or two in the afternoon.

The rest of her days were spent at the Aquinnah Public Beach, reading gossip magazines and baking in the sun, counting down the hours until dinner. When she got back to the cottage each afternoon, she headed straight to the outdoor shower, waiting until the salt had been rinsed from her hair to take off her bathing suit and admire the deepening glow of her tan lines as she lathered her skin with a bar of Irish Spring.

One evening after her shower, she came upstairs to find a small stack of papers left for her on the bedroom bureau. They were job postings, printed from a desktop at the Chilmark Library, where Moira worked. Never intended to be read on paper, the printed web listings were ill-formatted, with little exed boxes where images should have been and awkward, midsentence line breaks. Many of the jobs, most of them retail or waitressing, had been posted months earlier and were surely filled by now. It was far too late in the season to be looking for a summer job.

Cara shrugged off the gesture, but didn't like the way it made her feel, regardless of Moira's intention. The implication was that she should be doing something different, that she was wasting her life away, following the same mindless routine day after day, complicit in her own dilapidation. It was a notion she was reluctant to acknowledge. The threat of anxiety that would inevitably accompany any attempt at a planned future was enough to keep her adrift.

Moira, meanwhile, was persistent. When Cara continued to ignore her not-so-subtle nudges, she decided to take matters into her own hands, using her personal powers of meddling and gossip wrangling to manipulate the situation. On a rainy afternoon late in the month, she timidly asked Cara if she'd mind driving her to the fish market. She was having another ocular migraine and didn't feel comfortable getting behind the wheel. Naturally, Cara obliged, intending to wait in the car once they'd parked. But Moira insisted she was having trouble seeing. Would Cara mind coming in with her? She wasn't sure she'd be able to read the menu.

As they waited in line together, Cara read the prices out to her aunt. Bluefish was on special. The tuna was $21.99 a pound. The swordfish was $17.99. There was sand on the floor and the place was filled with the musty, metallic smell of fresh fish meat, scales, and blood. The fridges to the side of the line were stocked with things like cocktail sauce, lemons, and homemade smoked-fish spreads. Photos of proud fishermen in yellow rubber overalls adorned the walls next to neon T-shirts for sale, with silk-screened swordfish on the front and the shop's name and phone number on the back. Cara eyed the lobster tank in the corner and resisted the childlike urge to take a closer look.

When they reached the front of the line, Moira told the older woman at the counter that she was going to buy some bluefish and cherrystones. But first she had a question.

"I ran into Jane Newman at the farmers' market over the weekend and she was telling me that her daughter, Angela, who works here, has to leave for soccer preseason next week."

The woman nodded as she eyed the crowded line behind Moira, growing visibly anxious.

"And so I was just thinking, if you're looking"—Moira turned to Cara, resting a hand on her shoulder—"that my niece, Cara here, might make a good replacement."

Cara was mortified. It wasn't just that Moira had tricked her, going so far as to *lie* about an ailment to force Cara to come with her, but that she was treating her, quite publicly, as if she were a teenager, too young and meek to speak for herself like the adult she should be. She wanted to roll her eyes and reprimand Moira from the side of her mouth, but understood that doing so would only underscore her immaturity.

Cara prepared to apologize to the woman, embarrassed to have given the impression that they even for a second thought she was qualified to take on such a job. Fish people were tough and gritty—they'd take one look at her, she was sure, and immediately deem her too soft to handle the work, whether she was or not. And to presume that the shop hadn't yet found a replacement for this Angela person—and then to ask about it in the middle of a busy afternoon shift . . . the whole thing was so humiliating.

So it surprised her when the woman looked her up and down, her eyes big and blue, framed by sun-cinched skin, and asked if she was available through October. She pronounced October with a heavy local accent. *Octobah.*

Cara hesitated. She had no idea how long she would be staying on the island. Summer was one thing. Even September wouldn't be all that weird—you could still feasibly go to the beach in September, could still swim and wear sandals and grill outside. October was different. October was fall. She'd never once intended to stay that long.

"Oh, yes. She's not going anywhere," interjected Moira. "She's already graduated from college. She has a degree in fine art."

"You ever worked in a fish market?"

Cara shook her head, too stunned to speak.

"But she's reliable," Moira promised. "And quick on her feet. Aren't you, Bear?"

"I know how to shuck oysters," Cara blurted out. "And I'm not afraid to get my hands dirty. You know, with, like, guts and stuff."

Moira smiled, victorious, nodding in agreement.

"Why don't you come by tomorrow morning?" said the woman. "Ask for Mona."

There were two sources of revenue at the market: the fish counter and the kitchen. Customers visited the fish counter to purchase items to prepare and enjoy at home—tuna steaks, cod fillets, fresh live shellfish, and the like, all of it packaged up in white butcher paper and thick bags designed to block odors and prevent seepage. The kitchen was the place to go for ready-to-eat meals to be enjoyed out on the neighboring beach or at one of the makeshift tables built from old fishing crates along the docks out back.

Mona showed Cara how to work the register and took her in back for a quick tour. The kitchen area housed steaming vats of clam chowder and lobster bisque and buckets full of shucked lobster meat, crab cake filling, and quahog stuffing. The stove was already busy with big black pots of boiling water and shallow pans filled with steamers. A narrow doorway led to a cold, all-white space resembling a very smelly operating room where they carved up the fish and stored the shellfish—oysters, littlenecks, cherrystones, quahogs, mussels, and steamers—in giant, fizzing tanks with plastic tubes of various sizes sticking out of them.

Cara found herself wishing she'd thought to bring a pencil and paper with her as Mona listed off the purpose of each station. It was apparent that Mona was not the sort of woman with the time or the patience to have to explain something more than once. She owned and managed the shop with her husband, Rich, who could usually be found in the back of the house, cleaning and preparing fish and helping fisherman to unload at the docks. He also made a point of chatting with tourists and making sure everyone was happy. Rich was the pal. Mona was the enforcer.

Cara started out working the kitchen register with Graham Rabinowitz, a Columbia grad from Brooklyn. While one of them rang up sales at the register, the other ran food, scooping out cups of chowder and bisque and preparing the occasional lobster roll or stuffed clam when things got busy. Carlos and Adriano worked the kitchen—both of them Portuguese immigrants with wicked senses of humor—while Charlie, a Cape native, and Martin, from Cameroon, worked the other counter and helped Rich with the fish.

Cara's first few weeks at the shop were hectic. Sweaty. Stressful. Exhausting. While the kitchen counter had few patrons in the morning, Cara and Graham stayed busy with the prep for the day: unloading and breaking down deliveries; stocking the fish counter with ice and fillets; breaking down lobsters and extracting the meat. The crowds would start with the lunch rush around 11 a.m. and carry on through the evening when people came by on their way back from the beach to pick up dinner to cook at home, or to eat in Menemsha while they watched the sunset over the Sound.

One day during lunch, Cara listened with feigned sympathy as a customer chewed her out for taking too long to serve him his order. The man was thick-necked and sunburned, with sunglasses on Vineyard Vines Croakies around his neck.

"Sorry, sir. I'll check on those for you, sir," she assured him politely while he sighed in exasperation.

She went into the kitchen to find Graham, who was busy ladling chowder, and asked about the status of the guy's precious steamers.

"They're ready now," Graham said, pointing to a pot on the counter. "Just pull up the bag and ladle out some broth. And don't forget the hot butter. I was going to bring it out for you, but the family at the counter just ordered a billion cups of chowder, sorry."

Cara thanked him, prepared the plate as he'd directed, and rushed outside to find the man. But along the way she tripped on a hose and dropped the plate, soaking her shirt with oily butter and spraying her legs with hot broth. She let out a squeal from the pain, the liquid searing her skin. The man watched as the steamers, in their webbed plastic sack, tumbled to the ground.

"Are you fucking kidding me?" he demanded. "Those better not be my steamers you just tossed all over the floor."

"I'm so sorry, sir," Cara said, scrambling up. "I'll get you some more broth. I think the steamers are okay, though." Encased in their sack, they hadn't spilled out when they hit the ground, and she genuinely thought they were salvageable. The man, who furiously walked out without paying, did not agree. And neither did Mona, to whom he complained on the way out.

"A word of advice? Don't offer a patron food that has been spilled all over the fucking ground," Mona chastised Cara afterward. "Understand?"

Cara nodded, holding back tears.

"Unbelievable." Mona shook her head as she walked away.

Cara couldn't stop herself from crying. It wasn't even that she'd fallen. Mistakes happened. But what had she been thinking, trying to serve the man the dropped clams?

"Look, that guy was an asshole," Graham said, noticing Cara's mouth starting to quiver. He yelled back to Adriano in the kitchen, asking if he could work the counter for a sec, and led Cara by the arm to the walk-in freezer. "You okay?" he asked. It was so cold Cara could see his breath as he spoke. He had to stand with a hunch so his head wouldn't bump the ceiling.

She nodded. "I think any tears I had are probably frozen now."

"This is the best place to be if you ever need a breather," Graham said. "I think it's the only place within a five-mile radius that isn't crawling with self-important tourists."

Cara laughed.

Graham was tall and slim with bony shoulders and overgrown, curly brown hair. He wore green plastic glasses with his light-blue market T-shirt and khaki pants. Cara wondered how he had ended up at a place like this.

"I should get back to the counter," he said. "But take as long as you need. And don't worry about Mona. She's not as scary as she seems. Just doesn't really have a filter, so you never know what's going to come out of her mouth. And she's tougher on girls. I think it's some kind of weird competitive thing."

Graham left, and Cara took a few breaths to compose herself. She managed to make it through the rest of the day without any more mistakes—or tears.

The next morning she came in extra early in an attempt to show Mona how committed she was. She was in the back assembling to-go boxes, when Mona came in an asked how her handwriting was.

Excellent, Cara thought, but what she said was: "Pretty good, I guess."

Mona handed her a slip of paper with a handful of menu items scribbled on it. "These are the specials for today. Grab the footstool and update the chalkboard menu behind the counter."

Cara's face lit up. This was the best assignment she could possibly imagine getting at the shop. She dug through the drawers by the register where she remembered seeing chalk and grabbed a cloth to wipe the old list of menu items from the chalkboard.

She separated the board into three main sections—fish, shellfish, and ready-to-order entrees—stylizing the lettering of each heading. She drew a pile of clams next to the shellfish section, and a lobster roll chock-full of meat next to the list of fresh-prepared items. Adriano came out from the back to admire her handiwork.

"Look at this, we've got the next Picasso here," he joked. "What are you going to draw for the fish section?"

"Well, the special is bluefish," Cara said. "But I don't actually know what one looks like."

"Here's a hint: it's *blue*."

"Yeah, I got that," Cara said. "But is it just, like, a normal-looking kind of fish, or is it more like a flounder or something? How big is it?"

"Hang on," Adriano said, disappearing behind the thick plastic curtains. "I'll be right there."

When he returned, he was hefting a dead, fifteen-pound bluefish by the tail.

"Here you go, babygurl. Here's your bluefish."

In the end, Cara's rendering of the bluefish looked like any other generic fish, so the life model was hardly necessary, but at least she knew now.

When Graham walked in and noticed what Cara had done, he raised his eyebrows and nodded in approval. "That looks awesome," he said.

Cara shrugged. "Thanks. Can't say chalk is my usual medium, but I think it came out all right."

"I could never do that. I'm a horrible artist."

"Yeah, well, if you ask my college professor, I'm an excellent drafts-man but a mediocre artist."

"Meaning . . . ?"

"Meaning, I'm technically skilled, but my creativity is lacking."

"Sounds like a shitty professor to me."

Cara laughed. "Maybe."

"My family owns a gallery in West Tisbury, and there are always pieces there that I think are awful—like, *really* awful—that sell for tens of thousands. And then there's other stuff I *love* that sits unsold forever. It's so fascinating to me how different people's tastes can be."

Cara felt a prickle of excitement.

"Your family has a gallery?"

"Yeah. The Spinnaker Gallery? Most people know it as the place with the giant copper osprey nest out front."

Cara nodded, though she didn't know it. "Well, if they ever need an assistant or something, let me know. Believe it or not, the fish market wasn't my first-choice job."

Graham hesitated.

"I should have mentioned . . . it's actually closed right now. My grandfather—he's the one who manages it—he's been sick, so we're trying to figure out next steps. We'll probably sell it, unfortunately; but if not, then yeah, we could definitely use the help."

"Oh, I was just kidding," Cara said. "Don't worry about it."

"Hey, but I could still take you there," said Graham. "To the gallery. Only if you wanted to. It's not really set up with anything, but it's a cool space, and there's still some work on the walls. You free after work?"

Cara hesitated. She pretended to think through her plans for the evening to see if she could make time for a visit.

"Yeah, I could probably swing that."

Now that the kitchen staff knew about Cara's artistic talents, they got a kick of out commissioning her to draw different people and items in their downtime. After the lunch rush, Adriano demanded that she draw his portrait, so she did a quick sketch with a Bic pen and a napkin. They all loved it so much they hung it up on the wall in the back.

After close, Cara walked with Graham out to his blue Volvo station wagon so that he could drive her to his family's gallery. When they got in the car he apologized for the "mess"—an empty to-go coffee cup and a couple of old receipts, which he quickly swiped up and stuffed into a little fold-out trash bin strapped to the back of the passenger seat.

She could still smell the relative newness of the tan leather interior. Cara had to move a copy of David Foster Wallace's *Infinite Jest* so she could sit down.

"Impressive," she said, gesturing to the book.

"Oh, don't be fooled." Graham laughed. "I just have that to look smart. I've been schlepping it around for years. I'm never going to finish it. Nobody warned me about the footnotes."

He plugged in his iPod and quickly paused the Sara Bareilles song that came on. Cara thought she detected a hint of blood rushing to his cheeks, but chose not to call him out. He asked Cara what kind of music she liked, and she told him anything was fine. He spent an endearing amount of time scrolling through his library before settling on Arcade Fire's *Neon Bible*. She admittedly preferred this to Brendan's taste, which veered more toward Metallica and Rage Against the Machine.

She couldn't tell exactly how old Graham was. A few years her senior, she guessed. Despite working at the fish market, he had the air of someone with his act together. He'd initially seemed nervous, but there was something kind of attractive about Graham's confidence and posture as a driver, an easy slouch with one hand on the wheel. He was so tall that his seat had to be a full foot back from where Cara's was, just so he could fit. His thick brown curls blew in the breeze from the window.

The gallery was in a large converted barn. Graham clicked on the lights as they walked through, illuminating the space's high vaulted ceilings. Track lighting hung from glossy wooden beams along the walls, drawing attention to metalwork sculptures atop little white obelisks and a few scattered paintings still on display. Cara and Graham's footsteps echoed as they moved through the building.

"We told these people they could come pick up their work, but they never sent anyone to get it," he said. "It's amazing to me how someone could be so successful that they don't even care where all their artwork is." He pointed to a sizable photorealistic oil painting of a pair of yellow galoshes propped next to a doorway. "This one alone is worth about twenty thousand dollars."

"I can't imagine ever selling a piece for that much," she said, staring up at the canvas in awe.

"Not to be a pessimist, but if there's anything I've learned, it's all about who you know," Graham said. "This artist here, for example, was making about a hundred fifty dollars a pop on her watercolor paintings. Then she met my grandmother in aerobics class, who connected her with my grandfather, and now she's got her pieces in here going for about three thousand each. Now, she's probably not going to show at MoMA anytime soon, but she makes a decent living."

"What about you?" Cara asked. "You seem like you know a fair amount about art."

"Well, I think it's a fascinating world. I'm a filmmaker, though. At least, I'm trying to be. I'm hoping to go to film school in the next few years."

Graham turned from the painting to look at Cara.

"I should mention that my grandfather is also in the industry. Leo Rabinowitz?"

He nearly winced as he said it, like it was some shameful secret. Cara shook her head. She'd never heard the name.

"*Out of Africa*?"

Cara had never seen *Out of Africa*, but it felt more polite to pretend she had. "Of course!" she said. "That was him?"

"He was part of the production team. That's the film he's most known for. He's been retired for a few years now. Came out here and opened the gallery—it's sort of been a pet project of his. Not sure what we'll do with it when he . . . when he's gone."

"I'm sorry he's sick."

Graham gave her a smile. "Thank you. It's okay. He's ninety-two. He's lived a good life."

Cara could understand why Graham was out here on the island. It made sense that he would want to spend time with his grandfather, especially since it sounded like the man had been a real role model for him. But she still couldn't figure out why the hell he was working at the smelly, grimy fish market. If this gallery, with its soaring ceilings and $20,000 paintings, was a "pet project," the family had to be loaded. It was unlikely that Graham *needed* the petty cash he was earning.

But she couldn't ask about that. She decided on a subtler, less intrusive set of questions. "How long have you been living here? On the island, I mean."

"Well, let's see. Maybe a year and a half?"

"I hope you haven't been working at the fish market that whole time. . . ."

"Not the whole time," Graham said with another smile. "Maybe about eight months? The pocket cash is nice, but I honestly just needed something to do, someone else to talk to. And you have to admit, Mona and Rich are going to make some pretty awesome film characters one day."

There it was. Kind of. He was working at the market because he was bored, with the added incentive of finding some fodder for his future movies. She wanted to make a dig about his being a prince among peons, observing her, Adriano, and the rest of the crew as if they were research specimens or something, but she held back. Even if that was the truth, it wasn't as if he acted that way—like he was better than the rest of them.

Cara felt at ease with Graham and appreciated his interest in all different kinds of art—visual, literary, music, film. They were only just getting to know each other, but he struck her as motivated, curious, and thoughtful. He was someone she could imagine having substantive conversations with.

"What will you do after?" she asked, genuinely curious.

"After my grandfather passes?"

Cara's chest tightened. "Sorry, I didn't mean it like that. I just meant . . . you mentioned film school."

Graham waved her off. "That's okay. I know what you meant. And yes, I do want to go to film school. But I'm hoping to travel first. There's this town on the northern coast of Peru, where the local fishermen have supposedly been surfing the waves for thousands of years on these little boats handmade out of reeds. I don't know why, but it fascinates me. I've been totally geeking out over it from afar. So, I figure after a few more months at the fish market, I'll have saved enough for the trip."

"More fishermen, huh?"

Graham laughed. "Yeah, I suppose I've got a bit of a theme going."

"You could do a documentary," she pointed out. "About fishing practices all over the world. Or at least in a few places."

She paused. Was this even a good idea?

"You could interview Dean and Owen," she added.

Dean and Owen were two of the market's most reliable vendors. Salt of the sea, New England born and raised.

"Can you imagine?" Graham exclaimed. "I couldn't get more than five words out of those guys without an f-bomb. I'd have to bleep out the whole thing."

Now it was Cara who laughed.

He asked, "Were you there that day that Owen held up a huge tuna for a little boy—he had to be, like, five—and said, 'Check out the teeth on this motherfucker!'"

"I missed that one," Cara said, "But I *was* there the time he waved a giant live eel at this pretty blond woman who was watching and asked her if she wanted to give him a hand taming his eel."

"No," said Graham, shaking his head. "No, no, no."

"Yes. I'm pretty sure he winked at her too. It was so uncomfortable."

They continued through the gallery out back to a garden patio dotted with sculptures. Cara stopped at a bronze figure of a crane.

"I have so much more appreciation for sculptures like this now that I've taken a metalworking class," she said. "Turns out sculpture is way harder than it looks. I was so bad at it."

"Would you stop?"

"What?"

"Saying you're so bad at everything! You said you were a bad artist, but I saw what you did with that chalkboard. And those portraits you did of the kitchen guys today? You're obviously good."

"Yeah, but I'm *actually* bad at sculpture."

"Okay. Sure. I'll be the judge of that. You have any of your stuff on the island?"

Cara felt disappointed that she didn't. "Not really. Just some sketchbooks and stuff. I started a few pieces when I first got here, but I haven't been doing as much painting as I'd hoped."

"Would you be willing to show me sometime?"

Cara thought of all her sketches of Brendan. Now she was the one blushing.

"Maybe. They aren't really done."

Graham guffawed. "I don't care!" he said, giving her a playful shove. "I'd love to see whatever you have. Even if it's the worst, ugliest, most awful art I've ever seen."

When Graham drove Cara back to Moira's, they sat in his car in the driveway, the chirping of crickets announcing the onset of twilight. Their time together had been casual, platonic—two friends from work hanging out. That's it. So why did it now feel like the end of a date? Cara grew anxious about her exit strategy. If Graham had simply given her a ride home from work, this wouldn't have been an issue; she'd have gone on her way with a quick *See ya,*.

But now, having spent the past hour and a half with Graham, she felt like she should at least hug him or something, and the longer she sat there the more it felt like he might just lean over and kiss her. Because she knew Graham wanted to kiss her, in the way girls can just feel these things—especially when the guy likes the girl more than she likes him. But she couldn't afford herself the time to think about whether or not she *wanted* him to kiss her, because she knew that she couldn't let it happen. Because she was with Brendan. End of story.

So she gave him an awkward pat on the leg, thanked him again for showing her the gallery, and exited the car without looking back, noticing that Graham stayed in park until she'd safely made it inside.

Out on the porch with Moira and Ed, Cara only half-listened to Moira's story about the CEO from General Mills who was supposedly buying up property in Chilmark left and right. She suspected Ed was only half-listening too.

Her adrenaline was still on high from those final moments in the car. She felt oddly flustered by the whole thing, replaying the good-bye in her head, feeling like she'd just blown it. *Blown what?* she asked herself. If anything, she'd casually signaled to Graham that she wasn't interested—which she wasn't. Also, he probably hadn't even thought of it that way. It was just a silly good-bye. Still, she continued to feel anxious and unsure, worried that things would be weird with Graham at work the next day.

"Are they talking about it? At the fish market?"

Cara had to blink to bring herself back to the present.

"What?"

"The Cohens. Selling their house to the General Mills guy. Are people talking about it?"

"Oh. No. I haven't heard anything," Cara said, picking a fleck of old paint off the wicker of her chair.

She hadn't mentioned Brendan the whole time she was with Graham this evening and wondered if maybe she should have. She would find a way to mention him at work tomorrow. For sure. Just to be safe. It was weird that she hadn't already.

She thought about Graham's hopes to visit Peru. Why didn't she try to do something like that? It made her start thinking about life beyond the island again. She could spend a few more weeks working at the market, and then make her next move. Maybe it was New York City, or maybe it was somewhere else. Maybe she and Brendan could travel together to some exotic locale, instead of him going off on his own and leaving her behind, listening to Moira drone on and on about boring island gossip.

I t wasn't until Labor Day weekend that Cara seriously began to contemplate her next step. The shift was prompted by a visit with Lindsay, who was in Falmouth with her family for the weekend. Cara made plans to ride the ferry across the Sound to Woods Hole to meet her for brunch.

Lindsay showed up to the Fishmonger in workout clothes, still sweaty and red-faced from the run over. At college, she had been all-American in lacrosse, and she always, whether intentionally or not, made Cara feel like she should be dedicating more time to exercise. When she ordered the egg-white omelet with feta and asparagus, Cara felt compelled to get the granola parfait, even though she'd been eyeing the french toast with strawberries.

"Isn't it strange to think that people are back at school now?" asked Lindsay, unspooling her silverware from the napkin it was rolled in. "Without us?"

Cara nodded. "It definitely feels weird not to be going back."

"I mean, it's not like I necessarily want to go back. You know? It's just crazy to think how easily a place can live on without you. Like we've already been replaced."

Cara had little desire to go back to school. She was happy to be free from the burden of homework and papers and exams. But she found herself missing the sense of routine. The guaranteed next step. The prescriptive, cyclical nature of academia.

"How's your internship going?"

Lindsay sighed. "It's fine. I love the work, but the pay is still shit. I applied for assistant editor last month and didn't get it."

"Sucks. I'm sorry."

"And the girl they gave it to had never even worked in publishing before. She came from, like, an ad agency or something. But she went to an Ivy so I feel like that's why they hired her."

"So annoying."

"They're keeping me on for another semester though, so I guess that's good. My position was supposed to end in September."

"That's great," said Cara. "At least you have something. I need to get a job."

"What about the fish place?"

"I mean a *real* job."

Lindsay slapped her palms on the table and leaned toward her. "Come to New York!"

Cara shrugged. "I've been thinking about it."

"Oh, Cara, we would have so much fun. Everyone is there. I see people from school all the time. It's like college but without homework. I mean, don't get me wrong. New York City is a shitshow. It's exhausting. But I love it too. It's so fun. I'm pretty much always drunk. Which is horrible, I know. I will probably die when I try to run my half-marathon in October. But it might be worth it."

"I've only ever been there once, but I remember loving it," said Cara.

She didn't mention that she had been eleven at the time, there to see *Cats* on Broadway with Drew and her parents.

"I actually think living in New York should be required for everyone under twenty-five. Don't give me that look, Cara, I'm serious."

"I don't think I could afford it."

Lindsay's energy deflated. She took a sip of her iced tea, staring down the sides of her straw at her ice cubes. It wasn't clear which was more embarrassing: having parents who couldn't afford to pay your rent, or having parents who could and did. To be fair, Cara didn't know for sure that it was Lindsay's parents who were paying her bills, but it wasn't as if she had the funds to cover them on her own.

Lindsay's face perked back up. "Listen, you could wait tables or something! Until you can find a job at a gallery."

"But I've never even waitressed before. I mean, not really."

Cara mentally debated whether the fish market qualified. She castigated her early-summer self for not getting a job sooner. She could have saved enough for a least one month's deposit by now. Instead she had spent every free minute with Brendan, a decision she was now beginning to question.

"You could start as a barista or something. Whatever. It's New York City. There's a restaurant on every corner. And you're pretty. Someone will hire you. You can stay with me as long as you need."

The thought was enticing, but Cara hadn't told Lindsay the whole story. She needed to admit the real reason she was hesitating. She needed to tell her about Brendan.

For reasons that were only now becoming clear to her, she'd chosen not to tell her best friend about him. All morning, she'd been on the brink of confiding in Lindsay about Brendan. She'd looked forward to it the whole ride over, thrilled to be in the presence of a close girlfriend to whom she could spill the details about her romance. But each time the opportunity arose, she held back.

Because Brendan and Lindsay existed on two different planes. Lindsay was real. She made sense. She fit into the life Cara had always imagined for herself. Brendan wasn't. Didn't. And now, backdropped by the world of Lindsay and New York City and veggie omelets and underpaid interns, Brendan's luster was lost. The mundane superseded the exceptional, and Cara worried that if she conflated the two worlds, the trance would be broken. Like turning the light on in a dark room once full of extraordinary possibility.

"There's something else," Cara said finally, gripping her fork tightly and pushing the food around her plate. "I've been dating this guy."

Dating? Certainly there was a better word to describe what Cara and Brendan had been doing. But that was the word that came out.

"What? Who is he? Can I meet him?" Lindsay was giddy with excitement.

"His name is Brendan. He's in the military. Special Forces, actually."

"Ooh, sexy."

"He's overseas right now, otherwise I would have brought him," Cara said, knowing full well she would have done no such thing.

"So what's he like?"

"He's funny. *Super* attractive."

"Have you slept with him?"

Cara blushed. "Yes."

"Yes? Like, lots of times, or just a few times?"

"Like, lots of times."

"So you're full-on *dating*."

"I mean, yeah."

"How am I just now hearing about this?" Lindsay demanded.

"I don't know. I wasn't sure what it was at first. I thought it might just be a fling. But now? I don't know. It's gotten more serious, and I don't know if I could go to New York without him. I'd feel really guilty leaving."

"Guilty or sad?"

"Maybe both? Wait, what do you mean?"

"Is the issue that you would feel guilty about leaving him behind? Or would it make you sad not to be with him? Are you holding back because you'd feel bad for the guy, or because you genuinely love him and want to marry him and have all his babies and would desperately miss being apart from him for even a second?"

"Somewhere in between?"

"Okay . . ."

"No, I really like him. And I do think I'd miss him. I miss him right now."

"Okay, but isn't he not even here? I mean, on the Vineyard? Right now?"

"Well, no. But he's coming back."

"Does he live on the island?"

"Kind of," Cara hedged.

"Kind of?"

"I don't know. He's sort of . . . transient. I'm not really sure where his home base is. If he even has one."

"Well, then, what difference does it make if you live out here or in New York? It sounds like he travels a lot anyway."

"Yeah. . . . It's hard to explain. But you're right. It's at least something worth talking about, though I don't see him ever wanting to live in New York."

"Why not?"

"He's just not a city person. At all."

Lindsay put her fork down and swallowed a gulp of iced tea from her straw.

"Listen, the way I see it, if it's meant to be, you'll find a way to make it work. I say you try New York and see what happens. Either he'll follow you or he won't. And even if he doesn't, you can do long-distance and see how it goes. I just don't think it's fair that you have to sit around waiting for him. Plus, the summer is ending. Do you really want to be on Martha's Vineyard once the weather turns? I've been on the Cape in the off-season, and it's pretty bleak."

"Yeah, that's true. I guess I just need to think about it a little more."

After brunch, Cara and Lindsay got frozen yogurt and walked to the aquarium to see the seals while Cara waited for the next ferry. There were two spotted harbor seals in the pool lying on a slab and sunning themselves like a pair of overstuffed sausages on a grill.

"Do you think they're happy here?" Lindsay asked. "It's such a tiny pool."

"Yeah, but aren't they damaged? Or sick or something? This isn't a normal aquarium. It's a research institution. I don't think they'd keep the seals here if they didn't need to. They take care of them and rehabilitate them until they're ready to go back to the ocean on their own. At least, that's what my mom used to tell me. Maybe she was making it up."

"No, you're probably right," said Lindsay, stepping away from the railing. "Should we head over to the dock?"

Spending the morning with Lindsay made Cara feel like one of those seals. Except instead of living her life in a tiny pool, she passed her days on a tiny island, waiting for the moment when she was emotionally ready to be released back out into the ocean with Lindsay and her other friends.

Cara fished out her return ticket from her tote bag and hugged Lindsay good-bye at the ramp to the ferry.

"I think I'm going to do it," she said. "Come to New York, I mean. If you were serious before. About me maybe staying with you."

"I would love that," said Lindsay. "For real, I would. You have to come. Promise you'll come?"

"I promise. I'm excited."

Cara made a timeline for herself. By October—at the latest—she would leave the island and head to New York City. She'd taken no specific steps toward this goal, but her mentality had shifted. Her mind was made up. She had something to look forward to now. She could spend her days sleeping and eating and lying in the sun and not feel guilty about it. There was a destination in sight. "I'm moving to New York in October," she could say, if anyone asked.

Her only hesitation was Brendan. The memory of him, and the enormous role he had played over the course of her summer, was the Achilles' heel of her plan. It was amazing how quickly he had gone from being the most important person in her life—someone she truly loved and *needed*—to being a phantasmal token of nostalgia, a person whose memory filled her with giddiness, but whose true worth she now questioned. In the absence of any means of communication, it was as if he had died, and she no longer had any way of assessing whether or not her feelings for him could be trusted.

Because maybe Brendan wasn't as great as she thought he was. Maybe she had been so lonely when they'd met that she'd clung to him out of desperation, and not because she truly loved him. Besides, weren't people supposed to know when they were in love? If she truly loved Brendan, in the way she'd always imagined love would be, she wouldn't be questioning things in this way. Love was supposed to be certain. Obvious.

But maybe he really was that incredible, that alluring. Maybe she was only trying to convince herself otherwise now as a matter of convenience. Her decisions were easier without him. It was easier to believe that their connection had been nothing more than a summer fling. But it was also disappointing.

Cara's thoughts bounced around in this way, until she was able to come to what she deemed a compromise but was really a postpone-ment of judgment. She wasn't bound to the island, she realized. Her intent to leave did not necessarily mean that she was also leaving Bren-dan. Brendan himself had encouraged her to go wherever she wanted. He would find her, he'd said.

This was just the test she needed. It was good that she was moving. Her departure from the island would give him the opportunity to prove his sincerity. If what they'd experienced together was in fact true love, he would find her. He would find a way to be with her again.

The prospect of life in New York City gave Cara a sense of purpose that she hadn't felt since she'd arrived on the island. She started getting up earlier and running again. She went through her clothes, jewelry, and shoes, making piles of what to keep and what to donate. She threw out empty sunscreen bottles and bathing suits whose interior elastic was starting to peek through, and borrowed Moira's car to go buy makeup and a new purse in Oak Bluffs. Afterward, she went to the Chilmark Library and used a computer to purchase two tickets: a bus ticket from Woods Hole to Boston, and a seat on the Amtrak from BOS to NYC. Her last day on the island would be September 30.

Brendan came back the same way he'd arrived, drenched and drip-ping with seawater, naked as the day he was born. It was an hour before dawn. Cara had been dreaming about jellyfish. Everywhere she swam they were there, their tentacles wrapping around her wrists and ankles. It scared her until she realized that it didn't hurt.

She woke suddenly, as if reacting to the presence in the room. She sat up, checking her forearms for signs of stings. She could hear the ticking pendulum of the grandfather clock downstairs. Her bedroom was steeped in darkness. The floor creaked under Brendan's weight. She whispered his name. She felt his cold, wet hand on her shoulder. She reached out and held his waist, her palms sliding against the droplets on his waxy skin.

"You're back," she whispered.

"I'm back."

"Why are you all wet?"

"I swam here," he said. "I couldn't wait."

"You're so cold."

Cara moved over in the bed and drew back the comforter. Brendan's body triggered a chill through her own. They lay on their sides now, facing each other, gleaming, keeping their voices hushed.

"How did you get in?"

"The back door was open."

"What about the dogs?"

"They picked their heads up when I came in, but didn't seem too interested."

"Oh. Maybe they remember you."

"Or they're just horrible guard dogs."

"I feel like I'm dreaming."

"Me too."

"Did you just get back?"

"Yeah."

"Aren't you tired?"

"Yeah."

Brendan turned her over and wrapped his arms and legs around her, his heels resting on the tops of her feet. Cara gasped.

"You're so cold."

Brendan held her tighter. "You're so warm." He pressed his cheek into her neck and nuzzled his cold nose beneath her ear.

"How did you know I'd still be here?" Cara stared through the darkness toward the window.

"I didn't."

Cara didn't ask Brendan where he'd been or how he had gotten here, to her aunt and uncle's house, in the middle of the night. Or why he hadn't called or emailed before. Surely he had flown in or docked somewhere other than the Vineyard, someplace where he was permitted to access the internet and use a phone, to tell her he was coming. And what about the water? He said he had swum there. From where? How far?

Now was the time to tell him about New York. She was leaving in just over a week. She tried to imagine how he might react when she told him. She liked to rehearse tough conversations, playing out the various possible scenarios as a movie in her head well in advance—but she hadn't anticipated him coming back before she departed, so she wasn't prepared. And while she was relieved to have avoided a situation where Brendan might have felt abandoned or blindsided, she now found herself faced with an even more complicated dilemma: whether or not to invite him to New York. Would he even want to come if she asked? And if he did, where would he stay? She couldn't impose on Lindsay like that.

Brendan started kissing the side of her neck. The feathery blond hairs at edges of her scalp stuck softly to his lips.

"I missed you so much," he whispered.

He pressed his groin into Cara's backside, sliding himself against the space between the dimples of her lower back. She let him reach down under the covers and brush off her shorts. He entered her from behind and slid his hands up into the warm pocket of air beneath her shirt. Cara's nipples stiffened.

"I love you," he said.

"I love you too."

"Let's make a baby."

The words jerked Cara from the moment. She was fully alert now, letting out a nervous laugh. Brendan continued on unfazed, hugging her body close to his. Cara was conscious of her own cold rigidity against Brendan's warm embrace, like a metal fork in a bowl of pudding. She wanted nothing more than to relax down into his body, but her racing mind kept her body tense.

Brendan finished and rolled away, dripping a slippery trail of semen down Cara's legs and into a pool of wetness on the bedsheet. Unlike Cara, he was never bothered by the messiness of sex. But this was no time to worry about cleanup. She looked over at him, eyes closed and panting, beads of sweat on his forehead. She wanted to rouse him and ask if he had been serious, when he said what he said. Did he mean now, or someday in the future? Or perhaps never at all? Maybe it had just been dirty talk, a suggestion so forward and unlikely that it turned him on.

Cara tried to let it go and fall back asleep, but her mind couldn't move past it. After a few minutes, she rolled on her side and laid a hand on Brendan's shoulder.

"Hey," she whispered.

He didn't respond. She pressed her hand down harder and gave his body a gentle shake.

"*Hey.*"

Brendan groaned.

"Were you serious? Before?"

"Hmm."

"You said you wanted to make a baby. Did you really mean that?"

Brendan opened his eyes and turned to face her. Cara wondered if he could see the panic swirling inside her.

"Of course."

"But you don't mean now," she said, pushing through a single ripple of laughter to lighten the air. "Right?"

Brendan smiled and rested his hand on her cheek.

"It doesn't have to be today," he said. "Or the next day. Or the day after that. But for me, there's no reason to wait. I've found you. I love you. I will always love you. That's it."

"I'm not sure it's that simple."

Brendan closed his eyes and snuggled closer.

"Babies are incredibly expensive," said Cara. "And I don't know what you get paid, but I'm pretty sure there's no way we could support a child."

"Money's not an issue," said Brendan.

"What do you mean?"

"Nothing. Let's just go to sleep."

"Not until you tell me what you mean."

"I mean, it's not something you need to worry about," said Brendan, exasperated.

Cara hesitated, not sure if she should ask what she wanted to ask.

"Because you don't care about money, or because you actually have money? Because as much as I love the idea of living in a fantasy world where money doesn't matter, it's not realistic. We have to be practical."

Cara knew well enough by now that Brendan was an idealist. That was what she loved about him, the way he navigated through life without contemplating every decision, operating purely on instinct and desire. Because she was the opposite. And in this particular instance, she felt compelled to rein him in. Brendan didn't see things like a normal person. He was naïve in some ways.

Brendan sighed. "Because I have it."

Cara sat up. She could hear someone stirring down the hall but ignored the sound.

"What do you mean, you have it?"

"I have money," Brendan said quietly, as if he were ashamed. "It's not something you need to worry about."

"What?"

"How many times do I have to say it? I have money. A lot of it, actually. I've been saving."

Cara let this sink in. She wasn't sure she believed it, but she wanted it to be true, in spite of her conscience reminding her that she wasn't supposed to care.

"Don't look so shocked."

"But the boat. And your clothes." She laughed now. "You've been wearing that same old stained T-shirt since the day I met you. You *know* the one I mean."

"Well, technically I was naked when I met you. Technically I'm naked right now."

"Yeah, okay, smartass. You know what I'm trying to say. If you have money, why are you staying in an old sailboat in your friend's driveway? Why are you living off of root beer and Fritos?"

"Because I like root beer and Fritos. And I don't care about that kind of stuff. You know that. And like I said, I've been *saving*. That means not spending my money on stupid shit. Besides, the boat's got all I need. I thought you liked the boat."

"I do—but, Brendan, if you've got as much money as you say you do, you should be staying in a hotel. Or a house. At least somewhere with a real bed. It doesn't make any sense."

"Maybe not to you."

Cara knew there was truth to what Brendan was saying. He wasn't a materialistic guy. She believed that. But she knew that couldn't be all of it. Either he didn't actually have the money he claimed—which, she reminded herself, didn't matter either way—or there was something else, another reason he didn't want to spend it.

"Did you get the money from them? From the people who did this to you?"

"Some of it, yeah. They paid me well, relatively speaking. But even then, I didn't need it."

"What do you mean?"

"It's family money. From my mom's side. When she died, it came to me."

Cara pulled back and nodded with eyebrows raised. "Wow. Okay."

"I know what you're thinking," said Brendan. "I can see those wheels turning."

"What?"

"It's not like I grew up in a mansion eating bonbons or something."

"I didn't say you did."

"Yeah, but you're confused because I don't seem rich."

"What? Okay, now you're really misreading me."

"It's okay, I'm not offended. But let me explain it this way: having money is not the same as spending it. If you looked at our bank account, we were rich as shit, sure. But I never knew it. My mom was really frugal. She didn't want to spend it. I don't know what her deal was. The point is that we had money, but to all intents and purposes, we were poor."

Brendan rolled back over onto his stomach and used his arm to pull Cara in closer.

"Do we have to talk about this now?" he asked, his voice muffled by the pillow. "I just got back. Can we just cuddle?"

Cara wanted to remind him that *he* had been the one to start up this conversation in the first place, having the audacity to offhandedly suggest that they have a baby in the middle of sex, mere minutes into their reunion after a six-week hiatus. But she refrained, relieved to have an excuse not to talk about New York, still sick with the anticipation of sharing her new plans with him.

Tomorrow. She would bring it up tomorrow.

2014

Cara checks the mail on her way back into the house, and amidst the usual catalogs and bills she finds a 5x7 save-the-date card with a smiling couple on the front. They are holding hands in Central Park, and a pug wearing a bow tie sits at their feet.

The woman on the card is Lindsay. Lindsay, her best friend from college, glowing with happiness. She doesn't recognize the man in the photo. He's not someone she knows. The last she heard from Lindsay, she was dating that lacrosse player from Lehigh. Zach. She wonders who this new guy is, where they met, what he's like. She looks more closely at the card. He is, of course, tall, handsome, all-American—just the sort of man she would expect Lindsay to marry.

She is surprised to receive it, this request that she block off a day in the future, April 25, 2015, to witness and celebrate the marriage of her friend and this man—*Conrad*, the card says. *Save the date for*

Lindsay and Conrad. She has not spoken to Lindsay in at least four years. She wonders how she even found her address. The card is an extended hand, an olive branch, of which Cara feels completely and utterly undeserving.

After the incident with Micah and Brendan, Lindsay had been a good friend, or as good as a friend can be when she too is still trying to figure out who she is. But as Cara had with all others in her life, she had resisted Lindsay's offers of help, choosing instead to use the Atlantic as a shield for her grief, until the phone finally stopped ringing.

She looks at the card one last time and tosses it into the recycling barrel next to the house. She appreciates the gesture, but knows she will not be in attendance on April 25, especially in light of all that has been happening these past few days.

The house smells like bacon when she gets inside. The table in the breakfast nook is set for two with buttered toast triangles, poached eggs, avocado slices, and crab cakes on each plate. A pitcher of orange juice and a basket of muffins are set to the side. The bacon is still on a greasy paper-towel-lined plate next to the stove. Cara glances at the digital screen of the microwave, and her heart sinks. It's almost noon.

"Graham?"

She wanders from room to room searching for him. She yells his name again as she bounds up the stairs, two at a time. She finds him in the bathroom shaving.

"Long run?" he asks, sliding the blade down below his left sideburn. He stretches his mouth into a distorted oval.

"Graham, I'm so sorry. I lost track of time. If I had known you were going to make breakfast, I would have come straight home."

"It's fine, Care. Don't worry about it," he says. "Food's probably still good if you're hungry."

"I am. Come eat with me," she says, wrapping her arms around his waist.

"It's almost noon. I've got to get over to the gallery to help Giovanna set up for tonight. But you should eat."

Graham rinses his razor and clanks it down on the sink before grabbing a towel and wiping the leftover cream off his face. He pulls away from Cara with just enough roughness to let her know he's upset.

"I'll come with you," she says. "I was going to help Giovanna with the flowers."

"They were delivered this morning," says Graham. "I'm sure it's done by now."

Cara feels a lurch in her intestines. "Well, there've got to be other things I can help with."

Graham secures his top button in the mirror and turns around to face her.

"Listen, Care, I know you forgot about tonight and it's fine," he says. "You've clearly got a lot on your mind. Just stay here, enjoy the breakfast, and I'll see you later—*if you feel like it*. You don't have to come at all if you don't want to."

"Of course I'm coming," says Cara. "I've been looking forward to this."

This is a lie. Not only did Cara completely forget about the opening tonight, she also hates going to these things—a fact not lost on her husband. Still, she's alarmed by her own absent-mindedness. The summer opening is one of the gallery's biggest events of the year. They've been preparing for it for months, and yet all this time it's seemed like something in the far-distant future. She can't believe today is the actual day.

"Graham, you can be upset with me for missing breakfast this morning. I'd be mad too if I cooked for you and you never came home to enjoy it. You don't have to pretend like I forgot about the opening and that's why you're mad. I didn't forget. And it's not like I've been running around complaining about having to go. I want to go. My own work will be on display. Of course I'm going to go."

"Just promise me you won't come unless you genuinely want to," says Graham. "I'd rather not have you there at all if you're just going to be miserable the whole time."

"I'll be there," says Cara, knowing full well that she'll be miserable the whole time. "I'll go with you now. I just need to shower real quick."

"I've gotta go. Just meet me there later."

"You can't wait fifteen minutes?"

"No, I can't. I should have been there an hour ago."

Graham looks like he's about to sprint downstairs and out the door, so she finds something to say that she knows will stop him.

"Is this because of this morning? Because I didn't want to have sex?"

Graham stops at the top of the stairs.

"What? No. Look, I just need to go. This has nothing to do with you, or this morning, or last night. I've just got to go. I will see you later. Or not! You don't have to come."

His voice trails off as he disappears from view and huffs out the door, leaving Cara alone and guilty. Now she really has no choice. She has to go to the opening tonight.

2008

After a quick swim, Cara and Brendan waded back to their chairs to let the sun dry them off. The droplets slid off their arms, leaving tiny traces of salt on their hair and skin. It was unseasonably hot and humid that day, so they'd set up their beach chairs in the shallow waters over a sandbar, letting the coolness of the ocean permeate their bodies through the veins on their ankles and feet. A soft breeze blew along the water's surface.

Cara hadn't been able to relax all day, strangled by the tension of dread growing behind her sternum. She started to wish that she'd never seen Lindsay—never made plans to relocate to New York. The promise of change and excitement suddenly didn't seem worth the difficult conversation she knew she needed to initiate with Brendan. For days now, she'd continued to put it off.

The revelation that Brendan had money was a significant one, and

Cara could hardly deny the feelings of excitement and possibility that it provoked; but these feelings were sickened by the recollection that in five days she was planning to pack up her things, leave the island, and start a new chapter in New York City.

"Listen," she said, taking a deep breath. "There's something I need to tell you."

If Brendan was worried, he didn't show it. He remained reclined in his chair, eyes closed, his neck resting on the back rail.

"While you were gone, I visited my friend Lindsay. On the Cape."

"Oh, yeah?"

"Yeah. Anyway, she lives in New York. And we were talking about it, and we decided it might be fun if I moved in with her. In New York."

Brendan sat up now, taking off his sunglasses. Cara didn't want to look at him. Suddenly all she could think about was Brendan's father. *The victim. The woman.* A murder of passion. A body in the ocean. Her pulse quickened.

But this was Brendan. He wasn't his father.

"New York City?"

"Yeah."

"Is that something you'd consider?"

"I've got a train ticket from Boston this Tuesday," Cara said quickly, watching Brendan's eyes widen. "But you could come with me! We could both go. It would be fun."

"I don't want to go to New York," said Brendan. "And neither should you."

His reaction was disheartening, but hardly surprising. It was difficult to imagine Brendan in New York, or any city for that matter. She wondered if this was how people thought of her too.

"I know it seems sudden, but you wouldn't have to leave on Thursday. I could go and you could come meet me when you're ready."

"Have you ever been to New York?" Brendan asked, wincing. "Do you know what it's like?"

"I mean, yeah. Of course."

"It's dirty and crowded and maddening. It will suffocate you."

"I think you're being a bit dramatic."

"Maybe."

"Well, then, what do you expect me to do, Brendan? You said I could go wherever I wanted when you left. You said you would come find me."

"Yeah, so I could rescue you and bring you back out here. Or somewhere else where the air is clean. Somewhere by the ocean. Anywhere."

"Well, technically New York *is* by the ocean," Cara said quietly.

Brendan used his eyes to let her know how he felt about that logic.

"I don't have any friends here," said Cara. "I don't do . . . anything. Except work at the fish market and spend time with you. And then you go and I'm alone again."

"Look, if you want to go to New York, you should. By all means. But don't go this Thursday."

Brendan reached over to tuck a piece of hair behind Cara's right ear.

"Stay here. At least until my next deployment. I know you think you're missing out on something, but you've got it all backwards. You and me, living out here together in this beautiful place like we have been . . . this is the kind of life people dream about. One day, you're going to realize that."

Cara took in a deep breath and considered the idea. In this moment, the last thing she wanted was to leave Brendan. The decision had been so much easier when he wasn't there, alive and present by her side, looking at her with his dark eyes. But she'd told everyone she was going to New York. Lindsay was expecting her.

"I already bought my ticket," she said in a final, feeble attempt at persuasion.

"I just got back, and you want to leave?"

"No. I don't know."

Cara's resolve began to crumble. She felt herself gravitating toward the decision that caused the fewest ripples, that scared her the least. That was looking at her now, in a way that somehow managed to thaw the icy barriers she'd built up around herself. For as much as she'd been looking forward to New York, fantasizing about it on a regular basis, the astringent reality of packing her bags and finding her way through not only the city, but a new way of life entirely, made her sick with anxiety. It was one thing to say she was moving, and another thing to actually move.

Brendan grabbed her left hand with both of his and looked at her with an excited smile spreading across his face.

"Marry me," he said.

"What?"

Cara laughed, looking around as if to check whether anyone else had heard what she had.

"*Marry me*," he said again, leaning in closer.

If he had made more of a scene, set up a sequence that implied even the slightest bit of forethought, gotten down on one knee, even—ring or no ring—Cara might actually have said yes. But the obvious spontaneity and casualness of the question kept her from taking it seriously.

"Don't be crazy," she said, her thoughts drifting back to the baby question a few nights ago. She'd thought that was behind them.

"I'm serious," he said, getting off his chair and kneeling down in the water in front of her. He was on two knees, not one, but that almost made it cuter. He held her hands in his.

"I can't. You know I can't. I just told you I'm leaving, and your solution is to propose?"

"Shit. You're married already, aren't you? I knew it was a possibility, but I'm not going to lie. This is very disappointing."

Cara couldn't believe he was making a joke in a moment like this, but she laughed in spite of herself.

"Brendan! You can't just ask me to marry you like this. Like it's no big deal."

"Why not?"

"Because it *is* a big deal."

"Okay, okay. You're right."

Brendan inched forward on his knees, wedging himself between Cara's legs and leaning his forehead against hers. The touch of his hand on the curve of her waist sent a blaze of pleasure through her body.

"Remember what I said? The other night? I meant it. I love you, Cara. And I want to build a life with you. And I'm going to do whatever I need to do to make that happen."

Brendan's certainty was both perplexing and soothing. She couldn't understand how he could possibly be so sure of something like this, but she was glad that he was. It made everything seem simpler.

She could physically feel herself letting go. Relaxing the tension in her neck. Unraveling the angst in her chest. Slowing the flow of adrenaline through her legs. She hadn't realized until this moment how nervous she'd been feeling about going to New York.

There was another option now—another way forward. Brendan was potentially a free pass, a ticket to the front of the long line of twentysomethings working to build a future for themselves. In lieu of treading the traditional paths of self-discovery and personal exposure, Cara could now cling to the prospects of Brendan's apparent wealth, which offered an alternative she'd never thought possible.

She knew she couldn't come out and ask about the money directly. To do so would be uncouth. But she needed the reassurance, regardless of how ugly or selfish her motivations might be. Because there was love there too. She was sure of that now. Real love. And didn't that counter-balance things?

"But where would we live?" she asked innocently. If they were going to do this, they couldn't go on this way, with him in the boat and her at Moira and Ed's.

"Wherever you want," said Brendan.

And that was enough.

2014

Nearly all her life, Cara has dreamed of this. Of being right where she is in this very moment. Here, in a gallery, surrounded by her own artwork and a mass of faceless people there to see it. Isn't that the goal of every artist? Most will tell you it's not. They'll say they're happy enough just to be able to create, that the validation of others is simply an added bonus and not the end-all, be-all. Making art without having to worry about money. That's the ultimate goal.

But what about the other stuff? Like the *New York Times* reviews and the magazine interviews and the cocktail parties and the introductions and the speeches and the exhibition installations and the lecture invites and, oh, right—the collectors willing to purchase your work for sums of money so vast they actually make you laugh out loud.

Cara assumes that every artist, every creator, must dream of these things at some point, imagining how they'll look and what they'll say in each scenario, and how their loved ones will react (shock? jealousy? adoration? approval?). But not many of them get to live out the fantasy. Most never get to see whether their colored-in vision of success matches the tracing they created all those years ago.

Cara has, though. At least to some extent. She isn't world-famous. Certainly not. But there are people in the art world who know her work. People who recognize her name. Still, her success has never felt like she once thought it would. She's traveled more places and met more people than she ever would have otherwise. And no, she hasn't had to worry about money, although she also has Graham to thank for that; even if she never sold a piece of art, she would have been financially sound by his side.

To all intents and purposes, her life hasn't changed. *She* hasn't changed. Rather than looking forward to the appearances and interviews, she dreads them with a fierce anxiety. Because she still isn't good at picking the right makeup tones for her skin, and she still hears her professors during critiques telling her that her work makes them feel nothing, and she still raises her voice into a girlish octave when she's nervous, and she still doesn't know how to eloquently end a response to a question, regularly defaulting to an awkward "so . . . *yeah!*"

Her family has flown out for a few shows. Though it's clear her father thinks the art world is all a racket ("It's . . . nice," he once said, tilting his head and furling his brow at one of her darkest, most abstract pieces), she knows he is proud of her and pleased to see her filled with purpose. Lucia has, somewhat surprisingly, put a few of Cara's pieces up in her and Stanley's condo, and has said for years that she'd love to have Cara come in and work with her students sometime.

Her younger brother is the most receptive among the family, expressing great admiration for her ability to be "truly vulnerable" with her art. Drew has in recent years found minor success in the music industry as a beat-maker, creating and recording sounds in his bedroom to sell as kits to producers. One of his beats was just featured in a Jason Derulo song. Cara didn't know who Jason Derulo was, but she immediately downloaded the whole album in support of her brother.

As her success has broadened and her shows have grown more frequent at galleries across the Northeast, however, she has stopped inviting her family, understanding they couldn't possibly make it to every event. So here she stands, alone, on the biggest night of the year for the gallery she co-owns, shifting from foot to foot in her heels. She can already feel her bangs getting heavy from the sweat and oil on her forehead. She tucks the hair behind her ear and takes a sip of wine. And another. Lots of small sips feels less aggressive than a few big gulps. Intent on looking busy, she carefully considers a piece of artwork along the north wall of the gallery as if it's the first time she's seen it.

"I was with the artist when he painted that one," says a voice behind her. She looks over her shoulder and sees Evangeline Sumner in her signature white-framed, cat-eye glasses. They're too big for her face and would look ridiculous in any circle outside of this one. But here in the gallery world they are chic, elegant, cool.

"Evangeline. Hi," says Cara, going in for a tepid skinny-girl hug.

Evangeline smells like lemons and mint. She is thin, with what is by all accounts a fit, attractive physique, but her nose is too big and her eyes too close together—unfortunate facial characteristics that forever prevent her from being the beautiful woman at the party. She makes up for it with her fashion sense, however, the perfect balance of avant-garde and classic sophistication. Tonight she wears a fitted crop top and pencil skirt set that makes Cara's floral sundress seem girlish and unrefined by comparison.

"When did you get in?" Cara asks.

"We took the two forty-five boat."

"Oh, which B&B are you in?"

"The Green Barn," says Evangeline. "In Chilmark. It is so fucking idyllic, every minute is a page out of a Hardy novel. The stone walls, the lighthouses, the sea grass. I can't tell you how good it feels to be out of the city. I may never go back."

The timbre of Evangeline's speaking voice is low and centered in a way that only an educated, esoteric woman's voice can be.

"The owner cooked us freshly caught bluefish tonight. And for breakfast tomorrow they're making lemon-cranberry waffles. I can't have gluten, but it's still adorable."

"Well, I'm sure you can at least sneak a taste."

Evangeline smiles a tight, closed-mouth smile, and Cara fake-laughs through her nose.

"Anyway," Cara says, "you were saying you know the artist?" The threat of uncomfortable silence negates all conversational preference.

"I do. Patrick is my uncle's partner, and he painted this at their villa in Capri. I remember when he was working on it. A friend of theirs had recently died of AIDS and the two of them were still grieving. Seeing it now, in its complete form, I think it really does convey the emotional turmoil that results from losing someone so young, in such an ugly way. It's very powerful."

Cara wonders if Evangeline has ever truly grieved.

"Yes, it is," she lies. She is relieved to feel Graham's hand on her lower back.

"You made it," he says, giving her a kiss on the forehead. She'd like to think this is an indication that he's no longer mad at her, but knows it's just his public persona taking the stage.

"I was just talking with Evangeline," says Cara. "Have you guys seen each other yet?"

Graham nods.

"I came by earlier to help set up," says Evangeline. "Is this the tie we got in Nice?"

She looks Graham up and down and takes the liberty of straightening his bow tie.

"I don't know. Is it?"

"It definitely is. We got it the day we went on that boat ride. And there was that obese American woman who dropped her camera in the water and then made like it was the boat captain's fault."

Graham nods and starts to laugh, his eyes closed in memory. "Yup. You're right. And then her husband actually took a swing at the guy. What a weird trip."

"Yes! They were insane," says Evangeline. "Anyway, it was the same day. We got off the boat and ducked into the textile shop where we picked out your tie. I can't believe you still have that thing."

"Was this when you guys were studying abroad?" asks Cara.

"Yeah. We're talking almost fifteen years ago," says Evangeline. "He is such a hoarder. I hope you make him clean out his closet every now and then."

"Who're you calling a hoarder?" asks Graham. "This is a great tie. I love this tie."

"I bet you still have that tattered old *Star Wars* poster that was in your place in Bushwick, too."

"Number one: that is an awesome poster," says Graham. "Number two: it's probably worth a lot of money now."

"So you still have it."

"Hell, yeah, I do!"

Evangeline rolls her eyes.

"See what I mean?" She gives Cara a knowing glance. "Total hoarder."

Cara fake-laughs as if she and Evangeline are somehow bonded by their shared understanding of Graham's secret tendencies—his love of old things and his general reluctance to throw things away. In reality, of course, it is this very dynamic that divides them and prevents them from ever truly being friends. As long as Graham is in the picture, they will always be competing over who knows him better.

An older man approaches the trio then, putting a hand on Graham's shoulder and apologizing for the interruption. "I just wanted to say hello," he says.

He's tall and thin with a gray goatee and a shaved head. He and Graham shake hands.

"Alan. I'm so glad you could make it. You know Evie. And this is my wife, Cara."

Cara gives him the customary air kiss, a move she'd never in her life executed before meeting Graham and his people.

"Honey, this is Alan Schafer. He owns a gallery on Newbury Street. In Boston."

"I was just looking at your pieces," Alan tells Cara. "They're lovely."

"Oh, I didn't realize your work would be up tonight as well," comments Evangeline. "I'll have to take a look."

It's the sort of remark that feels like a dig, but one that Cara could never successfully justify as such to Graham.

"They really do mimic the sensation of being underwater," says Alan.

Cara thanks him and lets herself enjoy the compliment. It feels good to receive praise from an industry professional who isn't her husband.

"Cara's ex-husband could breathe underwater," says Evangeline.

"I'm sorry?" Alan looks perplexed, but interested.

Cara's breath catches. "Oh. No, that's not totally—"

"He was in the military and they did all these experiments and surgeries on him," Evangeline continues before Cara can interject. "And apparently it enabled him to actually *breathe* underwater. Right?"

She turns to Cara with eyebrows innocently raised.

Cara's vision blurs and her jaw feels stiff and heavy. Her throat is so dry she can't swallow, let alone speak. Graham tenses up beside her.

"C'mon, Evie, quit pulling his leg," he says with a chuckle. "You know those were just tall tales."

Cara knows that nothing she says now can alleviate the awkwardness of this conversation. Her face is too red, her discomfort too obvious. But she gives it a try anyway, mustering a soft chuckle of indifference.

"No, see—I think what you're thinking is . . . He was one of those free divers—those people who train themselves to swim down to incredible depths?" says Cara. "And he wasn't my husband. Just—an old flame. *You know.*"

She laughs and takes another swig of wine.

Cara doesn't know how much longer she can keep up this charade. Graham squeezes her shoulder and audibly asks if she'd mind coming with him to check on the caterers.

The back room is filled with stacked crates of glasses and plates and strangers in white aprons and black bow ties. The space is loud with clinks and shouts, sizzles and chops. The waitstaff and Giovanna, mid-conversation just a second ago, snap to attention when they see Graham and Cara enter the room.

"How are we doing? Everything okay?" Giovanna asks in her Italian accent, using her smile to disguise her sweaty brow and flushed cheeks.

"We're great. Just keep doing what you're doing," says Graham as he rushes by. He ushers Cara by the shoulders to the corner. She is a ticking time bomb.

"Thanks for telling Evangeline all about Brendan, Graham. That was really fun."

"Look, she shouldn't have brought it up like that. And I promise you I will talk to her about it. But try not to turn this into something it's not. It was a botched attempt at conversation. That's it."

"No, Graham, that's not it. That was completely humiliating for me and she knew it. She brought it up on purpose, just to make me squirm and us fight. Like we are now. So, congrats, *Evie*," Cara yells in the direction of the main hall. "*You did it!*"

"Is that really what you think? Evangeline is one of my closest friends. Why would she want us to fight?"

"Because she resents me for taking you away from her. She always has. For years she kept you in her back pocket, just in case she needed you. Just in case the perfect, amazing douchebag man of her dreams never came along. And then one day she woke up and she was in her thirties, and she started to realize that that guy was never coming. That *you* were that guy all along. But it was too late. Because of me. I fucked up her life plan and—*believe me*—she lets me know it every time I see her."

"Okay. This conversation has gone far beyond . . ." Graham puts his hands up and shakes his head. He takes a deep breath.

"Here's what we're going to do. We're going to go back out there and we're going to lead a brief welcome toast and then you can go home and go to bed. I'm not trying to diminish the importance of this conversation—we need to have it—just not here. Not now."

"Oh, so *I'm* the one who has to leave."

"What, as opposed to me?"

"No, as opposed to *her. Evangeline.*"

"Don't be ridiculous. What, do you want me to just walk out there and tell her to leave because she mistakenly touched on a sore subject?"

"Mistake or not, we wouldn't even be having this conversation if *somebody* hadn't told her my whole life story."

"She's my friend. We talk. What do you want me to say?"

"I want you to admit that she's in love with you and that she very clearly goes out of her way to make me feel uncomfortable. She purposely brought up that story to make me feel stupid and you know it. No, actually, I take it back. She's not in love with you. She's possessive of you, in this almost creepy, motherly way. It's not even that she wants you for herself—she still thinks she's too good for you. She just doesn't want anyone else to have you."

Graham glances toward the doorway back into the gallery.

"I can't do this right now. Stay. Leave. Do whatever you want, but I can't spend the whole night hiding back here. We can talk about this at home."

Graham starts to walk away then pivots midstride, coming back to Cara and hugging her.

"I'm sorry," he says, "I love you," before releasing her and heading back out into the exhibition.

Cara feels like a trophy wife, standing at the front of the room next to Graham, smiling but not saying a word. She isn't one, she knows that. And Graham doesn't treat her like one. And maybe she's just let Evangeline get inside of her head more than she should have. But then Cara wonders, for a moment, if this is where she's supposed to be. To others, her life now is a dream. A fantasy. Thanks to Graham—and the occasional painting commissions *he's* helped her accrue—she's free to spend her days as she pleases, wandering the paradise that is the Vineyard, painting and drawing, going to farmers' markets, exploring tide pools.

So why does she still feel so sad?

As Graham speaks to the audience, inserting the self-deprecating but charming jokes necessary to secure their affections and dollars, Cara looks at the sea of faces and realizes that they are all her husband's people. Few are year-round islanders, and none are her friends or family. She knows she should allow them to be her family—that they'd let her if she wanted to. But she's not sure that she does.

She and Evangeline will never be real friends. Of this, she is certain.

But how often do they even see each other? Two, maybe three times a year? She wishes she could just let the woman's sly little digs roll off. And she usually does, but this time feels different.

Lots of people know about Brendan and Micah. The kidnapping story made the local news in Boston. But only a select few know the whole story. Over time, Cara has learned to be very careful about whom she divulges the other details to. Because apart from the grief she's experienced in losing Micah, the worst thing she's ever felt in her entire life is the burning sense of humiliation and degradation whenever someone looks at her like she's crazy. The way the cops and the psychiatrists and the investigators had all looked at her when she'd confided her beliefs about Brendan. Shock, mixed with pity, mixed with the tiniest hint of amusement.

She hadn't felt that with Graham. At least, not in the beginning. She'd felt like she could trust him. So when she imagines him, now, imparting her story to Evangeline—of all people—Cara feels a knot of shame in her chest. She wonders how he might have framed it.

Oh my god, Evangeline, you're never going to believe this story. . . .

I need some advice, Evangeline. I'm really worried about my girlfriend. . . .

Evangeline, the girl I'm dating is batshit crazy. Listen to this . . .

No matter how it came up, Cara hates that it did. It's understandable that Graham would have needed someone to talk to—specifically someone who didn't know Cara—but did it have to be Evangeline?

As a follow-up to everything that's happened recently, with Dean's story and the visit to the old house and the whale figurine, the encounter with Evangeline feels like a wake-up call. The story and the whale are mere coincidences. Tricks of the mind.

As she directs a plastered-on smile to Graham and looks out adoringly over the audience, Cara makes a promise to herself to let it all go. She's been too deep in her own head lately. She was so good a few days ago. She should try to get back there. Pretend like the past two days never happened. She and Graham can go back to trying for a baby and continue building their life together. And when she's feeling down, or confused, she can channel that into her art. That's what she'll do. That's what'll make her feel better. Tomorrow she'll spend the day in the studio and get the stress and emotions caused by Dean and Moira and the whole stupid Evangeline episode out on canvas.

And then it happens, the timing so preposterous it feels like sabotage. It hits her like a pulse of electricity, the physical punch landing hard and round on her stomach but growing thinner and brighter as it travels down her arms and legs. She's sure she's imagining things. She has to be. Must be the wine. Must be the stress. Must be the exhaustion. Must be the hope, bubbling up again, unrelenting in its haunting.

But then she blinks, and he's still there, unmistakable, looking right at her. His hair is long and tied back and he has a full beard now, but she knows it's him. She lets out an audible gasp and drops her glass of wine to the floor. The silence that follows reverberates well beyond the sound of the shattering glass. Everyone is looking at her. Graham tries to grab her arm but she pulls away, pushing through the now-murmuring crowd toward the back of the room.

She shoves though strangers, searching their faces for the one she's sure she just saw. He must have gone outside. She hurries out into the night where bored gallerygoers have gathered for cigarette breaks and fresh air, uninterested in the remarks of the gallery owner and his wife.

Cara pulls off her heels and runs into the street, the asphalt somehow soothing on her sore feet. *He was here. Where did he go?* She looks in every possible direction for a trace of movement, growing panicked with each passing second. She consciously tries to slow her thoughts and consider where he might be. Not the street, but the woods. Behind the gallery.

Her heart thumps in her ears. She makes her way around the side of the building and through the trees, taken aback by how dark it is. Her eyes haven't yet had a chance to adjust. Dried-out twigs and upturned stones jab into her feet, but she keeps going, reaching her hands out in front of her to feel for trees. She is afraid to say his name out loud, so she whispers it instead. It is the loud sort of whisper utilized only in moments of urgency.

"Brendan. Brendan, I'm here. It's me.

"Brendan."

2008

Cara tried her dad's cell first, knowing full well that he wouldn't answer it. He was one of those people who constantly kept his phone off, fearing that if he left it on he would drain its battery and render it useless. Cara and Drew had repeatedly explained to him that a turned-off cell phone was just as useless as a dead cell phone, because no one could reach you either way, but the logic never quite sank in.

When, as predicted, the call went straight to voicemail, Cara dialed the landline instead.

She was relieved when her dad, and not Lucia, answered the phone. "Hi, Dad," she said. "It's me."

Cara knew her news would shock him, and shock wasn't an emotion she'd ever elicited in him before. Growing up, Cara had naturally been an obedient child, as so many young girls are. It wasn't that her parents were strict or reprimanding; it wasn't fear that kept her in line. Rather, it was the prospect of her parents' adoration and attention that kept her motivated. She lived for their praise and approval, her anxious desire to please a constant driving force.

That was why it felt so exciting—so thrilling—now to let all that go. She had made a decision—a spontaneous decision—and the adrenaline in her system made her bold. She could feel the change within herself, but that wasn't enough. It wasn't real until someone who knew the old her, someone who *really* knew and loved her, was also witness to the change.

It was 11 a.m. on the Vineyard, which meant it was only 8 a.m. in Glendale. Her dad would be sitting on the patio out back, enjoying the morning air before it got too hot to be outside. It was odd to imagine him there, surrounded by sand and saguaros, while she was out here by the ocean.

"How you doin', kiddo? All packed for the big city?"

The conversation steered to the issue at hand sooner than she'd expected. Cara started to pace, the phone feeling hot on her cheek.

"Actually, there's been a change of plans."

"Oh?"

"Yeah. I've decided not to go to New York after all."

"But you were so excited. What happened?"

"I changed my mind. I'm going to stay here instead. I'm going to live here. On the island."

"With *Moira*?"

"Well, for a little while, yeah. But eventually we'll find our own place."

"We?"

Cara took a deep breath. Her heart was beating fast, but she was smiling hard.

"Yeah. That's why I'm calling. Dad, I have some news."

"Okay . . ."

"I'm engaged," she said, almost laughing as the words came out. "I'm getting married."

Cara bit down on her lower lip and stared at a bathing suit top on the floor as she awaited her dad's response. His silence was charged. He let out a stunned guffaw.

"Honey, I . . . I can't tell if you're being serious. Are you pulling my leg?"

"Nope. I met someone and we've decided to get married. Not right away! Don't worry. But we love each other and we want to be together. Here, on the island."

"So you're serious."

"*Yes*, Dad. What do you think?"

"I don't know what to say, Care. It seems pretty sudden."

"Well, to you, yeah. But it's not like I just met the guy this week. We've been seeing each other the whole summer. I just never told you about him. His name is Brendan. He's in the military—Special Forces, actually."

Cara heard her dad let out a less-than-happy sigh.

"It's fine that you're with someone. That's great. But I don't see why you have to stay on the Vineyard," he said. "I was really hoping you'd end up going to New York. We were really excited for you."

"I know. But Brendan hates New York. Like, really hates it. And I'm starting to realize, I really like this place. Have you ever been here in the fall? The weather's amazing and there are fewer people. . . . It's really beautiful."

"Does Moira know about all this?"

"Yeah. Well, kind of. Not all of it. She doesn't know we're engaged. She knows Brendan, though. I wanted to tell you first."

"Well, I appreciate that. But I don't know about this, Care. What about Lindsay? Isn't she expecting you?"

"She was, yeah. But I told her I changed my mind. It's fine."

When Cara told Lindsay that she wasn't coming to New York after all, Lindsay had taken the news surprisingly well; it was the engagement that had stunned her. *But we're only twenty-two. . . .* Cara still found herself pushing the phrase Lindsay kept repeating out of her head.

"I know it sounds crazy right now. But I've put a lot of thought into this. And it's not like we're running off and eloping or something."

As soon as she said the words, she realized this wasn't something she was fully prepared to promise. An elopement could be romantic.

"At least, I don't think so," she amended. "I don't know. We just decided all this last night."

"Why don't you come home? Spend a few days here. Lucia and I will pay for the flight."

Cara recoiled at the thought. Arizona was not home. "Why would I go to Arizona?"

"You've been cooped up on that tiny island for so long. It's become your whole world. I think it would do you some good to get out and clear your head. Get some perspective."

"I thought you would be happy for me."

This was a blatant lie, but Cara wanted to make him feel bad.

"I just want you to think about this a little more, before you make any major decisions. I don't want you to throw your life away to be with this guy. If he really loves you like he says, he should have no problem with you going to New York. Seeing your friends. Getting a job. Following your dreams."

"Dad, be realistic. If I go to New York, chances are I'll end up living in a dilapidated apartment with a zillion roommates, managing someone else's schedule and going on coffee runs all day. Probably making no more than I do at the freaking fish market. At least here I have time to make my own art. Build my portfolio. That's what I ultimately want to be doing anyway."

"Look, I can't force you to do anything. But will you think about coming out here? No matter what you decide, we'd love to see you. Bring the guy if you want! Brendan. Whatever."

They eventually came to a compromise, with Cara agreeing to fly to Arizona for Thanksgiving, mostly so she could see Drew and so the three of them (four, if you counted Lucia) could be together as a family. But her cooperation was not without resentment. If her dad was so concerned, why couldn't he come out to the Vineyard himself? Why had he insisted that *she* visit *him*? If he just took the time to meet Brendan and reacquaint himself with the beauty of the island, maybe he would begin to understand her decision. Maybe he would remember why their family used to make the trek out here, summer after summer. Why they loved it so much.

But that was just it. He didn't want to remember. The idea of returning to a place that reminded him so much of his dead wife was too painful to bear. They both knew that as long as Cara was on the island, her father would never come visit. And that's what scared them both the most.

When Cara approached her, Moira was hunched over her needlepoint magnifying glass, a giant lens with an adjustable neck that Cara and Drew used to play with as kids, their teeth looking huge and monstrous through the thick, warped glass. Moira was working on a throw pillow that read *Caution, Dog Can't Hold Its Licker*, with a big black dog sticking out a giant, floppy pink tongue. Cara sat down next to her and forced a laugh.

"That's hilarious," she said, even though she found it tacky.

"Isn't it? I found this site on the web with the best patterns. People say needlepoint doesn't take any skill, but I don't care. It soothes me."

Moira's enthusiasm for the craft went without saying. The house was covered in throw pillows and footstools and hanging canvases—pretty much anything that could have been customized was. Even the dogs' collars had little stitched names on them.

Cara's heart was beating fast. She needed to tell Moira about the engagement.

Moira obviously knew about Brendan, but Cara and Moira had never actually had a real conversation about him or Cara's feelings toward him. She just hoped that Brendan's unexpected late-night visits hadn't bothered Moira, or Ed, for that matter, who suffered from severe sleep apnea and was at this very moment napping to make up for a restless night's sleep.

"So Brendan came back Thursday night."

Moira glanced up from her needlepoint with raised eyebrows. "More like Friday morning."

Cara cringed.

"I know, I'm sorry. I didn't know he was coming. Did he wake you? I feel bad. I'll tell him he can't just show up like that."

"It's all right. You've only got a few more days here anyway. Have you told him yet? About your plans?"

"Well, kind of. I did, but . . . I think I changed my mind."

"Oh?"

It was now or never.

"Brendan just asked me to marry him."

Moira didn't flinch. She kept on with her needlepoint, her fingers moving delicately over and under the canvas.

"And what did you say?"

"I said yes."

Moira looked up now, a warm smile on her face. "You really like this boy."

Cara wiggled her toes and shrugged. "Well, yeah. *Obviously.*"

"Love is a beautiful thing," Moira said, placing a hand on Cara's knee. "I'm very happy for you."

Cara could have let the conversation end there—hugged Moira and returned upstairs to sketch in her journal. Perhaps it was Moira's kindness that prompted Cara to do what she did next, an unconditional warmth and acceptance that made her feel safe.

"Do you think it's too fast?"

"Oh, Bear. Who am I to set the pace? Only you can know what's right."

"My dad's not thrilled."

"You told him?"

"Yeah, I just called him. I was so excited. I couldn't wait."

"Well, don't let his lack of enthusiasm get you down. You know you better than anyone else. And if you feel, deep in your heart—without a doubt—that Brendan is your person, then Brendan is your person, and no one else can tell you otherwise. Simple as that."

Without a doubt. Cara always had doubts. About everything. Were there really people out there who went around living their lives without a knot of question marks perpetually shadowing their every move? She looked down at the floor, feeling slightly nauseated. Did the fact that she did have doubts—even if they were just a few, small, probably silly doubts—mean that Brendan possibly *wasn't* "her person"?

Sensing Cara's hesitation, Moira leaned in closer and asked, "Do *you* think it's too fast?"

"Well, I mean, there's no denying it's *fast*," Cara admitted. "But it's also . . . I don't know. I love Brendan. I *know* I love Brendan. He always makes me feel so special and so lucky and so happy. But sometimes . . . I worry about him."

The words were scary to conjure but a relief to release.

"You mean with his job?"

"Yeah. Sort of. It's just that sometimes, he gets in these moods. And he turns into this completely different person. It's like, one day he'll be his usual self, funny and happy, and then all of the sudden, the next day, he shuts down. It's like the light goes out of him. Even his voice is different. He just seems . . . sad. It's happened two or three times now."

"Well, have you asked him about it?"

"Not directly, no. I just thought he was in a bad mood at first. Like how anyone gets down once in a while. You know? But it's happened a few times now, and I'm worried about it. I think he might have PTSD or something."

PTSD. Post-traumatic stress disorder. Cara's understanding of the affliction came entirely from books and movies, sad tales of soldiers returning home from war and struggling to reintegrate to ordinary life. Nightmares. Hallucinations. Alcoholism. A half hour or so of googling had left her confident that this was what plagued Brendan. Yet she had little idea what he actually did when he went overseas, let alone the ways in which those experiences affected his life back home. She assumed that his missions were perilous and stressful, and that this took an inevitable toll on him. Perhaps this was the reason he was always running away to the water, disoriented or triggered somehow, lost in a moment of recreated panic.

"Oh, Bear, everyone has bad days," said Moira. "We all deal with them in different ways."

"I know, but how am I supposed to know if it's just a bad day or something else? I mean, what if he has a serious problem?"

"Sounds to me like the two of you need to have a conversation," said Moira. "That's all. Tell him what you're seeing and thinking. Ask questions. If he wants to talk, he'll talk. You may find that it's nothing."

"Yeah. Maybe."

"In any case, does this mean we get to have you with us for longer, I hope?"

"For a little while, at least. Is that okay? Only until we can find our own place."

"Of course it's okay! Stay as long as you need. We love having you. You know that."

Cara thanked Moira and headed up to her bedroom. She barely made it up the stairs before she started to cry. Moira hadn't said anything wrong. To the contrary, she'd been completely supportive of the engagement and seemed unbothered by Cara's misgivings about Brendan. What Cara should have been feeling was consolation and relief. Instead, she felt a profound sadness, the ache overtaking her in one powerful surge.

Because she realized now that there was really only one person she wanted to talk to about Brendan: her mother. She needed her mom, and she couldn't have her—couldn't confide in her or seek her advice. Her mother would never know Brendan, never witness their life together. And it hurt, this grief, this pain of knowing that she would forever live with a void, no matter how hard she tried to ignore it, or fill it up with love from other people. It was always going to be there.

Cara took a deep breath. She couldn't talk to her mom, but she could try to imagine what she might say. Surely she would recommend, as Moira had, that Cara talk to Brendan, tell him how she was feeling. It was a prospect that filled Cara with angst. She knew it was a conversation they needed to have, but that didn't make it any less scary. Because there were still so many what-ifs. What if she offended him? What if she lost him? Or worse, what if she learned something she didn't want to know?

September gave way to October and the island began to shed its summer skin. The late-season visitors, the retirees, the childless couples—all those unbound by the demands of the academic cycle— were gone now, leaving solitary rubber flip-flops, empty oyster cracker packets, and broken beach umbrellas in their wake. The fish market was lucky to get a dozen patrons each day, and most of those were local fishermen and service workers, folks who made a living out of maintaining the estates of summer wash-ashores. Mona reduced Cara's hours to two lunch shifts a week, which usually entailed hours of mopping, restocking, and playing card games with Adriano. She never saw Graham anymore.

By early November, it was getting too cold to sleep in the boat. Cara bundled herself in layers of cotton sweatshirts and fleece blankets, doubling up on socks and starting some nights off with a knitted hat. It amazed her how Brendan continued to sleep in his underwear. He argued it was actually warmer that way, and tried to convince Cara to do the same, claiming that the natural heat of their naked bodies was the best defense against the cold.

Cara traced the outline of the whale on Brendan's back with her finger.

"What's the story with the whale?"

"My tattoo?"

Cara told him yes, though it wasn't the tattoo itself she cared about. Seeing it now reminded her of the book she'd found with its strange collection of photos and migration charts. Weeks ago, she'd gone back to the boat to search for it after Brendan had gone overseas, only to discover that he'd locked the cabin. She'd told herself it wasn't her he was locking out, that it wasn't the book he was protecting.

Because the truth was that that book, with its dense perplexity, still haunted her. She could understand Brendan's post-traumatic symptoms, emotionally taxing as they were on both of them. While his reactions didn't always make sense in the context of a given moment, when you layered on his life story and everything he'd been through, they did. But the book didn't. No matter how much she tried to minimize or explain it, she never felt like she understood it.

Cara continued to trail her finger over the tattoo. It looked like a pen drawing in blue ink, a clean, linear outline with individual dots in place of shading. She wondered if that made the application process more or less painful. The whale's tail was up on Brendan's shoulder blade, and its big block head leveled out at the base of his back, as if taking a deep dive.

"Why whales?" she asked again.

"Isn't it obvious?"

"I guess so. I mean, I get the whole breathing underwater thing."

"Well, whales can't actually breathe underwater."

"Oh, right. I'm an idiot. But they're mammals. Living underwater. Like you. Is that it?"

"Kind of, yeah. I feel a connection with them. I've seen them. Out there."

Out there. Cara couldn't begin to fathom the full reality of what those two words meant. She felt a tightening in her chest. She always did when Brendan talked this way, about what it was like to be underwater. It scared her to think about it, him living under the surface for indefinite periods of time. It struck her as dark, and lonely, and eerie. And as much as she tried to imagine it, to really envision what it must be like, to conjure an accurate understanding of Brendan's experience was utterly impossible. She could try to snorkel and even scuba dive, but she could never truly know. He would forever be alone in his knowledge.

"Is that why you have that book?"

Cara's voice almost broke as she asked the question, her throat suddenly dry and taut. Brendan wasn't facing her, but she could feel his body stiffen.

"What book?"

"That book I found. When I was helping you clean up."

Brendan stayed quiet.

"I know I shouldn't have looked. I didn't read anything, just flipped through the pages."

"I don't know what you mean."

"Yes, you do. I asked you about it before, remember? It was this big old *Where's Waldo?* book. And the pages were filled with maps and charts and pictures of whales that someone had pasted in."

"Oh. Yeah. That. That's just an old thing I made when I was younger. I don't know why I even still have it. I should just throw it away."

The explanation made sense. Why had she ever thought otherwise? Of course he'd made it when he was younger—that should have been obvious to her the moment she'd opened it up. She too could remember scribbling over the pages of her favorite picture books as a child, slapping Lisa Frank stickers in places they didn't belong.

And yet, she couldn't quite let it go. She sat up. Brendan remained horizontal, facing the wall.

"So why do you still have it? Why did you bring it with you out here? Of all the things?"

"I don't know. It's sentimental, I guess. Why do you care so much?"

"And if it's so old, why were there scissors lying on top of it when I found it? Do you still add to it?"

Brendan turned suddenly toward her, nearly knocking her off the narrow bed platform.

"Jesus, Cara, I don't fucking know. All right? Why are you so obsessed with this?"

"I'm sorry. I was just curious."

"Well, let it go. I'm trying to sleep. It's fucking freezing."

"Fine."

Hurt, Cara scooped up her blankets and tossed her pillow to the single berth across the cabin. Were it not so cold, and so late at night, she would have climbed out of that boat and ridden her bike all the way home. Instead, she slid out of bed with Brendan and curled up in her own bed, the cushion cold beneath her belly. She fell asleep waiting for him to apologize.

C ara could see her breath when she woke up. Her throat stung when she swallowed and the tip of her nose was white with cold. She craved water, but didn't want to leave the warmth of her bed. She remembered their fight—if you could even call it that, it was so stupid—from the night before and looked over to Brendan's side of the boat. He wasn't there. She checked the time on her phone: 5:52 a.m. Where had he gone so early?

She heard a shuffling overhead. Someone was up on the deck. She groaned to herself and pulled a knit hat down over her ears. She wrapped a flannel blanket around her shoulders, shivering, crept out of bed, and pushed open the hatch above the staircase, peeking through the crack until she saw Brendan, sitting folded into himself in his boxer shorts—the ones with little chili peppers on them—arms wrapped around his knees. Cara burst through the door and wrapped her blanket around him, holding Brendan close in her arms.

"Brendan, what are you doing out here? What's wrong?"

He'd been crying. His eyes were lined with pink and the vein on the left side of his forehead was engorged. His skin was rough to the touch with goose bumps. She tried to flatten them out with the friction from her hands, rubbing back and forth across his shoulders.

"It's cold. Come back inside."

"I can't. I can't think in there."

"Okay. Well, can I bring you some clothes?"

Brendan stood up. "I need to go," he said.

"Go where? Brendan, what's going on?"

"I just need to think," he said. "Figure out my next course."

He was pacing now, running his hands nervously through his hair.

"Is there anything I can do to help you?"

"No. No, it's safer if you don't know anything."

"Should I be worried? You're scaring me. Why won't you look at me?"

"I'm sorry. I need to go. Yeah, I need to go."

Brendan turned his body to climb down the ladder, and Cara grabbed his arm.

"Wait, Brendan. It's six o'clock in the morning! Where are you going?"

Brendan pulled his arm away, making no attempt to check his strength. Surprised by the force of his resistance, Cara lost her balance and fell back hard onto the deck. She called out Brendan's name, pleading with him to wait, but could only watch as he ran down the road, his silhouette disappearing into the blackness of the surrounding trees, backdropped by the glow of dawn.

Cara felt paralyzed by shock and indecision. She didn't know whether to chase after him or wait at the boat for his return. He'd been running so fast, she'd never catch him. But she could hardly sit and wait in the boat. Not with the flashing pulses of worry and fear racing through her head. She needed to do something.

She picked up her phone and dialed. It was the only thing she could think to do. Mental state aside, Brendan was physically okay—at least, he seemed to be. She'd seen him down before, but there had never been an episode quite like this. There was a terror radiating from him, made all the more concerning by the fact that, to her, its source was invisible.

Twenty minutes later, Moira's Buick appeared at the pull-off. Cara climbed in the front seat. Moira passed her a thermos of tea.

"Chamomile," she said.

Cara thanked her and took a sip, burning the tip of her tongue.

"Now, which way did he go?"

Cara pointed, and Moira drove the car slowly along the road while Cara looked for Brendan out the window. They followed Middle Road all the way to Chilmark before taking the turnoff to Menemsha. They drove to the end of the lot by the beach and scanned the sand and the jetty for any sign of him, but the only people out were a few recreational fishermen and joggers. It was hardly surprising. The likelihood that Brendan would have already made it that far on foot was slim. But she didn't know where else to look. There were dozens of little streets he could have turned down. She told Moira to head home.

Back at the house, Cara curled into a ball on the couch in the den, still in her sweats. She let the steam from the coffee Moira brought her envelop her chin and face and patted the cushion beside her so that Angus would jump up and cuddle. Moira sat down in the chair across from her.

"Thank you for coming to get me. I didn't know what else to do."

"Of course, Bear. You know you can always call."

"I've just never seen him like this. It scared me."

"What about what you told me before? About the post-traumatic stress."

"I don't know. I mean, maybe. Is that how people with PTSD act?" Cara asked. "It was like I wasn't even there. He wouldn't even look at me."

"I'll tell you what I think," said Moira. "I think the boy needs rest. Time to live his life without having to travel overseas and kill people in the name of Uncle Sam. That's what I think."

Cara had never thought of Brendan's missions like that. She always imagined him as more of a spy, using his power to infiltrate areas and obtain top-secret information, collecting data and files. Moira made it sound like he was an assassin.

Cara wasn't sure what she should be more worried about: Brendan's mental state or the real possibility that he might be in danger—and not just when he was on a mission, but all the time. Were there people out there trying to get him? Capture him? Harm him in some way? *Kill him?* The idea seemed so farfetched, especially in a place as wholesome and safe as the Vineyard, that it hardly scared her.

"I wonder if maybe it's time he saw someone," Cara said.

"Like a shrink?"

Cara nodded. "A psychiatrist. Yeah."

"Has he tried running?" Moira asked. "Or what about something like tai chi? There was a period in my life when tai chi really saved me."

When it came to medicine, Moira had always fallen more toward the extremely liberal end of the spectrum. Symptoms of depression and anxiety were afflictions best treated with meditation, exercise, and teas. Americans were grossly overmedicated, she often said.

Cara had seen a therapist once, though she'd never thought of him that way. He was just Mike, her college's health and wellness counselor. She'd never intended to visit the health center, but it had been mandated after she'd gotten her stomach pumped just weeks into her freshman year. The whole thing was humiliating. Until it wasn't.

Mike was one of those gentle giant types, a former Division I football player whose personal struggles had over time softened both his muscles and his demeanor. He gave the impression of having seen it all, and had a warmth to his eyes that made her immediately trust him. Having been through his own battles with alcohol and depression—a fact he openly shared with the students who visited him—lent him an air of credibility and fostered respect.

Their initial conversation naturally began with the subject of drinking, but quickly—seamlessly, a testament to Mike's skill as a counselor—transitioned to the issue of her mother's death. Cara could still remember what a relief it was to talk about it, the release somehow so much easier with a stranger. It was okay to talk about herself for an hour. It was okay to be sad.

Cara thought again about Brendan's book. The migration patterns, the maps and charts, the diagrams, the scribbled notes in the margins. The amount of time and energy and enthusiasm evident in the researching, and the cutting and gluing, and the placement of images and words, was as astounding as it was alarming. The book's existence loomed like a mysterious dark spot just out of view. And each time she slipped and allowed herself to think about it, it appeared bigger and muddier than it had before. But she couldn't acknowledge it openly just yet. She wasn't there. Not yet. She was still too afraid. Too hopeful. It was probably nothing.

Cara stood up to get more coffee. When she got to the kitchen, she had to brace herself on the counter. Her head suddenly felt like a medicine ball, her stomach a hot glob of dough. She ran to the first-floor bathroom and crouched over the toilet, gagging just once before vomiting out a smooth stream of liquid. She went to bed after that and slept on through to the evening.

The nausea and fatigue stayed with her for days, symptoms she attributed to her depression and worry over things with Brendan. Every time she tried to get up and make herself do something, she just felt sick again. She knew she was hungry—starving, even—but few things appealed to her. It wasn't so much that she felt ill. It was more just a sense of feeling off—of something not being quite right.

It wasn't until the fourth day of this that she realized what she had done. How, in a moment of reckless abandon, she had made a decision that would impact her life in ways she could never imagine.

She tried to remember now, weeks later, why she had done it. Why she had chosen to pop her pills in their plastic trays through the circular little films of aluminum, one by one, into the toilet with hardly a sound as they hit the water and fell through to the porcelain below. Because the dream—the lackadaisical, haphazard fantasy of making a baby with Brendan—was real now. Cara was pregnant.

The next time she saw Brendan was when he showed up at the fish market with a box of fudge from Murdick's. He looked like the same old Brendan again. The color was back in his cheeks and his shoulders were rolled back at their usual angle of confidence. He was wearing a brown leather jacket that Cara realized she'd never seen before.

"I journeyed all the way to Edgartown to get these for you," he said, sliding the box onto the counter. "Can we talk?"

"I can't. I'm working."

"Oh, I'm sorry. Is this a bad time? Am I pulling you away from the other customers?"

Brendan gestured to the empty room behind him as the hum of the refrigerator filled the space.

He was being obnoxious, but he was right. It was just Cara and Adriano there today. No one would care if she abandoned her post behind the counter for a few minutes.

They sat on the edge of the lobster tank, exactly the way Cara had constantly admonished summer patrons *not* to do. The lobsters crept and crawled over one another, seemingly in a daze, except for a pair in the corner looking ready to spar.

"Check out these two guys." Brendan pointed. "They're about to go at it. My money's on the pink guy," he said, referring to the pink rubber bands wrapped around the creature's claws. "We should take the bands off. Really see what they can do. Take the gloves off, if you will. You guys ever do that?"

"Can't say we do. No."

"Why not? Let these guys have some fun before they hit the pot."

"You mean let them mutilate each other? I don't want to watch that!"

"Oh, but it's okay to boil them alive?"

Cara sighed. "You said you wanted to talk?"

"Right. Sorry. Yeah. I wanted to say that I was sorry. For the other day."

"What *was* that? I was really worried."

"I don't know. I just . . . I let the stress get to me, you know? I wish you didn't have to see me like that. I'm not usually like that."

"So that's it? You were stressed? It seemed like more than that."

"I don't know what else to call it. I got a message. In the middle of the night. It caught me off guard."

"What kind of message?"

"Just some information. I wasn't expecting it. It's nothing you need to worry about."

"How could I not be worried? I wake up to find you huddled in a ball, crying, with no clothes on, talking nonsense. And then when I tried to talk to you, you literally ran away from me."

"That's not how I remember it."

"Well, that's what happened."

Cara considered her next words carefully. "Have you thought about talking to someone?"

"I talk to you."

"No, you don't. You aren't telling me anything."

"Because I don't want to scare you."

"At this point, I can't think of anything you can say to me that's going to make me more scared than I already am. So if that's your concern, we're way past that."

Brendan drew closer and spoke in a low voice. "Okay. I'll tell you what's happening. But know first that I would never let anything happen to you, okay? So please don't worry. You're not in danger."

"Okay . . ."

"What's happening is that there are people. Who know about me.

Who know about—*me*." Brendan put a hand on the crook between his chest and shoulder. "And I got a message a few nights ago saying one of these people might be on the island. *Here*."

"So what does that mean? Who are these people? Would they hurt you?"

"No. I mean, it's not like they're trying kill me or anything. We think they probably want to study me. Learn how my body works. See if they can do the same thing to someone else."

"You mean, make them able to breathe underwater."

"Yeah."

"Who are they?"

"The people?"

"Yeah."

"We think it's the Chinese."

The bell of the front door rang, and Cara asked Brendan to wait while she dealt with the customer who had just entered. But her mind was far away from the actions she was performing as she took the patron's order, put her gloves back on, and measured out two pounds of swordfish.

She felt like she was in a movie—a *thriller*, Brendan's words the lines of a tension-packed script. Add to it the fact that as he told her this, an embryo grew inside of her. Their baby. She needed to tell Brendan she was pregnant, but how could she, given the conversation they were having?

Cara wrapped the fish in parchment paper and stuck it in a bag with a lemon.

"Did you put the tartar in too?" the man asked.

"Oh, sorry."

Cara grabbed a pair of plastic cups and pumped globs of tartar sauce into them from the container on the back counter.

She thought about what Brendan had just told her. Despite the intensity of the situation he'd described, Cara couldn't deny feeling a slight sense of relief. Her pulse was racing, to be sure, but the revelation had allowed her to put aside her more troubling suspicions about Brendan's behavior. Now there was a new thing to fear—but it was something obvious and pronounced. An easily identifiable threat that evoked adrenaline rather than angst, excitement rather than dread.

As soon as the customer left, Cara joined Brendan back at the tanks. She imagined him like those lobsters, stuck in a tank while strangers poked and prodded at him. It was no wonder he was afraid. She grabbed his hand in a sign of solidarity. As a thank-you for finally sharing the truth.

"So what happens now?" she asked him.

"My commander's going to send some guys to check it out. See if these guys are who they think they are. Odds are they aren't. Probably just Asian tourists. I don't know why I got so freaked out. I'm embarrassed."

"Don't be embarrassed. It's just me. I want you to be able to talk to me. Okay?"

"I might have to go away," Brendan said. "Just for a little while. Until this is all cleared up."

"Where would you go?"

"I don't know. Maybe back to the base. They don't tell me anything until they have to. It would happen quickly. I might not see you before."

"But then how will I know whether you're okay? Whether you left on your own or if someone kidnapped you or something?"

"I'll leave you something. A note or a message. So you'll know."

Cara selfishly thought of the baby. If Brendan went away, when would she tell him? Assuming she *would* tell him. She'd discovered the pregnancy early, meaning there was still time. He didn't have to know that there'd ever been a baby at all. Not if she didn't want him to. Because what reason did she possibly have to bring a child into her life right now? After everything that had transpired over the past few days, the idea seemed preposterous. Why had she ever convinced herself that it would be a good idea to get pregnant?

This wasn't something one decided next to a tank full of crustaceans in a smelly old fish market. But Cara did know one thing: she wasn't ready to tell him yet.

"You aren't going to keep it, are you?" Lindsay spoke in a whisper, her shock skimming the surface of dismay.

"I don't know. I mean, no. Of course not."

"Wait. Go back. Was this by accident or on purpose?"

Had Cara already given herself away? She'd never expected Lindsay would even think to ask such a question. Because Lindsay was the kind of person whose reactions were based not on what she imagined made sense for the other person, but on what she herself would do if she were in the same situation. Which was why, after much contemplation, Cara had decided to call her this morning. She needed to hear Lindsay tell her she shouldn't keep the baby.

"By accident! I screwed up my pills—which you know I never do. I think my routine's just so all over the place here. I got confused. And so then my period was all messed up and I was spotting and stuff, but I figured I'd still be fine. And even when I didn't get my period on time, I just thought it was because I'd missed those pills. So then I bought a pregnancy test, literally just to put my mind at ease, and then I saw the results and I freaked out."

There. The lies were done, and Cara felt like she'd delivered them convincingly. From here on out, this would be her story. The truth was that she'd intentionally stopped taking her pills the day Brendan asked her to marry him. Looking back, the decision felt stupid; but in the moment, she'd been excited. The uncharacteristically spontaneous move felt consistent with the new life she felt she was building for herself—that she and Brendan were building together. They were in love and impassioned and ready to live a life others only dreamed of. So why not throw caution to the wind and go all-in? Wasn't that what Brendan had said he wanted?

"Well, I guess your strategy worked then," Lindsay said.

"What strategy?"

"Convincing yourself that you were infertile. Like you said earlier this summer, after graduation. You said you thought that if you just imagined a future where you couldn't get pregnant, it'd be less likely to actually come true."

"Oh, yeah. Right," Cara said. Had she really said that? It felt like such a long time ago now.

"Guess you might have believed it a little too much."

Cara put a hand on her belly. It was impossible to imagine, growing another human in her body. She'd gone through pregnancy scares before. Not the real kind, but the early, irrational variety of panic experienced only by girls for whom sex is still new. Once, when she was a freshman, she'd made Charlotte Savignano drive her to the local Walmart to pick up a pregnancy kit. She wasn't even a close friend, but the casual manner in which Charlotte described giving head to three soccer players in one night somehow made her the most qualified, in Cara's mind, to chaperone such a mission.

Cara could remember sitting on Charlotte's bed, fingers coated in orange fuzz from nervous Cheetos eating. And they weren't even regular Cheetos, but the "flamin' hot" variety that made the corners of her mouth burn. Meanwhile, the indicator stick sat perched on the box it had come in, looking like a UFO next to Cara's yellow Forever 21 shopping bag and a framed collage of photos from Charlotte's senior year at East Rockaway High.

Of course, the test ended up being negative, bringing Cara's emotions from terror to self-admonishment in a matter of seconds. She couldn't believe that she'd been so naïve as to actually believe she was pregnant, despite being a diligent oral contraceptive user. Even just an hour before seeing the negative sign on the test, she'd been convinced that her stomach had grown—that she'd felt movement inside of her, as if such symptoms were apparent so soon after conception.

"Does he know?" Lindsay asked.

"Who?"

"The *father. Brendan.*"

Cara thought of Brendan at the fish market yesterday, with his little box of fudge. She couldn't help it. The thought of him still filled her with giddy adoration.

"Oh. Not yet, no. You're the only one I've told. You can't tell anyone."

"I won't, I won't."

There was a pause before Cara spoke.

"Linds, I'm freaking out a little bit."

"I don't blame you. This is a big deal. Do you want me to come out there? I'm coming home for Thanksgiving. Have you made an appointment? For when you'll do it?"

Cara felt sick. Where was she going to make an appointment? On the island? This wasn't like college where she could just show up at the health center and cry to the nurses.

"I'm supposed to fly to Phoenix next Wednesday."

"You are? I thought you hated it out there."

"Yeah, but I haven't seen my dad and Drew for a long time. And I figure that with the pregnancy thing and all that's been happening with Brendan . . . I just decided it would be good to be with family."

"I think you should try to do it before. Just get it over with. Then, when you get to your dad's, you can just relax and recover without this hanging over your head. You know? And it'll be good for you to have a change of scenery. Think of it as a desert getaway. It'll give you some distance from Brendan—who I don't think you need to tell, by the way.

I know it's like—it's his baby too—but whatever. He doesn't have to grow it in his fucking body. At the end of the day, it's your choice. And this way you don't have to see him right away. You'll have time to process and feel better about things. Because it's going to be weird at first. It's going to take you some time to heal."

"Have you ever had one?"

"No, but there was a girl on my field hockey team in high school who did. It was tough. Like, she bled for a while, but she's fine now. She played field hockey at Bucknell."

The conversation was going exactly as Cara had hoped it would. Because now she truly was leaning toward getting an abortion, and doing it before she left for Phoenix, as Lindsay had suggested. The scenario she'd laid out, with the desert as an escape, as a place to heal, was compelling.

After she ended the call, Cara got on her bike and headed out to Gay Head, to the place where she'd met Brendan. If she was going to say good-bye to the tiny spark of life that was apparently growing inside her, she didn't want to do it surrounded by latex gloves and human anatomy posters and fluorescent overhead lights. She wanted to say good-bye here, by the ocean.

It was late in the day. The afternoon winds were calming down and the sun was beginning to cast elongated shadows of seagrass and boulders in the sand. Cara climbed up on a rock with a smooth, flat top, and hugged her knees into her chest. She kept her gaze forward as she cried, not bothering to wipe her face. The sea in front of her sparkled, oblivious.

Brendan disappeared again, just as he'd hinted he might. He left behind a plastic sperm whale figurine, like the kind Cara and

Drew used to play with in the bath, with a rolled-up yellow Post-it in its mouth.

I'm OK. Back soon.

Cara decided it was probably for the best. The more time she spent with Brendan, the more likely it was that she would tell him about the baby. And once he learned the truth, Cara knew he would do everything within his power to make sure the baby was born. He would be so excited. So happy. She could never ruin that for him. Better to follow Lindsay's advice. What he didn't know couldn't hurt him. Besides, maybe his departure was a sign. She couldn't talk to him even if she wanted to.

Baby. Every time the word entered her mind, Cara had to catch herself. It wasn't a baby. Not yet. It was an embryo. She had to keep reminding herself of that.

Her flight out of Logan was scheduled to leave at 1:17 p.m. on Wednesday. She caught the five o'clock ferry out of Vineyard Haven on Monday, and took a bus to Boston, using money she'd saved from working at the fish market to book a two-night stay at a hotel near Boston University.

The Planned Parenthood where she'd booked her appointment was just around the corner. Lindsay had told her about it. She'd never been, but her friend Kelsey had gone there to get tested for chlamydia after a vacation with her family in Europe, where she'd "fooled around" with one of their tour guides. She didn't have chlamydia, as it turned out, and she said the people at the clinic were nice.

Cara was already awake in her hotel room bed when her alarm went off on Tuesday. Acting on autopilot, she got out of bed, washed her face, brushed her teeth, put on some sweats, and headed to the lobby. Three of the five plastic cereal dispensers in the sad Days Inn breakfast area were empty, leaving her to choose from Froot Loops or cornflakes. The doctors had told her to avoid dairy, however, so she grabbed a paper coffee cup and ate the Froot Loops dry. As suspected, they were stale.

After breakfast, she went back up and watched an old episode of *Saved by the Bell* in bed, one in which the crew from Bayside High decided to create a call line to help other kids with their problems. She'd never seen this one, and braced herself for a caller dealing with an unplanned pregnancy. But this was *Saved by the Bell.* That was too serious—thank god. She wasn't sure she could handle that right now. Instead, the episode centered on Zack and his difficulty processing the fact that the girl he'd asked out over the phone was in a wheelchair. As she watched, Cara actually felt uncharacteristically sympathetic toward him. She had to leave before the episode was over. She didn't want to miss her appointment.

It was a sunny, cool morning, and the streets were empty. All the college kids who lived in the area must still have been sleeping. There were beer cans strewn across the sidewalk and empty pizza boxes left on front stoops. An old man hosed down the sidewalk in front of his restaurant. A severe-looking woman in an orange and blue Adidas marathon jacket flew by her. Cara looked for numbers on the buildings as she passed, and realized she was on the wrong side. She was looking for 176. She needed to get on the even side.

But when she came to a crosswalk, she kept on walking, no longer bothering to keep track of the address numbers as she moved. She walked and she walked all the way to the Charles River. Her phone rang and she silenced it, deleting the voicemail as soon as she saw the little "(1)" appear on her inbox. She didn't want to hear it, the gentle voice of the receptionist asking where she was. She felt guilty for not answering, but rationalized that they must be used to this kind of thing. The no-show. The guilty silence of a girl who's changed her mind.

Cara sat down on a green wooden bench facing the water. It was colder here, by the river. She wrapped her coat tighter around her body and rested one palm on her belly, while the other hand clasped the whale figurine she'd pulled from her purse.

It didn't matter how many times she said it, how logical and pragmatic she tried to be. It *wasn't* just a fetus inside of her. It was a *baby*. A tiny person that was half Cara, half Brendan. A brand-new human being. For the first time, Cara shamelessly allowed herself to indulge in the daydream of her body swelling with life. The woman who appeared in her mind's eye was beautiful and radiant and oozing with happiness. It was her, as an excited mother-to-be. And maybe it was hormones and hope, or fear and loneliness, but she knew, in that moment, that she wanted to be that woman. That she was going to be that woman.

Cara followed the esplanade trail as far as she could before getting to the footbridge that would lead her back to her hotel. When she arrived at her room, she drew the shades, called down for mozzarella sticks and buffalo wings, and ordered *The Da Vinci Code* movie, even though she still hadn't read the book, which was something she never did. That was the kind of day it was.

The next morning, Cara packed up her things and caught a cab to Logan Airport. It was time to go see Dad and Lucia.

2014

Cara wakes up thinking of Micah, her sweet little baby with his Michelin Man wrinkles and corn-silk hair. It makes her remember why she's been pushing these thoughts back for so long. Thinking about him is painful. It physically hurts to remind herself of all she's missed in his life, the same way her own mother has missed so much of hers. She will never help him learn to sound out words or balance a bicycle. She never got to see him at two, three, four. He'd be almost five years old now, but even if she were to see him again, she can never have those years back.

It kills her to think that the two of them could walk right by each other and not even know it. She likes to believe that she would feel something, that their connection as mother and son would not go unnoticed by either of them.

She can hear Graham downstairs and anxiously anticipates the conversation they both know they need to have. Her feeling of dread has become all too familiar of late. There was a lot of shouting the night before.

She forces herself out of bed and grabs a duffel from the closet. She starts with just a few items, then changes her mind and adds more clothes, tossing in her toothbrush, extra contacts, and almost all of her underwear. She pulls on jeans and a 1999 Black Dog T-shirt, ties back her hair, and heads downstairs, bag in hand.

Graham is at the kitchen table reading the paper with an enormous cup of coffee. There are purple pockets under his eyes.

"Hi."

"Morning."

"I'm sorry about last night," says Cara, still standing. "I really am. I totally lost it and I'm so sorry for embarrassing you like that."

Graham nods but doesn't look at her or say anything.

"I'm going to go to Moira's. I don't know for how long."

This gets his attention.

"You're leaving? Are we really at that point?"

"It's not about you and me, Graham. It's about him. He's here. I saw him."

Graham sighs, and Cara can tell he's thinking the same things he said last night.

If he's here, then how come no one else saw him?

If he's here, why did he show up last night only to suddenly disappear, nowhere to be found?

And then there are the words he didn't say, but that she knows he must feel:

If he's here, will I lose you?

"So then let's call the police," Graham suggests, his voice gentle. "Or the coast guard. All of them. Let's at least get the word out. If you really want to find him, they can help us."

The fact that he is even willing to humor her, to look for this man she knows he selfishly does not want to find—his wife's former lover— speaks volumes about who Graham is as a person. He is willing to do anything for her.

Cara swallows down her guilt.

"I can't do that," she says. "I've thought about it and I can't."

Graham's face drops. "Because you don't want him arrested."

Cara doesn't respond.

Graham takes off his glasses and rubs his eyes, leaning his head down into his hands. A part of her wants to run to him and hug him— tell him that she's sorry, that she'll stay—and things will go back to how they were before she found the whale: easy, peaceful, uncomplicated.

But she can't.

"I'm sorry, Graham. But I need to do this the right way. I don't want to spook him and risk having him disappear again."

"Please just stay. I know I said a lot of harsh things last night, but I was angry. You have to understand that. You know I didn't mean it."

"I know you didn't," says Cara. She hadn't meant a lot of the things she said either, but that doesn't mean they didn't hurt each other.

"You know I love you more than anything."

Cara nods. Her smile is sad.

After Cara had dropped the wineglass and run outside, Graham had rushed out to find her. She, of course, was hysterical, shouting about how she'd seen Brendan. How he was just there and couldn't have gotten far. He'd urged her to come inside and she'd refused, traveling deeper into the woods, desperate to find the father of her absent son. She can only imagine now how she would have looked to all the gallery guests, barefoot and sweaty with mascara running down her face.

It was 3 a.m. before Graham finally got her home, where the shouting match really got started. When was this going to end? he'd demanded. Every time he thought they'd made progress, he said, they took another huge step back again. It was exhausting. And this time, she'd taken it too far. She'd embarrassed him in front of hundreds of people, when she never should have been there in the first place. He'd told her this. He'd *told* her she didn't have to go—that she wasn't in the right mindset for it—yet she'd gone anyway. And look what had happened.

In response, she'd accused him of being image-obsessed, and hit him with a backhanded apology for not obeying his sage advice to stay alone at home behind closed doors—the crazy woman in his attic. Over and over she'd reiterated that she hadn't been hallucinating—*I. SAW. HIM.*—to which Graham replied, *Then, WHERE. IS. HE?* The argument cycled on a continuous loop, the same familiar sections replaying as if on cue, until they were both too tired to keep going. Cara retreated to the living room to sleep on the couch—which inspired a whole new round of arguing over who possessed that right, who was the true martyr. When Cara refused to leave the couch, Graham took to the chaise in the study as if to one-up her. Cara waited until he was asleep before giving in and retreating up to the bed.

"It's not for forever," Cara says now, hefting her duffel higher up her shoulder. "I just need some time."

A pill of tears lodges in her throat, and she exits through the side door. She can't help but notice how beautiful their kitchen is as she walks out. The built-in fridge, the white marble countertops, the herb garden by the window. And then there is Graham, her kind, smart, adoring husband, alone at the table, looking scared and deflated. She hates that she is hurting him.

She squeezes a folded piece of paper in her hand, digging her fingernails into her palm, before slipping it into her back pocket, hopping on her bicycle, and riding away.

2008

Lucia brought out a platter of homemade cheese empanadas and set them on the coffee table next to the array of chips and salsa, nuts, cheese and crackers, and shrimp cocktail.

"Lucia's empanadas are the best," Stanley said. "You've got to try one."

"Try it with the *ají* sauce," Lucia said, nudging forward a small bowl of chunky orange liquid.

"Careful, though, it's hot," warned Stanley. "I thought I could handle spice, but Lucia . . ." He raised his eyebrows in a show of awe.

"This one is not so spicy," said Lucia. "I made it special. I know you don't like it too hot."

Although Spanish was her native language, Lucia was completely fluent in English, her accent indetectable save for the softness of her *l*s and the precise annunciation of her *t*s.

The empanadas were browned and crispy with little globs of white cheese oozing slightly from the sides. Cara didn't want to give Lucia the satisfaction of eating one, but she couldn't help herself. She ate one, and then another, disappointed by her lack of self-control. Lucia looked pleased.

The *ají* sauce made Cara sweat. It wasn't particularly hot outside— not for Phoenix—but Cara would have appreciated some air conditioning. Lucia only liked to turn it on when absolutely necessary. At about five feet tall and probably no more than one hundred pounds, she was always complaining of being cold. Today she was dressed like she was about to go skiing. In addition to the silver bracelets and the diamond-studded cross she always had around her neck, she wore thick, fuzzy, microfiber socks, yoga pants, and a light-blue cashmere sweater, soft and uniform without a pill on it.

Cara chugged a glass of water and grabbed another empanada, her third. They were really good.

"Jesus, don't choke," Drew teased.

"Lay off me, I'm starving," Cara shot back, doing her best Chris Farley impression.

"Drew, come on, don't talk like that," Stanley said, as if Drew were twelve and not twenty years old.

Cara gave Drew a questioning look, and he rolled his eyes.

"Spoke the Lord's name in vain," he whispered to Cara with a smirk. "Lucia doesn't like that."

Cara widened her eyes to convey her shared annoyance.

Cara was excited to lay the hammer down and tell her dad and Lucia about the baby. She'd played the moment over and over in her mind on the plane and was actually looking forward to seeing the look of shock on their faces. She suspected Lucia would be excited, in her wholesome, maternal way. Her dad would be horrified, but he wouldn't be able to show it. Not in front of Lucia. Horror and dismay wouldn't fit with the new persona he had created for himself, even if that was what he was truly feeling. And Cara was sadistically eager to witness the outward projections of his internal conflict.

It was Drew she was nervous about. The news was going to freak him out. She just hoped it wouldn't feel like a betrayal. Like she'd broken the cool big sister code of conduct by doing something seemingly so irresponsible and, on top of that, irreversible. Because a baby was going to change things. Cara and Drew wouldn't be the kids anymore.

Cara stuck to her plan to keep quiet about the whole thing until the main event: Thanksgiving dinner. Sure, she was making it more dramatic than it needed to be, but she knew dinner would present an opening unlike any other and she wanted to take advantage of it.

It was a lifelong family tradition. Every year, after everyone was seated at the table but before anyone took a bite, each person was required to share one thing that they were grateful for that year. Cara used to wonder if her parents had come up with the idea sheerly for their own entertainment, as Drew's and Cara's answers as children had run the gamut of superficiality and materialism. Drew had shared that he was thankful for his Sega Genesis at least three times, and Cara usually said she was grateful for their dog, Loretta, and her private phone line in her bedroom (this was huge; all her friends were jealous). As they got older, they defaulted to "friends and family," each fighting to go first so that the other person didn't steal the line.

Like everything else, the tradition had taken on new meaning when their mom got sick. The misfortune had taught them to be grateful for the little things, like time spent together as a family at the beach or the health and ability to play sports with friends. If anything positive had come out of their mother's death, it was the capacity to be truly and sincerely grateful.

By the time dinner came around, Cara had completely given up on her attempt to snub Lucia by not eating her food. It all looked too good. As Cara had learned over the past few years, Lucia took Thanksgiving seriously. The dishes Cara's family had historically served from a box, can, or packet were all prepared from scratch when Lucia was at the helm. Fresh cranberry sauce; homemade stuffing; real turkey gravy. Before Lucia, they *never* used to have real turkey gravy.

As they filled their plates and sat down, Cara grew nervous. She could feel herself beginning to sweat, and she clenched her hands in her lap to keep them from shaking. She considered backing out. She could tell them later, individually, she thought. There was no need to make a big splash like this.

Stanley spoke first, sharing his gratitude for having both his children home for the holiday. It was hardly a groundbreaking revelation, but Cara found herself blinking away tears. Lucia said she was grateful for the love of God, and for her son, David, who was spending Thanksgiving with his father, and for her students, whom she loved, and the joy they brought her every day. Drew was thankful for his advanced music production class, which was taught by a super cool professor with exciting industry connections.

Cara, at her insistence, went last. She glanced around the table, as her dad, her brother, and Lucia patiently awaited her thoughts. It didn't seem right that she was making this announcement alone. She missed Brendan. She wished he were there, next to her, holding her hand under the table, the two of them beaming with love and elation.

She took a deep breath and stared ahead, unable to look at any of them.

"I am grateful for . . ."

". . . my baby."

Her lips felt numb as she said it. She looked down at her lap and made a show of resting her hand over her belly button, scooting her chair back just enough so they could see.

"Due in August."

Drew let out a tentative laugh. "You're joking, right?"

Lucia's mouth was agape. Stanley gripped the edge of the table with his fingers, leaning forward ever so slightly.

Cara shook her head. "Surprise," she said sheepishly. "I'm pregnant."

It was the first time she'd said it out loud, at least now that it was real. The time on the phone with Lindsay didn't count.

Lucia got up and came over to hug her. Cara had never been so glad to have her stepmother in the room.

"This is the happiest news," she said, tears in her eyes. "Stanley, isn't this the happiest news?"

They all looked over at Stanley, who looked completely and utterly stunned.

"It is. Yes, of course it is," he said. "I'm just surprised, is all. I didn't know that you . . . well, I just . . . It's great. It's great news."

Drew didn't say anything. He just stared with his eyebrows raised like they'd been glued up there, and his lips folded in on themselves. Cara looked at him, giving him an opening to say something, but he didn't take it.

"Well, I don't want to hold up dinner," Cara said. "*Eat*. Please. The food's getting cold."

She knew there were so many questions they wanted to ask. She could practically see the wheels turning in their heads. But there was something about being at the formally set table, it being a holiday and all, that seemed to prevent them from delving any deeper into the matter. As if dinnertime was sacred and any clarifying questions would have to wait until the dishes were cleared and the sun had set.

After a few moments of awkward silence, punctuated only by satisfied murmurings about how good the food was, Stanley found the nerve to speak up.

"And the father, I assume, is . . . ?"

"Brendan."

"Brendan, that's right." He turned to Lucia. "I think I told you about him. The boy Cara met earlier this summer. Military guy, right?"

"Sounds like quite the summer romance," Lucia said.

"*I'll say*," Drew said, and everyone ignored him, but the jab hit Cara like an ice pick to the chest.

"Well, we can't wait to meet him," Lucia said.

"He's wonderful," Cara said. "You'll love him."

Lucia and Stanley nodded.

"And will there be a wedding?" Lucia asked.

Stanley gave her a look of admonishment.

Holy, law-abiding Lucia. She just couldn't resist.

"Eventually. I guess," Cara said. "We haven't made any formal plans yet."

She chose not to share the fact that Brendan himself still had no idea that he was going to be a father. And it made her feel a little sick inside to know that she'd told her family before she'd even told him. In retrospect, she wished she had told Brendan as soon as she'd found out. But that was before she'd decided to go through with things—to *keep the baby*, as people liked to say, as if the unborn child were an old piece of furniture or a plate of leftovers in the fridge.

And now she had no way of reaching him. Not really. She could call or text him, but that didn't seem right. She wanted to tell him in person, to see his face when he heard. And every moment she had to wait felt like torture.

After cleaning up dinner, Cara and Drew drove out to the Mountain Preserve to walk off some of their meal. Cara closed her eyes on the ride over while Drew drove, blaming the tryptophan for her fatigue. She just wasn't ready to talk yet.

It was still hot out when they arrived, but the lack of direct sunlight made conditions bearable. The land was aglow in the way only a desert sunset can be, the surrounding cacti casting tall shadows along the trail. They hiked up to an overlook and sat on a sandy pink boulder, the lights of the sprawl below just beginning to twinkle.

"So are you totally freaked out?" Cara asked. "Honestly."

"Honestly? Yeah, kind of. I just don't get it. It feels so out of nowhere."

"I know."

"Like, you are *pregnant*. You're going to have a *baby*. With a guy I've never even met before. That you've only known for a few months!"

"I know. It's crazy. Even I think it's crazy."

"What's his name again?"

"Brendan. Oh my god, Drew, you'll love him. I mean it. He is *so* funny. Like, he gets our humor, you know? I really think you'd get along. You should come visit! Maybe over your winter break."

"I'm sorry, but I have to ask. Did you mean to . . . I mean . . . Was this a mistake, or . . . ?"

"The baby?"

"Yeah."

Cara thought about it. "No. We both wanted it. I can't explain it."

"But why now? I mean, do you even have a job? And where are you going to live?"

"I think we might buy a house. On the Vineyard."

"Aren't houses ridiculously expensive there?"

"Yeah, but Brendan has money saved. He's paid well, for his job. What he does is dangerous, you know, and he's compensated for the risks he takes."

"And that doesn't concern you? The danger?"

"No, it does."

"So why not just wait? Live together first? See how it goes?"

Cara shrugged and laughed.

"I don't know. Everything you're saying sounds practical to me. I guess it was just kind of a heat-of-passion kind of thing."

"Ew."

"No, I mean, I'm so in love with him. I *know* that he's the one for me. And all I've ever wanted to do is be able to live somewhere beautiful and make art. And start a family. And I can do that now. *Right now.* So I guess I just don't see the point of waiting."

"Don't you want to enjoy your twenties? Go out with friends . . . travel?"

"Well, yeah. Of course. But it's too late now. This is what I've chosen." Cara gestured down at her belly again.

"Are you scared?"

"Oh, *so* scared. Terrified. I have no idea what I'm doing."

"I'm going to be an uncle!" Drew said, laughing finally.

"So you're okay?" Cara asked. "With all of this?"

"I'm not *mad*. It's just a lot. It's going to be weird seeing you . . . pregnant. Like when you begin to show."

"It still doesn't feel real," Cara said. "It does more, now that I've told you. But still. I don't think it's hit me that my belly is actually going to grow."

"Well," said Drew, looking out over the city below. "Things are certainly going to be different."

Cara broke the news to Brendan on a cold December night, the first bitterly cold night of the season. He'd returned to the island just a few days after Cara had, showing up at Moira and Ed's front door at six in the morning with the beginnings of a beard and a new winter jacket. It had been a false alarm, he told her, the people they saw on the island. They'd looked into it and given him the all-clear. Cara didn't have to worry. They were safe.

Cara had been so preoccupied she hadn't even been thinking about all of that—the drama surrounding Brendan's most recent departure. The truth was that she'd grown used to his absences, sudden and sporadic, always for indefinite periods of time. It had simply become a way of life for them, though she wondered if she'd still feel that way once the baby arrived.

In lieu of sharing the news right away, Cara decided to wait, feeling like she owed it to Brendan to make the moment special. She wasn't really showing yet, but sometimes when she looked in the mirror she thought her belly looked bigger. It was still too early to differentiate pregnancy from a bit of bloating. In any case, Brendan hadn't noticed anything.

On the chosen night, Cara convinced Moira and Ed to go out to dinner with friends so that she and Brendan could share a private, home-cooked meal together. She'd told them the news a couple days after she got back from Phoenix. It was clear they were shocked. Moira had frozen in place in the middle of feeding the dogs, the bowls overflowing with kibble, but the tears in her eyes had been happy tears. Moira and Ed had never had children; Cara had never asked why, but she imagined it wasn't for lack of trying. She liked to believe that her announcement had brought them some joy.

Later that day, Moira had knocked on Cara's bedroom door and asked if she could come in, and the two of them sat side by side on the bed.

"I know you don't like to talk about it, and I don't want to stir up tough emotions," Moira began, "but I've thought about it, and I want you to know how proud and excited your mom would be by this news."

Cara couldn't get any words out, so she'd nodded, doing her best to smile.

"I still remember when she told me she was pregnant with you.

She was so excited. I'd never seen her happier. You reminded me of her this morning."

"Thanks," Cara had managed to say.

"And I know it's not the same—no one can ever replace your mom—but I'm here for you. Whatever you need."

Cara felt herself getting choked up again now, reliving the moment. She shook out her arms and took a deep breath to bring herself back to the present. She needed to focus on dinner—on telling Brendan.

Cara didn't really know how to cook, but figured she could follow a recipe. She sifted through Moira's stacks of old *Bon Appétit* magazines, looking for ideas. Ultimately opting for classic simplicity, she went to the Stop & Shop in Vineyard Haven and purchased ingredients for broiled petite beef filets served with blue cheese (pasteurized, because that was apparently something she had to pay attention to now that she was pregnant), garlic roasted potatoes, and creamed spinach.

The smoke alarm went off once, but only because the juices and oils the potatoes were cooking in had begun to burn; the potatoes themselves came out unscathed. The creamed spinach was more like milky spinach, and the steak was cooked well-done. Cara had been so worried about undercooking the meat and making both of them sick that she'd left them in too long.

This night also came to be the night that both of them learned that Brendan did not like blue cheese. Despite his best efforts to pretend otherwise, he failed miserably at hiding his distaste, and Cara gave him permission to scrape the melty chunks off his piece of meat.

"I mean, the steak was a little tough, but at least it was edible," Cara said when they were done. "And the potatoes were good, I think."

"I loved it all. Delicious potatoes. Best steak I ever had," said Brendan. "Five stars. And the green mush was good too."

"You mean the creamed spinach?"

"Is that what that was?"

"Yes."

"Well, it was the best creamed spinach in the whole wide world. I mean it."

"You are so full of shit."

"I am so full of delicious home-cooked food."

"I missed you."

"I missed you too."

Cara felt a flutter in her chest. They were alone, together, full on mediocre home-cooked food, sitting across from one another at a candlelit table. This was the moment. She took in a deep inhale, unable to withhold the edges of a smile, and opened her mouth to speak.

"Look! It's snowing!" Brendan stood up and pointed to the window.

Cara looked. Sure enough, there were soft white flakes visible in the glow of the floodlights outside.

Brendan jogged to the entryway to get his coat from the stand. Alone at the table, Cara felt herself deflate. Brendan tossed her coat on the table.

"C'mon, let's go outside!"

"Why?"

"It's snowing!"

"Yes, I see that."

"Don't you want to see it?"

"I can see it just fine from the window."

"When have you ever seen snow on the Vineyard?"

"Well, never. But only because I've never been on the Vineyard in the winter. It snows here all the time. Why are you so excited?"

"I want to go see it. Over the water."

Cara grabbed her coat and stood up.

It was freezing outside, and surprisingly dark. Brendan hugged Cara close to his side, and rubbed one hand up and down her arm trying to keep her warm while the other guided their path with a mini flashlight.

Brendan had insisted that they head down to Squibnocket to see the snow over the water.

When they reached the beach, they sat on the top of the stairs leading down to the sand and switched off the flashlight so their eyes could adjust.

"See? Isn't this nice?" Brendan asked.

Cara could hardly see the snow through the darkness and her hair was getting wet from the flakes landing on her head. Here by the water, the wind was much stronger, and her eyes were beginning to water as it blew into her face. Wincing, she peered out over the water and could just make out the lights of ships on the horizon. She could only imagine what it must be like to be out there on a night like this. She wondered if Brendan had ever done anything like that.

Cara turned to look at him, and he smiled like a giddy little kid. She could feel his body trembling with cold next to her own.

"I'm pregnant," she said.

This wasn't how the reveal was supposed to go, out here in the cold, with the wet ocean spray and snow blasting their faces. They were supposed to be sitting together at a candlelight dinner with plates of succulent steak. Or curled up under a blanket by the fireplace, cozy and warm.

This wasn't how any of it was supposed to go. Not even close. Lately Cara had vacillated between feeling totally enthralled and empowered, and feeling completely lost and confused. She could hear the warnings and criticism of others—even her former self—urging her to snap out of it. To take caution. To get back on the charted course. And she usually told them to fuck off. Because she was fine. She was happy. She was living life as it was supposed to be lived.

This was what she told them. This was what she told herself.

Brendan was ecstatic. He asked her about a million times if she was serious, before picking her up and swinging her around, sloppily kissing her face with cold lips. He set her down and skipped toward the water like a child, punching a fist in the air as he leaped, shouting with elation, a cloud of his warm breath lingering in the cold night air. When he was done celebrating, Brendan returned to Cara and held her face in his hands.

"I love you," he said, tears in his eyes. "I love you so fucking much. You know that? It's crazy. You make me crazy, I love you so much."

"No, *you* make *me* crazy, you lunatic."

"I know. I know. But you love me too, right?"

"Of course I do."

"And now we're going to be a family."

"There's no going back now."

C ara had hoped her dad and Lucia and Drew would come visit them on the Vineyard for Christmas, but she never actually invited them. She felt like it was their responsibility, not hers, to propose the idea. It would have been the right thing for them to do. She was pregnant, after all, and she had just traveled all the way out to Arizona to visit them. It was their turn to return the favor.

But even as they expressed disappointment over the prospect of not being together for the holiday—a first for all of them—the solution of gathering on the island never seemed to occur to them. Or it did, but they simply didn't want to come. Cara suspected that it was fear that kept her dad away. It would be too painful for him to return to a place with such strong associations with her mother. Too many reminders of the way things had once been.

She tried to understand where he was coming from, but also felt that his decision to lean on pure avoidance as a shield was not only weak but childish. If she, a young woman who'd lost her mother at far too young an age, could handle the emotional weight of returning to the island, so could he.

The easier answer was to blame Lucia. Cara liked to think that her dad truly did want to visit, but that Lucia was holding him back, preemptively jealous of the feelings of love and affection the island might conjure for her new husband's deceased wife. The mother of his children. The woman she could never compete with.

But Lucia had little influence over Drew. His decision not to visit was purely his own, even if, as Cara assumed, his reasons were purely financial. If he'd only expressed interest, Cara would have found a way to help him, using her own money—though she didn't have much—or whatever Brendan was willing to offer to make the trip possible. But he seemed firmly settled on spending the holiday with Lucia and their dad, in spite of all of his complaining in previous years about how they'd made him go to Christmas mass, and how celebrating Christmas in the desert was like "pizza without red sauce."

Cara spent Christmas Eve mentally reassuring herself that she was better off where she was, on the island with Moira, Ed, and Brendan. Christmas was just a day, anyway, a milestone for people to look forward to so their lives weren't quite so monotonous. The older she got, the more it had become a letdown each year, the hype never quite living up to the reality. She told herself it was just the hormones that were making her cry, as she privately splashed her face with cold water in the upstairs bathroom.

On Christmas morning, they exchanged modest gifts, a ceremony that took less than fifteen minutes. Cara gave Moira and Ed a grid of small painted portraits of each of their pups—which Moira absolutely adored—and for Brendan, she'd framed the unfinished drawing of a cormorant that she'd been working on the day that they met at Gay Head. Brendan gave her a necklace with a gold-painted shell on the end, and Moira had knitted her an alpaca wool sweater, and booties for the baby. Ed gave them all carved wooden boat tree ornaments.

It was simple but nice, in a way that made Cara feel guilty for feeling disappointed—for wanting more. She'd just never expected that at this point in her life, she would already be sacrificing holidays with her family. Well, Moira and Ed were family, to be fair, but they didn't practice the same traditions that she, her father, and Drew had always shared, like watching *It's a Wonderful Life* together on Christmas Eve, filling their stockings with copious amounts of chocolate of all different brands and varieties—the weirder the better—and writing *Santa* in disguised handwriting on the From section of the tag, forcing the recipient to guess who'd selected the gift for them. She wondered if her dad, Drew, and Lucia had done these things without her.

Later in the day, Cara and Brendan went exploring. That was the beauty of the off-season on the Vineyard. Docks, jetties, and beaches that were closed off and guarded by uniformed men in beach chairs in the summer were suddenly left abandoned and open to the casual stroller. You could spend hours wandering through other people's yards and peeking through their windows, each estate in an almost dormant state until summertime. Wicker deck furniture sat in living rooms and garages with large stacks of cushions on top. Clotheslines hung empty, naked without their vibrant beach towels to dress them. Boogie boards, shovels, and little plastic trays in the shapes of sea creatures waited in baskets, still caked with sand from warmer days.

Cara liked to close her eyes and imagine what these places would be like when they awoke. A golden retriever lying in the sun on the back steps. Bocce balls and badminton birdies left in the grass from the night before. Soapy sand on the floor of the outdoor shower. Sea kayaks and Sunfish pulled up on the sand, ready for launch at a moment's notice. Clambakes down at the beach, everyone in hoodies and flip-flops. Cocktails on the deck over a fresh plate of quahogs. Sun-bleached hair and tanned skin. Tangled fishing rods surrounded by stray scales. Ice cream for dessert every night.

One house they looked in still had an incomplete puzzle depicting a lighthouse on the dining room table, ready and waiting for next summer. In the front of the house was a sort of rotunda with floor-to-ceiling windows and a giant compass rose stained into the floor. They counted four fireplaces on the first floor, though they'd seen seven chimneys. Thick, sturdy wooden beams ran through the ceilings like veins, and a stunning, oversized painting of a clammer's skiff in brilliant tones of turquoise and orange and blue hung above one fireplace. Just looking at it inspired Cara to want to paint.

"What kind of people do you think live here?" she asked.

"Waspy ones," said Brendan, and Cara nodded.

"I bet they live in a huge house outside Boston," she said. "He works in finance and she quit her job in marketing to take care of the kids, but still does freelance design work. But not because she has to. Just so her brain doesn't melt. And so she doesn't have to refer to herself as a stay-at-home mom. Or feel guilty about how much she spent on her liberal arts education."

"You think they're happy?"

"No. Actually, yeah."

Anyone with a house like this one had to be happy. And this wasn't even their main home. It was the second home, vacant and empty—save for the occasional caretaker—for the vast majority of the year.

Brendan turned to face her now, concern in his eyes.

"Hey, are you okay?"

"Yeah, I'm fine."

"But even, like, the whole Christmas thing?"

Cara shrugged. "Yeah, it's fine."

"You miss your family, though."

"I mean, yeah. Kind of. I don't know. It's weird. I'm sad when I really think about the fact that it's Christmas and remember that my family's not here. But in the actual moment, it's fine. It's no big deal. It's just another day."

"You seemed sad this morning."

"Did I?"

"Yeah."

"I hope Moira and Ed didn't notice."

"I'm sure they understand. And think of it this way. This is our chance to have our own Christmas. Make our own traditions."

Brendan laid a hand on Cara's belly, and she smiled.

"Yeah, you're right."

They held hands as they continued to walk. They had to go a long way to get to the next house, but Brendan insisted upon it, leading them through low grassy dunes, which had browned with the winter cold. Their feet crunched over dry tumble-seaweed, and the hollow carcasses of wind-tossed crabs. Cara picked up a black, hard plastic-like pouch with two tendrils on each end. The inside was empty, but when she shook it she could hear flecks of sand tumbling inside like a little maraca.

"Drew and I used to call these alien eggs."

"They're all over the place out here," Brendan said. "Must have been a UFO crash nearby. You should probably stay close. They're clearly multiplying."

"Aren't they weird, though?" Cara asked. She started to visualize a large-scale painting of one of the sacks, resting in the sand. She ran her finger over the subtle indentations and creases of the dried-out and slightly deflated shell and considered the blues and grays she might use to render the three-dimensionality of it.

"They're skate eggs," said Brendan.

"Is that what they are?" Cara had always known they were the remnants of some kind of egg sac, but not what kind of creature left them until now. She wondered how Brendan knew. If he'd ever seen one as it was meant to be, soft, wet, and organic. Alive.

By the time they reached the house they were on the western edge of the island, looking north over the Sound just opposite Pasque Island, the beach in plain view, calm and bright. The house had a midcentury modern look to it, with an asymmetrical roof and a whole wall of windows, rectangles and trapezoids of glass framed by wooden panels. The structure was raised, with a deck wrapping around two sides. It had the island's signature cedar shingles, whitewashed by the salt and the wind, and a robin's-egg-blue door.

They walked up the steps to the porch and peered inside. The place consisted of one big room with an open kitchen, a dining table, and a small living area around a stone fireplace. The walls and cabinetry were unpainted save for the drywall between the beams of the vaulted ceiling. The furniture looked straight out of the seventies, with mustard-yellow cushions and an orange shag rug.

"Hey, I wonder . . ." Brendan walked around to the other side of the deck and tried the door. It swung open without a sound.

"Brendan, don't," Cara said, looking over her shoulder. "This is someone's house. We can't go in. If it's open, that probably means they're still here. What if they come home and find us inside?"

But he couldn't be stopped.

"There's obviously no one here," he said. "Someone just forgot to lock the door."

Checking for witnesses one last time, Cara followed Brendan into the house.

It smelled like salt and mold and old musty books. The floors creaked as they crept through the interior, peeking around the one wall to find a small bed and a toilet and bathtub tucked in the corner. The wooden framework of the walls was stacked with old paperbacks like *Anne of Green Gables* and *The Catcher in the Rye.*

"Oh my god, check out this fridge," Cara said, admiring the mint-green, art-deco-style appliance. The unit had smooth, rounded edges and the kind of handles that clicked open and closed with the press of a button. She ran a finger over the plastic of the hanging lamp in the kitchen, a bright-green shade that looked like the hats from the Devo music video for "Whip It."

Brendan stood by the wall of glass with his hands on his hips. Cara came up behind him and leaned against him.

"What do you think?" he asked.

"It's quite a view."

Brendan put his arm around her and whispered in her ear: "It's ours."

She turned to look at him, skeptical.

"What?"

"I bought it."

"You bought what?"

The answer was obvious, but Cara was so stunned she sincerely couldn't believe it. Not for a moment had she thought that Brendan might be bringing her here for a surprise like this. She stared at him, wide-eyed, and he clearly loved every second of it, his own eyes lighting up with excitement.

"But what about all this stuff?"

"Came with the house. We can get rid of some of it, if you want. Like that clown painting. We're definitely getting rid of that clown painting. But I figure it gives us a start. Until we can get our own furniture."

"Wait, so you're renting it or you bought it?"

"*I bought it*," Brendan said with a laugh, pulling her into him and kissing her. "It's our home."

Cara laughed, though her cheeks were wet with tears.

"Sorry. It's the hormones," she said. "I love it. I think I'm just in shock."

"I know it doesn't have seven fireplaces. Or a compass on the floor. But I think it's got more character. Now that I think about it, I'm an idiot for bringing you to that place right before here. Pretty much setting you up for a letdown."

Cara laughed and shook her head. "No, stop. It's perfect."

"And believe me, it's worth a hell of a lot more than it looks."

"Oh, I don't doubt it," Cara said, wondering how much he had paid for this place. She was too young to have any real sense of how much real estate cost, but knew that houses on the Vineyard—by the ocean, no less—were not cheap.

"I don't understand," she said. "How are you affording this?"

"Don't worry about it."

"You say that, but it makes me nervous. Can you just assure me that you came by it by honest means?"

"Yes. I told you. I have family money. The place was foreclosed. I got it at auction. There were a lot of other bidders, but I won." He laughed. "I honestly didn't even know what the inside looked like when I bid on it, which I'll admit was a risk, but I kind of love it. I mean, I feel like we're in fucking 1975, but I dig it."

Cara looked around the room and allowed herself to imagine the two of them making a life there, playing at being adults. Cooking dinner at the stove. Eating at the table. Reading on the couch. They could put a crib in the hutch next to the bed. She was due in August, so the weather would be warm when she delivered. She pictured herself pacing the porch at dusk with a bundle of blankets, the baby warm and sleepy in her arms.

"This is our home," she said.

She spent the next hour walking in circles around the house, grazing her hand across surfaces, opening and closing doors, fingering trinkets, smelling pillows, and petting rugs. She couldn't believe this place was hers. Theirs.

When she was done exploring, she sat on the floor by the window wall and stared outside. The next house over was far enough away that it felt like they were on their own private island, surrounded by water, sand, and sky. She grabbed a damp, moldy pillow from the couch and rested her head upon it, falling asleep right there on the floor.

Winter in Vermont brought snow. Winter on the Vineyard brought wind. Cold, biting, unrelenting wind. On the rare occasions that it did snow, the flakes were wet and tiny—little pinpricks of moisture pushed sideways by the violent air swirling in from the sea. One couldn't know whether it was coming from the water or the sky. The view outside the windows was white and opaque, the image of soft, fluffy flakes falling gently from above a distant memory. A luxury.

Cara had always been proud of her ability not just to endure winter, but to embrace it. She and her friends had grown up snowboarding or skiing or both. They put snow tires on their cars every Thanksgiving and took them off at Easter. They knew how to turn the steering wheel into the slide when the rear of the car started to spin and were unfazed by the unsettling crunch of antilock brakes. They'd felt the sting of snow on their bare skin from harebrained midnight snow angels in between bouts in the hot tub. The winter didn't hinder them; it invited them.

There was no denying the beauty of it, the way the snow here settled in drifts between rippled mounds of sand, the surrounding ocean a slate gray with crusty white edges. In the absence of summer growth, the water was as clear as it would ever be. But the island winter was a different breed of season. It was flat and scrubby and diluted in a way that was somehow more repellent than the dense, voluminous winter of the Green Mountains. The weather forced them inside for days on end, inspiring a modest depression that could only be cured by venturing out into it, which was the last thing either of them wanted to do.

At first it was cozy. Brendan would build a fire in the fireplace and the two of them would sit on the couch wrapped in blankets drinking coffee (decaf for her) mixed with Swiss Miss with whipped cream on top. But as the winter wore on, the remoteness of their home became increasingly evident. They would go days without speaking to anyone, until it was time to drive Cara into town for one of her appointments, the only thing that seemed to bring any structure to their lives. Brendan had bought them a car, a used 1999 Toyota Camry, to take the burden off Moira, who'd hitherto been generous enough to chauffeur her niece back and forth.

Every few weeks, Brendan would have to leave again for trips overseas or training on the mainland, leaving Cara alone in the little house by the sea. She used the time to paint, taking advantage of the house's giant windows to view the frozen landscape without having to step foot outside. But even this sometimes exhausted her. She was plagued by migraines and found it impossible to sleep at night, never comfortable in the limited positions her new body availed her. She'd wake up in the morning, groggy and sore in places she never knew existed.

She wanted to cry and complain and feel sorry for herself, but recognized that she was undeserving of pity. She had chosen this. She had done this to herself. Admitting defeat would only validate the arguments of those who had tried to warn her—Drew, Lindsay, her father. She imagined her friends from college and Vermont, living their ordinary lives, their struggles inconsequential in the grand scheme of things, unlike the heavy burden she mentally and physically carried with her at all times. She was glad they couldn't see her, alone in her house on the island. She had to believe that it would be worth it in the end. That the joy and fulfillment she would feel when the baby arrived would surpass the fun, carefree life she was currently missing out on.

They'd originally planned to keep the sex of the baby a surprise. There were so few genuine surprises in life, Brendan maintained, and they should seize this opportunity to share one. The observation was as romantic as it was compelling, so Cara went along with it as long as she could. Until the day came when she realized that she could no longer go on without knowing. She yearned to be able to humanize the person inside of her, fantasizing about what her child would look like, and act like, and sound like. She did it without Brendan knowing, cornering the nurse after one of her ultrasounds.

"Please," she begged. My husband doesn't want to know, but I do. I need to know. I don't know how much more of this I can take without knowing."

The lie of the word *husband* came out easily.

The nurse looked nervously over her shoulder. "You sure?"

"Yes."

"It's a boy. You're having a boy."

The words sent a shiver through Cara's body. Then came the tears. Then came the smile.

"Thank you," she whispered.

It was only then, as the sense of surprise tinged with mild skepticism hit her, that Cara realized she hadn't been quite as neutral as she'd thought with regard to the baby's gender. Up until that moment, knowingly or not, she'd been convinced that she was having a girl; now the whole image had changed. Now she faced the task of reorienting her inner musings and daydreams.

A boy. It wasn't so much that she was disappointed. To the contrary, she was ecstatic to finally know for certain. It was almost as if she'd just found out she was pregnant all over again.

"I found out," she said to Brendan that night over pizza and root beer.

"You found out what?"

"The baby's gender."

Cara took another bite of pizza. She'd once found pizza with pineapple a vile concept. Now she couldn't get enough. Brendan still thought it was gross, so he'd gotten mushrooms and pepperoni for himself, a combo that now made Cara want to retch. Pregnancy cravings were real.

Brendan coughed, stifling a near-choking swallow of dough.

"No, you did not." His tone was serious, but he couldn't hold back his smirk.

"I'm sorry, but I needed it, Brendan. You know I needed it. This has been so hard for me, and I thought if I just knew the sex—if I could just find out who was inside me—that then maybe I could make it through. That maybe it'd be a little bit easier. And it worked! It *is* easier. I'm more *excited* now!"

Brendan sat back, crossed his arms, and shook his head.

"Are you mad?" she asked.

"I'm not mad, but . . . I don't know. I wanted us to find out together. At the same time."

"I know. And I'm sorry, but I couldn't help myself! The nurse was there, and you were away, and I couldn't wait anymore. I grabbed her and I made her tell me. I know I shouldn't have done it, but I'm not like you. I don't even *like* surprises."

There was a pause. Brendan took a swig of root beer and opened his mouth at the end of his swallow, producing an audible reaction to the bubbles hitting his throat. He tipped back his chair, balancing it on the two back legs like the hyperactive boys in elementary school used to do.

"So let's hear it then."

Cara perked up. "You want to know?"

"Do I have a choice?"

"Of course you do! I don't have to tell you anything. If you want to keep it a surprise, I won't let it slip. I swear."

Brendan laughed. "Is that right?"

"Yes."

"We've still got five months to go, pretty mama. Alone. In this house. And you think you can hold a secret like this that long? Potentially the biggest secret of your life?"

Cara could think of a bigger secret.

"You don't think I can do it?"

"Just tell me," he said.

"You want me to?"

"Yes."

"I don't know . . ." she teased. "You said you wanted a surprise."

"That was before. Things have changed. Let's hear it." Brendan slapped his hand down on the table with a nod.

"I'm not sure I want to tell you. I'm still offended that you think I couldn't keep a secret. I think I ought to prove you wrong."

Brendan got up and crept deviously toward her.

"I think you should just tell me," he said, edging closer.

He reached around and started to tickle her, compelling Cara to leap out of her chair. When she started to make a run for it, he picked her up and tossed her over his shoulder. Cara banged her fists on his back, laughing so hard she could hardly catch her breath.

"Put me down," she demanded. "Think of the baby! Our child!"

Brendan tossed her softly onto the bed and pinned her down.

"I've got you now. Don't think I won't use these," he said, wiggling his fingers dangerously close to the sides of her rib cage.

Cara didn't last long. She was paralyzingly ticklish. She screamed with giggles as he squeezed her sides, until she couldn't take it any longer, her body exhausted from the stimulation.

"I surrender!" she shouted between breaths, her eyes wet from the elation. Or torture. She wasn't sure which. "I'll tell you. Just stop tickling me. All this excitement is confusing the baby. This is a lot of commotion for him."

"Are you kidding me?"

"Well, I don't know. But I bet he can feel *something*."

Brendan sat up, rigid, holding his head with his hands. His hair was a mess, little tufts sticking up in the back.

"It's a boy?"

It was only then that Cara realized what she had done. Sometimes she felt like the baby was sucking up all her brainpower, inhibiting her ability to process thoughts and make clear decisions.

"Oh my god." She laughed. "I didn't even mean to do that. I swear."

But Brendan wasn't listening to her.

"We're having a boy?"

There were tears in his eyes now, goose bumps along his forearms.

Cara nodded. "Are you surprised?"

"I don't know."

"I was. I really thought it was a girl. Shows what *I* know. But isn't it great to know now? Now we can talk about names. And all the things we want to do with him. And what we think he'll look like. And what his voice will sound like! Isn't this great?"

"It is," Brendan said. "It is great. But I'll tell you, it's a good thing I decided to let you tell me. You managed to keep that secret for . . . what was it, three minutes? Four minutes?"

"I can't believe I let it slip like that," Cara said. "I hope I didn't ruin the moment."

"Nah. It was perfect," Brendan said. "I mean, yeah. If you hadn't snuck behind my back, we could have, like, let the suspense build for months, and then found out right when he came out, when our emotions were at their highest, and we were seeing him for the very first time, his little wiener poking out. But this was way better. Really. Just as magical. Maybe even more so."

Cara shoved him.

"*I'm sorry!*" she said. "I told you, I couldn't help it."

"I guess it's all right. We can try again with the next one. Or, let's be real, maybe the one after that. Third time's the charm, right?"

2014

On the night of the gallery reception, through the duration of her awful fight with Graham, Cara had had a trump card. A get-out-of-jail-free card. Proof that Brendan was back.

She'd found it in the woods behind the gallery, where she'd discovered a hand-carved humpback whale, suspended from a branch with fishing line. Just behind the whale, tucked into the hollow of a white oak, was a note with two words written on it: *Squib Pond*.

Rather than share her discovery, Cara had snapped the whale loose, buried it in a pile of leaves, and shoved the note into her bra for safekeeping. And she'd continued to keep the note a secret, even as the tension between her and Graham had grown increasingly tight.

She knows she should just tell him. The note itself is concrete evidence that Brendan is back on the island—proof that it was not, in fact, a hallucination that caused Cara to drop that glass. And yet, despite the painful accusations of insanity and obsession directed her way, she's chosen to keep the discovery to herself. *Why?*

When she gets to Moira's, Cara parks her bike and throws her bag on the front stoop, not bothering to go inside. The dogs bark and she ignores them. She walks around the back of the house to the old boating shed and slides open the wooden track door. Sweeping away cobwebs with a stick, she squints and waits for her eyes to adjust to the darkness. She's relieved to see Uncle Edward's old dinghy, *Archimedes*, resting keel side up in the corner. The shed is filled with salty tackle boxes, nets, life preservers, and outboard motors with long dried-out barnacles on the blades. She shoves things aside with her legs, creating a path for the boat.

The dinghy is heavier than she hoped and makes a scraping sound against the concrete flooring of the shed. She's able to drag it out and flip it over, revealing a long-abandoned hornets' nest, clumps of spiderwebs, and scrambling earwigs inside. She grabs a pair of oars and uses them to clean out the hull, wiping the residue onto the grass. She tries and fails to lift the boat up with her arms and resolves to drag it, tossing the oars inside with a thud. The volume of the sound startles her and she utters an "ow," as though she's channeling the pain of the little boat, though she herself feels no actual physical pain.

She has to stop four times to catch her breath and stretch, forearms burning from the tension of the boat's weight against her own. She winces every time the dinghy goes over a rock, sure that the hull will be covered in scratches when she's through.

When she makes it to the water's edge, the gray skies above make good on their threat to rain. It's a light rain, but the drops feel cold on her bare arms.

After bringing the dinghy afloat, she holds it as steady as she can and awkwardly climbs aboard, nearly toppling over into the shallow water. She's forgotten oarlocks, but wouldn't know how to maneuver them if she had them anyway. So she rows the boat like a clumsy gondolier, using a single oar to navigate out on the water. Her path is meandering and full of oversteers and spins, but it'll get her where she needs to go. The island should only be a few dozen paddles away.

The small patch of land is surrounded by marsh and pond and covered in shrubs and brush. Cara wonders if she'll be able to recognize the bare cake of sand where she and Brendan set up camp that one night. They'd paddled out here in a kayak, the two of them squished into a hole meant for one with a tent and sleeping bags hastily strapped to the front and a cooler full of Bud Lights, hot dogs, and burritos held precariously on the top of Cara's head. They'd managed to make it without spilling the food, but had had to lay out the sleeping bags in the sun to evaporate the seawater they'd soaked up on the journey.

As Cara pulls ashore, she is remarkably calm. It feels safe out here on this tiny island—if you could even call it that—nestled on the edge of Squibnocket Pond. The island trees are short and shrub-like, but big enough to hide a person who doesn't want to be seen. Cara makes her way through the mud and grass to drier ground and tries to remember where they pitched their tent all those years ago. There's a chance the ashes and charred stones from their campfire could still be there.

Brambles scratch against her calves. As Cara turns a corner, she sees a figure in all black, sitting on a log facing the water. She holds her breath and stops walking, then approaches the silhouette with caution, for fear of frightening him off.

For the briefest of moments, Cara considers turning back. She's been here before, in this moment, thousands of times in her mind. But now that it's here, despite countless mental rehearsals, she's terrified of letting it play out. She could leave now and get back on her original course. But then, perhaps that's exactly what she is doing. Perhaps this *is* her original course, and it's the past five years that she's been lost.

Brendan turns his head over his shoulder and looks at Cara with a casual glance, as if he's known she was there all along. Her whole body goes numb. She can't move. The muscles in her face freeze somewhere between a smile and a frown. Brendan stands up, then walks close to her and cups her cheeks with his palms. His hands are warm.

This. This is why Cara chose not to tell Graham about the note. Because even last night, in all the chaos, she knew deep down that she was unwilling to sacrifice this moment. Alone. With Brendan. In private. Had she shown Graham the note, he would have insisted on coming with her, which, she is sure now, would have changed everything. This moment, with the man whose visage still sends a satisfying reverberation from her gut to her shoulders—the man she feared she might never see again—makes all the fighting and crying feel necessary.

He's wearing a full wetsuit that looks about fifty years old. Sections are patched with mismatched fabric and threads from messy sewing jobs hang loose from their seams. His grown-out hair is tied back with a part down the center, and there are grays at his temples and in his beard. She can hear the air whistling through the hair of his mustache each time he inhales. His lips are dry and chapped, and the skin of his face not covered in hair is deeply tanned.

Brendan is the first to cry. His eyes gleam with liquid and the corners of his mouth shake.

"Hi," he whispers.

"Hi," Cara says back, her body rigid. She knows it's Brendan, yet their closeness unnerves her. It feels like too much too soon.

"You look the same," says Brendan. He grazes his fingertips over Cara's forehead and through the soft hairs of her bangs.

"You have a beard," says Cara.

"I do," says Brendan. "You like it?"

"Sure." Cara shrugs. "I mean, yeah."

Brendan laughs and wraps his arms around her, squeezing her tight against his chest. Cara feels allured by the potency of his scent, masculine and familiar, and breathes in as much of it as she can. A calming warmth spreads through her. The way he holds her—with his hands flat against the small of her back, pulling her midsection in close to his, his chest a perfect perch for her head—reminds her how it felt to be twenty-two and in love.

"I've missed you so much," he says into her hair.

It all feels so good. To be held like this. To hear that she has been missed. Cara wants nothing more than to give in to the languid flow of happiness and elation, ignoring the sharp traces of resentment, bitterness, and flat-out anger she's been harboring.

But there's a tug stronger than the pull of passion and nostalgia. Cara pulls away.

"Micah," she says, holding out her hand to steady herself.

Brendan looks at the ground.

"Brendan. Where is Micah? Is he alive? *Please*, Brendan. I need to know if he's okay. Either way, I need to know. *Please*."

Brendan's hesitation both tortures her and protects her. Cara is desperate to hear what's become of their child, but the prospect of finally learning his fate also terrifies her. There is a delicate safety in her ignorance that keeps her hope intact.

"Cara . . ." Brendan's eyebrows curve into a soft, sorrowful wince. He reaches for her hand, but she draws it back.

"No," she says, shaking her head. "No, no, no."

Her legs evaporate beneath her. Brendan crouches down next to her, enveloping her shaking body in his own.

"I'm so sorry," he whispers. His voice has a gruffness to it now.

Cara hasn't realized how much hope she's been holding on to until this moment. Hasn't she already conquered the darkest stages of grief? Denial. Anger. Depression. She's mourned and moved forward, allowing herself to start anew with Graham, all the while maintaining a safe spot for her firstborn deep inside of herself.

But now, it is as if she has lost Micah all over again. And not just her baby, but her five-year-old son. The boy she has for so long been hoping to meet.

"When?" Cara asks. "What happened?"

"Years ago," says Brendan.

"How?" she asks. "I want to know how."

"He drowned."

"But I thought . . . I didn't think you could. I thought he was like you. You said he was like you."

"I did too. He was."

Cara never believed that Micah was like Brendan. That he too could breathe underwater. It was impossible. A ludicrous idea. But not believing it, facing the truth, meant that Micah was surely dead. And so for years, as she is now realizing, Cara has clung to the hope that maybe, just maybe, Brendan was right. That Micah really was special. That Brendan wasn't crazy. No, not crazy, but sick. Confused. Lost.

That hope is fading now, quickly, without sympathy.

"You did this," says Cara, darkening. "You killed him."

"Don't say that. Please don't say that."

"Why did you have to take him away?"

"I was protecting him. And if I could go back and do it again, I would."

"You killed him."

"I *saved* him. I took him away him from those *people*. They were going to keep him inside a fucking lab for the rest of his life. I gave him freedom."

"And what about me?" Cara asks. "What did you give me? You left me here."

"You left me first."

"Because I caught you trying to drown our child!"

"It wasn't like that. You know that's not what I was trying to do."

"It doesn't matter. None of that matters anymore. You took my baby away from me. And now I'm never going to see him again. I can hardly remember what he looks like anymore. Do you know how heartbreaking that is?"

"I'm sorry, Care."

"Five years. Almost five years, I've been waiting."

Brendan reaches out for Cara, and she pushes his hand away.

"We can try again," Brendan says. "I'm ready now. I love you."

"What?"

Cara looks at the man in front of her. It's amazing how his words still have such an impact on her. He looks so tired. So weathered. She imagines what a hot shower and shave might do. A haircut. Fresh clothes. Medication.

"I said I love you."

"I heard you," Cara says quickly, trying to think. She can't decide what she wants.

"Let's start over," says Brendan, coming closer. But Cara backs away, shaking her head.

"I'm married now, Brendan. To Graham." Her voice wobbles. "I love Graham."

"I've seen you with that guy, you don't love him." Brendan laughs as he says this, wholly unconvinced. "He's a nice guy, sure, but you don't love him. He doesn't make you laugh. He doesn't get you like I do."

"Stop," Cara warns.

"I'm right and you know it."

"*Stop!*"

Cara looks Brendan in the eyes, breathing hard but not saying anything, his brown eyes staring back into her own.

"I never want to see you again," she says.

2009

Spring didn't come until May, the end of Cara's second trimester. The warmth was a relief, the neon-green buds on the trees a subtle pick-me-up. Walkers and joggers started to appear on the island streets. Shops that had been shut all winter began to open their doors, operating on limited schedules, getting ready for the rush of summer tourists.

Cara spent her mornings sprawled out on the floor of the deck in her hoodie and sweatpants, soaking up the vitamin D of the sun's rays, burning the skin by her hairline and on the bridge of her nose until it finally graduated to a tan. Something about the hard wooden surface felt therapeutic against her back.

She'd taken to eating a grilled cheese sandwich for lunch each day, even though the doctor had advised her to eat more leafy greens. What she really wanted was a bologna sandwich on white bread with lots of yellow mustard, but that was apparently on the do-not-eat list. She'd of course always known that pregnant women were supposed to abstain from things like alcohol and smoking and high-mercury fish. But deli meats? Soft cheeses? Coffee? No one ever talked about these things.

She'd been so good in the beginning, taking care not to ingest even a molecule of anything she thought might harm the baby. But over time she'd grown lax, allowing herself certain indulgences as a personal reward for enduring pregnancy. The bologna sandwich, when she finally had it, was all she'd hoped it would be. She felt so remorseful after eating it that she had to immediately throw away the remaining meat, squeezing dish soap over it in the garbage so she wouldn't be tempted to eat it out of the trash.

Temptations aside, the good weather energized Cara and gave her the boost she needed to leave the house. She took the car and swung by the fish market one afternoon, only realizing once she got there how much she'd missed social interaction. Mona gave her a big hug when she saw her, and Graham could hardly hide the shock in his eyes when he saw the size of her belly. Adriano, with his usual candor, asked who'd knocked her up.

She was disappointed when patrons started to come in and they all had to go back to work. In the old days, she could have taken a seat and hung out, reading a book or a newspaper. But it was different now that she was pregnant. She was too conspicuous. Women at her stage of pregnancy couldn't just hang out and blend in. It was expected that she should have something better to do, even if that something better was resting or eating or attending a yoga class. But Cara was tired of resting. Tired of reading. Tired of wandering around the house. She was feeling better than she had in months, and she wanted to take advantage.

So she invited Lindsay to visit. Lindsay and her boyfriend, Zach, whom Cara had never met. In the days before they got there, Cara frantically tidied up the house, stuffing clothes in drawers and reaching over her belly to try to wash the dishes in the sink. The work made her sweat. Her heart was beating so fast she needed to take a break on the couch. The skin on the tops of her feet bulged over the straps of her flip-flops like mayonnaise over a dropped spoon.

This was the first time in their friendship that Cara and Lindsay would experience anything like this. There'd been no unmet boyfriends or "other" friends in college. Aside from the occasional stray hookup (like Cara's senior week Simon Danews encounter), they ran in the same circles. Now they were both in serious relationships that had developed outside the familiar fold, relationships that had budded and eventually blossomed (quite literally, in Cara's case) without the other there to witness it, or to offer the sage, sincerity-soaked counsel that only a best friend can.

What if Lindsay didn't like Brendan? What if she didn't "get" him? But then, how could she, never having had the opportunity to meet him organically, without pretense, the way Cara had? The way they'd always met each other's flings—at a hungover Sunday morning breakfast in the dining hall, or a Beirut tournament at a frat party. Casual. Low stakes.

Instead, Lindsay and Zach's travel to the island had been arduous, beginning with a train ride into Boston, followed by a drive to Woods Hole, and a ferry ride across the Sound, the sheer length and complexity of the journey only adding to the anticipation. All of this combined with the fact that Cara was pregnant with Brendan's baby. Dramatic. High stakes.

And this was just one thread of the growing web of insecurities Cara now faced. She also wanted Zach to like *her*. And Brendan to like Lindsay. And to like Zach herself.

Lindsay put a hand over her gaping mouth when she saw Cara for the first time, effectively putting a dent in Cara's poise. She knew she looked big. But did she really look *that big*? Seeing Lindsay come down the dock, slim and toned, with a collarbone that seemed to glisten in the sun and the smooth sculpt of an indent beneath her deltoid and bicep, made Cara feel even more like a whale. Maybe this whole visit had been a mistake.

Zach was short but muscular. Even at rest, his calf muscles seemed to bulge, the bottom halves of his legs like chicken drumsticks. His hair was cut high and tight, his neck barely visible through the bulk of his shoulders. He had played college lacrosse, just like Lindsay—a face-off specialist at Lehigh.

Zach and Brendan shook hands when they met, and the formality of the gesture seemed comically grown-up, as if they were all playing parts in a movie.

Cara sat in the front seat while Brendan drove, with Lindsay and Zach in the back. They talked about the ferry ride over (it was a little cold with the wind, but pretty), and how Cara was feeling (humongous, but less nauseated), and Lindsay and Zach's summer plans (weekends at the shore, a week in Spain). Zach kept looking out the window and saying, "This place is awesome," which made Cara feel good, as if the whole island was hers to show off.

They went to the fish market for lunch; Cara had gone to great lengths to build anticipation for it, claiming they had the best fried clams in the whole world, and a steal of a lobster roll, filled with chunks of claw and tail meat.

Cara didn't recognize the girl they ordered from at the counter—a circumstance that was surprisingly disappointing—but it was Graham, sweet, kind Graham, who brought their food out to the docks. Brendan gave Graham a quick fist bump but otherwise ignored him. The two men had met before, and if Brendan saw Graham as any kind of threat, he certainly never showed it. Graham, on the other hand, exhibited a noticeable shift in mood whenever Brendan came around the shop, snapping at Cara for trivial things and making passive aggressive comments about her flirting when she should have been working.

Cara introduced Graham to Lindsay and Zach now, and he kindly presented them all with a quartet of oysters on the house.

"Oh, thanks, but I can't actually eat these," Cara said, gesturing down to her stomach.

Graham looked like he'd just served them raw fish chum by mistake.

"Oh, jeez. Of course you can't," he said. "I'm an idiot. You want something else?"

"No, no. I'm good," Cara said. She felt silly for even mentioning it. Why had she done that?

"It will be painful, but if I have to eat Cara's for her, so be it," said Brendan. "That is a sacrifice I am willing to make."

It was a stupid joke, but Lindsay laughed, which helped release some of the tension in Cara's shoulders. In fact, each time Brendan made Lindsay laugh, Cara felt better, as if that was proof Lindsay didn't hate him, and might even like him.

"Aw yeah, *is very nice!*" Zach said when Graham brought him his lobster roll, affecting a silly, accented voice like the Borat character from the famously outlandish film. Lindsay laughed, so Cara and Brendan did too.

"So, Brendan, remind me what you do?" Lindsay asked. Again with the strange adult formality.

"I'm in the army."

"Oh, cool, man," said Zach. "I've got a buddy in the army too."

Cara could practically hear what Brendan was thinking:

Holy shit, what are the odds? You want a cookie?

To her relief, he only smiled and asked what division the friend was in.

"Um . . . I'm not sure," said Zach. "He lives in Southern California."

"Yeah. I probably don't know him then."

The conversation was hardly riveting, but Cara was enjoying herself. She'd missed moments like this, eating lunch outside with friends, friends who were her age with similar values and upbringings and senses of humor. Despite her worries about everyone liking each other, it felt like things were going well. She was already dreading having to say good-bye to Lindsay and Zach when they left.

A boat pulled up while they were eating and a fisherman Cara knew came ashore. It was Dean, a frequent contributor of fish to the shop.

"Well, would you look at you!" he said, stopping by the table and gleaming at Cara. He nodded at Brendan. "Hey, pal, how are ya? How much longer, sweetie?"

"Twelve weeks," Cara said.

"Speak in English, I don't do math."

"Three months."

"Whew! Getting closer. You ready?" He looked more at Brendan than Cara when he asked.

"Ready for what?" Brendan asked.

"You didn't know?" Dean smiled. "That's a baby she's got in there."

"A baby? Like a human baby?" Brendan feigned shock. "And here I was thinking it was all these fried clams. . . ."

Lindsay and Zach laughed. That was at least three laughs now. Maybe four.

"You find out if it's a geoduck or a cuttlefish?"

Brendan laughed right away. Cara wasn't getting it, so Brendan answered for her. "It's a boy," he said.

Just now getting the joke, Zach slapped his hand down on the table and guffawed, looking at Lindsay to make sure she got it. She nodded and rolled her eyes, though Cara suspected that neither of them had a clue what geoducks and cuttlefish were. In fact, she was surprised that Brendan did.

"This was really good, Care. Thank you," Lindsay said when they were done eating.

"I'm proud of you for getting the fried clams," Cara said. "I know they're horrible for you, but wasn't it worth it?"

"Oh, *so* worth it," Lindsay said.

"*Great success!*" Zach said—again in the goofy Borat voice. He gestured toward the empty containers in front of them and threw his crumpled napkin on his plate. "I'm stuffed."

By the time they left the dock, the sky had grown overcast, prompting Lindsay to stop by the car for a fleece. As the sun disappeared, so too did the people, and the foursome soon found themselves alone on the small beach. They left their shoes in the sand and walked out onto the jetty, Cara and Lindsay in front with Zach and Brendan a few paces behind.

"What do you think they're talking about?" Cara asked.

"I have no idea. Does Brendan like sports?"

"He says he likes to play them more than he likes to watch them."

"Hmm."

"What?"

"I guess I just don't see it as an either/or thing. Zach plays sports, but he also loves to watch. Like, borderline obsessed."

"Does he have a favorite?"

"Probably football, but only because he does fantasy. Does Brendan do that?"

Cara realized she didn't know. She assumed not—she and Brendan didn't have cable. They didn't really even watch TV. And it had been months since Cara had been on the internet. It was like they lived in a different time, wholly separate from the place Lindsay and Zach had come from.

"I like him," Lindsay said. "Brendan. He's really funny."

"Thanks. I like Zach too. He's really great. He does that Borat voice. . . ."

"Oh, yeah." Lindsay rolled her eyes, blushing but laughing. "It's annoying, I know."

"No, no, it's funny!" Cara lied. "He's sweet."

There was a pause.

"So do you think he'll be a good father?" Lindsay asked.

"Brendan?"

"No, the fisherman guy at the dock. *Yes*, Brendan!"

"Yeah. I think so. I hope so. He's been really sweet through all this. I don't think I could have made it this far without him."

"You can say that again."

"Oh, stop. You know what I mean. He's been really helpful and attentive. When he's here, at least. He travels a lot."

"For the army?"

"Yeah."

"Where does he go? Iraq, I'm assuming?"

"I don't think so, actually, but I know he's been. Now it's mostly Asia. China, Korea—" Cara stopped herself. "I'm not actually supposed to tell you that. I know you're not going to call the government or anything, but maybe don't tell Zach, okay? I'm being ridiculous, I know, but he's pretty serious about keeping it confidential."

"Does he tell you secret stuff? Like what he does when he goes?"

"I think he might if I asked. But I feel like that'd be unfair to him. And also, I don't know that I want to know. It would probably just freak me out."

"Are you worried about him being away so much? When the baby comes?"

"Yeah. But I have my aunt here too. So that will help. I won't be totally alone."

"That's good. What about his family?"

"It's a long story. His mom died when he was a teenager and he doesn't have any siblings. His dad is . . . well, he and his dad don't really get along."

Before heading back to the house, they stopped at Gay Head to see

the iconic lighthouse, which, due to erosion, now sat so close to the cliffs it looked like it might one day fall down into the sea. Cara felt the same way, standing at the edge of the lookout point with her front-weighted body. There was a rail, of course, but she could feel herself leaning backward ever so slightly, just to keep a safe balance.

Zach took lots of pictures with his digital camera, a red, pocket-sized point-and-shoot. This was a rare sight for someone from Pittsburgh, he said. He was excited to show his mom. Cara found this endearing.

They spent the rest of the day back at the house. It was too chilly to sit outside, so they sat on the sofa and a couple chairs by the glass windows and played Monopoly. They'd found the box, which smelled like the 1960s, in one of the house's closets. Lindsay had the idea to turn it into a drinking game. She explained the rules she'd learned from her cousins: drink if you land on someone's property; drink three times if they own the whole set; take a shot if you land on a hotel. They drank beer for the minor infractions and threw back vodka for the shots. Cara drank root beer for everything.

The only time things got heated was when Lindsay tried to place a hotel on the Reading Railroad.

"I can do it because I own all four," she said, her words beginning to slur. "It's the same as any other property."

Zach was aghast. "I'm sorry, sweetie, but no."

"Don't 'sweetie' me. This is how we've *always* played it with my cousins. It's in the rules," Lindsay argued, gesturing toward the box and knocking over a drink with her arm. "Fuck, sorry!" She laughed, making a lazy attempt to help Cara clean up the mess.

"It is *definitely* not in the rules," Zach insisted. "Somebody tricked you."

He started rifling through the box, but the instructions had evidently been lost long ago.

"Think about it," he said. "It doesn't make any sense. You can't build a house on a railroad car."

"But it's not a railroad car. It's a rail*road*," Lindsay argued. "You can build houses along it because you own it."

"She's got a point," said Brendan, clearly entertained by the whole thing.

"No, she doesn't. By that logic, I could just buy the whole road and not let any of you put anything on it. There would be no game!"

"Yeah, but there's no 'road' section of the board," Lindsay pointed out. "Just the railroad. This is from, like, before roads."

Cara and Brendan exchanged amused glances. Both Lindsay and Zach were completely wasted.

"I'm from Pittsburgh. Okay?" said Zach. "Steel City. I think I know railroads."

Lindsay scoffed. "I'm sorry, but how is that even relevant?"

"My forefathers literally built railroads. Maybe even the railroad we took to get here." Zach's face was getting redder, his temples sweatier and sweatier.

"Oh, please, Zach. Your grandfather was a doctor."

"That's my *dad's* dad. My *mom's* dad was a miner. For forty years!"

Lindsay turned to Cara. "I'm sorry, am I the only one who's confused? How did we get to talking about miners?"

"What's confusing is how anyone could think you could build a house on a railroad. Can we just agree that that's retarded and totally against the rules?" Zach looked to Cara, the only sober one, to make the decision.

"I'm not getting involved," she said.

"Well, wait a minute," Brendan said, a wily look in his eye. "Let's talk this out. I think it really depends on how you look at it. Have you ever seen one of those houses they haul on the highway? The ones with the WIDE LOAD signs and the special escorts? Maybe this is like that."

"Also, some trains are really nice now," Cara added. "As nice as hotels, even. Maybe that's what Lindsay's hotel is. A train hotel."

Brendan's face lit up. "Yes! A train hotel! Good one!"

"I thought you weren't getting involved," Zach shot back.

Cara shrugged.

"You guys suck. I'm going to take a piss."

Zach went outside to the deck, letting the screen door slap shut behind him. The room filled with laughter behind him.

"I'm sorry," Lindsay said between sobs of laughter. "He's so wasted."

"Is he really mad?"

"No. He's fine. He's just drunk."

"Do you really play with that rule?" Cara asked.

"I mean, yeah, but only because that's how we always played it as kids. I'm sure it's not officially allowed."

Too drunk and tired to go anywhere, they abandoned plans to dine out and chowed down on hot dogs, frozen waffles, and Cape Cod chips for dinner. Zach passed out early on the couch, so Cara and Lindsay took a walk down to the water. It was dark by that point and the wind was shockingly cold, but the house was too small for private conversation. When they made it to the sand, Cara stopped walking and turned to her friend.

"I'm really scared," she said.

"What do you mean?"

"To have this baby. I'm really scared."

"Well, that's normal, I think. It'd be weird if you weren't scared."

"I just . . . . do you think I'm doing the right thing?"

Lindsay looked away. "Isn't it a little late to be asking that question?"

"Yeah, but I still want to know what you think. Do you think I'm making a mistake?"

"It doesn't matter what I think. It's your life."

"So you do."

"What?"

"Fuck. You think I'm throwing my life away."

"Wow. That's not what I said."

"But if you didn't you would say that. You would say, *No. Of course not. Of course you're not making a mistake.*"

"Look, Care, it's your life. You could have walked away from all this months ago, but you didn't. And you must have had a good reason for it, otherwise we wouldn't be here. Now, would I want to have a baby at this point in my life? Honestly? No. But that's me. Not you."

"But that's the thing. If you had asked me the same question a few months ago, I would have said the same thing. And even *I* don't know what's changed. I don't! It's like I've become this other person out here, with this whole different life, but I'm still the old me too. And I love Brendan—I do—but I always had you, and New York, as my escape hatch before. And now I don't. And sometimes I'm one hundred percent okay with that. And sometimes I'm not."

"I don't know what you want me to say."

"I don't either. I guess . . . just promise me you'll still be my friend after the baby comes. Things will be different, but maybe they don't have to be *that* different. We can still hang out and do fun things. Like we have this weekend."

"I promise. You're going to make a great mom, Care. You really are. You can do this. Now can we go back? It's so fucking cold and I can barely keep my eyes open."

Neither of them spoke again as they walked to the house. Cara tried to calm herself, but her mind continued to race. She wished she hadn't said anything to Lindsay. She'd broken her bluff, and now Lindsay, one of the few people whose judgment Cara valued—and feared—most, knew the truth of what was going on. That Cara wasn't the confident, overjoyed mom-to-be that she pretended to be. This had been her own doing, of course, but the circumstances didn't make her feel any less exposed.

They walked along the sandy path through the beach grass and the yellow light of the house appeared within view. A shadow glided past the windows. But the person making the shadow wasn't inside; he was outside, pacing back and forth across the deck, wearing nothing but a T-shirt and shorts. The closer they got, the more clearly they could hear his voice speaking, though his words were indistinct.

"Is that Brendan? Who is he talking to?"

Cara suddenly didn't feel cold anymore.

"Oh, yeah. I don't know. Let's maybe go in the side door. He's probably working."

"Working?"

"Yeah, I'm sure he just got a call. It happens sometimes. Let's go this way."

Cara grabbed Lindsay's wrist and practically pulled her around to the side of the house where they couldn't see Brendan anymore.

Cara had known something like this was a possibility, but her initial concern had dissipated when she'd seen how well things were going between Brendan and their guests. The social interaction had been good for him, she thought. Lindsay and Zach were a welcome distraction from his usual anxieties, which she'd realized had a tendency to peak when he was alone and idle.

But now there he was, shouting and gesturing to no one.

Cara brought Lindsay inside and helped her make up the Aerobed, stealing glances out back to make sure Brendan wasn't doing anything that might cause alarm. She needed to get out there to talk to him, to calm him down the way only she could.

"Okay! Blankets, water, ibuprofen . . . Can I get you anything else?"

She stood over Lindsay, eager for her to fall asleep.

"I think I'm all set."

"Great. Good night!"

"Wait, Care?" Cara's finger paused on the light switch.

"Yeah?"

"I'm sorry if I came off as insensitive before. I didn't mean to."

"It's fine. You didn't. I'm fine."

"It's okay if you're not."

"No, I am. Really."

Cara could see Brendan outside raking his fingers through his hair. She could hear him, even inside, and wondered how Lindsay didn't seem to notice.

"Thanks," she added hastily. "Don't worry about it. We're good."

"You sure?"

"Yep. Good night!"

Cara flipped off the switch and rushed out the back door. She caught Brendan by the shoulders and forced him to stop walking.

"Brendan. Calm down. You're okay."

Brendan's body stopped moving, but his eyes picked up where his legs left off, his pupils pointing everywhere but Cara's face.

"He has nukes."

"What?"

"Koh. Williams says a threat is imminent."

"Brendan. Look at me. *Look at me.* Whatever it is that's upsetting you, it's going to be okay. Whatever it is, we'll take care of it. Okay? But it's late. Let's get some rest and we'll deal with it tomorrow."

Brendan continued to look agitated.

"Breathe with me."

"I need to go."

"No, Brendan. Please."

"I'm sorry, but they need me. I'm the only one who can access the tunnels."

Cara could only watch as Brendan sprinted away from the porch and out toward the road. She didn't know what to do. Should she run after him? Call the police?

It was quiet. Lindsay and Zach were asleep inside. Cara felt her panic at seeing Brendan in such a state begin to subside. She was giving up. There was nothing else to be done. She collapsed into a beach chair and put her hands on her belly. She was exhausted.

The next morning, Cara woke up in her own bed to the smell of food cooking on the stove. She rolled out of bed, her lower back killing her, and peeked out into the main living area. Lindsay and Zach were still asleep, though Zach had migrated during the night from the couch to the air mattress with Lindsay. She was relieved to see Brendan in the kitchen making french toast. She walked quietly over to him.

"Hey. You okay?"

"I'm great," said Brendan. "Why?"

The scene felt surreal. Though it wasn't the first time something like this had happened, the shock of seeing Brendan so disoriented and then, just hours later, so normal, never went away. Usually it frustrated her. How dare he act like everything was normal? He could have gotten injured or killed last night, running out to the street that way, and now here he was making french toast, acting like nothing had happened. It wasn't just confusing; it was infuriating.

"*Why?*" Cara repeated, incredulous. "Because of all that stuff you said that night—Williams and Koh, and something about nuclear weapons. It was weird."

"Oh, that was nothing," said Brendan. "A false alarm. You want Mrs. Butterworth's or the real stuff with your french toast?"

Cara wanted to press further, but knew she couldn't. Not today, with Lindsay and Zach starting to stir on the Aerobed. Today she needed to join Brendan in the charade and carry on as normal, so that they could get through the next few hours without their friends suspecting anything amiss. So Cara took her cue, delivering her line like a character in a play.

"How dare you insult me with such a question! You think I would ever stoop so low as to ruin my delicious breakfast with *Mrs. Butterworth*?"

"Ah, right. Vermont girl," said Brendan. "Please forgive me."

After breakfast, they drove out to Oak Bluffs to kill time before Lindsay and Zach's boat. They made a special stop at Vineyard Vines so Zach could buy a hat with a pink whale on it. Cara urged Brendan to buy one too, citing his love of whales. He responded by mimicking throw-up noises.

Cara had anticipated a flood of sadness and loss at saying good-bye to Lindsay, but when the moment finally came, she felt only relief. The massive ferry blew its horn, and Cara watched her friend walk up the ramp, blond ponytail swinging in step. She'd been thinking that everything would change once the baby was born, that this weekend would be the last time she and Lindsay would spend together and still have things be the same. But she'd been mistaken. Everything was already different.

2014

"'m ready to call the police," Cara says, standing in the doorway, hands on her hips.

Graham is in his office at the gallery, sitting at the handmade table one of his artists made for him—the one from Seattle. A piece of glass with edges so thick it emanates a cool teal glow rests over a teak tray of sand and shells from Aquinnah—scallops, periwinkles, lady slippers, jingle shells. Graham gestures for Cara to sit down.

The table is covered with scans from Graham's latest meeting with dealers. The pictures are abstract, but vibrant with happy yellows and jubilant greens. Cara doesn't know if it's their resemblance to children's drawings or a jealous resentment of the feelings they evoke that drives her to push them aside. She doesn't want to look at them.

"Do you want to tell me what happened?"

"He's gone, Graham."

Cara's voice gives out. Graham pulls his chair closer to her side, the legs squeaking against the floor.

"Brendan?"

"Micah."

"Tell me what happened. I thought you were going to Moira's."

"I was. I did. And then I went to meet him. He left me a note. Last night." Cara drops the crumpled paper on the table for Graham to unfold. "I know I should have just told you. I don't know why I didn't."

Graham inspects the note. "Squib Pond?"

"We used to camp out there. Me and Brendan."

"I don't understand."

"I went there to meet him. And he was there. I talked to him."

"This morning. Just now. You *talked* to Brendan."

Cara nods.

"And you're sure it was him."

"He told me Micah's dead, Graham. He told me he drowned. Years ago."

"I'm so sorry, Care."

"I mean, I knew he was gone. We all knew it. But to hear it . . ."

"Where is Brendan now?"

"I don't know."

"Well, do you think he's maybe still there? At the pond? Did he tell you anything about where he's been staying?"

Cara shakes her head. "I was so angry. I couldn't stay there."

"Okay. Well, I know this isn't the news you wanted. That *any of us* wanted. And I'm so sorry, Cara. This is devastating. But at least now we have some closure. And once they find Brendan, this can all be over." Graham is smiling now, hope radiating from his eyes. "He'll go to jail— or wherever he needs to go. An *institution*. Whatever. And you and I can finally move on. Start over. Together. Like we planned."

Brendan. Jail. Institution. A splinter of preemptive guilt cuts through Cara's body.

"That's still what you want, right?" Graham asks her gently.

Cara feels herself nodding, but her mind is elsewhere, hit with the neon flash of an unexpected detour.

"Is there a specific person you think I should call? Do you have a number for Detective Sawyer?"

Graham's back behind his desk and on his laptop, gliding his fingers down the trackpad as he scrolls through the website for the local police station.

"Or maybe we should just call nine-one-one," he says. "What do you think?"

Cara doesn't answer. She stares down at the shells beneath the glass of the tabletop, her mind preoccupied with another image entirely.

"What's wrong? Am I going too fast? I know it's a lot, but I think we should do this now. While we know he's still on the island."

"Yeah, I know," says Cara. "It's just—I just thought of something."

Her gaze remains fixed, her voice monotone. She can't believe she's only just realized it.

"What?"

"Dean's guy—Jimmy. He said he saw a man and a child. Why would he say that?"

"What? Who knows," says Graham, sensing a weakening in Cara's resolve. "Guy was making it up, for all we know. Or maybe Dean got the story wrong. I'm still not convinced they saw anything at all, to be honest."

"Yeah, but it'd be a pretty weird coincidence, don't you think? They see something, and then Brendan shows up just days later? And he said there were two people. I *know* he did."

"I'm calling."

Graham starts to punch a number into his cell phone. Cara puts out a hand to stop him.

"Hold on. What if he was lying?"

"Who?"

"Brendan. What if he was lying about Micah?"

"Jesus." Graham drags his free hand down the side of his face with a sigh. "Are you ever going to stop torturing yourself? Micah's gone. He's dead. And I'm so sorry. I truly am. But you need to face that truth. Move on. In refusing to believe it, you're only making things harder for yourself. For us."

"You'd like that, wouldn't you?"

"What?"

"If Micah were dead. You'd like that."

"What? Of course not. How can you even say that?"

"You just want all of this to go away. You said it yourself."

Graham puts his hands up in defense. "Hey, that's not fair. Don't spin this around on me. I'm trying to help you. Of course I hope Micah's alive. *Of course* I do. But I'm also trying to protect you and make sure you don't get your hopes up just to get fucked all over again. I'm not the bad guy here. Brendan is. Have you forgotten that? *Brendan* took Micah away. Brendan's the one messing with you. Brendan *killed your child.* Why are you still trying to protect him?"

"I'm not trying to protect him. I just want to find Micah."

"Are you sure about that?"

"What? Of course I'm sure."

"Just tell me this. When you saw him, what did it feel like?"

"What?"

"You could have told me about the note. But you didn't. You let us argue on and on all night long, making me look like an asshole while the whole time you had this note—from him—in your pocket."

"So?"

232

"So . . . do you still love him? Is that what this is about? Honestly."

"I'm not even going to answer that. I need to go. There's someone I need to talk to. Please don't call anyone until I'm back. Okay?"

Graham looks at her without saying anything, chewing on his bottom lip. Cara knows he's desperate to keep her there, but to keep her in his life, he needs to let her go.

"Fine."

2009

The baby came right on his due date, August 5, 2009, at 6:25 a.m. All of his stats were average—average length, average weight, average amount of hair. But to Cara and Brendan, he was exceptional.

They named him Micah, for no real reason save for the fact that they both liked it. It reminded Cara of the shiny, brittle pieces of mineral she and Drew used to peel off one of the boulders in the woods near their house in Vermont. *Mica*, their mom said it was.

Micah was shiny and brittle too. Shiny in the way his skin and eyes seemed to emanate purity and light; brittle in the way he fussed and cried, his little person still so delicate and tender. The feeling of his warm, dainty head against her bare chest sent bursts of euphoria through Cara's body. She felt like she wanted to absorb him back inside of herself, where she knew he would be safe, and warm, and protected, where he would forever be her most loyal companion.

Every time she looked at him, she experienced a renewed sense of amazement. They had done it. He was here.

Cara's family arrived two days after the birth. She would never forget the sense of excitement she felt at hearing the wheels of their car crunching over the shells in their driveway. Holding Micah in her arms, Cara walked out to the porch with Brendan, the three of them in a shared embrace as doors opened and people began to emerge. Stanley was first, his body seemingly pulled by a force coming from the bundle in Cara's arms.

He walked fast, and then slowly, quietly, so as not to disturb the scene in front of him. No one else moved, watching as he paused, just a few feet away, no longer able to contain his emotion. The tiniest of sounds—something between a gasp and a sob—so acute you could almost miss it, escaped from his throat. He pressed a fist against his bearded lips. His broad shoulders started to jerk.

Cara approached him, holding out baby Micah.

"Do you want to hold him?"

Her father looked back at her with an expression of complete surrender. He couldn't speak. He nodded and put out his arms, taking the baby. He smiled through his tears, all the while laughing at himself. Laughing at the power of his emotions and the futility of his efforts to hide them. Laughing at the absurdity of having become a grandfather. And laughing at his foolishness in staying away from the island for so long, the senselessness of fearing something so welcoming and beautiful.

Even though Lucia was there, watching politely from the driveway, Cara knew her dad was thinking of Siobhan. Siobhan with her dark, frizzy hair and narrow blue eyes; her silver rings and sun-spotted chest; her bare feet and tiny wrists. The mother of his son and daughter, and the grandmother of the brand-new life he now held in his arms.

Cara thought of her mother so much during those first few weeks. The experience afforded her an even greater appreciation for everything Siobhan had done for her. For lending out her body in a way that was, Cara was learning, as pleasing and fulfilling as it was painful and draining. Because being a new mother was hard. So much harder than any knowing glances or personal stories could ever convey.

She wished her mom were there. Every day, she wished she were there, to help and to guide and to reassure and to laugh. Cara strove to emulate her in everything she did, calling on the memory of her mother to calm her in moments of utmost frustration and chagrin, and to share in those of tranquility and peace. She remembered how her mom used to sing her lullabies and stay with her in bed until she fell asleep, and the way she always used fun cookie cutters to shape Cara's and Drew's sandwiches—even when they were too old for that.

Her family stayed for two whole weeks. There wasn't enough room at the house so they'd piled in with Moira, who, despite any saltiness she might have been harboring for them, was beyond thrilled to have them there. They spent most of their time at Cara and Brendan's, however, staying well past when Micah was put down for bed, sitting out in the sun on the porch or gathered around the fire circle down toward the beach.

"He's very handsome," Stanley said on one such evening toward the end of their stay, throwing another log on the fire. Brendan and Lucia were inside—Brendan asleep, Lucia cleaning—giving Cara, Drew, and Stanley some alone time.

"Micah?" Cara asked.

"Your husband," Stanley said. "Very handsome man."

"He is. I agree."

Cara tried not to laugh. Drew wasn't so courteous.

"What the hell, Dad? Where did that just come from?"

"What? I'm just saying."

"Thank you, Dad. Brendan will be thrilled to know you think so," Cara said. Parents were so weird. And now she was one herself. "He's not my husband, though. Not yet."

"Are you going to have a wedding?" Drew asked.

"I mean, maybe. Yeah. But I literally just gave birth, so maybe give me some time?"

"Well, I for one hope you do get married," said Stanley. "When you're ready. And not just because I think it's the right thing to do, but because I like him. I think you got a good one."

Cara thanked him. It was nice to hear. Anyone who was around those first few days would have agreed. There was no denying that Brendan was going to make a great father. That he already *was* a great father. He was patient and gentle and, best of all, he already seemed to enjoy the act of parenting. It was almost as if he *liked* getting woken up in the middle of the night, simply because it gave him an excuse to hold his son.

But perhaps the biggest surprise had been Lucia, who had proven to be a quiet but invaluable source of support. Since she'd arrived, Lucia had done all of the shopping, cooking, and cleaning, always making sure there was something to eat for breakfast and never minding it when people preferred to grab and graze rather than sit down for a meal. She taught Cara the best way to dispose of diapers and was there to snatch up a dirty spit-up cloth or onesie at a moment's notice, running loads of laundry and leaving items folded on the bed that very same day. She was so wonderful, Cara found herself wondering how they would manage without her when she left, a feeling she never would have expected.

They heard shouts coming from the house. Cara stiffened. It was a man's voice. Her father and Drew were outside with her; it had to be Brendan—but Cara found herself praying it wasn't. Somehow, the possibility of an intruder felt less threatening than the alternative: Brendan having some kind of episode, here, now, with her family all there to witness it.

It was when she heard Micah crying that Cara really began to panic.

Her chest tightened and her arms went numb. She jumped up from her spot by the fire and bolted to the house. She heard her father and Drew calling after her, wondering what was the matter. Hadn't they heard the commotion?

When she got inside the house, Cara found Brendan and Lucia in the living area. Brendan was in his boxers, red-faced and glowering, with his knuckles clenched tightly over the top loop of his army backpack, which he dangled up by his shoulder. Lucia was backed up against the wall, arms up in surrender (or maybe it was defense), her hands visibly shaking. Cara glanced nervously over to the alcove where Micah had been sleeping, but was now screaming. She wanted to go to him, but felt paralyzed by the disorder of the scene in front of her.

"Oh, Cara. Thank goodness," Lucia whimpered, on the verge of tears. "I don't know what I did. Please help."

"*YOU* shut up," Brendan shouted, pointing at her in a rage.

"Brendan!" Cara said, snapping to face him. "What is *with* you?"

"She's a fucking spy!" Brendan said. "I caught her red-handed. Going through my shit." He threw his bag to the ground.

Stanley and Drew came in then. Lucia ran to Stanley and collapsed into his arms, twitching with every sob.

"What's going on?"

"Dad, just—get her out of here," Cara ordered. "In fact, all of you should just go. I'll take care of this. Just go back to Moira's. We can sort this out tomorrow."

"I don't understand. What happened?" Stanley sounded bewildered.

"I was just trying to do some laundry—"

"Oh, like hell you were," Brendan cut in before Lucia could finish.

"Brendan, *stop*," Cara said, trying to push him away from Lucia. His body felt stiff with obstinance. "Please, everyone just go. *Please.*"

"What about the baby?" Lucia asked. "Can we take him with us?"

"Don't you fucking touch him," Brendan sneered.

"He's okay," Cara said, hoping she was right. "I'll take care of him. Can you all please just go. I'll handle this."

"Yes. We're going," said Drew, practically pushing Lucia and Stanley out the door.

"But what about you?" Stanley asked from the doorway. "Are *you* okay?"

"I'm fine. I'll be fine," said Cara, though she wasn't sure. Brendan had had episodes before, to be sure, but never quite like this. And then there was the story of Brendan's father, a narrative that seemed to follow them wherever they went like a shadow, a warning sign. Did Brendan have it in him to kill? As a member of the military, she could only assume that he had. She'd never dared to ask him. What if she hadn't interrupted him and Lucia in time? And what about her own safety?

It was only when they heard the car engine start that Brendan seemed to relax. Cara ran to Micah and held him, rocking him and making shushing sounds to try to calm him. She looked him over for signs of distress—scrapes, bruises, spit-up, rashes—but there were none. He was fine, just tired. And probably scared.

Brendan was at the window, watching the car pull out of the driveway.

"What the hell was that, Brendan? What's gotten into you?"

"That woman was going through my things," Brendan said. "I *caught her* doing it."

"So what? Maybe she was looking for something. She said something about laundry . . . I don't know."

"No, she was looking for documentation."

"What?"

"She works for someone. I know it. I knew from the moment she walked in."

"*Lucia?*"

"Where'd you say she was from again? Colombia?"

"Ecuador. What does it matter?"

"I wouldn't believe that."

"Are you serious right now?"

"She tried to take Micah, too. You heard her."

Cara was lost for words. Nothing Brendan was saying made any sense. She wanted to shake him. She wanted to scream and cry and pound these crazy thoughts out of him herself. She felt so angry and frustrated and, most of all, exasperated. Because she couldn't fight it anymore. She couldn't go on downplaying the reality of the situation. She'd spent so much mental energy trying to convince herself that Brendan's odd behaviors could all be explained by benign or surmountable causes, but she'd run out of excuses with this one.

How had she managed to maintain this state of denial for so long? She told herself it was because she loved Brendan. The real Brendan, at least, not the person who was standing in front of her right now. This was someone else, and she'd finally reached the sad conclusion that arguing with him was never going to bring the real Brendan back.

"Let's just go to sleep," she said. "Can we do that?"

"We should probably check and make sure she didn't take anything else."

"I'll check," Cara said. "I promise. She's gone now and she won't be coming back. We don't have to worry."

"How can you be sure?"

"Because I told them not to come back. They're gone forever. We're safe now."

Cara knew better than to try to argue with him. It was like telling the little kids she used to babysit for that she'd checked the closet for ghosts. It was no use trying to explain to them that ghosts weren't real. Better just to tell them that you'd looked, and the coast was clear. The last thing she wanted was to upset him further.

241

After she'd fed Micah and put Brendan to bed, Cara sat with the sleeping baby in the rocker on the porch and stared out into the night. There were no stars visible, just an opaque, glowing grayness. Just a few weeks ago, she'd had her future all planned out. Now she couldn't see more than a few feet in front of her.

E arly the next morning, while Brendan was still sleeping, Cara scooped up Micah and took the car to Moira's. Her family was leaving that afternoon, and she wanted to say good-bye, and to apologize for the night before. She hated that their visit had ended this way. It had started off so well, and they'd come so close to making it through the visit without a hitch. If only Brendan could have waited another twenty-four hours to have his breakdown. Then no one would have been the wiser about his affliction, and Cara could have kept on pretending that everything was fine, that Brendan wasn't completely delusional.

She had to coach herself through the door, whispering out loud to herself that she could do this. It was just her family. She was going to be okay.

She felt better when she saw the five of them, all sitting in the den, drinking coffee and sharing a plate of muffins. Lucia was the first to approach her.

"Oh, there you are. We've been so worried."

Cara let Lucia hug her and passed off Micah, taking a seat in the high-backed chair near the fireplace. She noticed the suitcases, packed and ready at the bottom of the stairs.

"I'm so sorry, you guys. I'm so embarrassed."

She waited for them to tell her that it was okay—not to worry about it.

242

"Brendan struggles with PTSD," she tried to explain. "He has these moments sometimes where he just isn't himself. I think it has to do with things that he's experienced on duty. He's never told me what, but it's clearly affected him. I mean, we all saw it."

Cara had no idea if any of this was true, but what else could she say? She didn't want her family to think badly of Brendan. She wanted them to love him for all the same reasons she did, and it seemed they had been starting to until everything went so horribly wrong.

"I don't know, Care," Stanley said. "I'm not so sure this was PTSD. This was different."

"Isn't PTSD more like nightmares and stuff?" Drew asked.

"Well, yeah. That can be part of it," Cara started, suddenly acting like an expert, "but sometimes you can have these delusions too. Think you're somewhere you're not."

She was pretty sure she'd seen that in a movie, a character in a shopping mall who freaked out at the sound of the theft detection system going off. She wanted to convince them that this was what had happened to Brendan. He'd been triggered somehow. They couldn't fault him for that.

"I'm telling you, honey. This doesn't sound like that. Lucia, tell her what happened."

"Well, you all were outside by the fire, so I figured I'd stay behind and clean up a few more things before we left for the night," Lucia began. "I remembered how Micah had spit up on our walk by the beach, and I wanted to find the little bib Brendan had used to clean it up. Since he'd brought his backpack with him, I wondered if maybe he'd stuffed it in there. I didn't mean to snoop—I was just looking for the bib. I promise.

"And that's when Brendan came up behind me. He said"—she paused, lowering her voice—"he said, 'What the *f-word* do you think you're doing?'

"And so I told him, I was looking for this bib. And then he just went off on me, calling me a liar and a rat and a spy, and saying all these things I couldn't even understand about me being some kind of informant or agent or something. It was very strange. None of it made any sense. And he was angry as he said it. Really, really angry. His face was red and he was coming at me like he might hurt me. I was afraid."

"Does he do that sometimes?" Stanley asked Cara. "Get really angry really quickly?"

He said it in a gentle, cautious voice that made Cara want to scream. She knew what they were thinking. They'd come up with the idea that because he was angry last night, Brendan must have an anger problem, that he must be abusive, and that Cara was the quietly suffering victim of his abuse, too afraid to say anything about it.

But that wasn't it at all. Brendan had never hurt her. Up until last night, Brendan's behaviors had been worrisome and perplexing, yes, but never quite so frightening and never violent. This was an exception. They needed to understand that.

"No, he doesn't," Cara snapped. "He's never been violent like this. I'm telling you. He's just . . . he just . . . I think he needs some help. And I will make sure he gets it. Okay? And I know last night was weird, but please try to cut him some slack. It was a weird moment and I know he's sorry. Can we please just pretend like this never happened?"

"Cara . . ." Her dad shot her a look of pity.

"You were just telling me yesterday how much you liked him, Dad. Remember? He's still that same guy, he just needs a little help. And he'll get it. I know he will."

"We just want to make sure you and Micah are safe," Moira chimed in. "That's all that matters."

"And we are. I am telling you, we are," Cara said.

She surprised herself by how defensive she suddenly was of Brendan. She'd been so mad at him yesterday, and even this morning when she'd left the house. And now here she was sticking up for him, shrugging off last night's events like they were no big deal. Just an isolated incident. It was as if she'd forgotten about the fear, and the worry, and the striking revelation she'd had with regard to Brendan's mental state. Here, now, with her family, she only wanted to defend him. Maybe if she could just convince them that everything was okay, it would be.

She wished they had more time. She'd finally gotten them all together in one place, finally gotten her dad and Drew back to the Vineyard, and now any memory they had of the visit would be tarnished by this one unfortunate occurrence. It was devastating.

She knew she could probably convince them to stay. All she had to do was indulge in the story they'd created of her being a poor innocent victim in need of help and protection. But they'd been there two weeks already, and Cara was tired. As much as she longed to spend more time with her family, she also craved the quiet predictability of routine, and wondered if that was maybe what Brendan needed too. The two of them had hardly been alone with Micah yet, and she knew it was time for them to give the parenting thing a go on their own.

When she got back to the house, Brendan was asleep on the couch with his head tipped back and his mouth wide open. Even in this less than flattering pose, a rumbling snore coming out of his throat, she couldn't help but marvel at his athletic physique. His shoulders. His hands. His neck.

She rested Micah in his car seat down on the floor and snuggled up next to Brendan, nudging him awake. He flashed her a sleepy smile.

"Hi, you." Brendan wrapped his arms tight around Cara, pulling her close.

"Hi."

"Your family leave?"

"Yeah."

"Are you sad?"

"A little."

"Where's the little guy?"

Cara pointed to the floor. "It's just us now," she said. "You ready for this?"

"Baby, I was born ready."

2014

Jimmy Coughlin is young, maybe twenty-one, twenty-two. His hair is light and wavy and he still has a spattering of youthful freckles across his cheeks. He's right where Dean said he would be when Cara finds him, sitting at the bar at the Wharf in Edgartown, a half-eaten Reuben sandwich with fries and a Sam Adams on the counter in front of him.

Cara sits down on the stool next to him.

"Hey, you're Jimmy, right?"

Jimmy swallows his bite and nods, looking bewildered as to why this slender, green-eyed woman is interrupting his lunch.

"My name's Cara. I'm a friend of Dean's."

"Okay . . ."

"Listen, I have a question for you that might sound kind of weird, but it's really important that you tell me everything you can."

The boy shrugs. He looks nervous, as if he's about to be accused of a crime or something.

"Dean was telling me that you saw something the other day. Over by Gull's Ledge. Can you tell me about that?"

Jimmy's shoulders relax and his face brightens with excitement. "Oh, yeah, it was wicked bizarre! We're out there trolling and I swear I see what looks like two people swimming out in the middle of the ocean. So my buddy Sean gets the binoculars out, and sure enough, it's a guy and a boy. I could see their faces, clear as day. But the crazy thing is, there wasn't another boat in sight. We figured they must have had an accident or something. So we started to motor closer. So we could help. And then they just went under. Just like that. *Boom*. They were gone."

"But there were two of them? You're sure?"

"Definitely, yeah. You a reporter or something? Am I gonna be in the *Gazette*?"

"And it was definitely a man and a boy?"

"I mean, I'm shit at telling people's ages, but one of them was small, like a little kid. A fuckin' kid, out there in the water. Unbelievable."

Cara feels a burst of adrenaline. "And that was it. They went in the water and never came back up, right?"

"Well, as far as we could see. I'm not suggesting they were fucking mermaids or something. Don't make me look crazy. But it was weird, you know? Them being so far out there, with no boats around. And then they disappeared. All of a sudden. Just gone, beneath the waves. You know if the coast guard ever found anything? Like an abandoned boat or somethin'?"

"I don't know. Sorry."

Cara thanks him and gets up to leave.

"Hey, make sure you don't make me look crazy, okay? We fishermen got a bad rap as it is."

Cara waves and heads out the door.

2009

"I think he's like me."

It was late. Or early, depending on how you looked at it. Cara and Brendan had both given up on sleep and were sitting in the living area, staring at their own tired, gray reflections in the window. Cara couldn't remember the last time she'd showered. Her scalp itched and her nipples were raw. She rubbed her eyes and yellow flecks came off her lashes.

"What do you mean?"

"I mean, what if he somehow inherited it?"

"Inherited what?"

Cara was getting annoyed. She wished he'd just say what he wanted to say, instead of speaking in code words.

"You know . . ."

"No, Brendan. I don't know. What are you trying to say?"

249

"I mean, what if his lungs are like mine? What if he can breathe underwater too?"

"He's not."

"I think he is."

"Brendan, that makes no sense."

"But he's crying all the time. I think something's wrong."

"It's colic. We already know this."

"I know that's what they said. But I'm not so sure."

"Brendan, I promise you our baby didn't inherit your . . . whatever you want to call it. Which, by the way, you were not born with. So it would actually be impossible for Micah to inherit it."

"You don't know that."

"Pretty sure I do. You can't just inherit something that's not in your genes. That's like saying a baby can be born with holes in its earlobes because its mom has pierced ears. Your thing was surgical, Brendan. It can't be passed down."

"But when a mom does drugs, that affects the baby, right?" Brendan argued. "They gave me *injections.* Of I don't even know what. For a year."

"I am so done with this conversation." . . . .

"I'm serious. I'm worried about him."

"Okay, fine. Let's say you're right. Let's say Micah does have superhuman lungs and can breathe underwater. Why would that be the thing making him cry? What does one have to do with the other?"

"I think it's painful for him. The way he's growing. And have you looked under his arms? It looks really red."

"Okay, now you just sound crazy."

"That's not fair." His face darkened. "Don't fucking call me crazy."

Cara sighed. "I know, I know. I'm sorry. I shouldn't have said that. I think we're both just really, really tired. Let's try to get some sleep and we can talk about this tomorrow."

They went to bed after that, for a few hours at least, and the subject didn't come up again—not right away. It stuck with Cara though. One morning she actually found herself checking Micah's armpits, rubbing her fingers along the soft crease to look for abnormalities. His skin did look a little red. She grabbed some cream and gently massaged it into the soft pink flesh. When she was done, she stood back and looked down at her wiggly little boy, who for the moment actually seemed content.

"Mommy is losing her mind," she said in a baby voice, wiggling his feet with her fingers.

The fact that she'd even for a second let herself believe Brendan's theory was so completely ridiculous, she had to laugh at herself. It was amazing what sleep deprivation could do to you.

But that wasn't the end of it.

It happened in the afternoon. Micah had been much better lately, so Cara had planned a day out in Oak Bluffs with Moira. It was actually just a day of errands, with a stop for brunch on Circuit Avenue, but she had really been looking forward to it. She took a shower that morning, blow-dried her hair, and even put on some makeup. She was feeling good.

They spent most of the morning shopping. Cara bought Micah a onesie that read *We're gonna need a bigger boat* on the butt, with the *Jaws* logo on the front, and picked up a pair of earrings for herself. After a delicious brunch—a barbecue bacon cheeseburger with fries for Cara and huevos rancheros for Moira—they took a walk through Ocean Park, licking ice cream cones as they admired the iconic "gingerbread" houses, rows of Victorian-style homes with ornately trimmed roofs and porches in a rainbow of pastels.

Cara felt a little guilty for enjoying herself so much. She loved Micah more than anything, but it was nice to get a break from the poop and the crying and the staleness that seemed to have overtaken their house. And Brendan had finally agreed to see a psychiatrist, which made her feel more comfortable relaxing and indulging in a day off.

It was the Lucia episode that had done it. It was the motivation Cara needed to stand her ground and say what needed to be said: if Brendan wanted Cara and Micah to remain with him in the house, he needed to get help. There was no other option. Either he agreed to consult with a doctor, or she was going with Micah to live with her dad and Lucia in Arizona.

"I'm only saying this because I love you and I'm worried about you," she'd said. "I've been worried for a while now, and I just think it would help if you talked to someone. Someone who can help us understand why you've been having these episodes."

She'd stopped there, ready with a full list of evidence to support her assertion if she needed it—a full rundown of all the times she could remember when Brendan had acted strangely or given her pause, including his most recent suspicions regarding Micah.

But she hadn't needed it after all. Much to Cara's surprise, Brendan had nodded and agreed, without stipulation. He said he would see someone. Figure out how to manage his anxiety. That's what he'd called it—his anxiety—as if it were nothing more.

That was two days ago. This morning he'd gotten up with Micah and let Cara sleep in. When she woke up around nine, he'd cleaned up the living room and put a fresh load of laundry away. He told her he'd found a psychiatrist. His first appointment was on Thursday.

The relief Cara felt upon hearing these words was all-encompassing. This was what she needed: reassurance that someone else would be looking after Brendan. It was no longer her responsibility—and hers alone—to observe his behavior and somehow determine what was normal and what wasn't, all the while creating narratives in her head about what might be wrong with him. She didn't know. She wasn't trained to diagnose what might be troubling him

No. The issue would soon be in the hands of an expert, as it should be. Cara had done what she could do. The warning lights that had been flashing for months were finally beginning to fade. Perhaps now she could focus more on being a good mother to her son, instead of stressing about Brendan.

But the feeling was fleeting. Once again, she'd relaxed too soon.

When Cara got home, there was Brendan, hovering over a screaming Micah in the bathtub. They'd never bathed Micah in the tub before; he was still too little. Besides, he had his own little tub that fit right in the sink.

Even from the doorway, Cara could tell that there was way too much water in the tub. It was filled to the brim, practically overflowing. The sight of it incited a panic in her so strong she could hardly feel her fingers and toes. Because the instant she saw them, she knew what was happening. She knew exactly what Brendan was doing.

"Give him to me," she demanded, rushing over to the tub. She grabbed Micah from Brendan, who calmly let her take him, and pulled up the bottom of her sweatshirt to dry the baby off and warm him up.

"What the fuck were you thinking?" she asked, her heart still thumping. "You could have killed him. Do you understand that?"

"He can do it, Cara," Brendan said. "I know you think I'm crazy, but he can do it."

"Stop it. Stop talking like that. I don't want to hear it. I'm not going to sit here and listen to your wild delusions and act like they're normal anymore."

"I know you don't believe me, but I'm telling you he can do it. I had to try it. I *had* to, and I was right. It was incredible. You should see it."

Brendan followed Cara around the house as she gathered what she needed—a towel for Micah, a duffel bag, diapers, her phone charger. She couldn't even look at him, she was so furious. She grabbed the keys from the counter.

"We're leaving."

"Please don't."

"You've left me no choice. *You could have killed him*," she said again.

"I'm worried, Cara," Brendan said, frantic. "I think they might be tracking me. Have you noticed anything weird? A device?"

He started running his hands and fingers down his forearms, as if feeling for lumps.

"Brendan, you need help."

"And I told you I would get help. I'm going to get help. I promise I won't do this again. I just needed to know. I'm sorry, but I had to know. Please just don't tell Moira. Don't tell her what I told you. Don't tell anyone. I'm serious. If they find out, they'll take him. He'll be stuck in a lab for the rest of his life."

He grabbed her wrist now, just as she was getting out the door.

"Promise me you won't tell."

"I won't tell," Cara spat, pulling her arm away. She headed to the car, hurriedly fastened Micah into his car seat, and drove away.

This was it. There was no going back this time. At least, that's what Cara told Moira and Ed when she arrived at the house. It was one thing for Brendan to act out toward Lucia. It was another thing entirely for him to put Micah's life in danger in the way that he had.

"There was way too much water in the tub," Cara said as she explained to them what had happened. "He easily could have drowned."

"Do you think he maybe just didn't realize?"

"No, this was one hundred percent intentional," Cara said. "He knew what he was doing. He wanted to see what would happen if he put Micah's head underwater. Thank god I walked in when I did."

"But why would he do that?" Moira asked.

Cara hesitated. In her fervor, she'd forgotten that Moira and Ed knew nothing about Brendan's secret, a secret Cara no longer knew whether or not she believed. But how much context should she be sharing?

Fuck it, she thought. Cara was tired of protecting Brendan's secret. "There's something I never told you," she began. "About Brendan."

Moira scooted her chair closer and rested a hand on Cara's knee. "Is he hurting you?"

"No, no, no. It's nothing like that. It's . . ."

She started over.

"Okay, this is going to sound really crazy, but just try to listen."

Moira nodded and waited.

"So I told you Brendan is in the Special Forces, right?"

"Right . . ."

"Well, as part of that he's had some things done to him that make him . . . different."

"Different how?"

"I don't know how to say this without sounding completely insane, so I'm just going to say it. Brendan can breathe underwater. They did an operation on him a couple of years ago, and then they injected him with these special steroids that somehow made it possible for him to do this. There are these slits, under his arms, that filter the water."

Every word that came out of Cara's mouth made her less and less confident in the story she was telling. Every syllable felt awkward and misshapen, as if her voice wasn't hers, but someone else's.

"And you believe this?"

Cara searched her aunt's face for clues as to how she might be processing what Cara had just told her. Was she incredulous or curious? Supportive or concerned? If anyone in the world was going to believe her, it would be Moira, but maybe this was too much. Surely even Moira was astute enough to detect nonsense when she heard it.

"I don't know," Cara said. And she didn't. What she wanted to say was, *Of course not*. Of course she didn't believe such a ludicrous tale. Any sane human being would agree that there was absolutely no way Brendan's claims could be true.

But up until recently, Cara *had* believed it. She'd seen it with her own eyes.

Hadn't she?

"I think . . . I think it could be," Cara admitted. "If it's not true, then he's really good at holding his breath because I've seen it, Moira. I've seen him do it. At least, I think so. I'm so confused now, I don't even know what's true anymore, and the more I talk about it out loud, the more I doubt myself. But at one point, I did believe him. I'll admit that. But now he thinks Micah might be able to breathe underwater too, and that's what's worrying me. He was testing him. He was putting our poor baby's head under the water, to test him and see if he could breathe. And so maybe Brendan can breathe underwater. Fine. Maybe that is true, maybe it's not. But the notion that Micah possibly could too is just crazy."

"And so what happened?"

"What?"

"This afternoon. When Brendan tested Micah. What happened?"

"Well, I caught him just in time, thank god. So he's fine now. But he was screaming when I walked in."

Cara glanced over at Micah, now asleep in the old bassinet they kept at Moira and Ed's house.

"So you stopped him, before he had a chance to test his theory."

"No, I think he actually did it," Cara said. "Micah's hair was all wet when I walked in."

"And . . . ?"

"And what?"

"Could he, in fact, breathe underwater?"

"Well, no. I mean, I didn't see it, but—I mean, Brendan said he did, but I don't . . . it's impossible."

"But Brendan believes he can."

"I guess so, yeah. I was rushing out of there so I was hardly listening to him, I was so mad, but yeah. He told me he could do it. That I should have seen it. You don't believe that, do you?"

"You said you believed that Brendan could breathe underwater," Moira pointed out.

"Yeah . . . ?"

"So why not Micah?"

Cara laughed, incredulous.

"Because, Brendan's explanation actually seemed plausible. He's in the military, they did surgery on him, I saw the openings under his arms, and I've seen him underwater. But the idea that Micah could magically somehow inherit the same ability . . . that seems like a stretch."

"Brendan's personal story was unbelievable, and yet you believed it," Moira said. "You opened up your mind to the impossible once. What's holding you back from doing it again?"

Cara slept like a rock. She dreamt that she was underwater, swimming through a world of glowing green light and cursive plant life swirling all around her. Her father was there. And Lucia. And Drew. And Lindsay. And Zach. They were all swimming back up to the surface, moving in the direction of the daylight. She wanted to go with them, but her foot was tangled in seaweed. It was slimy but delicate-looking, and it should have been easy to break apart with her hands, but she couldn't seem to rupture it. She kept pulling on it with her fingers, using her fingernails to try to cut herself free, yet she remained tethered, despite the natural buoyancy of her body, which continued to pull her upward toward the others.

She realized, then, that Brendan was there too. He was swimming around freely, doing flips and spins and gliding through the water with ease. He invited Cara to join him and she told him she couldn't, that she was trapped by the seaweed, unable to move from her place at the bottom. Brendan told her she just needed to pull harder. If she just pulled a little harder, the weed would break. It wasn't that strong.

It was at this moment in the dream that Cara remembered that she couldn't breathe underwater like Brendan could. He was safe down there, but she was not. She started to panic, pulling and pulling on the seaweed as hard as she could, all the while worrying that she was exerting too much energy. She was going to run out of air soon. She was going to drown. Any minute now she was going to have to give in to the water, opening up her passageways and allowing it to infiltrate her body.

Shouldn't she have passed out by now? She must be dreaming. She *was* dreaming. None of this was real. She just needed to wake herself up.

Sunlight was streaming through the window when she opened her eyes. She checked the alarm clock on the nightstand: 8:35 a.m. This was late for her. Micah was always up by now. But he was quiet. Now that she thought of it, she couldn't remember having to wake up for him at all during the night. He would likely be starving by now.

The wood floor felt cold on her feet as she stepped out of bed and tiptoed over to Micah's crib. But he wasn't in there. More confused than alarmed, Cara considered the possibilities. Moira must have gotten him up. But how could she have done so without waking Cara? It had been an exhausting week, but still, it seemed unlikely for her not to have been roused.

Cara threw on a hoodie and sweatpants and headed downstairs. Uncle Ed was sitting in his recliner, reading the *Vineyard Gazette*. She asked him where Moira was, and he directed her to the sun porch.

"Oh, there you are," Moira said when she saw her. "Where's my little one?"

"I thought he was with you."

Cara remained calm, though she could feel the hair on her arms beginning to prickle. Surely there had been a misunderstanding.

"I woke up and he wasn't in his crib. Did you maybe move him in the night?"

"No, Bear, I never got out of bed until this morning, maybe around about six thirty?"

"And you didn't get him up?"

"No. I assumed you were both sleeping. Didn't hear a peep out of him all night. You're sure he's not in his crib?"

Cara's chest felt tight. "Would Ed maybe have gotten him up? Uncle Ed?" She hurried back to the living room. "Uncle Ed, you didn't by any chance move Micah last night, did you? Or get him up this morning? Did you check on him? At all?"

"No, dear. Was I meant to?"

Cara pivoted and ran up the stairs, skipping steps along the way. She swung open the door to her room—her mom's old room—and peered once again into the crib they'd put Micah down in last night. She was rifling through the blankets, as if he could somehow be hidden beneath them, when Moira entered the room. Cara felt something hard under the blanket.

"What is this?" she asked, holding the object up for Moira to see.

"Looks like a little whale."

"I know what it is, but where did it come from? Did you give him this?"

Moira shrugged. "Never seen it in my life."

But Cara knew what the whale was, and she knew how it had gotten there. This was a message, from Brendan. Somehow he'd managed to sneak into the room in the middle of the night, lift baby Micah from his crib, and steal him away without waking a soul. This whale was his way of letting Cara know it had been him. That Micah was okay. Of course, the idol was hardly reassuring.

"He took him," Cara whispered, sinking down to her knees. "Brendan. He was here. He took Micah."

259

"You think so? Would he do that?"

"I know so. He's sneaked in here before. He knows which room it is. He knows how to get in."

"But why would he do this?"

"He's scared people will find out about Micah. He thinks Micah has his gift, and he's scared people will come after him. He said something yesterday about Micah having to spend the rest of his life in a lab. I have to get back to the house."

But Brendan and Micah were not at the house. Nor were many of Micah's favorite things—his blankie, his pacifier, his onesie with the lobsters on it. While most of Brendan's things were still there, a number of his personal items were missing, including his backpack, the very same one he'd accused Lucia of rifling through. Desperate, Cara yanked open cabinets and searched under furniture.

After looking everywhere she possibly could, she headed outside, leaving Moira in the house while she searched under the porch and made her way down to the beach hoping to stumble upon any trace of them. Then she got back in the car and drove to Squibnocket, and Gay Head, and Menemsha, clinging to the hope that she might still discover them strolling down the beach or bobbing together in the water.

The water. This was what she feared the most. What if Brendan, in his desperation to protect their son, had retreated to the water? The ocean was Brendan's ultimate hiding spot; it was dark and expansive. It was where he went when he needed to be alone. Because he could. And now he seemed to believe that Micah could too.

That was what terrified Cara: the thought that Brendan, in his delusional state, could have brought Micah into the water with him. Her sweet baby Micah, drowned as a result of his own father's insanity. Never mind the fact that Micah was only a few weeks old. As if on cue, Cara's breasts started to throb. She needed to pump. Micah, wherever he was, needed to eat.

She went back into the house to splash cold water on her face, only to find the kitchen sink covered in blood, a knife discarded next to the drain. What could possibly have left so much blood? And whose was it? Horrified, Cara prayed that the blood was Brendan's.

She couldn't wait any longer. She ran to the phone and called the police.

When the officers got to the house, Cara was in a daze. They wanted to know what made her think it was the father. But Cara didn't even know how to begin answering them. Was she really going to sit there and tell them the whole story? So she told them about the whale—how Brendan had always had a fascination with the creatures, how he even had a giant tattoo of one down the length of his back. The figurine had been a message. He wanted her to know it was him.

They asked her where she thought Brendan might have taken Micah, as if she hadn't just gotten back from searching all of those places. So she told them to check the water, which of course raised further questions that she didn't know how to answer. She explained that Brendan had been subject to advanced military training. That if he didn't want to be found, he was highly skilled at ensuring that he wasn't. That he was particularly strong at diving. Could hold his breath for minutes on end.

"But there's more," Moira cut in. "Tell them, Bear. Tell them what you told me. They need to know."

Cara shot Moira a look. Was she really going to make her say it? What good would that do?

"If you've got more information that could help us in our investigation, I suggest you share it," the officer speaking with them said. He was young, and tall, with coarse strawberry-blond hair that looked like it would grow up and out instead of down if he ever let it get long.

Cara knew that if she wanted the authorities to have any chance at finding her son, they would need to search the water. And not just the surface, but under it. Below it. Within it.

She should probably just tell them the truth. If she did, this cop, the one with the crooked teeth and the Brillo pad hair, might just laugh in her face. But he might also check out the story, contact Brendan's unit and report him missing. And then maybe, just maybe, he would mention the bit about Brendan's wild claim. Just to be safe, just to be sure. And then, at last, Cara might know the truth about Brendan. She might know if the story was real.

"Brendan used to claim he could breathe underwater," she said at last. "It sounds silly, I know, but that's what he said. He said the military did a special surgery on him, gave him gills. And now he thinks our son can too, that he inherited the same ability."

The cop turned to the woman in uniform next to him and muttered something about the National Guard. The woman left the room, pulling a cell phone from her belt.

"Ma'am, was this pretty common for your husband? To make claims like this?"

"He's not my husband."

"Pardon me. Was it common for Brendan to make claims like this? Was this the only super ability he claimed to possess, or were there more?"

Cara wanted to laugh. She could think of any number of "super abilities" Brendan might claim to possess. Like being a super lover or a super dancer or a super father.

"No. No, it was just the one thing."

"And did he say or do something specific that led you to believe he might think your son possessed this ability too?"

"Yes. He said, 'I think he's like me,' and then yesterday I caught him trying to test out his theory in the bathtub."

"What about the sink? The blood. Any idea where that came from?"

"I don't know. Brendan had mentioned something about a tracking device. I once saw him feel along his arms for it, like it might be embedded under his skin. I'm wondering if, maybe, he was trying to get it out before he left, so no one would find him."

"Did you find any such device?"

"No, no. It's just an idea. Wishful thinking, maybe, I don't know. I'm just praying it's not Micah's blood," Cara said, collapsing into tears.

The cop sighed and shook his head, almost as if in apology to Cara. *You poor thing*, it said. *You poor thing for having to live with such a lunatic.*

"We'll get the blood tested," he said.

"Just promise me you'll check the water," Cara said, struggling to regain her composure. "You need to search *in* the water."

"We'll do everything we can do get your son back," he said.

"Are you going to call the army? Or Brendan's commander, or whatever? Maybe they can help."

"We've been in touch with his unit. Apparently Captain McGrath has been AWOL for a few months now."

This shouldn't have been shocking news to Cara, but it was. For as long as she'd been with him, Brendan had made it seem like he was still very much an active member of the military. The idea that he could have been hiding away with her on the island this whole time, without anyone else knowing, was astonishing.

But then, Cara had never met anyone else who knew Brendan. No friends, no family. As far as she'd known, she and Micah were the only people in his life. And now, it seemed, they were the only people who had known where he was.

"Is there anywhere specific that you think Captain McGrath may have taken the child? Any meaningful location or place you can remember him mentioning?"

"No. He never mentioned anything. But you need to check the water. If I know Brendan, that's where he'll be."

"I hear you, ma'am. It's just . . . well . . . the ocean's a pretty big place. . . ."

"Then get a helicopter. Circle the island with a submarine. I don't care how you do it, please just promise me you'll look for them. *Please.* Please find them."

Sensing her fatigue, the man passed Cara his card. Told her to call him if she thought of anything else—anything that might help them narrow the search.

But she could see in his face, and in the faces of his colleagues, that it was a lost cause. She imagined them talking about it back at the station, openly sharing their repulsion at the story Cara had shared. What kind of father would do a thing like that—hold his infant son underwater, just to see what would happen? A sick one. A deranged one. With that kind of setup, they might as well just sit back and wait for the bodies to wash up.

I t was almost three weeks to the day following Brendan and Micah's disappearance that Cara started drawing. She'd found a half dozen sticks of compressed charcoal in an old makeup bag and managed to locate a sketchbook she hadn't yet filled.

For days she'd been sitting alone in the house doing nothing. Sitting. Staring into space. Waiting. Her breasts ached. Her limbs felt numb. Any notion of time or space had disappeared. She had nowhere she wanted to go and no one she wanted to see. With Brendan and Micah gone, her life had been whittled down to pure, solid nothingness. Her only social interaction came via daily visits from Moira, who'd come by with food, toilet paper, and trashy magazines that Cara never read. After returning each day to find her home-cooked dishes uneaten, Moira eventually started bringing the only things Cara seemed to be eating these days: milk, cereal, string cheese, peanut butter, jelly, and bread.

Cara turned the charcoal piece on its side and dragged it down the page, leaving a staticky trail of black and gray. When she got to the bottom of the page, she started at the top again, rendering a new column. And another, and another, until the page was full. Then she repeated the process all over again, making the page darker and blacker with every sweep of the mineral to the paper. Little flecks of black crumbs started to fall off on the page. Her fingertips looked charred, the half-moons of her fingernails filled with black.

There was a soothing monotony to the task that allowed Cara's thoughts to wander in a way that was cathartic. She kept going, page after page after page, until her arms and legs were smeared with charcoal and the sketchbook was filled. Craving further release, she searched the house for more supplies, only to find she'd gone through the last of her paints weeks ago. All she was able to locate was a pack of crayons, a handful of pens, and a legal notepad.

So for the first time in weeks, Cara grabbed her keys from the dish on the counter and headed into town. She drove straight to EduComp and gathered all the supplies she could carry—oil paints, acrylics, canvases, colored pencils, charcoal, sketchbooks, paintbrushes, and sponges. She didn't know what she wanted to make, so she bought it all, making sure she'd have everything she needed all in one place.

"Are you enrolling in an art program?" the salesperson who checked her out wanted to know, surveying the quantity of supplies she'd purchased. Cara said no, just starting a new project. And just like that, she was back in the car, retreating to the seclusion of her home.

Moira couldn't understand why Cara would want to spend so much time alone at the house. It wasn't healthy to sit in there all day, she said. Too many memories, too many triggers. But Cara saw things differently. The house was the only thing she had left. It was the only thing in her life that was truly hers. It was her only connection to Brendan and Micah, and she wasn't ready to let it go.

Everyone kept telling her that she should get out of there. Get a fresh start. Hit the proverbial reset button. This was her opportunity for a "do-over." Do things over, but this time, go straight to New York, get a real job, don't fall in love with a mentally disturbed person, and don't get pregnant.

Of course, this magical opportunity for a reset was contingent upon believing that Brendan and Micah were gone forever, and that they weren't coming back. And Cara didn't believe that. Not yet.

The wildest thing she ever considered doing was driving out to the prison where Brendan's dad was incarcerated. She figured it was possible that he might know something about Brendan's whereabouts. Maybe Brendan had even visited him. Moira and Ed were highly against this idea, and they didn't have to work hard to talk Cara out of it. In the end, she'd been too scared, preferring instead to lock herself away in her house and wait.

What she did do was google Brendan using the Chilmark Library Wi-Fi, populating the search bar of her laptop browser with the few small details he had told her about his family. The story about his dad checked out. She found posted PDFs of old print news articles announcing the sudden and shocking resolution to the cold case murder mystery. The details were disturbing, but reading them wasn't nearly as distressing as what Cara would soon discover.

The papers described Brendan's father as the husband of Michelle "Shelley" Stone, one of the heirs of the Stone family trust. Cara researched the Stone family and learned of their eminence during the Gilded Age as shipping industry tycoons. She googled the name of Brendan's mother again, Shelley Stone McGrath, seeking stories of her fatal car accident.

Instead, she encountered dozens of articles detailing a series of frightening public disturbances involving Shelley Stone, who reporters described as "suffering from severe mental illness." On one occasion, she had arrived at a CVS armed with kerosene and matches, claiming they were selling products that were "giving us all cancer." In another, she had been found pouring hydrogen peroxide on another person's naked child. When prompted to explain herself, Ms. Stone said she was "cleaning the child."

The most recent article that Cara could find reported that Shelley Stone was now living in a treatment facility outside Boston. There were no articles about the drunk driving accident that killed her, because there had been no accident. Cara wasn't even sure that she had been a drinker. But this detail hardly mattered. What mattered was that Shelley Stone, Brendan's mother, was still alive.

Brendan had lied to her. And it was a powerful lie. When Cara learned that Brendan had also lost his mother, she'd automatically, as if by instinct, felt an intimacy with him that she hadn't with other men. She'd felt he was capable of knowing her in ways that others couldn't. And now she wasn't sure how to feel. Because she was already suffering through the betrayal, and the abandonment, and the hurt. The pain couldn't get any worse than it already was.

What she did feel now, which she hadn't before, was a sense of clarity.

No one had explicitly said as much to Cara, nor had she openly acknowledged the suspicion to herself, but she knew now. Brendan was schizophrenic. The paranoia, the confusion, the bizarre episodes, and that book—the odd book she had found with strange drawings and clippings of navigation charts and whale migration patterns. It was a disease widely known to be hereditary, and Brendan's own mother had it.

She should have known, should have seen what was coming. And she *had* known, hadn't she? On some level? All of this could have been avoided—Micah might still be with her—if she had just listened to her gut instinct. If she had just had the strength, and confidence, and self-determination to break free of Brendan's spell. She had been weak. Scared. She had allowed this to happen, knowing that her actions were irrational.

But knowing was not the same as accepting or believing. Even now, she refused to say the words out loud, choosing not to share her discovery with Moira, her father, the police, or anyone else. Because if her fears were true, and Brendan did suffer from schizophrenia, the likelihood of her ever seeing her son alive again was very small. A child that young needed capable, competent care, which in his current mental state Brendan would not be able to provide.

And yet she waited, still somehow, in spite of it all, believing they might at any moment walk through the door. It was as if she could feel them, out there somewhere, floating in darkness, but still very much alive.

Cara lugged a two-by-three-foot canvas to the kitchen counter and used a stool, a paper towel holder, and duct tape to jerry-rig an easel. She squeezed globs of oil paint onto a dinner plate—blue, green, black, yellow—and started mixing. Satisfied with the color palette she'd created, she took to the canvas, brushing on the paint in thick, oily globs.

It wasn't like her to work like this. She couldn't remember a time she'd ever applied paint to canvas without first sketching out a plan in pencil. It felt freeing to do so now, unafraid of what the outcome might be. Because for the first time, it wasn't about the final product for Cara; it was about the process. She wasn't creating something in replica of a photograph or a true-to-life image. She was rendering the intersection of a feeling and a vision, a picture in her mind of a time and place that might not exist.

The painting came out dark and blue, textured with raised veins of green. The color at the bottom of the page was opaque and dank, but as the eye traveled upward it softened, making way for a thinner sheen of color at the top, a hinting of light through a musty veneer.

This was where Cara imagined Brendan and Micah to be, surrounded by the cold black, blue, and green hues she'd created on the canvas. In looking at the piece, the viewer could see the world as Cara felt Micah and Brendan were seeing it, surrounded by water, yet somehow safe, somehow protected.

The painting was the first of many Cara would make over the months to come, each one offering an illustration of where her child and first true love might be at a given moment. It connected her to them, and gave her a sense of purpose she'd been looking for since long before she ever met Brendan or welcomed her dear Micah into the world. Nothing would ever fill the void their disappearance had left, but at least, through her paintings, Cara was able to penetrate it, explore it, and open it up for the world to see.

2011

The invitation was addressed to a Dr. Ian Crowley. *Dr. Ian Crowley or Current Resident*, it read. Cara had lived in the house for two years now, and she was still getting Dr. Ian Crowley's mail. She'd made up a whole story about him in her head, deciding he was probably a well-to-do surgeon in Boston who'd used the old island bungalow as his getaway, the place he went when he needed space from his wife and children. Who knew? Perhaps it had even served as a secret rendezvous for him and his mistresses. A love nest.

On the front of the card was a watercolor painting depicting a series of items a beachcomber might find: a rusty fishing lure; a piece of sea glass the color of pistachio; a lost glove; a deep-purple shard of clamshell, its once sharp edges dulled by the sea; a yellowed, dried-out egg sac—a curved spine of hollow disks.

Spinnaker Gallery—Grand Reopening, it said in bold but simple typography, followed by the date in smaller letters. Cara turned the card over and immediately recognized the address. This was Graham's grand-father's gallery, the one he'd taken her to that time after work. She wondered if his family still owned it and if he was in any way involved.

She hadn't seen Graham since before Micah was born. She wasn't sure she could even remember the last time. There was no casual catch-up meeting or good-bye before he left. After Micah and Brendan disappeared, it had taken months for her to feel ready to interact with the world again. By that point Graham had moved on, she assumed to film school in New York, as he'd planned.

Even now, years after Brendan and Micah's disappearance, Cara's emotions continued to fluctuate. On the good days, she'd manage to get herself up and out of the house for work, or even just a moment of sunshine on the deck. On the bad days, she couldn't get out of bed. She'd come close to getting fired a few times from her gig as a server at the Crow's Nest, a job she'd held for over a year now. On the really bad days, she wished to fall asleep and never wake up. She had, on more than one occasion, considered swallowing a bottle of sleeping pills, des-perate for a reprieve from the perpetual pain and guilt she felt.

But today was a good day. She was surprised she hadn't heard any-thing about the gallery's reopening at the Crow's Nest. The work was mind-numbingly slow in the off-season and gruesomely busy in the summer, but she made enough money to cover her utility bills and liv-ing expenses, and the schedule allowed her plenty of time to draw and paint. The place was frequented by locals who always had news to share about the comings and goings of the island, but no one had mentioned the Spinnaker Gallery.

Gallery openings weren't really Cara's thing, and this one was sure to draw hordes of snobby tourists and wash-ashores. Work was her so-cial time. She put in her hours, went home, ate a comped meal out of a Styrofoam container, and painted until she fell asleep. Sometimes, if the weather was nice and she wasn't working dinner, she'd fit in an evening walk on the beach, but that was as wild as she got. *Maybe* after-work drinks with the other servers, but she generally stayed out of that too.

The summer staffers were all around her age, but she felt much older. She related better to colleagues like Sue and Dana, the seasoned Vineyard lifers fifteen years her senior who didn't have to write orders down and could tell you the name and penis size of every fisherman on the island. They were the only other two who waited tables year-round like Cara did.

But the gallery invitation intrigued her, for reasons she couldn't explain. And her schedule was open. And she had to admit, she liked the image on the card. She could go, enjoy the art, and leave. The crowd—assuming there was one—might even be a good thing. She could blend in more easily. Others were less likely to notice her in a large group.

She thought about inviting Moira to join her. Uncle Ed had passed away in his sleep just a month earlier. Moira would likely appreciate the chance to get out and see people. On second thought, maybe it wasn't a good idea to bring Moira. She'd no doubt want to say hi to everyone she knew, trapping Cara in a never-ending circle of small talk. No thank you. She would find something else to do with Moira. She would go alone.

On the night of the opening, she decided on a long, shapeless black dress. She wore no makeup and let her hair air-dry, something she never would have done just two years ago, but things had changed. The last thing she wanted was to stand out.

As expected, the place was busy. Very busy. She had to park on the street, a substantial walk away. Whoever owned the gallery now, it was clear they knew how to market its appeal. Dozens of patrons spilled out onto the lawn and the sculpture garden in back, balancing little clear plastic plates of hors d'oeuvres over the mouths of their wineglasses. Cara was quickly provided with a glass of wine of her own by one of the servers, whom she luckily did not recognize, nor they her. She turned her body sideways to squeeze through the crowded doorway and made her way as fast as she could to the corner of the space with the fewest people.

The main gallery was lovely, achieving the perfect balance between elegant modernity and rustic authenticity. There was an open airiness to the room that made it feel less crowded than it was, and the lighting set a calming mood while still flattering the artwork. She recognized the work of the artist from the invitation. It reminded Cara of her own work, at least the way it used to be, the way she'd always hoped it came off to onlookers. Of course, Cara's style had since changed in dramatic fashion. Her college self never would have believed she'd be making the kind of art she was now—thick, heavy-handed, and much more abstract. But she was prouder of it now. Maybe it was true that the more tortured the artist, the better the art. Cara's own suffering and loss had certainly made her work feel more meaningful to her. How naïve she'd been before, rolling her eyes at what she deemed to be wordy, esoteric artist statements. She got it now, even if many of those she'd once scoffed at really had been full of it. The best art always had a story behind it.

She was feeling more relaxed now. She still hadn't seen anyone she knew—it was obvious from the hair and the outfits that not a single person there was a local—and now, halfway through her second glass of wine, she felt like she could be alone with the art, taking the time to read the description of each piece and truly understand what each one meant. When she'd made it through the sections that interested her, she started observing the people too, as if they were part of the show. There was a man wearing salmon-colored pants who couldn't bring himself to dedicate more than five seconds to a given piece, choosing instead to challenge his friends to "find the weirdest ones you can," and regroup. And a tall woman with a short coif and a dragonfly lapel pin who shed actual tears while admiring a black-and-white sketch of a great blue heron.

Cara was still playing this game with herself when she inadvertently locked eyes with Graham. There was no doubt: it was him, and he'd definitely seen her. But it was possible he hadn't recognized her. This was her hope as she quickly moved from her spot and attempted to blend back into the crowd.

She'd known this was a possibility. And if she was being completely honest with herself, it was part of the reason she'd come. She'd wanted to see if Graham would be there. If he'd look different or the same. If he'd remember her. If he'd remember that she was an artist.

Now she was hoping that he didn't. What was the point? What would they even have to talk about? There was no telling whether or not he knew about Brendan and Micah, and the last thing she wanted was to have to recount the whole story to him. Nor did she want to hear him say how sorry he was. This was why she avoided situations like this.

But then, why would he remember her? She was sure now he wouldn't. They hadn't seen each other for years. She decided it was time to leave anyway. She'd enjoyed herself more than she'd expected, and now she could leave on a high note and retreat to the house where she had leftover ravioli and an episode of *Grey's Anatomy* waiting for her.

She was headed for the street when she heard her name called. She kept walking, but stopped when she heard it again. It would be rude to ignore it. She reluctantly turned around and saw Graham coming toward her with a big smile.

"Cara? I thought that was you." He put a hand on his chest and announced himself, just in case *she* perhaps hadn't recognized *him*. "Graham. From the fish market. A few summers back?"

"Hi. Yeah, of course. Yeah, I remember you," she said. She could tell from his broad smile and innocent enthusiasm that he knew nothing about Brendan and Micah. No one who knew ever approached her like this.

"Are you still living here?"

"I am, yeah."

"Last time I saw you, you were about to pop." He looked past her, his eyes searching. "You got a little one running around here now?"

And there it was. The turn in conversation she dreaded most. But if it was going to happen, at least it had happened quickly. She could get it over with. It had taken years, but she could finally say it without crying, her go-to explanation for why she no longer had a child, every syllable and pause rehearsed to perfection.

"Oh, no. I actually—this is always hard to have to say in conversation—he passed away a few days after he was born. SIDS."

Sudden infant death syndrome, commonly known as the unexplained death of a child less than one year of age. To claim Micah had died of this was a lie, of course, but it was easier than trying to tell the real story. That story just elicited more questions. No one asked follow-up questions about SIDS. A bold few who didn't know better would ask what it was, but most took the cue.

"Oh my god, that's awful, I'm so sorry. I didn't mean to intrude."

"That's okay."

"But so, do you still work at the market, or . . . ?"

A tactful change of subject. Graham was still kind. Cara laughed.

"Oh, god no. Although I guess what I am doing now isn't all that different. I wait tables at the Crow's Nest. I split from Brendan, my partner, a few years ago. I don't know if you remember him, but things were really tough after the loss and it just didn't work out."

Better just to get this all out up front, before Graham could ask. Not that he would, but just in case. Because even if he didn't ask, he'd probably been silently wondering. Now they could just move on.

"But I've been waitressing and just—enjoying the island life!"

Enjoying the island life? What was she saying?

"My schedule gives me a lot of time to paint," she added. "So it's perfect for me."

"Yes! You're an artist. I remember that. You used to do all of our portraits. You were really good."

"Well, my style has changed quite a bit since then. But I used to have fun doing that. I can't believe you remember."

"I'd love to see some of your work sometime. I know a gallery that's always looking for new artists," he said with a smile.

So he *was* involved in the reopening. Or so Cara deduced from the smile.

"Oh, you're sweet, thanks. But I wouldn't dream of putting my work next to talent like this," she said.

"Oh, please. I'm sure it's amazing. I still remember your stuff. You've got the eye."

"Yeah, well . . . what about you? Last time I saw you, you were planning on film school." Cara didn't want him to think she was there to brown-nose him in hopes of scoring a show, even if, deep down, that very prospect might have been a big part of her decision to come that evening.

"Yeah, good memory! I did, in fact, go to film school. I just recently graduated, actually."

"Oh! Congratulations. Good for you. When can I expect your first feature to hit theaters?"

Graham let out a self-deprecating chuckle. "I wouldn't hold your breath. Plans have changed a little bit."

"Oh, sorry."

"Nah, that's okay. It's just . . . I think when I met you, I was probably into documentary, right?"

"Yeah. You were going to make a film about fishing, or something. I remember you were planning a trip to Peru!"

This inspired a hearty laugh from Graham. "I can't believe you remember that! Yeah, no, that didn't end up happening."

"No Peru?"

"No Peru. But only because I got to school and immediately fell in love with experimental film."

"Oh, interesting. Is that a far departure from documentary? I don't really know the terminology."

"Yes and no. Depends how you look at it. Basically, it's more on the artsy, avant-garde end of the spectrum. It's the kind of thing you're more likely to see in a gallery than in a theater, if that makes sense. And unless you're Salvador Dalí, it's probably going to be a lot harder to earn a decent paycheck."

Cara laughed. "Got it. That sounds neat, decent paycheck or no."

And it did. Cara quickly found herself forgetting that she'd wanted to leave the gallery.

"Can't say my parents are thrilled, but what are you going to do?" Graham shrugged. "That's how I got back here. This place was just sitting here, so I convinced my parents to help me fund a renovation and let me lead the place. I'm looking to manage the gallery remotely while also working on my own stuff on the side from New York—kind of like you were just saying. It may be a totally delusional plan, but that's my goal. I don't know how successful it'll be in the long run, but so far so good."

Graham gestured at all the people surrounding them.

"Well, I'd say you're off to a good start," Cara said.

"Thanks. Listen, I have to get back to mingling and stuff." Graham rolled his eyes to indicate that he'd much rather not. "But I'd love to see you again sometime. I'll take you out to dinner and you can show me your stuff."

Cara recoiled inwardly. "Oh, no, really, you don't have to do that. Honestly, I didn't even know you were going to be here. I just got the postcard and . . . Alice Granger, she's great. I just wanted to see her work in person. The gallery looks amazing though. Congratulations."

Graham blushed. "I didn't think . . . I wasn't . . . We don't have to talk about art. Up to you. I'd love to just catch up before I head back to the city. Talk about the old days at the market."

Cara hesitated, then shrugged. What was she so afraid of?

"Yeah, okay. Sure. Can I give you my number?"

2014

Cara is frantic. She fears she may be running out of time. Brendan was right there in front of her, and foolishly, she sent him away. Told him she never wanted to see him again. After all this time. And she worries that she's made a horrible mistake. Because she now has reason to believe that Micah may still be alive.

She's heard it from Jimmy himself. He saw *two* people—one of them a boy. And who else could that boy possibly be? So unless Micah suddenly perished within the last few days (which is a possibility too painful to dedicate any energy to considering), there is still a chance that he's here, on the island.

She knows she should let it go. *Stop torturing yourself,* she thinks. *You're giving in to the fantasy. It's just going to be more painful later. You're losing your grip on reality. Micah is gone. Micah is dead.*

As she drives south from Edgartown, Cara contemplates her next move. She could still send the authorities after Brendan. For all she knows, Graham already has. They could help her find Brendan and keep him in custody while they investigate what happened to Micah. But instead of turning off toward the house, she keeps going, instinct propelling her forward, driving faster than she should, flying past a couple on a moped.

She clenches her teeth when she sees the boat. She can't believe she is back here yet again, after being met with such disappointment just a day ago. Does she really think it's going to be any different this time? Has she lost her mind? Why must she continually torture herself in this way? And yet she cannot stop.

She pulls over, not bothering to remove her key or shut the car door, the alert bell dinging behind her. She approaches the vessel and pauses in deference to all the memories it conjures. She is nervous. Afraid of what she might—or might not—find. Slowly, she climbs up the ladder, then lowers herself through the hatch, muscle memory guiding her way. She touches her feet down gently, one at a time, and holds her breath.

There, asleep in the double berth, is a boy. She watches his chest rise and fall, and the world stops. She wonders if she's dreaming, if any of this is real. She is bewildered by the size of him. The girth of his torso and the lengths of his arms and legs. It is as if the soft clay mold of her little baby has been sculpted and stretched overnight, yielding a human that she barely recognizes.

But it's him. There is no mistaking it. The distance between the eyes. Brendan's aquiline nose. The tufts of hair that twist and curl in the damp island air. He is wearing a little wetsuit that looks like it may have at one point been black, but has since faded to gray. It is a detail that confounds her. She wants to reach out and touch him, but holds herself back. If she isn't careful, she worries he may vanish.

Something breaks inside of her—something that she has for years worked fervently to keep intact. And now, as it crumbles, she feels a great release. Here, in this dark, creaky, marooned boat, is the physical manifestation of all the fragile hope she has never once abandoned. There have been times when she's come close, to be sure, but somehow, she knew. She always knew. From the day he disappeared, Micah has remained with her, hidden away in this boat, lost in its own invisible ocean. But now she's found him. She's found her Micah.

Cara crouches by the bedside and reaches out to touch his cheek, her hand shaking. Micah's eyes slowly flutter open. When he registers Cara's presence, he sits up quickly, scooping in a frightened breath and backing away from her. The reflex breaks her heart. She is a stranger to him.

"It's okay, Micah," she says, the words so delicate they almost break. "You don't need to be afraid."

Everything in her wants to lean over and hug him close, to wail and to cry and to scream, releasing the grief that has been building up within her for so long. She doesn't want to frighten him, but the tears come anyway, choking her throat and blurring her vision.

Micah looks nervously around the cabin, eyes wide with fear.

"Do you know who I am?"

Micah shakes his head.

"I'm your mom," she says, trying to smile through the tears. "You're my son. I took care of you when you were a tiny little baby."

Cara searches Micah's eyes for a flicker of recognition, as if there's a chance he might suddenly remember her. But he remains expression-less. She reaches out for him, and he flinches.

"It's okay. I'm not going to hurt you," she says, stung by the rejection.

Micah is sitting up tall now, his back stiff and alert with caution. His eyes dart to the bow, to the stern, to the ladder, and back again. Cara fears he might jump up and flee at any moment.

"Are you looking for Brendan? Your dad?"

As soon as she says the words, Micah's eyes turn pleading with recognition.

"I know where he is," she says. "I can take you to him."

Micah looks unsure.

"You can trust me. I know Brendan." She moves closer. "And I love you, like Brendan loves you. We're a family. If you come with me, I can take you to him. I've got my car out front. We can go together."

Carefully Cara reaches for him, resting a palm on his cheek. This time, he lets her touch him.

"Come with me," she says. "I won't hurt you."

She leans forward and pulls him into her arms. His body is rigid, unsure, but she is holding him. She heaves a heavy sigh soaked with solace and pulls Micah in close, taking in the smell of his skin, the softness of his hair.

When she finally pulls away, he looks at her, more confused now than afraid, the depth of his innocence on full display. Cara stands up and reaches out her hand.

"Will you come with me?" she asks. "Please. *Please*. Will you come with me? Micah?"

The clock is ticking. Every noise from outside feels like a threat. The *whoosh* of a passing car. The rustle of leaves. At any second, Brendan could appear and ruin everything.

She takes Micah's hand now and squeezes it tightly with her own. Coaxing him along, gently but with urgency, she gets him up and out of the boat, letting go of his hand only once to get him safely down the ladder, before guiding him into the car and buckling him into the backseat. And then she begins to drive, still skeptical of what has happened. Every chance she gets, she glances back again through the rearview mirror to make sure Micah is still there with her in the backseat. That he hasn't vanished. That he is real.

Of course, Cara has no idea where Brendan is. She feels guilty for lying. The poor boy is clearly terrified, desperate to see his father, potentially the one person he knows and trusts. But Cara wasn't about to leave him there in the boat, nor could she risk waiting around until Brendan's return. She's waited too long for this. All that matters is that Micah is safe in her care. She resists the urge to call her family—Moira, her father, Drew—to tell them the good news, sure that if she does it will break the spell, compelling Micah to disappear into a cloud of dust the moment one of them lays eyes on him. She is tempted to snap a photo with her phone to show them. The boy has Siobhan's eyes.

When they get to the house, Cara leads Micah inside, narrating every move.

"And this is my house," she says. "It can be your house too, if you'd like."

Micah doesn't respond, and Cara worries she's jumped too far ahead.

"Are you hungry?" she asks instead. "I can make you some food if you like."

To her relief, Micah nods.

Micah takes in his surroundings with wide, curious eyes. Cara sits him down on a stool at the kitchen island and starts rifling through the cabinets for something to feed him. She jumps and nearly hits her head on the cabinet door when she hears him speak behind her.

"Dad?" he says.

"Your dad will be here soon," she lies. "Let's just get you something to eat first."

She makes him toast with cinnamon and butter, a warm, safe, and welcoming treat she is sure no child can resist, and serves it with a glass of milk. With every bite that he takes, she feels a stronger sense of achievement.

She hears the back door slam, followed by Graham's voice echoing through the house.

The boy looks up with alarm. Cara runs to the door to intercept Graham, signaling him with her finger on her nose to be quiet.

"You okay?" he whispers, squeezing her shoulder. She can see the relief in his eyes that she is back. She cannot wait to show him what she's found. To observe the look of shock and bewilderment on his face when he sees.

She leads him into the kitchen and proudly gestures to the young boy eating toast at the counter.

"I want you to meet somebody," she says. "Graham, this is Micah. Micah, this is my friend Graham."

Graham is stunned. He raises his eyebrows in question at Cara, who nods in acknowledgment, then waves at the child, unable to speak. He pulls Cara to the doorway where the kitchen meets the dining room.

"What's going on?" he whispers. "Whose child is that?"

"Mine."

Graham looks confused.

"It's Micah."

"Cara . . ."

"It's him, Graham. I know it!"

"You're sure?"

"One hundred percent. I found him sleeping in Brendan's old boat. It's him, Graham."

Graham still looks skeptical. Cara knows what he's thinking. He's thinking she's really lost it this time. That's she done something horrible. That she's kidnapped a child and is now holding him captive in their kitchen.

"Go look at him if you don't believe me."

Graham hesitates, then moves back into the kitchen. He stands on the other side of the island where he can get a good look at the child.

"Hey, buddy," he says. "Enjoying that toast? *Yum!*"

Micah looks at Graham, and then at Cara, swallowing his bite.

"Do you know my dad?" he asks.

As painful as it is to hear Micah ask for Brendan yet again, Cara is pleased to hear him speak a full sentence.

"Your dad is coming," she promises. "He'll be here soon."

Graham gives her a questioning look and Cara shakes her head.

"How about we watch some TV while we wait?" she proposes, curious whether her son has ever even seen a television. She leads him over to the couch and navigates to the Kids TV section of Netflix, putting on the first "boy"-looking program she sees, a computer-animated show about kid superheroes.

Micah is transfixed, mouth agape like a zombie, seemingly forgetting all about Brendan. Cara puts a blanket over him and watches him watch the show. She would be happy to sit and stare at him like this all day. And she does, for a while, until Graham snaps her back to reality, calling her back into the kitchen.

"We need to talk about this," he says.

"Okay, let's talk. But we have to talk here. I'm not leaving him."

"Fair. I just need a little more context."

"*It's him*, Graham. Do you still not believe me?"

"I'm not saying that. I'm still just trying to process all of this."

"Did you see him, though? I mean, did you really look at him?"

"Yes, and I can't deny it. He looks just like you. I can't argue with you on that."

"So?"

"So, if that's your son in there, why did Brendan tell you he was dead? What reason would he have to lie to you?"

"I don't know. Maybe he didn't want me to know," Cara speculated. "Maybe he's still trying to protect him, from whatever it is he's been trying to protect him from all this time."

"But then why contact you at all? Why come back now? Like this?"

"Maybe he was testing me. Seeing if I'd get back together with him without Micah. Maybe, if I'd reacted differently, he would have told me the truth."

"Where did you say you found him again?"

"In the old sailboat Brendan and I used to stay in. The one off of Middle Road. It was crazy. I don't even remember making a conscious decision to drive there. I just kept going and that's where I ended up. It's like something was pulling me there. And when I looked in the boat, he was there, sleeping peacefully, alone, as if waiting for me to come along."

"And that's what he was wearing? The wetsuit?"

Cara nods, the implications of this observation hovering in the air between them. Why would a five year old be in a wetsuit unless he were spending long periods of time in the water?

"But Brendan wasn't there," Graham says, getting back to the matter at hand.

"No. He has no idea. At least, I don't think so."

"So you're lying to Micah when you keep telling him that Brendan's on his way."

Cara pursed her lips. Graham sighed.

"I know you're not going to like this, but we need to call the police. We can't handle this on our own."

"No, please, Graham. Please, don't. What if they don't believe me? What if they take him away?"

"Look, I know all signs point to this being your child, but if it's not, we could be in serious trouble."

"But this *is* my child, Graham. He's here. Finally. In this room. Are you still not convinced? Do you still not believe me?"

"I do believe you, Care, I do. But there are legalities here that we need to deal with. Not only that, but we need to protect ourselves. What if Brendan comes here and tries to take him back? What are we going to do then?"

"Please, Graham, just give me one night," Cara pleads. "We'll call the police tomorrow. I promise. Just give me one night to be alone with him. Without all the noise. *Please*."

After four episodes of the kid superhero show, Cara and Graham feed Micah hot dogs and Kraft macaroni and cheese, which he appears to enjoy. He seems less afraid now, and when Cara suggests a hot bath followed by a warm, soft bed, he allows it. She is surprised by her lack of modesty when he peels off his grimy wetsuit and hops into the bath. She is again amazed by the human body in front of her, astounded that this growing person could be the same human she herself gave birth to years earlier.

After the bath, they put Micah in one of Cara's old T-shirts and a pair of cotton shorts she sometimes sleeps in; all of Graham's clothes are too large for Micah's small frame. Cara laments the fact that she doesn't have a book to read to him.

As they're tucking him in, he speaks again.

"Are the bad guys going to come here?" he asks. He looks so tiny in their queen-sized guest bed.

Cara and Graham exchange a worried glance.

"What bad guys?" Graham asks, and Cara ignores him.

"No. No bad guys can come here," she says. "This is a safe place. You don't need to worry."

Cara doesn't press Micah to elaborate on who these so-called bad guys are, because she already knows. The obvious, logical explanation is that Micah has been trained, by Brendan, to fear the police. That *they* are the bad guys he speaks of. They are the reason Brendan and Micah have had to live a life on the move, or so Cara imagines.

She suspects that Micah has been made party to Brendan's confusion, his ever-evolving fear that the government is looking for him, and not just because he kidnapped Micah, but because of his inhuman abilities, abilities he's convinced that his son somehow inherited.

Once Micah is asleep, Cara leaves the room for only a moment to grab a sketchpad and pencil. Refusing to leave his side, she stays in the room long after Graham goes to bed, sketching his angelic little face over and over from varying angles, desperate to capture the moment somehow. It is an experience she's waited a long time for, and one that she fears may never happen again. She wants to be awake and present for every second of it.

After a time, she does fall asleep, however, and is later awakened by the sound of voices downstairs. There is shouting, and the crash of something falling over, a kitchen stool maybe. Cara gets into the bed with Micah, who is still sleeping, and softly pets his head. He sighs and snuggles up closer to her.

She's known Brendan would find them eventually. He'd obviously been watching her, learning her whereabouts, observing the new life she'd made for herself with Graham. She hears his feet pounding up the stairs, with Graham following, pleading with him not to go up. Graham threatens to call the police, says he's dialing right now. He shouts a warning to Cara: "He's coming!" Cara listens as Brendan tries the door of the guest bath, then the hall closet, until she can see the shadows of his feet in the crack beneath the door.

But Cara isn't afraid. She's been waiting for this. Hoping for it, even. When Brendan opens the door, she can see a red-faced Graham coming up behind him. But he isn't quick enough. Brendan slams the door and locks it from the inside, ignoring Graham's warnings that the police are on their way. For a moment he just looks at them, Cara and Micah, cuddled up in bed together. He looks tired, but relieved.

"You found him."

Brendan gets into the bed on Micah's other side, and the boy wakes up. His face brightens when he sees Brendan and he wraps his arms around his neck, giving his father a tight, loving squeeze.

"My dad is here!" he says proudly.

"That's right," Brendan says. "And you know who this is?"

He points to Cara.

"This is your mama. The one I told you about."

"From the story?"

"Yeah, from the story. Isn't she beautiful?"

"Yeah."

Graham continues to pound against the door from the hallway, rattling the doorknob and throwing his body weight against the wooden frame.

"That guy better be careful or he's really going to hurt himself."

"I should let him in," Cara says, but she doesn't move. She knows this may be the only time the three of them have together, before the police come and everything gets torn to pieces. She's aware that she should probably be taking more advantage of this time, asking Brendan all her questions about where he's been and letting him feel, again, how angry and hurt she is.

Instead she turns to him, as Micah lies wedged between them, and tells him how much she's missed him. How she's thought of him every day that he's been gone.

"I missed you too," he tells her. "I was just trying to protect him. I didn't want them to get him."

"I know," Cara says. "And now?"

"Now, I'm tired," Brendan says, his eyes filling with tears. "I'm so tired of running. I don't want to do it anymore, Cara. I can't. I can't do it anymore. It's killing me."

"So why didn't you just tell me before? At the pond? Why did you lie to me about Micah?"

"I didn't know if I could trust you," Brendan said. "I've been watching you. You and your new life with your new husband and . . . I don't know. I was angry. I was confused. But I needed to see you anyway. And now, being here with you . . . with Micah . . . all of us here, together . . . I just want you and Micah to be happy. That's all I want, Cara, I swear to you."

"And we will be," Cara says. "You know I'll take care of him. I would never, ever let anything happen to him. You know that, right? No one has to know our secret."

Brendan nods and wipes his nose with his knuckles.

"Your guy called the police," he says. "They're going to take us away. Not just me. Micah too. Unless we leave now. I could probably take Rick Moranis out there."

Brendan glances at the door, and Cara lets out a little laugh.

"Graham looks nothing like Rick Moranis."

"Or we could try climbing out the window."

"No." Cara shakes her head. "Let's just stay here. For as long as we can. Will you do that for me?"

Brendan looks disappointed.

"You can't keep running, Brendan. It's not fair to Micah, and it's not fair to you. If you mean what you said about making me happy, then stop running. That's all I want. Please stop running. For Micah's sake, I beg you."

Cara pulls the down comforter over the three of them, and they hold each other in a charged embrace. They stay that way until the police arrive. There's a hard knock on the door, and Brendan turns to Cara.

"Do you want me to open the door?" he asks. "Is that what you want?"

"Brendan, don't make me choose like this."

"If I go with them, and leave you with Micah, will you be happy?"

"Yes," Cara says quietly—almost too quietly for him to hear.

"Yes?"

"Yes," she says louder.

He looks at her, giving her one last chance to change her mind. She returns his gaze for the briefest of moments before she has to look away. Her heart is breaking.

Brendan gets up slowly and makes his way to the door, still trying to call her bluff, but Cara is steadfast. She cannot bear to watch as the police put him in handcuffs and lead him away.

And yet there is a trace of relief in the madness. It is as if Cara is now the one living underwater, the lights and sounds all around her somehow muted. The police radio. The flashing lights. The frightened cries of her child. The water absorbs the pain and protects her from the full brunt of the impact.

She makes coffee for a police officer while they wait for the Department of Children and Families to arrive and pick up Micah. It makes no sense that they should have to take him away. She is his mother. She should have legal custody. But they tell her it is more complicated than that. They need to interview the child first. They need to confirm his identity.

She worries that this will damage her fragile relationship with her own son. That he will blame her for Brendan's arrest. That he will forever associate her with the fear and the pain and the confusion that all of this has roused.

Graham tries to assure her that it won't be long. That she should trust in the process. She thinks he might finally believe her now.

Cara watches through the window as the Water Street drawbridge in Woods Hole is tilted open to a steep slant, looking like the fin of a giant sea creature, ready to slap down upon the water with a splash. But of course it never does. An elegant sailboat passes through, and the massive chunk of aluminum, asphalt, and iron slowly lowers back into place as if it had never moved.

She sits back down in one of two leather-cushioned chairs that face the desk at the head of the office. The walls of the room are lined with what must be original dark-wood wainscoting below a grandiose coffered ceiling. The bookshelves are adorned with old books, the kinds with fabric spines in muted greens, crimsons, and browns, the authors' names and titles imprinted in faded gold lettering. She can smell the fustiness of their pages without having to open them.

This isn't the general's office, she's been told. In fact, it bears no military association and belongs to the Oceanographic Institution, which has generously offered up the space as a matter of convenience for today's meeting.

She wonders if they knew about the painting when they chose the room. It sits in an ornately carved, gold-painted frame on the wall that faces her, behind the large desk. Its colors appear murky and faded, the ocean a deep blue-green with gray and white bubbles of foam. A harpoon boat rides to the crest of a wave with the silhouette of a harpooner at its bow. His arm reaches back behind his head for leverage as he prepares to strike the giant creature before him: a furious-looking, deep-black sperm whale.

She stands up when she hears a knock, and is surprised when a woman walks through the door. She is dressed in full uniform, a crisp navy suit adorned with gold buttons and tiny pins of varying shapes and colors. Her hair is parted down the middle and pulled into a low, tight bun. She introduces herself as General Davis.

"Thank you for coming here today," she says as she sits. "And for taking the time to go through all the paperwork. I know it can feel like you're signing your life away, but I can assure you it's only for everyone's protection."

"I understand."

"Good. And so you also understand that no one is to know about this meeting, and that everything we discuss today must remain confidential."

"Yes."

"Good. Now that we have that out of the way, I want to tell you how sorry I am that you have had to go through all of this," the general says, stonefaced. "I know it can't have been easy on you or your family."

"Thank you."

"As you may be aware, Captain McGrath is currently being held for psychiatric evaluation at Joint Base Cape Cod. He has been charged with desertion."

"But given his condition, they can't possibly find him guilty, right? Brendan suffers from severe mental illness. He didn't understand what he was doing."

"He will likely plead not guilty but only by reason of lack of mental responsibility."

Lack of mental responsibility. The phrase feels unfair. Brendan is sick. His mind plays tricks on him in a way that is frightening and confusing both for him and for those around him. But in spite of it all, Cara still believes that he is the same person he's always been. A good person, who is caring, and funny, and charming. To label him insane negates all of that. It implies a loss of humanity that is as dangerous as it is disgraceful.

"Captain McGrath has been diagnosed with schizoaffective disorder," says Davis. "Do you know what that means?"

"You mean, like schizophrenia?"

"It's a chronic mental health condition, characterized by symptoms of both schizophrenia and mood disorders, like mania or depression. In this particular case, the patient appears to suffer from"—she looks down to read from the paper on her desk—"powerful hallucinations and delusions of grandeur, in addition to symptoms consistent with bipolar disorder."

Cara nods. Although this is the first time anyone has ever explicitly explained what Brendan suffers from, she has always known. The paranoia, the outlandish stories, the strange behavior. And that book. She never did get an explanation for that.

"Did McGrath ever talk with you about his involvement in the United States armed forces?"

"Sometimes. But nothing specific," Cara is careful to add quickly. "Just that he was a member of the Special Forces. And I knew he regularly went on missions to places around the world. And he'd sometimes talk about the toll it took on him emotionally. Or even if he didn't talk about it, it was obvious to me in his behavior. But he never gave me any details."

"No details whatsoever. Never disclosed locations, or names, or specific actions requested of him?"

"Not that I can remember, no. It was always a point of frustration for me. At the time, I thought he might be suffering from PTSD and so I worried about him. But he never talked to me about it. Said it was for my own safety."

Davis takes a deep breath, keeping her eyes on Cara.

"Did Captain McGrath ever try to convince you that he had special powers or superhuman abilities? Anything like that?"

"He did."

"Can you tell me more about that?"

"He said that he could breathe underwater."

Davis jotted something down on her notepad.

"And what was his explanation as to how he had acquired such an ability? Was it something he was born with? Something he developed?"

"He said that military doctors had performed surgery on him."

"And did he offer an explanation as to why they would do that?"

"Not really. I don't know. Just that it was an advantage, for the US to have someone like him. Who could travel underwater for long periods of time."

"I see. And did you ever witness Captain McGrath's alleged ability in action? Did you ever see him breathing underwater, as he claimed he was able to do?"

Cara doesn't know how to answer this question. There were dozens of times when she'd been convinced that Brendan was in fact breathing underwater. She had seen it. She was sure she had. And for years she'd never questioned it, until time and developing knowledge of his mental affliction started to creep in like clouds, so that she could no longer see those moments—those instances when she had been so sure—with genuine clarity.

"I don't know," she says. "I used to think so. If he was faking it, I could never tell. But over time . . . and after hearing what you're now telling me about his mental health issues, of course . . . it seems unlikely."

Cara waits for a prompt from Davis to elaborate, but she moves on.

"And aside from actually seeing him in the act, was there any directly observable evidence of Captain McGrath's having undergone the surgery he described to you?"

"Yes. He had these slits, under his arms," Cara explains, searching for a way to communicate the idea without sounding ridiculous. Without using the word *gills*. "Openings in the skin that he said helped with the filtration process. With his lungs."

"Thank you," says Davis, continuing to scribble down notes.

For Cara, there is a comfort in talking about this with someone so unfazed by what most would consider an incredible and dumbfounding tale. Davis seems very interested in the details Cara is sharing with her. And her questions hint that she knows more than she lets on. Cara scoots forward to the edge of her seat in anticipation of Davis's response.

Is General Davis about to confirm Brendan's story? Has it really been true all along?

Davis puts her pen down and sits up straight. Cara feels herself lean in closer.

"Ms. Hansen, as you know, a part of the reason I'm here today is to touch base with you and ensure that Captain McGrath never disclosed any military secrets. But I also feel it is my duty to clarify a few things for you, if I may."

"Please."

"I can confirm that Captain McGrath was, and technically remains, a member of the US Special Forces. At the time when you met, he was still very much an active soldier, and any calls of duty he described or mentioned to you were likely legitimate."

"Okay."

"However, I speak on behalf of the United States military when I tell you that there is no record of him ever having undergone a surgery of any kind that might instill in him the abilities he described to you. Any mutilations you may have witnessed were likely performed by Captain McGrath himself as a direct result of his psychosis."

The words feel like a door slamming in Cara's face. She's done it again—allowed herself to hope for the impossible, only to be disappointed.

"How long do you think he had it? The disorder."

"It's something you're born with. He's always had it. It's more a question of when the disease started manifesting itself."

"So when was that? How long do you think he was showing symptoms?"

"That's really a question for his medical team."

"Of course. Right."

General Davis crosses her arms across her chest and offers Cara a weak smile. "Are there any other questions I can answer for you, Ms. Hansen?"

Cara thinks about this. She can think of hundreds of questions to ask about Brendan's medical diagnosis and what it means, but clearly this isn't the time or place to ask them. So she focuses on the procedural aspects of the situation, trying to gauge what she can expect going forward—what decisions she will likely need to make.

"I'm just trying to wrap my head around what's going to happen to Brendan," she said. "Will he go to jail? Or be institutionalized, or what?"

"It depends on the findings of his sanity board hearing. That will dictate if and how he is tried."

This answer just leaves Cara with more questions—like what the maximum penalty is, and how his military charge of desertion intersects, if at all, with the kidnapping. But she can tell she's not going to get any more information out of General Davis today, despite her feeble attempts to appear helpful. The purpose of this meeting wasn't to help Cara; it was to make sure Cara didn't know anything important, and one thing's for sure—she doesn't. She hasn't known a thing for certain since the moment Brendan walked into her life.

Cara sits in the waiting area, folding and unfolding her shaking hands. She's starting to wish she'd allowed Graham to come with her, like he wanted to. But she'd fought against him. Told him she needed to do this alone, aware that in asserting so, she was hurting him, pushing him further away. She regrets it now. She wishes he were here to fill the empty chair at her side.

A young, large-chested woman with long braids, carrying a clipboard, enters from a side door and calls her name. She asks Cara how she's doing today in a cheerful voice, as if Cara were any normal visitor coming to see any normal friend or family member. Cara wonders if the woman knows any of the context of Brendan's story. The woman hums to herself as she travels confidently through the corridor.

She stops at a door labeled 216. The door has a small window into the hall, the long, narrow kind with a grid of crisscrossed lines along the glass. The woman taps on it, waves, and scans a card against the gray lock box to gain entry to the room. She tells Cara she'll be back in a half hour and holds the door open for Cara to enter. There is already an armed guard waiting inside. Beyond him, she sees Brendan.

He's wearing a white T-shirt and gray cotton sweatpants with flip-flops. He looks tired, and swollen somehow, but he stands and smiles when he sees Cara.

"There's my girl."

Cara looks nervously at the guard.

"Can I hug him?" she asks. The man nods.

Brendan wraps his arms around her tightly, and she returns the hug, but tentatively. She lets go before he does, letting her arms go limp while his remained wrapped around her, holding her body close.

"I'm so glad you're here," he says, whispering into her hair.

Cara pulls away, and they sit across from each other at a small round table. His beard has been shaven, making him look more like the Brendan she remembers, except he seems smaller somehow, more fragile. She notices jagged pink scars like slashes up and down the lengths of his forearms, remnants of his delusional attempt to remove a supposed tracking device five years ago. The bloody knife in the sink.

"It's good to see you," she says. "How are you doing? How are they treating you?"

"They're making me take pills."

"That's good," she says. "You should take them. They'll help you."

"They think I'm crazy."

"They don't think you're crazy. They think you're sick. There's a difference. You have a disease, Brendan."

Brendan recoils, ever so slightly. "So you believe them."

"It's nothing to be ashamed of," Cara says, avoiding the accusation. "It's hardly different from having something like diabetes or epilepsy or another chronic illness. Except in a lot of ways, this is better. With the right medication, it's completely manageable. You can live a normal life. Your health is otherwise perfect."

These are the very same words the doctors have told her. And each time she hears them, especially now, as she is the one who says them, she believes it a little bit more. And if it can make her feel better, maybe it will help Brendan feel better.

"But it's not the right diagnosis," Brendan says. "They think because my mom was a schizo that I am too, but I'm not. They think I'm making everything up, Cara. *Everything.*"

He glances over at the guard.

"All the things I told you, in private. They know about it and they think I'm making it up, but I'm not. You know I'm not."

The doctors had prepped Cara for this. They'd told her that while he was making progress, Brendan was still in denial about his diagnosis. It would take some time, and a lot of psychotherapy, they said. The good news was that Brendan did seem to be responding to the medication, but they believed he'd traveled so far into his delusion, lived with it for so long, that it was going to be very difficult for him to disassociate himself from it. They would keep adjusting his dosage until they got it just right. They'd explained to her that while treatment had the potential to be incredibly effective, it could take years before they found the optimal combination for him.

Cara wonders if the day will ever come when Brendan will be able to talk coherently about his affliction, and the actions it compelled him to take. She yearns to hear the clear, lucid, unobstructed version of his perspective, of what it was like to fall victim to the illness. If he knew that it was happening. If he could feel it. If it scared him. And, most importantly, where he's been for the past five years. What he did with Micah.

But for this, she is told, she will have to wait. Again, her most burning questions remain unanswered. Like how a person as troubled as they claim Brendan is could have cared for an infant on his own—and not just for weeks or months, but for *years*. It didn't make any sense. All they kept telling her was that schizoaffective disorder was a very complicated disease with varying levels of functionality from person to person. Still, they did acknowledge how extraordinary Brendan's case was. Similar stories had had much darker outcomes.

"It doesn't matter," Cara says. "All that matters now is that you and Micah are safe."

"How is he? Is he with you? Tell me he's with you."

"Not here, physically, but yes. He's been released to live with us now," Cara says. "And he's doing great."

Her eyes tear up when she thinks about it. Having her Micah home again is a miracle that never stops glowing.

"But he misses you," she admits. "He asks for you a lot."

"Will you bring him here? To see me?"

"Eventually. Maybe. Yes. Whenever the doctors say it's okay."

Brendan doesn't know it, but the doctors *have* said it's okay. It's Cara who doesn't want Brendan to see Micah yet. She isn't ready. As irrational as it may be, a part of her still worries that if she brings Micah back to Brendan, he might take him away again. Maybe not physically, but emotionally. She doesn't want to lose any progress they may have made.

She feels awful about it, keeping a child away from his father—essentially the only parental figure he's ever known. But that's just it. Cara is jealous. Micah is *her* son. He came out of her own body. They share blood and DNA and family history. And yet she feels like she's doing something wrong, like *she's* now the one guilty of kidnapping. It isn't fair. As Graham has repeatedly told her, she shouldn't have to feel bad. But she does.

Everything is so complicated now. Cara regularly tries to imagine her future, mapping out roles for Brendan, Micah, and Graham, but there are still so many unknowns. It's impossible to put all the pieces together. Brendan could be in the hospital for weeks or months, even years. And even if he does get released, there's no knowing when he might be back again. Even in the most successful of cases, she's been told, relapses are common.

The logical thing to do, or perhaps the most tempting, would be to forget about Brendan and raise Micah with Graham, maybe even have another child—grow their own little family. Process what's happened and move forward. She knows the road may be bumpy at first, but Micah is still young. She and Graham are still young. In a few years, everything could settle into a new normal.

But what kind of person would she be if she just shrugged Brendan off like that? Washed her hands of him and left him to rot in this hospital, perhaps for the rest of his life? Could she really live with that kind of skeleton in her closet? Yes, Brendan did a horrible thing. But did that make him deserving of total abandonment?

The alternative, of course, would be to keep Brendan in Micah's life, but as a peripheral figure. She and Graham would have full custody and, depending on how he was doing, Brendan could visit. He could maintain his right as father and harness a loving relationship with

Micah. People did that all the time, didn't they? Couples divorced and then, depending on the situation, they set up some kind of custody agreement. It doesn't have to be weird.

But it's hard for Cara to imagine. More than hard, it's disappointing. The life of a co-parent is not the life she'd always thought she'd have, and the loss of that dream—that vision of a traditional nuclear family with two (not three) parents, in the same home—feels like a sacrifice.

There is a third option, and that option looks at her now, imploring her to look back up at him.

"It's good to see you," Brendan says, as if he were reading her mind. He's always had a way of doing that, another of his superpowers, to be sure. "Those days with you, before—those were the best of my life. I want you to know that."

Cara hates him for saying this. But she also wants to tell him that they were for her too. That she still thinks about them all the time. That she still loves him. That's she's only ever loved him. That she's decided to leave Graham and run away with him and Micah. She'll get up from the table and hold his face as she kisses him and promises never to abandon him. She believes him, she'll say. He *can* breathe underwater, and all of this—the hospital, General Davis, his diagnosis—it's all a ruse, a government cover-up of one of the world's most incredible secrets. She will expose them, and rescue Brendan from their clutches. Together they will reunite with Micah and move back into their home, the one with the path to the ocean and the mint-green fridge. The three of them will run off into the sunset, laughing and teasing each other, just as they were meant to. They will finish their love story. They will finish their fairy tale.

Instead Cara smiles sadly and simply says, "Me too." She refocuses and takes a deep breath, bringing herself to standing.

"Take care of yourself," she says. "And give the doctors a chance. They're trying to help you."

At home, she turns off the car engine and sits in the driveway, closing her eyes and concentrating on her breathing in an attempt to regain composure. She wonders if her hands will ever stop trembling. There's no need to feel so sad. She hasn't just said good-bye forever to her soul mate. She hasn't done anything wrong yet—hasn't decided anything. At least, not definitively.

When she comes inside, she turns the corner into the living room to find Graham and Micah kneeling next to the coffee table with her Prismacolor pencils and loose sheets of printer paper scattered across the surface. They don't hear her come in. Graham leans with his right arm behind Micah's little curved back, peering over his shoulder at what he's drawing. They're talking in quiet voices. Cara can't hear what they are saying, but she feels a burst of warmth spread through her chest as she watches Micah turn his head back to look at Graham and smile, biting his lip with a mischievous glare as he begins a new drawing, Graham looking on approvingly.

That's when Graham notices her. He looks up at her and aims a little shrug and excited eyebrow-raise in her direction, as if to signal his shared disbelief at this tender moment between him and Micah. It's the first time the two have interacted this way, and she can tell Graham is pleased. She is pleased too.

She looks at her son and she wonders: could the sickness in Brendan be in Micah too? It seems so impossible, the idea that the beginnings of such a cruel and merciless disease could already be lying in wait within the happy, innocent boy in front of her. *Her* boy. She knows she is destined to spend a lifetime worrying, looking for signs, all the while cognizant of the fact that there is nothing she can do to stop it.

She decides not to tell Micah where she's been, and who she's seen, and joins him and Graham at the table, picking up a pencil and beginning the outlines of the first object that comes to mind. She starts with the tail and ends with the head, drawing a cartoonish spout of water coming out of the top of the creature's body.

t is the perfect beach day. The sun is high and bright and the breeze is strong enough to cool sweat and sweep away greenheads. The clouds move quickly, but the waves are only just starting to come up. She and Micah and Graham arrange their towels and chairs at the edge of the dunes, tufts of beach grass swaying in the wind.

Micah begs to go in the water—his little legs dancing with excitement.

"Not until we get your sunscreen on," Cara says. Anything to delay the moment further.

For weeks, she has avoided the issue, refusing to bring Micah to the beach, despite his repeated pleas. It's not like she thinks he's going to get in the water and swim away forever. Hell, she doesn't even know if he can actually swim.

It was Graham who finally convinced Cara to bring Micah to the beach. He suggested that it might actually give her peace of mind. She'd see Micah playing in the water and realize he was just like any other child.

The thought had made sense at the time. Now Cara's not so sure. Her adrenaline is on high, a panic attack waiting just around the bend.

She carefully rubs the sunscreen into Micah's cheeks, imploring him to stop bouncing so she doesn't get any in his eyes.

"Can we go now?" Micah whines.

"Hold on. Did I get your neck?" Cara asks. "Let me just make sure I got your neck."

"Pretty sure you got it," Graham says teasingly. "The boy's got enough sunscreen on him to protect all of us at this point."

Cara sighs and rolls her eyes.

Graham doesn't get it. Ever since she got Micah back, Cara has wondered: *What if Brendan is right? What if Micah can breathe underwater?* The implications would be almost too great to bear. If Micah demonstrated the ability to breathe underwater, that would almost certainly mean that Brendan could too. It would also mean that Brendan had been wrongfully diagnosed, intentionally or otherwise. It would mean Cara failed to believe and trust the person she once loved in the moment he most needed her to. It would mean they could have avoided this whole mess years ago, that day she found Brendan "testing" Micah's abilities.

Another person would have found a way to debunk the theory right away. Squash any looming delusions and move on. But for whatever reason, Cara couldn't do it. Wouldn't do it. She told herself it was out of safety concerns; she wasn't about to dunk her five-year-old son's head under the water to see what would happen. But really, she was afraid of discovering an undesired truth, a prospect that a tiny, hidden, locked-up section of her brain still believed might exist.

They'd asked Micah once, point-blank, but it was impossible to know if he'd truly understood what they were asking. He'd nodded in response, nonchalantly continuing to play with one of his trucks.

"But humans can't breathe underwater," Graham had said. "It's physically impossible."

"Did you go in the water?" Cara had asked. "With your dad?"

Micah nodded.

"Okay, now you're just leading the witness," Graham said. "This is stupid. He's five. When I was five, I would have told you I had X-ray vision like Superman."

And that had been the end of that. Cara had suggested bringing Micah to therapy to see if maybe they could learn more about all the time he'd spent with Brendan. Graham agreed it was a good idea, but wanted to wait. They'd only just gotten him back. They needed to let him settle in first.

The tide is high. Cara holds Micah's hand in hers as they approach the lapping waves. The water is cold on her feet and toes, but Cara barely notices. She picks Micah up now and holds him on her hip as she moves forward into the water. She does a little hop every time another wave rolls by. One of the waves gets her in the face. This makes Micah laugh. She wipes away the water from her eyes and licks the saltiness from her lips.

"Let me go," Micah says, starting to wiggle.

The water is only to Cara's midriff, but it still seems too deep.

"I want to swim, Mama. Let me go."

"Okay, but I'll be right here," Cara says. "You can hold on to me if you need me."

He's getting too squirmy to hold now. Seeing a lull in the waves, Cara releases her arm and lets Micah free. He can just barely touch, bouncing on his tippy-toes and doing the doggy paddle. But not once does he look afraid. He looks quite natural, in fact, using the buoyancy of the salt water to balance his body. And then, in a moment, he goes under, as if he's done so a thousand times before, and Cara watches the dark shape of his body as it glides through the water, above the sand and rocks and under the waves, like a creature of the sea.

Acknowledgments

I wrote *At Sea* in secret, the vulnerability of admitting to the world that I dared dream of writing and publishing a novel too terrifying to bear. But I never would have had the ability and determination to attempt such a feat without years of love and support from friends, family, teachers, and fellow writers.

Thank you to all of my writing teachers and fellow class participants at Hopkins School, Kenyon College, Harvard Extension School, and GrubStreet.

Thank you to my agents, Callie Dietrick and Wendy Sherman. Callie, I will never forget who pulled my work from the slush pile and quite literally changed my life. And Wendy, I truly do not know when you sleep. I have been so moved by the level of dedication and enthusiasm you have extended toward me and this book.

ACKNOWLEDGMENTS

From the very beginning, my editor Jackie Cantor has made me feel like *she* is the lucky one for getting the chance to work with *me* on this book, when in fact, it's the other way around. I feel so fortunate to have been matched with such a warm, thoughtful, and exuberant advocate and advisor.

So much energy and work goes into publishing a novel, and I am forever indebted to the incredible team at Gallery Books for bringing *At Sea* to life—in the midst of a global pandemic that has turned the industry upside down. Thank you to Aimée Bell, Jennifer Bergstrom, Eliza Hanson, Mackenzie Hickey, John Paul Jones, Andrew Nguyen, Lauren Truskowski, and the entire Gallery team. Thank you also to Lisa Litwack and her team for the exceptional book jacket design, and to Joal Hetherington for her keen and thorough copyedits.

Thank you to Katie and David Fedor for inviting me across the Sound to Martha's Vineyard and welcoming me into your island traditions. I never imagined that a place could enchant me the way that the Vineyard has.

My sister, Hallie Mueller, was the very first person to read *At Sea*, a privilege I would only entrust with the most compassionate and thoughtful of readers. Thank you for recognizing and respecting just how vulnerable it felt for me to share this work and for offering the heartfelt praise and validation that I needed.

So many of the scenic descriptions in *At Sea* are thanks to the countless coastal walks I have taken with my dad, Eric Mueller, whose creativity, humor, and powers of observation are traits I can only hope I've inherited. Thank you for showing me what it looks like to fearlessly follow your creative passions and live a happy, fulfilling life.

Even now, as an adult, I roll my eyes at my mom, Jan Lenkoski-Mueller's over-the-top enthusiasm for everything I create, but I also know that I would never have had the confidence and courage to write this book were it not for her love and support. Thank you for making this solidly average girl feel like she might actually be exceptional at something, and for taking me to Borders and letting me pick out whatever books I wanted.

My biggest deterrent from writing has always been a fear of missing out on time with my husband, Nate Fedor. Are there two people in the world who enjoy spending time together as much as we do? Thank you for playing so much golf and hockey so that I could fit in some FOMO-free writing time. I love you and the life we've built together.

I must also thank all of the friends and family members who have forgiven me for keeping this book a secret from them for so long. Your patience, understanding, and unconditional support is deeply felt.

And, of course, thank you to all of the readers and booksellers out there for reading this book and helping to spread the joy of reading with the world at a time when we all need it most.